With All My Devils

A Novel By

Michael Atticus O'Shea

Connie,

A thousand blessings upon you & everyone you care about. Hope you enjoy the read.

Michael O'Shea

Copyright © 2021 Michael O'Shea
All Rights Reserved

Cover Art by Francisco and Nuria Velasco-Sanchez
Instagram: welderwings@gmail.com

Find Michael Atticus O'Shea on:
Facebook : @michaelatticusoshea
Instagram : @atticusoshea
Blog : michaelatticusoshea.wordpress.com

Or Email me : atticusoshea@gmail.com

For

Kelsey Temperato, who provided the inspiration for my own journey of love and life that served as the foundation of this book.

For

Kevin O'Shea, who taught me a love of words, and stories.

For

Rhonda O'Shea, who gives a constant love and encouragement that I could not live without.

For

Adrianne, Rowan, and Conor O'Shea. You all are the reason I do everything I do.

For

Jesse Truitt, who gave proofreadings and critiques since the beginning of my writing journey. Corey Jepson, who first brought the book to physical existence at a critical moment.
Gerry Stevens, who provided near constant counseling and therapy.

Chapter 1

To be a necromancer, one must have had their heart broken. This is a prerequisite. Necromancy is a dark trade, and one must have an intimate understanding of sorrow to develop the craft properly, and to straddle the line between life and death. For her part, Coriander Lou was a naturally talented necromancer.

It is not common for parents to hope their child will grow up to be a necromancer. Cori's father was not unique in his concern for her daughter, though he did understand her interest. Both of them had their hearts broken when her mother went off to heal the sick during the outbreak of the Crimson Plague. A doting mother, beloved wife, and fierce Paladin, she was never seen again, and in some ways both Cori and her Father felt a deep sense of abandonment. Since those days, Cori has seen the unseen, and known the unknowable. It first began when she was hiding behind a neighbor's shed in a rowdy game of 'Ghost and the Graveyard'. The game took a more literal approach when Cori found herself hiding alongside a child she had never met before. The child whispered "hush", then disappeared.

From that point forward Cori began wearing black clothes clothes and started reading obscure books that caused concerned whispers with the local librarians.

Somewhat of a savant in the art, Cori's father was all the more disturbed to find the regular reanimations of roadkill, or Tywin, the once beloved family cat. With every passing year, Cori grew in her interest and in her skill. This all took a second seat to love for several years after high school, a time when Cori lost all sight of sorrow in the arms of another. Love soon gave way to betrayal, and Cori was left robbed of her closest confidants. It was at this pivotal moment that she saw a newspaper advertisement that would shape the course of her life from that moment forward.

Necromancer's Apprentice
**Looking for Specially Abled Youths for Entry Level
Necromancy Position at the St. Margaret's
Home for the Nearly Departed.
Standard Minimum Wage with Housing and Meals Provided
Apply Online at MagesGuild.com/OpenPositions/Necromancy/SMHND**

And all too quickly she found herself hundreds of miles from home, riding a train to the town of Remedy.

"Necromancer..." Her father had scoffed. He was a gardener by trade, and skilled in Druidry, and other life giving magicks. "I've put up with this nonsense phase for long enough. You can do so much better than that. Your mother would have wanted better for you."

Tristan, her father, berated her for weeks, insisting that Cori follow in her mother's footsteps as a Paladin, a fierce and holy fighter who can call upon divine energies in the name of healing and heroics. Her father had further stressed the point that the Higgin's daughter had already graduated college as an alchemist, having written a dissertation on human transfiguration.

"This *is* a lot like healing." Cori had explained, hoping to find some common ground, and so bridge the gap. "That's just it. It's just a different type of healing."

At this, her usually quiet and even tempered father burst into a fit of rage. "I don't want you going anywhere near that house." He had shouted at her, spittle flying from his mouth. It was a family tradition for the women of Cori's family to become a Paladin. The tradition ran several generations back. The only one who paved her own path was Aunt Monica who had become a Priestess, which wasn't the most rebellious deviation. But even considering this, Cori could not understand her father's response. "You'll tarnish your mother's name. You'll bring shame upon your whole family."

Cori's eyes swelled with tears, for it was much in her mother's name that she set out on this path. But her father, in his concern for his daughter, had salted a wound that was far from healed. It was a wound he knew and felt in his own way. But with those insensitive words, Cori set out with even greater determination that very same night, traveling hundreds of miles from home by train to the Southern Town of Remedy.

Cori studied incessantly during her journey, learning everything she could about the profession she intended to make her lifelong career. From necromancy's roots as a source of evil and villainy, to the kind and caring Lich king of the Renaissance, St. Andrew, who first used Necromancy for good. St. Andrew founded a whole city of the dead to serve as a way station between here and the beyond so that souls could 'pass on' with grace and ease. But no matter how much Cori studied, none of it seemed ready to prepare her for what lay ahead.

"Approaching Remedy" Came the call from the PA.

The Southern Town of Remedy sat alongside a cliff above Lake Talula which was nestled in a great canyon. Cori looked back along the train tracks from the station and saw the rusty old bridge she had crossed, and she shuddered. The bridge swayed gently in the wind, and a long overdue inspection sticker could be seen plainly from afar. It was a miracle that a bird could land upon it without causing it to collapse, let alone the train which Cori had rode in on.

It was a fresh spring day and much warmer than the frosty land Cori had rode in from. A fresh and fragrant wind blew from the mountains in the North, carrying both seeds and allergens, and there were many exotic birds that Cori could not name, singing bird songs in a language Cori had never yet heard. Cori thanked the train's conductor, and headed off the station into town.

Remedy seemed friendly enough. There was a piper dancing on a fountain in the square, tea and coffee being served behind an elegant and ivy woven iron fence, and people were driven two and fro by fuzzy rickshaws, lit with neons and bumping hip hop from the back seats. Old ladies smoked pipes while leaning on beanstalk trellises, and the children were tame in their play.

Cori wandered, and learned the shops and streets of this strange new town where she spotted hooligans sword fighting in an alley between two quizzically leaning buildings, one a haberdashery, and the other a purveyor of stuffed animals which were imbued with consciousness and the capacity to love. There were vendors hawking tarnished watches and thingamajigs from the backsides of carriages, and street side theatrical shows from a performing troupe of clown-human hybrids. There was much to see and the morning hours vanished with a glittering array of new sights, scents, and sounds.

    For lunch, Cori's nose guided her to Quintanilla's Produce Cafe where they baked savory bread. This alone served as an adequate meal with a pad of butter and some grilled asparagus on the side. It was at that cafe that Cori heard two men; shirtless, bearded, and wearing brightly colored suspenders; speak of St. Margaret's Home for the Nearly Departed. And though they were discussing their desire to purchase and renovate the building, Cori was able to pick out that it was only a few miles up the road that ran along the River Talula.

    Cori left immediately, ciabatta bread dangling from her mouth. River Road hugged tight, first to the cliffs above Lake Talula, then to the waterfall which poured into it, then to the river which fed the falls. It was near the falls that Cori happened upon a sign, choked by grape vines, that read 'St. Margaret's Home for the Nearly Departed;' told in a detailed script with a small ghost logo above it and an arrow pointing left.

    The miles of her hike melted as quickly as her morning hours had, and she strolled past budding meadows and lavish vineyards spotted with gothic farmhouses. From here she could spot those who may soon be her neighbors, either sitting upon their porches or keeping busy with yardwork.

    These structures grew fewer and fewer as the land elevated and the river grew more distant from up above. The trees grew thick with spanish moss which draped down over the branches. The buildings Cori passed no longer seemed inhabited, and some were downright ruinous. The road and cobblestone wall beside it was being torn apart by plantlife, and an unseasonable fog crept through the ivy. The fog here carried with it a scent like english gardens. It was through this fragrant fog that Cori first spotted a tombstone, down the hill and beside the river.

A chill set into Cori's bones. It was a little shiver up her spine that set the hairs on her neck on end. She had arrived.

She spotted the manor through the spanish mosses. It was up beside the road and on par in elevation. Down a hill and to the side was a graveyard at the river's elevation, and a small chapel beside that. St. Margaret's was an impressive structure of jutting parapets and crooked storm shutters, Victorian towers connected by arches and crumbling under the weight of disrepair. The very stucco of its walls was imbued with bone, as Cori recalled that the legends of the place told of the bodies of construction worker casualties being laid into its foundations and masonry. Cori couldn't get any easy grasp of its enormous size, but saw that it appeared to have three main floors, if you ignored the towers and parapets and crumbling upper pathways.

Like an enchanted Palace. Cori thought, and surely only one with a deep appreciation for the macabre would think so. Shingles fell even as Cori gazed upon it, and one of the boarded windows on the third floor shone a green light that pierced the eerie fog that roiled around the place.

Cori stepped cautiously upon the great front veranda to the arched and oaken doorway. *Rappa, tap, tap.* She knocked upon the door. From within Cori heard moaning and whispers. Goosebumps appeared on her left arm. Cori looked over.

The fog at her side coalesced into the shape of a girl, who drifted lazily in the air. The fog girl must have been no more than nine. Her head was bent to the side and she watched Cori curiously. Her body was out of phase with the world, much like television static. The ghost smiled, and held up her hand in a sombre greeting. Cori gulped, but smiled, and held up her own hand before the girl faded out of existence.

The doorway to the manor opened suddenly. "Who're you?" A round woman with painted black eyes and painted black lips and blue hair glared down at her. She wore a Hot Topic gown, with raven's feather shoulder pads. She stared at Corey's plaid pippy long stockings, then up to her grey dress and leather belt, and tee shirt; then to her wide brimmed and freckled nose and smoke stone eyes and unruly purple hair braided as best as it could be braided into pig tails. Cori just knew they'd get along.

"Hi, yes. I'm here for--uh...the apprenticeship." Cori said, trying to set about with an air of professionalism.

The woman raised a drawn-on eyebrow and stared down at Cori, eyeing her from head to toe, letting the silence elongate into terror. Then, she shrugged and walked back into the Manor. "Oh right, the new girl....Follow me."

Cori stepped cautiously into the foyer. The anticipation of several weeks of planning was finally relieved. It seemed a somewhat ordinary home. There was a mirror to the right and a doorway to the left that led into a family room with a blaring television. It was musty as old buildings often are, but the hardwood floors were a nice touch and there was a dreamy mysticism that hung like clouds in the air. The walls were draped in wallpaper that Cori's grandmother would have thought was out of style, and hung with disturbing paintings. Cori held her gaze on one that depicted two renaissance cherubs, faces all serenity, while one cherub made to cut the others ear off with a pair of scissors. Another painting was of a woman being burned at the stake, all while she grinned maniacally. Cori did a double take when she realized this one was not a painting, but a photograph. The tables in this front room were adorned with taxidermy creatures and sculptures of bone. And all of this might have set Cori on edge if it weren't for the warmth emanating within the place, like a grandmother's cottage.

Cori was then led into a charming kitchen, just a short walk down from the foyer. It was an appropriate size for such a manor, but it was made more quaint by herbs and plucked ducks hanging from pieces of driftwood in the rafters. There looked to be pizza ovens laid in the bricks and what must have been two recently purchased fridges that looked out of place with their sleek modern design. Central to it all, a cauldron hung by a chain above a fire, cooking ramen noodles.

Cori's guide opened a door to a grand stairwell that lifted up several floors. A gentlemanly spectre hung by a noose from the rafters two stories above, his tongue lolling. Cori gasped. It was all so vivid and real.

"George, get down from there. Damnit, I thought we were past this."

The ghost screamed, fell to the ground floor with a thud, and disappeared. Then Cori's guide bellowed "Maya, can you log something?"

From deeper in the house Cori could hear a voice calling. "Log what?"

"George has started hanging himself again."

"Got it."

It was difficult for Cori to take in further from the stairwell, traumatized as she now was. All she could register was a great stained glass dome at the top which was set about with arcane sceneries and dark design.

Cori's guide, whose name turned out to be Dana, led her through the hallway at the top of the second floor stairway and on through a maze of turns. Dana warned Cori several times about traps lining the hallway. Traps that she would likely have to memorize. There were secret passages as well. Dana opened what looked to be a tiny doorway in the hall which opened a normal sized doorway leading into yet another stairwell. Onwards to the 3rd floor, and past a room filled with the stench of rot, they finally reached a door that Dana waved Cori on through.

The room was a formal office space covered in a creative mess. "New girl." Was all her guide said before the door was shut, and Cori was left alone with the scent of musk and beeswax.

Cori was certain that there was someone else in the room with her, presumably seated in the large red leather executive chair behind the desk, facing away and hiding whoever might be in it. The walls were covered in black and white photographs, all taken at odd angles. There was a tilted tornado in one, the corner of a sculpture in another, with a water glass front and center. One seemed only to be a close texture shot of bark, with a busy ant carrying a leaf. Amongst these photographs, a cat clock ticked its eyes back and forth and swung its tail. Shelves were filled to capacity with tomes, scrolls, notepads, binders, and bells. Above the chair hung a single unicorn skull, it's horn made entirely of quartz crystal. Behind Cori, a door covered in dozens of different styles of locks.

The chair turned, flowing of its own volition. Hands clasped upon his knees, a gaunt wizard spun then stopped himself abruptly as he gazed down at Cori. One could tell he was a wizard because of his silk robes and gaudy jewelry. His long salt and pepper hair and long beard set upon his angular face, and his eyebrows crested ferociously. His lips curled downward into a frown. Long bony fingers tapped together as he faced Cori, blue eyes piercing passed her oval glasses and through her silver irises and into her very soul.

"Why, hello." He said, his voice more effeminate than Cori expected.

"Hi there. We did an interview over the phone? I'm Cori?" She wasn't sure why she phrased it as a question. She was terrible with interviews. And tests. Then the silence stretched until Cori was forced to say, "I'm here about the necromancer apprenticeship."

"Arrrrre you now?" He raised his sharp eyebrows even higher at her and widened his eye, peering ever more deeply. "Well, thank the spectre of death. You cannot imagine how short staffed we've been." The wizard waved his hands through the air, electricity crackling between his rings of sapphire and emerald, which matched his robes. "I AM the MEISTRO of this house, the Master Necromancer, Absalon of the Thousand Eyes they've called me in some realms. But here in the Mundane, you may call me... Morris."

"Nice to meet you, Morris."

"I imagine it is." He said. "Let's get this over with. Previous job experience?"

"Uh...none." Cori said.

"Skills?" He asked.

"Necromancy?"

"Good answer. Accolades?"

"...No." Cori was beginning to blush.

"Coriander, would you tell me what you believe your strengths and weaknesses are?"

This was a question Cori had been prepared for. "Well, I like to think I've got a strong sense of empathy...So I suppose that would be my strength."

Morris made a 'tch' sound. "Debatable." He said, but Cori continued.

"And for weaknesses...I can sometimes be too soft spoken. Like, I think I need to speak my mind more." She said.

"Intriguing." Morris said. "And where do you see yourself in five years time?"

"You asked that over the phone interview." Cori said.

"I gave you a phone interview?" Morris asked, showing a measure of genuine surprise, then apathy. He adjusted a skull ring on his hand with jewels for eyes. "Well, why don't you refresh my memory?"

"Well, I'd like to be quite a bit more skilled with necromancy, maybe work my way up in the company. I wouldn't be opposed to starting a family by then." Cori said, then found herself surprised she had said it. That last bit was something she hadn't even voiced in her own mind before. She pulled on her stockings absentmindedly.

"How quaint." Morris said, then leaned forward in his chair to look at her more directly. "Cori, would you regale me for a moment with why, exactly, you are here."

Cori stared at Morris and blinked for a few moments. "I uh--- am here for a job."

"No, no, no. Ugh, you've no sense of poetry." Morris said with a wave of his hand, emitting sparkles as he did so. "In the grand scheme, Cori. Why are you here in the grand scheme?" Cori still looked confused, so Morris pressed more firmly. "Your goals. I'll start...I'm Morris. I like animals, and Reese's peanut butter cups. My mission is to someday take vengeance upon the Arch Lich of Babylon for burning down my childhood home and raising my family as animate corpses. I feel like working here as supervisor will help me hone my skills for battle, but also sometimes I just get fat and lazy and I've worked here for far too long. What about you?"

"Oh, wow. Uhm...well...I'm Cori. I like reading and video games. My mission is….to be...a really good necromancer… and--"

"Next." Morris called out. "You're fired."

"What?" Cori's heart dropped.

"Not for realsies. But you simply must do better than that."

"I'm not really sure how…"

His tone became sarcastic. "Whyyyy would you like to be a 'really good necromancer', Cori?"

"Because...I want to heal things. My mother was a healer. Her name was Margaret too, so your advertisement called to me. I'd like to be a healer like her, but on my own path and in my own way. It makes me feel like maybe I'm connecting with her...somehow."

"Warmer. Go on."

"I-- I don't have any very long term goals," Cori said, "but I suppose I'll consider myself a really good necromancer when I feel like I've truly healed one soul."

"And what would truly healing a soul entail?" Morris asked.

"I don't know yet exactly. Maybe, bringing them back to life? Like, all the way back to life."

"Hmmm...Interesting." Morris said, looking at Cori quizzically. "If I'm being honest with you Cori, that's not quite what necromancer's do. Paladins heal souls, and bodies. Paladins bring creatures back to life. We necromancers give comfort to the dying. We reanimate bodies so that the dead may say goodbye where they may not otherwise have had the chance. But it is a thankless job, and often tedious. If you'd like me to refer you to the local Chapter of the Order of Paladins, I'd be more than happy to."

"No, no. I'm sorry I grew up learning the traditional methods of healing in my family, and that's how I think sometimes." Cori said, thinking of all the times her father tried to teach her the golden laced magicks of traditional healing. "But like I said, I want to forge my own path."

"An admirable desire." Morris held out his hand, and Cori shook it instinctively. "It is nice to meet you, Coriander Lou. I hope you find what you are looking for."

"You can just call me, Cori." She said.

Morris glared, then smiled. "Your eyes are like iron. I like it. Now, for however long it may take you, I shall be your teacher; and you, my newest apprentice. Of course, you'll be among kin. You met Dana already. She's a peach, but not terribly talented in the arcane. Then there's Maya, my prodige. Derrick...he's a bit of a queef. Sammiel, a dark, brooding type. Usually works the night shift. Tres chic." He snapped his fingers and stood from his chair. Cori was taking note that whenever Morris said an even vaguely foreign word, he would pronounce it in an exaggerated accent that often was nothing similar to it's actual linguistic origin. "Follow me. Where was I? Ah, yes. There's Kitsune, our resident Jiangshi. Or, Vampire, just not quite your westernized sort, or so she'd tell you. Obviously, she's on night shift. She's technically undead herself, but we're really hurting for staff. Oh, and can't forget Luke. Also night shift. Sweet old geezer. He might as well be undead for how long he's got left in those bones." Cori scurried along behind Morris as he continued to speak. "Unfortunately, that's all we've got for now. Even *with* you we'll be short staffed. People just aren't willing to work with decaying flesh like they used to be. Hello, Nigel."

  Morris stopped in front of an open doorway where a barely decomposed zombie stood and moaned, rubbing his fingers around his belly button and chewing on his bottom lip, which barely had any lip left. The zombie raised his hand, and Morris gave him a high five. "Say hello to our new staff. This is Cori."

  Cori raised her hand and gave a small 'hello', and the zombie snapped his teeth at her.

  "Now Nigel, stop that." Morris said playfully, swishing his silky red robe as he turned, but then as they walked away he bent down to Cori's ear, "Do be careful. It's only ever happened once, but he did eat the brains of one of our staff before." Cori gave a horrified gasp as Morris chuckled. "Don't worry, he only got one good lick before I stepped in. Damian is fine now, and has mad good worker's comp covering him for the rest of his life. Only lost his comprehension of numbers. A real good deal, I'd say."

  "Your room will be in the East Wing." Morris continued in his tour guide voice. "I've placed wards on all the staff bedrooms, so it'll be the one place in the house where you can actually get some peace and quiet. In your interview you mentioned that you liked reading, and we had a room open just next to the library, and I thought that'd be nice for you. Are you comfortable with interdimensional portals? There'll be one in your closet. Don't worry, it's relatively safe."

  Cori struggled to enjoy the idea of her own library against her pressing visualization of the pain that would come from having your skull bit open by a zombie, or the lurking horrors that might await just beyond the confines of this reality. But she managed to say "Thank you" as they kept up their walk back downstairs, through a recreation room filled with arcade games, a pool table, a bar, a hookah, and the detailed chalk drawn geometries of forgotten witchcraft

"Next to your room is Sarah's...she's a bit of a banshee some nights but she'll be your best friend before you know it. Watch out." A chair flew towards Cori, and exploded in a shower of splinters with a flick of Morris's wrist and a fork of lightning. "Ho ho! Who was that? Bah, invisible. Come now, who was that? Oddie, I know it was you. Oddie is a poltergeist. Keeps you on your toes, that one. But he's got a real talent for arranging furniture."

Cori already had the urge to run. It had only taken a few minutes for the house to erupt in such chaos. But she didn't have enough money for a train ticket home, and that rickety bridge the train crossed to arrive seemed to be the greater danger.

"Derrick get off your phone, you sick lard!" The disgust in Morris' voice was apparent, though there was a small smirk at the edge of his lips. "You're still on probation."

Derrick's face might have been somewhat non-descript if not for the lip rings and eyebrow piercings and heavy egyptian eye makeup darkening an already dark and youthful face. His hair was in a poorly tended faux hawk, and dyed acid green. He did not look up from his phone. He had his feet kicked up onto the pool table. "I never signed your damn probation letter, Morris. I was having a bad week, Morris. Will you get off me?"

"You missed your shift three days in a row." Morris hissed.

Derrick looked at Cori then back at Morris. "You know I was in a bad place." He said.

"I'll put you in a worse place to give you some perspective, then. Now get your ass downstairs. Sol's binding will wear off any hour now, and you know how he gets if he even spends a minute without a body. And change your damn clothes. No flip flops! I want to see mid-level Necromancer gear. You look like a tween."

Derrick groaned, and swiveled in his chair but did not get up. Morris waved his hand, producing a small firecracker explosion.

Derrick hopped up and walked away until Morris waved his hand and produced another *crack* and another, trailing Derrick as he moved faster and faster.

"I'd kill him, but then we'd just wind up having to take care of him." Morris said, and Cori had trouble deciding if he meant it or not. "Moving on." Morris said as they went past the rec room into the halls beyond.

"Um, I'm not too sure I'll be able to...I haven't really done..." Cori couldn't phrase her thoughts properly. "This is all a bit over my head..."

"Nonsense. Your aura flares with brilliance. Shush that noise. Wait!" Morris held a hand out in front of Cori in a sudden halt. "No...it can't be..." Morris faced a door that was bending on its hinges at the end of the hallway, covered about by protective sigils which were popping and burning now, one by one. "Run." He whispered. Then he yelled, "Ruuuun."

The door burst open. Shadows full of gnarled maws and gnashing teeth spilled forth violently. Ghastly figures and a tsunami of ectoplasm tore at the edges of the walls. Morris frowned and his eyes widened with madness as he cast a shimmering blue shield against which the demonic host crashed.

Cori ran away, fast as her little legs would carry her.

"Your past does not define you!" She heard Morris shout to the creature of darkness, his voice shaking the very walls. "Calm yourself!"

Cori tried to find the front door. She wanted to leave this place, but she became lost in the maze of halls. Spectral faces grinned at her and cackled as she passed, and Nigel the Zombie snapped at her but lost his jaw in the process. The paintings looked at her as she passed and there was an unholy wailing from every direction. Candles levitated and shadows danced in the corner of her eyes as she ran and ran.

She tried to back track, but found herself downstairs in the library Morris had spoken of. Panting as she slammed the door behind her, Cori spied the ghastly little spectre she had first met on the front porch. The girl was quietly reading a book, but looked up and smiled. She had big circular glasses, too big for her face, and she had a little red bow in her hair. The ghost girl stood upright and approached. "You're the new girl. I'm Sarah." Her voice was a mournful whisper, but sweet. "What's your name?"

"Cori." Cori replied breathlessly, still afraid of what horror might assail her now, but trusting the child. "You're Sarah? Morris had said…"

The ghost drifted close and softly placed a small and incorporeal hand against Cori's, producing a chill. "We're going to have our rooms next to each other, right?"

Cori hesitated, but nodded. There was such hope in the question. The girl's eyes were bright and wide.

"Good." The girl said. "You seem nice." And with that, the ghost girl Sarah faded from the world.

Alone, Cori stood and caught her breath. She put her hands on her knees, stretched a bit, and took assessment of her situation. The library, a place of peace and possibility, brought a steadiness and familiarity into Cori's mind. The soft glow of the candelabra and the woodsy scene from the great but grimy windows at the edge of the room lent further to the calming atmosphere. Cori was alone with the several plants that adorned the shelving.

Cori took a deep breath and assessed her situation. She had come here to do good work. She had come to give help to those undead whom the world had cast aside. Good work is rarely easy. *That girl seemed sweet*, Cori thought. It hardly seemed as though she needed any help, but then, Morris had said she was like a banshee on some nights. Why might she be bound to this mortal coil? Cori asked herself.

"You the new girl?" Came a voice from behind her, bringing even more surprise to Cori's already fragile heart..

"Yeah…I think." Cori sighed, and turned around. "Hi, I'm Cori." A woman stood before her that was about Cori's own age, but with a deeper set maturity and keen eyes. Her skin was dark, and her hair was woven and strung about with brightly colored string. She had a septum piercing, and dark red lips against bright teeth. She wore metallic skull anklets set upon woven harem pants, and a chainmail corset.

"I'm Maya." The woman said. "Looks like you got spooked, huh?"

Cori sighed. "That'd be an understatement."

"Don't worry. Everyone does when they first get here. First day jitters take on a whole new meaning in this place." Maya approached and offered Cori her hand, which Cori shook. "You'll get the hang of it though. You need a minute?"

Cori could feel that her face was drained of all blood, and that she was sweating, and that she was panting, but for all this she said "No, no, I'm good." Her voice cracked while she was saying it.

Maya laughed and offered Cori a waterskin which contained a sweet and golden liquid. Cori drank it, and felt some of her life return. "Well, if it means anything to you, you couldn't have come at a better time. I wouldn't blame you if you bust out of here, but it'd be a huge help if you stayed. Most of us are on half a year without any days off. You good?" Maya asked.

"Yea, much better." Cori replied.

"Well, the least I could do is show you to your room. Then, if that doesn't convince you, hell I don't know I'll have to bribe you or something. I really need a day off." Maya laughed, and smiled in such a way that it seemed a bribe in itself. "Come on, follow me. Maybe there's a rag in there we can wipe all that sweat off your face."

Chapter 2

"Oh...it's lovely."

"Honey, don't lie." Maya put her hands on her hips.

Cori's new bedroom was consistent and pure in its adherence to a dusty abandonment aesthetic. There was a window caked with grime, a bed with no mattress, a single hanging empty light socket, and a hearth piled with ash besides a bath basin and some cookware. There was also one unmoving skeleton covered in cobwebs. Cori let out a small yelp.

"Sorry," Maya saw where Cori was looking, and grabbed the heap of bones and threw it over her shoulder as a few smaller pieces fell to the floor. "Damnit. I told Morris to get this place ready for you. He's up there in his office looking at memes." Maya said as her phone pinged. She showed Cori her phone, which had a case of scarlet geometry. "He literally just sent me a meme right now. Look at this. It is literally a meme about how he should be doing work instead of looking at memes. Whatever, don't worry about the skeleton, it's just one of the vessels we use for the reanimation. This used to be Kamayla's room."

"Kamayla?" Cori asked, looking out the window of her room to see what sort of view she'd have once she cleaned. She was fairly certain she could make out the graveyard and the river beyond.

"A resident ghost. She moved on." Maya said, her face a mix of wistful pride and grief.

"Oh...how--?"

"I mean, really that's our main job here, I'm sure Morris told you...well maybe Morris told you. We try to help them work through...whatever it is they have to work through. Some take longer than others. Some I'm not convinced will ever really move on."

"Yeah, he touched at that a bit. I'm not entirely sure I understand. I'm just kind of rolling with things at this point. I thought moving on was when they died and became ghosts." Cori said and Maya looked at her quizzically.

"Nah, nah, nah, girl look. So you die but then your spirit comes out and goes through to the Betwixt. There's all sorts of realms in there, heaven and hell and everything in between. But spirits 'move on' when they're no longer 'in between'. They're all the way gone, past the Betwixt. They usually have some unfinished business or another, and we help them work through it."

"You'd think they'd teach you that in school." Cori said.

"They don't teach you anything in school." Maya replied harshly.

"No kidding. I know about mitochondria though, so there's that. But so, what happened with Kamayla? What did she have to work through?"

"Ya know, sometimes we don't even know what does it. Kamayla started talking about her past a lot. She kept mentioning the way she'd dance with her husband when they first met. So I went out and found a few albums from back in her day. The third one must have struck a chord with her."

"That sounds nice enough." Cori said. "And so uh, where they go when they move on?"

Maya looked at Cori and raised an eyebrow. "I suppose that's hard to say." Maya said. "I mean, no one knows. But I've never really thought *they* go anywhere. There is no more 'they'. There's all sorts of places they can go 'before' they move on. They can go around all the Betwixt...the whole cosmos. But...I'm not sure there is anything once they pass the Villa..."

Something caught in Cori's throat, and she was no longer able to speak.

"Which of course makes it sad." Maya said as her eyes focused through the window on the far horizon. "You get really attached... But they're at rest, and that's important. Listen, I'm gonna go yell at Morris for not having anyone clean this room. Then I'll get you a mattress and some cleaning supplies, alright?"

"Thanks." Cori whimpered, and gazed out the window of her new room.

Maya came back shortly with a broom and a dustpan, and Cori set to work. First to go were the spider's webs. "I'm sorry. It's not you, really. It's me." Cori said to the scuttering arachnids who whispered curses at her from below. Then she set to the floor.

Maya returned a while later, carrying a mattress with Dana. "Hey, so I snagged this from Morris's room." She said, panting. "Figured it would be a good way to make him pay. He's got the best mattress in the house. Firm, European style. Certified organic, somehow."

Dana chuckled, "He's gonna be pissed."

"Serves him right."

"Oh, thank you." Cori said.

"Maya, you think we should give her the new hire orientation?" Dana asked in her doleful way. Cori noticed that through her makeup, Dana had eyes like a basset hound. "You know Morris won't."

"What, that dumb video that uses old timey animation to show how necromancy works?"

"Well yeah, that might be a good idea. But I was thinking maybe we could do it in a way that doesn't suck."

"Not a bad idea, Big D." Maya replied "Alright. Cori, what do you know about Magick?"

Cori hadn't been prepared for a quiz, but the answer was obvious enough. "Well...its a system of turning thought into reality, right?"

"Alright, but any middle school student knows that." Maya said with a knowing look. "What else?"

"It's...creativity but without a physical medium such as a canvas." Cori replied.

"What is the canvas, instead?" Dana asked.

"Energy?" Cori said, quickly, then more certainly. "Your body's energy. Its ether, its aura, or its will."

"Alright newbie." Maya said, nodding. "But then why does magick utilize so many formulae?"

"Oh, I mean, I know a number of formulae, if you want to know them." Cori said. She was beginning to sweat.

"No, no, no. Why?" Maya asked

"I don't know." Cori responded.

"No problem, not a lot of people do, but it's important. It's because magick relies on your mind's capacity to believe. Every addition to a spell or ritual, every sacred geometry or formulae which describes an entity in mathematical detail assists in your minds capacity to believe in what you're doing." Maya said, flourishing her arm with this great revelation.

"I did not know that." Cori admitted under her breath.

"And of course all formulae work to describe the realms of the Betwixt." Maya was beginning to talk like a college professor, and she pointed to her temple. "Do you care to tell me the connection between this and belief?"

"I know." Dana said, swooshing her hair back and forth.

"I...do not."

"That the Betwixt which they really ought to have taught you all about in high school is really a collective unconsciousness that feeds upon the belief of the residents of all the many worlds of the Cosmos." Maya said. "Boom. Mic drop."

"I feel like this is a lot to take in." Cori said, sitting upon her new mattress, then thinking better of it and standing back up.

"Well its important stuff." Maya said. "Now your job is going to be utilizing psychological tricks that conform to your beliefs and allow you to perform wonders such as reanimating a corpse. We reanimate a corpse with a binding for a soul. We put their little souls into skeletons and remind them of their names and keep them busy and try to find what last pieces of business they have, so that they can comfortably move through all this collective belief into the final sphere, the Villa of Ormen. You follow?"

"I think I'm getting dizzy." Cori said, and sat back down on the bed again.

"It won't be the last time." Dana wallowed.

"I'm gonna head to bed now." Maya had told her, "Sweet Dreams, Cori. Nice to have you on board."

"Don't let the bed bu--" Dana began. "Maya, you don't think Morris set any traps on the mattress, do you?"

"No...no. I mean...why would he?" Maya asked, but she didn't look like she had convinced herself by the time she left. "Best of luck with the cleaning."

Cori had never really had much to clean before. Her father had always been so good at it, so she knew how to keep things clean that were already clean, but had no experience in the realms of renovative cleaning. But it was that same inexperience with true grime that motivated her. She feared sleeping even one night so surrounded by the lurking presence of all these dust bunnies. What would they do to her lungs? Plus, it seemed the only way for her to escape the jarring revelations about the afterlife that Maya had been bombarding her with.

It was late in the night and Cori was sweating profusely when she finally proclaimed "There, done." It was far from done, but it was all she'd be able to do. The floors resembled hardwood. The bed was made and ready. There was a lightbulb hanging from a wire, and Cori had plugged her nightlight into a wall socket. The hearth was ready for new wood, should it be needed. The attached bathroom was now usable, even if the toilet seat was missing. She hadn't been able to scrub the chalk drawn geometries from the walls of the closet, but after some calculations she discovered these were, as Morris had told her, a portal to the Betwixt. There were no longer any spiderwebs, and the window produced only minimal visual obstruction. Done indeed.

As she lay on her new mattress, trying to invoke sleep, Cori felt the lurking fingers of an uncalled-for despair. A low growling could be heard echoing through the room. She looked down at her trembling fingers. "Oh merciful God above, I forgot dinner."

The house was no quieter than it had been during the day, just darker. There were still moans and howls, and footsteps both walking and running, and rappings upon walls and doors. However, now Cori was quite alone, lost in a maze of halls, set with a desperate lust for food. If there had been any need other than food, she would have found a way to stay in her room all night. But for food, no concessions could be made.

Creeping quietly, Cori hugged tight to the walls where the floorboards creaked the least. She made her way down her hallway and to the spiral stair which she approached cautiously. In the library, she was not alone. Candles were lit in the dark, and books were being organized, floating from one shelf to the next.

Cori took a deep breath and stepped down the spiral staircase slowly, trying not only to stay quiet; but to pretend that she was not at all part of the room and didn't even, in fact, exist. This she had always done quite naturally, even before Maya's suggestions of magick as a system of manipulating beliefs. In school, everyone had called Cori a ninja for her proclivity in the arts of stealth. She could be actively talking in a conversation without being noticed by anyone.

Ghosts do not fall for such tricks.

The books finished their floating arrangement, and all movement in the room ceased. Cori had reached the bottom step, but was halted by the sudden shift. A chill passed over her, and the air became thick. Cori stepped down further. It was just Sarah, right? Sarah seemed the sort to haunt the library.

"Hello…?" Cori said, trying to start a dialogue with whatever phantasms might be in witness. But there was nothing. Only silence responded as Cori continued creeping forward, acting as though this was all quite normal. She looked out the grand library windows, hoping for some comfort of nature, but saw only a foggy night time forest and tombstones lit by a flickering floodlight. Just then, deep from within the manor, an organ sounded a discordant note. Cori was paralyzed with fear when a rush of air which blew out all the candles, and left the room in perfect darkness, all except for one door at the opposite end.

I'm going to have to run for it. Cori thought, her heart was pounding through her chest, sweat dripping. But before she could finish that thought, the door started closing ever so slowly.

Cori leapt forward, racing towards the last vestige of light. From behind she could hear the patter of footsteps drawing close behind her. A moan filled the air and gained in pitch as her pursuer came ever closer. Cori ran to catch the closing door of the library as the sound of books flapped off the shelves. She reached the knob, and flew out into the brightly lit hallway, slamming the library door behind her.

"Hey."

Cori shrieked.

"Whoa, whoa, whoa. Sorry, didn't mean to scare ya." To Cori's left was a solid human. He wore long black robes, bound in leather straps like so many belts. Arcane tattoo's wound their way up his neck, and his shoulder length hair, shaved on one side was a striking silver that matched his ethereal green eyes. "I'm Sammiel. But most people just call me Sam." He said, his voice like rusty tin. "You must be the new girl."

"Yeah. Cori."

"Are you...afraid of ghosts?" He asked, chuckling and trying to peek behind Cori.

"What? No." Cori tried to laugh, and brushed her hand against her cheek which was glistening with sweat and tears.

"You just ran out of that room bone white, and slammed the door behind you."

"I've been around plenty of ghosts." She said, more firmly now. "That one was just…"

"Just?"

"Scary." Cori said, as she looked down at her feet.

"I see."

"It turned off all the lights. I couldn't see anything."

"So, you're scared of the dark then." Sammiel said, his eyes curling mischievously.

"I suppose that might be closer to the truth." Cori said, resenting this plunge into her psyche.

"I hate to tell you, but two of your shifts are going to be night shifts."

"What?"

Sammiel nodded, grim yet with the same mischievous spark in his eyes. "You're my relief for one of them, and Luke's for another. What were you doing out of bed anyway? It's really late."

"I needed--" But Cori's stomach answered loudly before she could.

"I see." Sammiel smirked with lips of pale pink gossamer. "Come on, I'll show you to the kitchen." And Sammiel led Cori through the halls. She was relieved to see they were more brightly lit in this part of the house. Sammiel trailed a mysterious scent behind him, strong, of herbal musk. Maybe Frankincense. Cori took note from behind of his odd gait, and secretly made fun of his fashion choices.

They hadn't been too far from the kitchen, and Cori felt as though she could replicate the directions again on her own. *Left out the library, right past the creepy baby painting, through the secret bookshelf door at the end of the hall, on through the dining room with the levitating candelabra, exit the door on the right, take a left, then another left at the weeping demonic bust, then it's the door at the end.* Easy.

The kitchen held a position in the house much akin to a heart. From what Cori could tell, it was as near to central as anything could be on the first floor. It was well lit, and comfortable, and warm; aside from the ectoplasm oozing from the far wall. There was Nigel the zombie at the table eating microwave sausages, a ghost combing her hair in the mirror with fluctuating fanaticism, and another pale spirit who oozed blood down his neck at all times like a waterfall. The blood was so vivid, Cori could not tell if it was physical. This was the most activity Cori had seen in a single room yet, and it brought some comfort to the mysteries of the night.

"Say hi to Cori, everyone." Sammiel said as he daintily sat at the table. Nigel grunted, and neither of the ghosts so much as turned their heads. "They'll get used to you. People come and go a lot, so it takes a while before they really bother to get to know you."

"Well, I look forward to it." Cori said, trying to maintain some semblance of positivity in the face of her gnawing hunger which reached into her mind like tendrils out of The Great Abyss.

Sam pointed to the zombie. "That's Nigel."

"We've met."

"And the lady in the mirror is Jacquelin. And the one at the fridge is Ernie."

"I'm sorry to interrupt but I need to eat before I kill someone." Cori said as she made her way to the cupboards and started opening them at random. Every word her new coworker spoke made her despise him more as he kept her from her prey and the ultimate satisfaction of her nocturnal desires.

"Oh, right yeah." Sam said as he watched Cori plunder the cupboards, disturbed by Cori's brazen salacity. "Knock yourself out."

"Do I just grab anything?" She asked, already stuffing crackers in her mouth.

"Yeah, go crazy."

There were all sorts of unique things to be found in the kitchen. Curry Pop Rice, Squid Munchums, Country Soured Toast, Chips Galore, Fraggle Pudding, Eye of Newt, Schlanger's Canned Meats, Nuggat Waifs.

One thing above all others stood. "Whaaaaa--?" Her sparkling eyes lay upon a wholesale tub of frozen sweet and sour chicken.

"Oh yeah, Morris is mad for sweet and sour. I wouldn't touch it though." Sammiel tried frantically to reach out and stop Cori, but to no avail.

"Morris can bite my ass. What's he gonna do, fire me?" It was testament to Cori's depraved appetite that she could speak so boldly.

Sammiel crossed his arms and smiled. "Well, in that case he usually has a smaller load thawed and ready in the fridge."

Cori threw open the fridge and tossed aside every condiment and tupperware that stood between her and her deep-fried gold. There. *Glory of Glories.* "Got any lemon?"

"Uh...? Yeah, bottom drawer."

Cori popped the chicken into the microwave then doused them heavily with lemon. The first bite scalded her tongue, but she ate just as fervently through the pain.

"Well, I guess I'll leave you to that." Sammiel said, backing away towards the front hall and scratching his head. "Nice meeting you."

Cori hardly registered his words, but when she regained her standard state of consciousness she found herself alone in the kitchen, feeling naked and shamed.

Chapter 3

Cori woke to a fist pounding at her door. She strained her eyes against the first light of dawn, trying to shake off strange and feverish dreams. She wasn't at all sure how she got back to her room, frenzied and drunk on sweet and sour chicken as she was. It was all a blur of MSG and grease. "Who is it?" Cori asked, but the only response was more pounding. Cori thought perhaps more spooks were coming to torment her, but that didn't matter quite as much in the daylight. Cori did have some experience with ghosts and their ilk, afterall.

"One minute, One minute." Cori hastily threw a silken robe from her pack over her shoulders and opened the door.

It was Morris. His face was red, but he looked as though he were trying very hard to keep composure, and his voice was measured and calm despite a lurking ferocity. "I have been informed that you ate some of my sweet and sour chicken. Is this true?"

Cori looked back on the intoxicated stupor that hunger had brought her into the night before. She cringed. "I'm sorry, I had forgotten to eat dinner last night. I can be a little brash when I'm hungry."

"Whatever it is that you turn into when you are hungry, I would like to impress that I am three times more horrifying when someone indulges in my sweet and sour chicken." Morris hissed.

Cori tried to say 'sorry' again but her mouth seized and a lump developed in her throat. Cori couldn't stand being yelled at, and though Morris had not yelled, it came close enough to bring dew to her eyes, which she attempted to stifle and hide.

"Oh...Oh no. Don't do that. No, no, no." Morris flailed his arms around and looked for someone to help. Then he reached out his hand and distantly patted Cori upon the head as if she had the flu. "There, there. All's well. No tears."

Cori made to wipe her tears away, and suppressed a sniffle.

"No, stop, you fool." Morris said, and pulled a vial from his sleeve. "Collect them. Tears are a hot commodity. Healing, you see. People will buy them for a mint."

And so Cori lifted a vial to her eyes and collected her tears and offered them to Morris who shook his head and motioned them back to her. Cori looked away, tucked the vials into her satchel, and tried to gain composure while doing what she could to hide the red flush in her face. She said, "I'm sorry about the sweet and sour chicken. It's my favorite."

"Stuff and nonsense." Morris replied, his rage disintegrated. "Your favorite you say? Hmmm...I'll tell you what. If it makes you happy...you may have...one pint of my sour chicken a day. But you must tell no one!"

"Every day?" Cori's wet eyes glittered with the prospect.

"But tell no one. The second even one of the others is allowed to dip their frail fingers into that succulent gold, all of them will be clamoring for it like howler monkeys."

"Deal."

"Pinky promise?" Morris's eyes were wide and his voice held the airs of great importance.

"Pinky promise." Cori said, and they shook pinky's on it.

"Come. It is time for your training to begin."

"Well, okay, lemme get changed first." She said.

"Of course, of course."

Cori came out a minute later, wearing a turquoise summer dress with a wide brimmed black hat and sunglasses, for she could already feel the southern heat as the bright sun rose higher in her window.

"Ah, hmm...yes...Is that all you have to wear?" Morris asked, looking at Cori as though she had four arms.

"Yup, pretty much. I only brought one pack with me." Cori said, uncertain why she would need to explain herself. "I've been looking forward to the day I could wear it. I thought it looked nice."

Morris grumbled, then led Cori through the route she had learned to the kitchen, rambling the whole way about the importance of the color black and the symbolism of skulls, and how you should dress for the job you want, but even more importantly dress for the job you have. He himself was wearing a dark cloak, decorated with silver chain link.

They proceeded through the kitchen and into the greenhouse, which dropped Cori's jaw a few inches. It was the only place inside the manor that felt lively. Cori had thought she'd now be living her life in a haze of shadow and miasma, but the greenhouse felt golden and woodsy. She was surprised to find Dana sans makeup and wearing jeans and dirty gardeners gloves, wiping her brow of sweat and tending to the budding sycamores next to the hemlock.

"Oh gosh." Dana said. "Don't look at me. I'm a mess."

"I didn't know we had a green house?" Cori exclaimed, running her hands along the petals of the petunias. "Am I allowed in here?"

"Does the dress code mean nothing anymore?" Morris asked to the sound of a lone cricket.

"So long as you take care of my babies." Dana said, emitting a maternal frown of worry and love. "Are you interested in gardening?"

"Uh, yes!"

"Well, I could show you around sometime. There's a lot to take care of between the greenhouse and the backyard."

"Are you ladies done?" Morris asked, his eyes fixed on his phone, which was ensconced in a purple velvet case. "I thought I was training a necromancer, not Martha Stewart."

Morris led Cori out of the greenhouse and through a long back patio where an empty rocking chair was creaking back and forth. Cori and Morris followed a brick path through a well tended though overgrown garden and wove their way down a wooden stair that led to a cemetery perched peacefully along the riverbed. Some of the tombstones at one corner were half submerged in stale river water. Clouds by this time had rolled in to ease the heat of the day to a dull overcast, with small shafts of light gliding lazily across the tombstones. Many of the graves looked freshly dug, and some were done haphazardly, with shoes or hands still sticking through the mud.

"We use the cemetery often, so we tend to keep the graves shallow." Morris said, noting that Cori's eyes were trailing to the semi surfaced cadaver limbs. "People donate themselves to our cause in their will. We use the bodies for a number of things. Replacement bones for the few residents who enjoy using skeletons. Bones can be so fragile. Then, Nigel needs a new body from time to time. Do you know how to reanimate a corpse, Cori? Reanimate...not bring back to life. You know the difference, right?"

"Yes, of course. I've only reanimated small animals before." Cori said, embarrassed and adding, "But I've never been able to practice with a human before."

"Then you're already more skilled than Dana." Morris said, giving Cori a little golf clap. "Good for you. Humans aren't so different. The largest obstacle is in the mind. We presume that humans must be so different from small animals, and we block ourselves with the expectation that it will be incredibly difficult. Not so. It is all approximately the same. You still need a spirit to bind to the body, or a construct if you wish to control it yourself. You still need to rig the bones with the strings of animation, and utilize some basic logic matrices. It works the same way for both zombies and skeletons. Then, you connect the strings into their proper places in the central ego matrix of the spirit or construct. Voila! The only difference is that some extra energy is required to properly animate a human. With a squirrel it does well enough to just give it some of your own life force, but with a human there needs to be a power source if the spell has to hold for a while. We use maelstrom charged quartz here, then place it in either the belly of the cadaver or the skull of the skeleton. Allow me to demonstrate."

Morris put on his theatrical airs once again, and thrust his hands into the air. A nearby tombstone shifted, and the earth lifted, and a comically crisp corpse with empty eye sockets came through the dirt and brought an electrified stink to the air.

"Poor sap died in a flood. Forgot to cut the power on the fuse box. Zzzzzzap." Morris chuckled, then put his hands together as if he were holding a ball, and an electric blue data sphere grew visible. "I'm going to make a very simple construct, created with the sole purpose of dancing, and then dissolving after one minute. Never forget that with constructs. They must be programmed to dissolve. And, for such a short duration as this, we won't need a power source."

"Got it." Cori nodded, in awe at the swift and natural way Morris was able to create a construct. Cori had never been able to make one before. It required detailed and analytical thought. It required a great deal of memorization, and spatial visualization. These things she did not have in excess.

The matrix orb floated over to the cadaver and lodged itself inside its chest. Then, from Morris, thin white strings like spider silk grew from his fingers, and drifted eloquently into all the limbs of the cadaver. Still connected, Morris twitched his pinky, and the arm of the cadaver flailed. He closed his eyes in concentration, and flicked his middle finger, which caused the whole body to shiver. "Obviously..." Morris said, his eyes still closed, "One must have a very thorough understanding of anatomy. And one must also have the finely attuned senses necessary to properly probe the body and mind. Listening is key. One must listen to every vibration, every twitch, every nuance within the body. Ah, there we go."

The silky threads detached from Morris's fingers, and the body lifted its head. Then it flipped itself onto its feet and began a skillfully choreographed dance. Though there was no music, the dance itself was so clear in its rhythm that Cori felt she could hear the tune.

Cori laughed and Morris smiled, and soon the corpse collapsed with a final groan to the Earth.

"Now you try." Morris said.

"I wouldn't even know where to begin. I don't know how to make a construct."

"No? I'll send a tome over to your room later today so you can learn. It's certainly not mandatory. You can bet your ass Derrick hasn't ruffled the pages of a book since grade school. But you know, Cori, a lot of people come through here, and most of them are nincompoops. On the rare occasion that someone isn't, it's usually apparent as soon as they walk through the door."

Cori waited for a moment for Morris to continue, but he didn't. "I see...so you're saying I'm not a--?"

Morris looked startled. "Oh no, I haven't the foggiest. It wasn't at all apparent with you. That's why it's especially important that you study."

Cori's shoulders drooped, and Morris placed his attention elsewhere. Cori began to walk off as Morris studied the cadaver he had animated and muttered about how Derrick would need to get on shovel duty and bury the body once more. At the edge of the graveyard and near the river bed stood the small stone chapel Cori had seen when she first arrived. She had always found chapels to be peaceful and pleasant places, and everything else around this manor had been so lovely. She walked towards it to see if she could take a peek within.

She heard the flapping of robes as Morris swooped in front of her. "No, no, no. The chapel is strictly off limits."

"Oh, what? Why?"

"It's Kitsune's room. She'll lick out your eyes if you come into her room without invitation. Especially in the daytime." Cori pulled her hand back from the doorway slowly, before Morris said, "Now off with you, small one. Shoo, shoo. Go find Maya, she will train you in the more mundane natures of this position. Oh, oh...and, staff meeting...next Tuesday. Not this Tuesday. Some guy from HR is going to be here."

Cori walked around the manor's grizzly brick exterior and into the front door, passed through the dank foyer, which led into the family room, which led into the parlor, which led to a smokery, which led to a dusty ballroom filled to the brim with nearly deflated balloons. From behind the ballroom bar, a skeleton struggled greedily with the cap of a bottle of rum. Cori quietly offered her hand to the grateful spook, and opened the bottle which he then chugged.

"Sol, right?" Cori asked, and the skeleton nodded. "I don't think we've been introduced but Morris told me a little about you." Sol offered his hand which Cori then shook. Then, he clattered and cackled like a delighted imp. Cori smiled instinctively. "Say, you wouldn't know where the stairwell is, would you? I need to find Maya."

Sol pointed to a doorway, then grabbed Cori's hand and led her to it. He pointed down the inverse hallway, which twisted gravity to its spiraling course. "Thanks." Cori said while Sol popped another swig of rum. Checking doorways as she went, Cori opened a door to a dark room. In it, a man sat cross legged, and intently watched the static white noise on a TV. His neck craned, and his head snapped in reverse to stare at Cori with a wide and toothy grin. There were no eyes in his gray and moldy face. Cori closed that door as quickly as she could. A shiver formed in her spine. She took note of the number 113 scratched into the wood above her head. Most of the other doors in the hall had numbers scratched into them, but one door had a fire escape sign next to it; and Cori presumed this to be a stairwell.

Cori entered and looked up the white painted stairwell, and found it higher than she had expected. And lower. "There's a basement?" Cori went downstairs and found a doorway, chained and padlocked. "Curiouser and curiouser." She muttered to herself.

Back upstairs, she found her way to the second floor. The layout was not at all the same as it had been below. Here, she found herself in a doll maker's workshop. Fabrics, paints, glues, clutter, and dozens of dolls, lit only distantly by the brightness coming in from the light of the windows of the stairwell. Cori skittered her way to the door on the right as quickly as she could, and found herself amongst masses of fabrics and mannequins and dresses.

It was all becoming too much. Cori felt short of breath again, drawn inward to her anxieties. "Maya." She called, as loud as she could manage with the knowledge that at any second she could be assailed by the undead, but there was no response.

More doors, more hallways; each more bizarre than the last. One room might appeared to be a torture chamber, while the next one over appeared to lead into a nocturnal garden from another world. It was from within this room that Corey heard a haunting piano melody that was simply too enchanting to resist.

From within the eves of this starry garden and behind moonflowers and irises gleamed the melody from a white piano played deftly by a skeleton strung about by wreaths and flowers. The skeleton slammed its bones into the keys and let out a long wail.

"Oh stop that, you need to be able to play in front of other people if you're ever going to perform for an audience." Maya said. "Hiya Cori, this is Franklin."

"Hi." Cori said, and Franklin clacked his teeth.

"Okay, try it again." Maya said, and Franklin began playing a melody, melancholic like the long void between the stars in the sky. Cori stayed silent and watched Franklin perform, and at the end, both of the living applauded the dead. "Bravo! I didn't expect you to actually do it with anyone else here. That's a huge step, Franklin!" Maya clapped Franklin hard on the spine, throwing the bones forward into the piano. "Sorry. Cori, Franklin here has been practicing to do a live concert."

Franklin stood up and nodded and bowed, then offered his bony hand to Cori, and Cori shook. "That was really beautiful." Cori said, and Franklin tapped his feet in a delighted fashion

"Franklin played piano his whole life, and always wanted to be a musician, but was always too afraid to play in front of anyone aside from his family." Maya said. "We got lucky. We usually don't get that much information, but his daughter brought him here just a couple months ago and they knew exactly why he was still bound to this world. Seems like a cut and dry case."

Franklin went over to the door and pointed to it. "Yeah go ahead, you're free for the morning." Maya said, and Franklin left the room. "You shadowing me today?" Maya asked Cori.

"Yeah."

"Surprised you found me. Can't have been easy."

"Definitely wasn't easy." Cori said, laughing. "Why the hell is there a room full of dolls?"

"Right?" Maya said. "I told Morris, I told him. You can't put a room full of creepy ass dolls in a creepy ass manor. It just isn't right. But art is one of the most common ways we help any of the spirits, so there's a room for almost anything you could think of, and if there isn't I'm sure Morris would let you make one."

"I'm sure I'll be able to think of at least ten things."

Maya gave Cori a wink. "Yeah, you're going to do just fine here. Come on, follow me."

They left the room and Maya took Cori on yet another tour, this time through the East Wing. Maya made an energetic tour guide, and it quickly became apparent that she had that rare sort of personality that could show happiness with the same ease as the sun shines light. She smiled and joked and bobbed her head with every small observation. "Now don't work your panties in a knot trying to figure the layabout. I still don't know how to get around some places. Watch your head. Got a bump from that lamp last week, hoo."

"Wack."

"So you'll get a schedule. We'll give you a caseload with a few spirits to visit each day. Some of them we know what helps them, some of them you're going to try to figure out." They passed into what appeared to be a windowless candy shop where Cori swore she saw that same smiling spectre from Room 113 behind the counter for just a moment. Maya continued. "But even if we think we know what they need, it always helps to listen to them, their whispers. You might figure out something new that we don't know already." Then they passed into a new hallway, and Maya opened the door to a room full of records and filing cabinets. "This room's warded, so it's another room where you can get some peace and quiet. Great for screaming, hah. We have records in here of every ghost that's ever passed through this house. So when you get your caseload, I'd say you start with this room and research a bit before going to see everyone."

"I don't have to read all of that do I?" Cori asked, staring at the shelves and shelves full of thick manilla folders, brimming with papers.

"If I'm being real with you, Cori, I haven't read a single one of them." Maya said, slapping her knees as she laughed. "But do as I say, not as I do. Just read a little whenever you work with someone." They left the archives behind. "Now, I don't know if you saw the basement door yet. Off limits. You won't get a key, but don't you try any 'alohomora' shit either."

"All these off limits places, why can't I go in the basement?"

"Well, that's where we keep the spirits that reach a sort of...point of no return. It's a labyrinth that runs beneath the whole estate, and maybe even a little farther. I dunno, I've never been down there. But if the spirits become so dark that they start dragging others down with them, or pose a threat to the staff, and there's really no hope that anyone can find, we have to put them down there. At least until arcana improves or some buddha comes around offering free exorcisms. The spirits turn into demons, basically."

"That's so sad." Cori said.

"Yeah...Keiran is gonna go down there soon if nothin' improves."

"Keiran?"

"Yeah, Morris has been having a lot of trouble with him. Real powerful spirit, too. Busted up a door last night."

"Oh him? I saw that..."

"It's a shame, he's the best when he's calm, but he's been turning into...that...more and more often." Maya frowned thoughtfully, then regained her smile. "You know anything about embalming?"

"Not a thing."

"Your lucky day. Come on."

Maya guided Cori next door and walked her through all the oils and chemicals and the necessity of keeping cadavers fresh. She showed her the importance of cadavers in the process of helping spirits say their goodbyes to the mortal coil and to finally rest in peace, and introduced Cori to the staff rumor mill.

"Okay, okay, you're gonna hear it here first. I'm a big old gossip. You want the tea, you're coming to me. So who have you met so far?" Maya said, wrist deep in an autopsy she was performing in an effort to give Cori a better understanding of anatomy. "Yeah, see, there's the lymph nodes. Slippery little suckers."

"I think I've only worked with you and Dana and Morris. I saw Derrick once though." Cori said.

"Okay, so Morris is our boss and so I respect him on that level, but the dude is losing touch. I just don't think he cares anymore, so the whole ship is kind of sinking around him. That's less fun gossip. I'm gonna take his place when he finally goes though, mark my words. Dana is more fun. You can see it when you meet her, sad sweetheart. She's the mama of the bunch. That said, there are at least five different men who visit here to see her."

"What?" Cori slapped Maya's arm, causing some spillage in the anatomy. "Don't even."

"Mhm. That girl is looking so hard for a baby daddy." Maya said, removing her bloodied gloves and washing her hands. "Can't tell with the makeup, but she's like mid thirties. Those ovaries are screaming, but they are just picky as hell or something. I've got no idea. Give her half a minute and she'll trash talk each and every one the guys that come around. One is in and out of prison, another one is just looking to be friends, another one really wants her but he's her least favorite, etc etc."

"Huh."

"Then I like Dana and all, but then she gets all warm and cozy when Sammiel's around. And it's like...girl let up, you got five, you don't need six. But Sammiel's a real professional sort, so that's hopeless." Maya said, then began showing Cori a makeup kit. "You can use makeup if you want to make the cadavers look alright. Most times we're all lazy and don't mind the sight of decay, but your call. I'll show you how at least."

"Thanks. And yeah I met Sammiel too, duh." Cori said. "Definitely one of the more attractive guys around here. If you're into that sort."

"Well, I don't know about you, but I'm into gorgeous men, myself." Maya said. "And its not all looks with Sam, but... I don't know, he doesn't really seem to have any ambition or know what he wants. He just stays up in his room most times and plays around. But whatever, enough about him."

"So then, Derrick. He's cute, but he's a big flirt, and he's got this one girlfriend he breaks up with every other week, so don't get any ideas."

"Not really my type." Cori clarified, recalling the piercings and acid green mohawk.

Maya honed her focus onto achieving the perfect eyeliner on her corpse. "There. Now, of course there's Luke. Sweet old man, likes poetry. You would never guess that he was like this hard ass warrior when he was young. He's got a couple of Berserker tattoo's on his arm that he'd be glad to show you, along with a bunch of scars. And from what I heard, he only ever learned Necromancy after the Crimson Plague so that he could properly guide on the souls of his dead wife and child."

"Oh my God, that's so sad." Cori cupped her hand around her mouth.

Maya nodded, and set down all her tools. "Yup. Then there's Kitsune. I don't even know where to begin with Kitsune. You just have to meet her. Come on. I'm going to show you my room. We can take a break, maybe have some tea."

Cori and Maya left the embalming room, came back the way they came and climbed up to the third floor using a stair hidden behind a false wall.

"Tons of secret passages in this place." Maya said and unlocked the door at the top of the stair. She unveiled a room of bohemian fantasy. A room covered in red fabrics and dark stained wood and antique lamps, hanging plants, and macabre curios on shelves next to a well cultivated selection of books. It was all lit easily by a skylight and several crystal clear windows that reached up a few floors as the room wrapped around into the tower Cori had spied from the outside. "So this is my room…"

"What." Cori said, barely keeping her jaw off the floor.

Maya flashed her teeth. "Don't worry, mine looked a lot like yours did when I first got here. But you know, we don't pay rent living here, so even though the pay is kind of shit, we do wind up with a bit extra. Annnnnd I have an online shopping addiction."

Maya's voice was drowned by Cori's curiosity as she lay her fingers on a shrunken head and her gaze panned left to a bat encased in glass. Wherever books couldn't fit on shelves, they stacked upon the floor. *The Final Doorway, Twelve Principles to Reanimation, Possession: Tips and Tricks for the Aspiring Artist, Spirits Wail: Healing for the Earthbound Dead, Advanced Cantrips.*

"You're really into this job, aren't you?" Cori asked Maya.

"Yeah." Maya bobbed her head and acted coy for a moment, but her passion broke through. "I mean it's like, what's more important? Death is just about the only guarantee in life, right? But some people get screwed out of doing it right. So, if you wanna help people, maybe you could be a doctor, or Paladin. But no matter what, your patient or clergy will eventually die. Your healing will eventually not matter. But here, what we do is really the final and most important healing. And I'm sorry, but Morris won't be here forever. And when the higher ups come around looking for a new supervisor I'm gonna make sure they know who the right girl for the job is." Then Maya took on a subtle frown. "Sorry, my mouth is just running all on its own today."

"No, that's...exactly how I feel. I mean, I wouldn't have been able to put it so eloquently... My mom was a healer." Cori said, frowning and looking up into the tower windows. "But I wasn't the priestess or Paladin sort. I don't have too much of a talent for healing… or anything really. But I can see and talk to ghosts, so I felt like this would be the most healing thing I could do for the world. And my mom's name was Margaret, so when I saw this newspaper ad, it just felt like...like it was meant to be."

"She pass on?" Maya asked.

Cori sighed. "I guess. It was during the Crimson Plague. She was a Paladin so she had to leave to help heal people and stop its spread. She didn't come back."

Maya wrapped Cori in a warm and tight hug, then pulled back to look in Cori's eyes. "Yeah, we're gonna be cool, you and me." She said with a soft punch to Cori's arm, and Cori smiled at her new friend.

Chapter 4

Cori spent a few days shadowing Maya and learned the routines of the house. She learned to renew the binds on bodies, and to cast aether shields, against which spirits could not stand. Her power grew so that she didn't need a nap every time she cast a spell. She made a strong intention to read the book on constructs, 'Etheric Algorithms in Practice and Theory', that Morris sent to her, then forgot about it. Instead, she read more of the resident's files than she intended to, finding them not so much a tedious chore as she expected, and more of an entertaining pass time. Hundreds of mini-biographies that sat unappreciated in a totally silent corner of the house, just waiting for company.

Cori became more comfortable with her job and surroundings, and though most shifts still invoked mortal terror in her at some point or another, the thick airs in the house became less foreign and the apparitions grew less jarring. She learned how to listen for the toilet abomination before it would reach out to grab her, and learned enough morse code to have basic conversations with Penny, the little blind sprite who lived in the walls. And just as Cori began to think she'd be able to get used to the place, it came time for her to shadow for the night shift.

Cori had tried to explain her fear of the dark to Morris. Morris responded kindly, and brought her a heavy flashlight from his desk in his office, grinning as though the problem were solved. "May it serve you well. And here. Our St. Margaret's Brochure. It's got a map. Now, you will report to the kitchen at twenty four hundred. Kitsune will meet you there." Morris said, then sat and lost himself to mindlessly clicking between two emails on his laptop while Cori glared at him. Then she put her map and flashlight into the leather satchel she kept as a purse. "Don't let her steal your soul." He added, carelessly.

41

Cori tried to sleep in advance of her late shift to prepare her body and mind for the trials to come, but no sleep came to her, and she was unable to stomach the smell of pickled feet of valerian root Dana that had prescribed from the greenhouse apothecary. Instead, Cori wandered the halls so as to avoid the library past dark. She took Serpent's Pass, the winding corridor out the balcony of the library, which slithered in a curvature that was unnatural for walls. She then found herself near Keiran's apartment. Several new sigils replaced the old broken ones, but Cori could have sworn she perceived movement along the wooden grain of the door. The hallway stretched like a childhood nightmare and Cori took the first door she could to the recreation room besides.

Even in this brightly lit room of arcade games and dart boards, something was different past dark. It was quieter, and that lent itself to a more ominous atmosphere than the constant wailing and shrieking of the spectres of daylight.

"I need to learn to do this." Cori said to herself, more to hear her own voice than for the actual reminder. "One step at a time."

The air was thicker at night, and filled with illusion. Cori knew the landmarks and the halls she was walking through, but she kept getting lost all the same. She intended to scrounge some late night snacks in the candy shop, but found herself at the door to the Ossuary at the other end of the house. Something wasn't quite right with her head in these nighttime hours, and as she looked back down along the hallway, she found Ernie, transparent, legless and hovering, blood spraying as his neck twisted rapidly in all directions.

Seeking refuge in the Ossuary, Cori darted into a room of skulls and sculpted bone arranged into a Chandelier and fountains which trickled with a soothing song of water. Cori pulled out her map and flashlight, for the Ossuary's candlelight left much to be desired, though the incense was religiously pleasing.

"Okay, where are we?" Cori said, still insisting on talking to herself. "This is nonsense." The map revealed a manor which was an anomaly of architecture that didn't work by any standards of design. And, unsure of how she found herself here, she discovered she was in the Southwest corner of the Manor. The main stairwell was just a short distance away, just past the bottomless pit. Cori could get there so long as Ernie wasn't still out there, twitching his blood all over the place. She could use some defensive magick if he was going to be weird, but she didn't want to tucker herself out before the night shift. She was plenty tired enough as is.

Cori peaked open the Ossuary door. Ernie was not down the hall, though his blood could still be found covering the wallpaper. Silence. Nighttime.

A great moan issued forth, and Cori beheld Ernie's ghastly visage just inches from hers in the other direction, as he spread his neck wound and covered Cori in his crimson humours. Cori reflexively wove an aether shield, an energized blue bubble of her own aura structure, which saved her from much of the torrent and allowed her a quick escape to the twisting halls by the bottomless pit and into the main stairwell which led straight into the downstairs kitchen.

Cori was gibbering mindlessly when she entered the kitchen, covered in blood. She collapsed into one of the kitchen island's bar stools and laid her head down on the hardwood countertops. Sol was in the kitchen too, bound in a skeleton as he so often liked to be, and Cori hardly noticed him till he started clacking around the kitchen. Cori didn't lift her head to see what the commotion it was, but she heard the pitter patter of clinking utensils and pouring of water and the rush of steam and the fragrant morning aroma of freshly ground coffee beans.

Sol clattered to Cori and slammed a shot glass of hard espresso in front of her. Cori looked at the plastered and toothy grin of her skeletal companion and felt tears rising behind her eyes.

"For me?" Cori asked, and Sol nodded a bony rattle.

"Sol...that's incredibly sweet." Cori said, and she heard Sol's tell tale cackle from behind the world of sound. Cori sipped at the bitter draught and felt life return to her veins with every passing caffeine molecule. By the end of the shot, she felt electrified and alive. Somewhere nearby, she heard George hang himself off the stairwell, and then the peculiar sound of gears turning. Whirring contraptions and a *clunk, clunk, clunk.*

A door swung open, a door Cori had never noticed on the Eastern Wall of the kitchen. Crawling from within, a metallic claw grabbed the ceiling door frame. Upside down, a clockwork spider dug sharp legs into the ceiling. Hanging from this brass machination, seated firmly in the cushioned cockpit of the steampunk whirligig, a gray haired corpse pulled levers and twirled devices and piloted the spider to release its grip, which then landed deftly on the floor.

Or, not a corpse, Cori started to notice. Just a very old man. "Luke, right?" Cori asked the loosely skinned goblin. Cori thought for a moment that Morris hadn't been exaggerating so much by calling him 'nearly undead'. She reprimanded herself for the thought, and tried not to smirk at the old man's expense.

"What a night to be alive, isn't it? O look at all the fire folk sitting in the air!" He wheezed as he looked through the kitchen window, then held out a shaky hand and Cori shook it. His automaton powered down as steam whistled out an exhaust pipe in the back, and the legs lowered Luke's seat down. The old man had a long pointed and sparse white beard that looked as though it could have belonged to Morris a few centuries ago. His chin jutted apart from the rest of his face, and his eyes were beady and wet. He wore a dapper leather jerkin over a white dress shirt. His brass spider walker, Cori noticed, had gilded roses at the edges. "Might I have the pleasure of guiding you through your new job tonight?"

"Oh, I think I was supposed to meet Kitsune here." Cori said, looking back and forth for the jiangshi Morris had described.

Luke's automaton jittered and spat its way to life, lifting and clicking its way across the floor to the doorway it had come from. "Come along. We've got Martha, Keiran, Oddie, and George tonight." Luke said as though he hadn't heard a word.

Cori followed along, unwilling or unable to insist that she wait for the one she was scheduled to meet. Cori followed the skittering automaton through east-wing halls into a magnificent cabin room with a second floor landing, and grand tapestries and filthy persian carpets. A chandelier hung center, and vaulted windows were skillfully cut, if a bit grimy. There was a chess table, and an electric faux-leather massage chair. Cobwebs decorated the room without prejudice, though this was the way of it in most rooms.

At one end, above the fireplace mantle, a portrait hung of a young puritanical woman wearing wool coats and a straw bonnet, her hair blowing forever in the wind. She stood upon the precipice of a dark cliff, a raven blowing in the wind by her side. The mantle was decorated like an altar.

"I know we're not supposed to have favorites," Luke said, "But Martha's a sweet gal. Could set an old man's heart purring just like he were in school again."

Martha's painted face turned a coy look at Luke and smiled deviously. Luke coughed out a laugh, and Cori felt as though they were sharing a private joke.

"Nice to meet you Martha, I'm Cori." Cori said, almost offering her hand to the portrait, then thinking better of it. "I'm going to be working the night shift from time to time."

Luke smacked his lips a few times, his wet beady eyes barely holding themselves open. "Thing about Martha you need to take care with…"

Cori waited for the rest of his statement, but Luke's eyes were shut, and soon his breathing turned soft and slow. Cori's heart picked up pace as she looked between Luke and the portrait. Martha held an even more devious stare, now focused solely on Cori.

She hadn't read Martha's case file yet. But so far the things you needed to 'take care with' with residents at St. Margaret's often involved death, disfigurement, possession, and soul-eating if Morris was to be believed about this girl Kitsune that Cori was supposed to have followed.

All remained still and quiet, and eventually Martha took her devilish stare off Cori. Cori couldn't muster up the gumption to wake an old man from his midnight rest, even if it was on the clock. Instead, Cori took a seat on the couch and started clicking the flashlight on and off at different objects about the room.

The room could be lit adequately, but Morris had a strict policy regarding the manor's electric bill. It was his way of offsetting his raucous use of summertime air-conditioning. As such, all lights at night time were dimmed to ten percent capacity. This barely made a dent in the darkness of the manor. Many of the rooms didn't even have windows. The cabin room did have its vaulted windows however, through which the moonlight shone.

Cori clicked her flashlight about, and tried to avoid looking at her phone while on the clock. It was a terrible habit she didn't want to entertain, especially during training. Then, with another click, she noticed a flutter at the edges of her vision. She turned her flashlight to a dark corner of the room where she had thought she had seen it, but found nothing. She flicked her flashlight off, and squealed.

In the shadows, Cori spotted a red eyed teen crouched in the corner peering at her, a girl who had not been there half a second prior. Cori flicked her flashlight on again, but the corner was once again empty.

Cori's eyes were wide, and her limbs were frozen in a panic. Her breath was heavy, and she could feel the color draining from her face. Hot breath fell on her neck from behind.
Cori turned slowly and found those dark red eyes, half an inch away from her face. The face melted away, oozing into black oil. Black oil which then formed like clay into dozens of bats. Bats which then flapped and squealed and tangled into Cori's hair, then came to her front and formed into a ball. Here, they melted once more and transfigured into the shape of the girl she had seen before.

"Hi." The girl said, and Cori lost consciousness. Awakening some time later, she found a nose nearly pressed against her own. "Hajimimashite Kitsune-des, dozoyoroshiku."

Cori was no longer so taken aback. The blackout had done its job, a full reset which allowed Cori to process information rationally once again. "You're Kitsune? But you're…" Cori said, horrified that she was about to say *'caucasian'*. The farthest east this girl's blood could have come from would've been Poland, Cori thought. She instead settled on saying "You're...Not undead," as this girl did not appear to be the horrifying Jiangshi vampire she had been made out to be. Just a small and pale girl, a bit like Cori herself was though just a touch shorter, but with longer black hair, cut into bangs. She wore a french maid lolita top, but her wrists were covered in colorful rubber bracelets, some charged with magicks. Between this, dozens of hair clips, and delicately decorated nails, the girl didn't strike such an ominous figure.

The girl kept her voice unnaturally high and airy. "Ohhhhh, the bats didn't give it away?"

"Well Morris said you were a Jiangshi, so I just imagin--"

"Whhhhhaaaaaa? Kuuuuso!" Kitsune said as dark energies crept along her veins. "Baka gaijin." Cori wasn't quite sure how to place this girl, or this situation. Esoteric horror seeped from her every pore, and Morris had said she'd lick out anyone's eyes if they dared enter her chapel, a crypt which was also her bedroom. And yet, for all this and more, she just seemed odd. "I am not Jiangshi, I am Kyuuketsuki."

Cori cursed Morris under her breath, then said "I'm sorry, I didn't know."

The girl took on new airs in an instant, becoming suddenly cat-like in her mannerisms and speech. "It's not like you could have known. Morris is ignorant."

This girl has got to be a pisces. Cori thought. "Well, nice to meet you Kitsune."

"Why didn't you meet me in the kitchen?" Kitsune asked.

"Oh, Luke told me to follow him." Cori said, and Kitsune stared at her till it became uncomfortable and Cori was forced to elaborate. "So I did. Follow him, I mean...Into here. This room."

"Why?"

Cori responded with a quiet, "I don't know."

"Well then, follow me now." Kitsune said then strut forward, regally, past Luke who was still sleeping. "I'll be taking her from here, Luke-san."

"Who?" Luke woke and sputtered, and Kitsune didn't answer.

"Thanks for your help." Cori said as she passed Luke by, but he paid her no mind. So she let herself follow Kitsune while repressing all questions of 'why?' in favor of trying to figure out Morris' tonal context when he said 'Don't let her steal your soul.' *It must have been a joke, right?* But Cori and Kitsune were alone in the endless corridors of the manor. Anyone who heard Cori scream here would just assume it was Oddie or Keiran or Agnus. St. Margaret's was always filled with screams, Cori learned quickly enough.

"My brother boiled my cat alive when I was thirteen." Kitsune said after pausing in a room filled with furniture covered by white linens. "Did you know that?"

"Oh, my God."

"He made me watch."

Cori stood for a moment, flummoxed. She had barely learned the girl's name. Words slipped from her mouth, "That's heavy."

"What's your trauma?" Kitsune asked, leading Cori through the hallways which contained rooms 111 through 117.

"I'm not entirely sure what you mean."

"Sure you do. Everyone has at least one."

Cori looked back and forth, as if there would be another person in this dusty room with them, ready to save her from this conversation, just waiting to be found. Instead, Cori chose a favorite method, deflection and distraction. "So, who's next on the list?"

Kitsune glared at Cori for a moment or two before saying, "Agnus. Do you know about Agnus?"

"Maya had said something about her before, I think. I can't quite…"

"Of course Maya would say something, Maya is *terrified* of her. I would be too, if I were human."

Cori stayed silent for a moment, aware that only flimsy flashlight filaments separated her and total darkness. "She can't be that bad?"

"Oh, but she is." Kitsune said, and led Cori through the kitchen to the opposite end. Kitsune opened doors for Cori, and inhaled deeply as Cori passed by. They went up a set of rickety stair well Cori had not yet taken before. There were a lot of those. "Osoroshīdesu. She died in the Crimson Plague twenty years ago."

"Can you give me some...clues? On what to do?"

"You'll only learn through experience." Kitsune said, as they made their way to the third floor now. "Now shush, and be careful of everything you say. She can hear everything in her halls, and she will hold a grudge if she hears something she doesn't like."

Cori started to hold her breath, feeling like even that might be in offense to this newly waiting horror. The third floor corridor that belonged to Agnus was eerily blue. The wall paper, the upholstery, the lampshades and the carpets of all different shades of blue trimmed with gold. Tasteful, but disquieting. All this together with a thick miasma lent an oceanic atmosphere, and even the light of Cori's flashlight quavered as though it were underwater.

Kitsune took on a formal tone as they walked through the hall, "This is Agnus' bedroom, her study, her bathroom, her doll's bedroom. For the most part, each night, Agnus will give you instructions on how to best care for her doll, Vivian. The best thing for you is if you do it all without question." At the end of the corridor, Kitsune opened the door to a room like an attic, where a gray haired old woman sat, and the rest of the objects in the room were floating gently, as though suspended in water.

Agnus's chair turned slowly with the grinding screech of wood on wood, moving of its own volition as Agnus continued to brush her doll's hair. A battered crone, white of eyes and of curled and permed hair, several teeth sat jostling about in her slack jawed mouth while she stared cataract into her own dolls hair, mumbling. She sat fetally in her rocking chair, swaying back and forth. Then she stopped, and looked up at Cori, her eyes nothing but empty pits reaching back into the furthest abyss. Agnus tilted her head as though curious. Cori tried to introduce herself, but found her throat had dried up.

The furnishings dropped from their suspension just as Agnus's chair grated forward against the ground and rushed towards Cori like a predator.

Cori shut the door just in time, as Agnus had launched from her chair, lunging. Cori took a deep breath as Kitsune chuckled from the side, but Agnus began pulling herself through the solid wooden frame quickly enough, clawing rabidly at the floor, her ethereal body strong enough to leave physical scratches in the wood. This spirit, Cori noticed, was nearly as physical as a living person if you ignored the way she was halfway suspended through a wooden door.

"Agnus, this is our new staff." Kitsune said, stifling her giggles, as Cori ran with all the fear of death at her tail, through the hall with Agnus crawling upside down, her limbs at unnatural angles, and snapping at Cori's heels. "Her name is Cori. She's going to be working with you."

Agnus stopped and stood dumbfounded, her widening eye holes boring into Cori's heart as it palpitated, and the sweat began to pour out her pores.

"Okay, Cori-san, Agnus is going to probe for your greatest fear." Kitsune said. "Just relax."

The lights went out. All the bulbs shattered, even for as little light as they gave, but Cori's flashlight too was shattered, and the room was struck blank but for the labored breathing Cori could hear coming from Agnus. Cori, on the other hand, could hardly breathe at all.

"What lurks in the dark?" A quivering elderly voice said this as it stalked invisibly around Cori. "What lurks beneath?" The floor fell out from under her, and Cori was floating. "What lies in the depths of the Ocean?"

The Ocean. The great black chasm that Cori saw now, filled with secret and unimaginable creatures.

"Deeper." Agnus' voice said, and Cori could see nothing. Darkness became her sight, and darkness grew into her ears and over her skin then slithered its way into her mind. Cori was alone in the void, emptiness all around her. Or was she alone? What slithered beneath her ankles in that void? What could exist in that space, where not even the stars could shed their dying light?

Cori could not breathe, and though there was no point of reference, she knew that she was being pulled downwards, down into some formless maw which hungered to extinguish that light that lay within her.

"No, no, please no, pull me out. Please, pull me out." Cori screamed.

She woke to Kitsune pinching her arm, hard, and twisting. "Ow, damnit. Stop." Cori said as she regained composure and grounded to reality, and Kitsune smiled and gave a little peace sign and winked and bit her tongue.

"I think she likes you." Kitsune said, helping Cori to stand.

"I did not get the same impression." Cori moaned.

"You don't know her very well." Kitsune shrugged, and walked off.

"Did I die?"

Kitsune turned around suddenly. "You're afraid of the dark, aren't you?"

Cori nodded.

"I'll remember that." Kitsune said, then, "Listen, Agnus probably won't come out again with you around, but I still have some things I need to do with her and Vivian. Go take a break in the kitchen."

"Oh, okay...you sure? I feel like--"

"Sarimasuuu~..." Kitsune said, and Cori didn't know what that meant but she sounded as dismissive as a cat who has been pet long enough for one day.

"Thank you, Kitsune."

Kitsune held her two hands like paws, and pretended to lick at them.

"You have to have a bad memory to work here." Maya had told her during one of their shadowings. *"Whenever something awful happens, you need to be able to just forget about it."*

Cori hadn't liked the thought of that when she had first heard Maya say it, but it was sounding more important to her now.

Cori did her best to find her way back down through the East Wing Halls and into the kitchen. And by the time she got there, she was in perfect denial that anything scary had happened at all. Sammiel was sitting in the kitchen, Ernie hovering just over his shoulder, hardly visible.

"Ernie's a little faded tonight." Sammiel said, gazing into his phone as he sat at the kitchen table, his long silver hair reflecting the electric blue glow. His phone case was clear, and exposed a number of circuitry and gears and arcs of lightning underneath, the working machinations of his smart phone.

"Oh, hey...Sammiel. Yeah, Ernie spent all his energy bleeding on me earlier." Cori said, glaring at Ernie, who did not make eye contact. "Hey, I thought you were supposed to be off tonight. It's like 3 am."

"Yeah...yes. I'm off, but I live here...and I don't have friends, so I like..." Sammiel said, his eyes curling as he looked up at Cori. "Y'know...I'm pretty much nocturnal at this point."

What a weirdo. Cori thought. *Just look at that stupid silver hair. Just gonna shave one side of it, huh? Last decade much? And who the hell just wears a robe made of belts?* The silence stretched till Cori said, "So do you normally just...chill in the kitchen like this?"

"Well, I go into town sometimes, but I can't really stay awake in the day, and the town is pretty quiet this late at night except for a few places. Then yeah, I dunno, I just study. Practice Magick."

"Cool, cool. What are you studying?" Cori asked and leaned against the table.

"Necromancy." Sammiel said, raising his eyebrow and smiling.

"Well yeah, obviously." Cori flushed. *Who the hell does he think he is?* "But like, what have you been learning most recently?"

"I dunno, I'm pretty into cosmology and the planes. So, I usually just practice inter-dimensional math and sacred geometry. Sometimes I make homunculi."

"Oh, whoa. You can make homunculi? That's not even Necromancy, is it?" Cori asked, looking at Sammiel with more intensity than she had before. "I didn't take you for a brainiac."

"Okay, so maybe I do a lot of magick." Sammiel said, and laughed like rusted tin. "What about you, what are you into?"

"Necromancy." Cori said, and they both laughed.

"So, this must be some sort of dream job for you, huh?"

Cori hesitated for a time. "Yes and no. Tonight's been a little rough, not gonna lie."

"You were shadowing Kitsune, right?" Sammiel tried to stifle a smile. "That can make things a little difficult."

"It was more Agnus than Kitsune that made it difficult, but I did have a little trouble placing Kitsune. I feel like I have a lot of questions."

"I think we all have a lot of questions. So, don't feel bad."

"Okay, so like, do you know if she's...like, is she japanese, or...?"

"She grew up in Remedy, and Morris knows her mother and father, David and Rita Miller. They are very white."

"Okay, that's about what I was expecting. And what about--"

"The vampire thing?" Sammiel asked. "I don't know much about it, but I would be careful around her. She usually keeps to herself. I do know she needs to drink blood or steal qi or whatever. Then one time we had an asian dude who started working here. Good guy, and great cook, but I warned Morris there was gonna be trouble with Kitsune."

"What happened?" Cori asked.

"She started like watching him in his sleep and stuff. Super weird. She'd follow him at a distance and run away whenever he looked at her. He quit pretty shortly after. We're lucky he didn't take legal action."

"Okay, keep an eye on Kitsune." Cori said. "Noted."

"Don't tell her I said that." Sammiel said, holding up both his hands and exposing more esoteric tattoos on his palms.

"I'm pretty good at keeping secrets." Cori said.

"That so? You heard anything about me, yet?"

"So what if I have?" Cori put on a coy smile, and her blood pumped heavier in her veins.

"Just hope it was good. It's nice. I get along with everyone here. But you give me that vibe like you're someone I would have hung out with in high school."

Cori found herself nodding without intention. "Yeah, I could see that. We might have been part of the same mall walking group."

"Between that and the fireside camping." Sammiel added.

"You too?"

"A couple of underage beers in the starlight, yeah."

"Well damn, I guess we would have been pals." Cori said.

Sammiel smiled. "Good thing we still can be." Then he stood up. "I'm gonna head off for the night. See ya on Friday at Duke's."

"What?"

Sammiel turned around with a confused frown, and pointed at Cori. "The Duke's Downfall? The Tavern. We're all going out. Maya was going to invite you."

"I haven't seen her today." Cori said.

"Well, consider this your invite then. Friday at Seven. See ya, Cori." He said, then left the room.

Cori was dismayed to find herself now alone in the kitchen, with Ernie staring at her, murderous intentions in his gaze. That, and there were tons of snacks, and Cori was bored. It began with the peanut butter chocolate wafers then made its way to a fried pack of Cheesy Darnel's. Some lemonade and some Twisty Chips. Kitsune returned just before Cori started making another late night espresso. At her arrival, Ernie yowled and fled the room. Together, she and Kitsune resumed the night shift against Cori's crushing weariness. They paid an uneventful visit to Jacquelin, who spent the time weeping as she looked into her mirror. Kitsune texted on a phone, the case of which was composed of thousands of eyes peering through a dark mirror. Then, they went down to the graveyard and exhumed a body, which was strangely exhausting work that Cori hadn't expected to be in her job description.

"Can't we just pull them up with magick?" Cori asked Kitsune, panting and wiping mud off her brow, which left only more mud on her brow.

"Nope, sorry. It's against regulation." Kitsune lied, lounging on a lawn chair from behind Cori, watching in comfort.

Dawn's light began to rise and Kitsune announced she was off for the night.

"It was nice working with you, Kitsune." Cori said. "See you at Duke's Downfall."

"Who said you were invited to that?" Kitsune said, with a snarl. "Experienced staff only."

"What? Is that why Maya didn't invite me herself?" Cori said. "But Sammiel...?"

Kitsune picked at a fang with a long nail. "Oh, is he hitting on new hires again?" Kitsune asked. "Well. I guess it's not up to me."

Cori left her shift feeling a mingled sense of victory and despair. She couldn't help feeling the sorrow at Kitsune's harsh words. But Cori had been to high school before and knew one couldn't always take such words at face value. Reserving judgement for further information, Cori went to bed, wondering at what the next day's mysteries might bring.

Chapter 5

Cori walked into the staff lounge just off the first floor front hall at 7:54 am, one day following her night shift. Maya was sipping a coffee and Derrick was chattering excitedly about nothing in particular with an energy drink all his own. The staff lounge was one of the places in the house that was warded against spirits, which ought to have made it a comfortable getaway, especially considering the corporate computers which had been hacked and made to play online video games. As legend tells it, however, it was receiving just a bit too much use and Morris was forced to make a pact with one of the dire spiders from the Deep Halls of Albahazred. Now, from time to time, if staff were caught snoozing or playing games, a face sized spider had a tendency to land on the perpetrating offender. Cori would have avoided this dark room entirely, with its rattling chains, rusted walls, steaming pipes, and arachnid legends, except for the fact that staff were required to clock in here, as well as check their shift schedules.

"Keiran?" Cori asked. "This is my first shift alone...I've never even worked with Keiran while shadowing someone. What is this?"

"Keiran's great to work with as long as you know some good battle magick." Derrick said, karate chopping the air. "Want me to teach you anything?"

"I'm fine, thank you."

"From what I've seen she's a lot more skilled at magick than you." Maya said from behind her earbuds.

"Is that a challenge?" Derrick asked, his grin growing wide. "If you guys wanna wrestle me or anything, I'm down. Right here, right now."

Maya rolled her eyes. "Cori, you know any good spells to use against our friend here?"

"*Arachnea Cutis.*" Cori said, taking a long and loud sip of her own coffee while she glared at Derrick. That's what they had called it in the tome she had found in the basement of the school library in the ninth grade. "It grows spider eggs in the skin."

"Pfft, I don't care about spiders." Derrick said.

"It's either that or my spell, *Shrinky Dink*." Maya said, her gaze lowering. Derrick tried to laugh off the threat, but Maya's eyes conveyed no joke.

"Seriously though, I don't feel like I'm ready to handle Keiran at all." Cori said.

"Morris believes in baptism by fire." Maya said, sipping on her fresh kona, blended with coconut oil and cacao, sliced mango by the side with a bowl of oatmeal for breakfast. "He only started having new staff shadow their first shifts after I laid into him about it."

"Then Damian got his skull opened by Nigel and Morris blamed you for it." Derrick said, mischievously.

"Yes, thank you for the reminder Derrick." Maya said, pursing her lips. "Damian had a chunk taken out of him on Derrick's watch, and while Morris did write Derrick up, he still insisted that the problem was that Damian didn't get a proper baptism by fire."

"But new staff still shadow on their first shifts..."Derrick responded.

"That's because I threatened to report Morris if he stopped."

"He really needs to get his balls out of your purse." Derrick said.

Maya paused and gave Derrick a look that started off as intimidating, but then grew in fury and fervor, as shadows danced through the room and cackling whispers muttered curses. Maya grew in size as Derrick shrank, and still the glare held.

"I don't mean to interrupt," Cori said, her hands shaking in anticipation, "but what do I do?"

"Well...that's hard to say." Maya said. "Just do what you normally do. Ask Keiran questions, chat with him, get to know him. Hopefully shit won't get real. But if it does, you'll start to get confused. The thing that always helps me the most is just repeating my name."

"Yeah, that works for me too." Derrick affirmed, snapping a selfie shortly afterwards. His phone case was a clear container of oozing and bubbling alchemy that shifted and mixed as he turned his phone.

"So he'll kind of get theatrical on you." Maya continued. "Start acting out the uh...the suicide... Then once that's done, that's when he gets violent. But that's *if* there's an issue."

"I mean, I've only seen Keiran once, and he was a tsunami of shadows that Morris could hardly hold back." Cori said.

"Keiran's not usually like that." Maya said.

"I mean, 'usually' is a pretty vague term." Derrick said. "Keiran's not like that every single day is more accurate."

"That's just because you're always looking for a fight when you go to see him." Maya gave Derrick that same look, this time causing him to flinch. "I can't remember the last time he had an issue while I was around."

"Oh, come on--" Derrick began.

"Derrick...bye." Maya said, waving him off. "Cori, you can text me if you need *anything*. Just hold your feet steady, and repeat your name in your head as often as you can. And uh...bring a coat."

Not feeling at all comfortable with what she was about to do, Cori left the staff lounge. *Okay, Keiran haunts the second floor, near Morris' office so maybe Morris can keep an eye on things. That's comforting, at least.* Cori thought this until she made her way up through the steep stairway, where George contemplated once again jumping from the rafters. Here, Cori found a sign on Morris' door, 'Reese's run, be back in a few hours'.

Cori broke out into an angry sweat. She pulled out her phone and found her conversation with Maya and pounded her fingers down on the touch screen.

"Morris left. Got a sign on his door, 'reese's run'. Wtf?"

"Baptism by Fire" Maya responded. "He knows what he's doing."

Cori nearly threw her phone, but took deep breaths instead and just placed one foot in front of the other. *Look at you now.* Cori thought. *A week ago you wouldn't have been caught dead doing this.* She made her way down the stairs from Morris' office and into that ominous hallway she now found herself going to great lengths to avoid. *Stupid Morris with his stupid...first shift give me the hardest damn ghost in the place.* She thought these things as she proceeded very slowly down the bitter length of Keiran's hallway of paper sigils.

Reaching the door, Cori gave a faint knocking. Nothing. Another knock, just a bit louder.

The door knob turned on its own, and slid open. A frigid draft blew from within that gave her the heebie-jeebies. She had forgotten a coat.

Cori had read Keiran's file. From what she had seen of the spirits she knew, the files were always mismatched from reality. But there were some facts to be found across the hogwash that could prove useful. Cori felt confident in only a few facts: 'Keiran is an old and powerful spirit with an angsty suicide. Like George, he plays his death on repeat. He can be kept away from this illusion, but once he has it, he almost always becomes violent. However, as dangerous as this violence can be, the main risk Keiran poses is in the way those around him, whether they be spirits or human, tend to become consumed in his illusion. Keiran was brought to St. Margaret's back when it was still St. Jerome's, shortly before the outbreak of the Crimson Plague. If his danger to those around him continues or increases, there will be no choice but to seal him away in the labyrinth beneath the estate.'

Cori slipped into Keiran's room. There were no rooms in the manor that struck Cori as being as unpleasant as Keiran's. It had all the attempts at a semblance of normalcy. There was a couch and a coffee table and a ceiling fan and a fridge and a microwave and a small canvas that said 'Home' in cursive letters. But there was not one surface within the apartment that Cori would be comfortable touching. Not for fear of dirt or grime, but for the fear of some hidden taint. It was a windowless attempt at recreating a city apartment, but something felt inverted about it. It was not the ordinary fear of ghosts and the unknown that stalked Cori, nor even the darkness of the windowless room. It was instead the perception of sardonic rot that one couldn't find the source of.

"I've heard about you." Cori heard a voice whisper. It was just out of reach, like a radio in another room that wasn't tuned correctly. "You're Cori." He said, and made his appearance from his apartment hallway, levitating into the main room while Cori's legs turned to jello. He could have been a handsome young man, and though highly desaturated, Cori thought she could make out a glint of red to his long messy hair. He had messy teeth and a gaunt face and hollow eyes, but these things seemed products of a long withstanding sorrow. Keiran clutched at his arm as he moved from the hallway and turned towards Cori, but he did not make eye contact. "You look so...familiar."

"Yes." Cori said, her voice quivering even as she puffed out her chest. "I'm the new staff. And you're Keiran."

"You're scared." Keiran hovered in circles around Cori, and Cori shook her head. "It's okay, you can be honest with me. You don't have to stay. I don't want to hurt anybody. I'm used to being alone."

Cori stared at Keiran for a moment. She had expected many things of him, but not the degree to which he could evoke sympathy. "Well, I don't want you to hurt anybody either. That's why I'm here to help you." Cori responded.

Keiran looked up at her. "You can't help me." He said with wide, sad eyes. "No one can help me anymore. I'd eat you alive." Even this was said not with threat, but with despairing resignation.

Maya's voice came to mind. *"Just hold your feet steady."* It probably wasn't the way she intended it, but Cori was going to stand her ground. "Well, I beg to differ."

Keiran backed away and disappeared, and the television turned on to static, where his face could be seen once more, speaking through the static. "We can only help ourselves, wouldn't you agree? But I can't help myself...I don't think I even want to help myself."

"You're very forward." Cori said, trying to imagine how her mother might have acted if she were doing this, even though she could hardly remember how her mother acted at all. "I'll try being forward too. They've told me absolutely nothing. I have no idea what to expect here, and I'm kind of nervous, I'll admit. But you seem nice, maybe you can talk me through this a little bit?"

Keiran tilted his head. "Maybe." He said, then the television shut off and he disappeared.

Cori looked around for a moment, tapped her foot, then said, "Just as bad as Morris." *So is that it? Am I done? No chance I'm going to guide him through to final rest on my first visit, right? Its only been a couple of minutes though. And I'm doing good. No need to cop out now.* Alone in the room, Cori noticed how easy it was to let her thoughts sink. *I see what Maya meant about getting confused. I can hardly...* "I am Cori." Cori said to herself, trying to remind herself that she had no real cause for sorrow. Something didn't feel right. Her vision swam, and she felt a terrible despair. But Keiran appeared a moment later from the hallway.

"I lose myself, sometimes. You can fight all you want on the outside, but it's the inside you need to worry about. Your thoughts. When it starts, you'll begin to lose yourself. You have to know who you are."

Is that what I need? It struck Cori like a rock. That's the defense? *But, who am I?*

Cori. She tried to think in reply, but she knew that was an unsatisfactory answer.

"You should leave." Keiran said, as though in response to her thoughts.

Baptism by fire. "No. This is great." Cori said. "Now I get to learn things about both you and me." *That's what mom would say, right?*

"I don't want to hurt you."

"And I'd bring you back to life if I could. But sometimes we just have to deal with the cards we're given." She said. Keiran looked down and to his right, back up at Cori, then back down again. Then Cori asked, "So, what do you do for fun around here?"

"Fun." Keiran said, as if the word tasted strange on his tongue.

"When was the last time you went outside?"

"I don't go outside."

"Well, there's problem number one." Cori said.

"I'm not allowed outside."

"Did Morris make that rule? That's stupid." She said, but quickly texted Maya. "Why isn't Keiran allowed outside?"

"Too dangerous." Maya texted back with a little skull emoji.

61

"Too dangerous inside too." Cori typed. "Whats the diff?"
"Remedy."

"Well shit." Cori said out loud. "Okay, so maybe not outside. Keiran?" She looked around the room and behind the couch for some reason, and found no soul.

Keiran's whisper rounded Cori's head. "I'm tired. I'm just so tired..."

The ghosts did often get tired with too much talking or carrying objects or playing pianos or whatever interaction they had with the physical. Often, that was the key moment when staff decided that the job was done. "Okay, great. Well, I feel like that went really well." Cori called out to the empty room. Relief nearly washed over her, but she wasn't standing in the same room she had been in before. "Keiran?"

"I'm just so tired…" Cori and Keiran said in unison. And the weight was not the exhaustion felt before sleep, but the weariness of Atlas as he longed only to release the world, his burden, in final rest. Cori knew this feeling too well, and too quickly she and Keiran were one.

Together they stood in a dark foyer in the early hours of the morning, dread rising as their heart sank, knowing what they would find. Candles lined the corridors and there was a new smell in the house. *But we knew this was coming, didn't we?*

Keiran and Cori's vision turned red as they looked upon the scene, and together they saw their lovers bedded with their friends, each viewing their own personal experience, superimposed and as one.

"Get the fuck out. Get the fuck out of my house. Stay the fuck away from them." They screamed. "Stay the fuck away from them you sick piece of shit."

But the violence was too great, too consuming. "Get the fuck out." It wasn't said in warning. It was said in pleading. Keiran knew they could only contain themselves for so long. Cori knew they could only contain themselves for so long.

Silence passed between Keiran and his wife. Silence passed between Cori and her boyfriend. Their sorrow was met only with disdain, and both were left alone to weep in an empty house with only violence in their veins, and the greatest weariness. It was both her boyfriend's house, and the house she lived in as a child on the night her mother left her forever. The night her mother abandoned her forever.

I'm Cori. She thought.

The sorrow transcended tears.

Who's Cori?

Days passed, and it only grew worse.

Cori is a necromancer.

Each day, what seemed to be a rock bottom was only scratching the surface. They simply did not have the will to bear it all.

I'm Cori.

And each day they found new strength, and tried harder than the one before.

But who is Cori?

But each day that strength faltered, and it was never enough. Life only grew heavier.

I am...will...

Until Keiran found themselves in a tub with the kindest looking blade that they had ever seen.

What will?

And tested it against their skin.

The will to fight.

I don't want to die.

I am Cori.

And pressed it deeper.

What's worth fighting for?

Until it made a small cut.

Life.

And all that was left was to make the final cut. The deep one.

I'm Cori, and I fight for life.

"I'm Cori, and I fight for life." She said from inside Keiran's bathtub, reoriented once again within St. Margaret's. She looked around, and a chill passed through her. A loneliness like she had never known trickled from her veins as she saw the cut in her skin and the blade dripping blood from her hand.

Get help. Came the small voice of reason. Cori texted Maya. "I need help fast"

"I'm sorry." Keiran whispered from nowhere and everywhere.

No. Not the dark. Cori thought, but she was unable to move, to speak, or to act. *Not the dark.* It enveloped her senses, cut her off from touch and cut her away from her body. Soon, Cori could not hear. She could not feel her own breath.

Her thoughts silenced, and all that she was became fear. The horror lay in wait in the void.

Their soul ascended like a rocket, her and Keiran, enmeshed in the sky. Up, up, up through the Bardic layers of the Betwixt and all its strange astral realms, their frequencies growing higher; silence enveloping their mind. Cori's body was far below, and far gone.

They shot above St. Margaret's, and pierced through heavenly planes of sunny green. Then above floating islands in a sea made of golden starlight nectar, full up of rose pedals, flowing oceanic in all directions. Cori wanted to see these places more closely, to run through their glades, but Keiran held her fast. Further up they flew through a strange and formless realm where they became a tragic melody, a place where everything existed as sound and music. And further still they flew into a visually overwhelming crystalline cosmic realm, wholesomely alien, a place where Cori could see worlds beyond worlds with color beyond imagining.

But things changed as they rode higher, and Keiran brought Cori to a quiet place. So quiet, Cori couldn't hear herself think. It was a distant and cold world, lit only by the eclipse of a dying star.

"The Villa of Ormen." Keiran said with reverence, his eyes full of tears, and scared.

"Keiran. Please. I don't want to be here." Cori said, averting her eyes, trying not to look at the structure before her.

"But you do, Cori. I felt it. In your dream. You're just like me." Keiran replied. "You've tasted despair just like I have. You've lost those closest to you. Your lover. Your mother. It's time the pain stopped."

"I'm scared."

"I am too." Keiran said, his voice full of empathy. "I've been waiting for so long for someone like you. Someone who will come with me. I didn't want to go alone."

"I don't want to go." Cori pleaded.

"You won't be scared anymore. Never again. You'll never be sad or scared or lonely ever again." Keiran said. "Look at it, Cori." Cori had her eyes shut tight. Keiran took his fingers and tried to pry them open. "Just look at it. It'll be alright. It's beautiful."

"I don't want to."

There was a great roar in the otherwise silent world, and it quaked all the land. Keiran turned to look, but was blasted in his face with a ball of sonic energy. "Keiran, you let her go." Cori heard Maya yell, her voice all righteous fury.

Cori did not dare to peek, but as they existed in a frequency higher than sound, she sensed more than enough to gauge the raging battle. Keiran's acrid flesh melted beneath blow after blow of fierce magick, then screamed as he snapped his jaws and swiped his claws at Maya. Maya dodged on deft feet, dancing gracefully, deflecting blow after blow. Keiran's body enveloped in flames of black and red, but Maya grew thousand arms of aether, and wrapped and bound Keiran before he could unleash his full fury. Cori could not make out what happened next, and did not want to until she felt her gentle touch as Maya caressed her face, and wrapped Cori into a hug. "It's okay, it's okay, we're going home." Maya said, and they crashed. Downward they fell through harsher realities and louder places and lower frequencies, then slam!

"Shh, shh, baby girl, it's alright. You're alright. We're gonna be able to fix this up, no problem." Cori could hear Maya's voice from afar, and the sounds of a woman screaming. Her own screams, as it turned out. Cori saw her own body, then saw Maya binding Keiran into a box, and chaining it. Cori swam against a current, reaching desperately for the body she saw below.

Pain in her wrist.

Pain was good, Cori thought. Pain kept the darkness at bay. Darkness. The darkness behind her eyes was so much brighter than the silence at the Villa. Cori was back in her body once again, she knew. She dared herself to open her eyes.

"That's good, yeah, you're a fighter. That's good. Look at you. You're comin' right through this." Maya said.

Cori managed to let out a feeble, whimpering voice, "Help me put that curse on Morris. The spider one."

Maya laughed, and Cori felt a tear drop hit her face. "I bet I can find something even nastier, if you want."

Cori smiled, then opened her eyes to Maya's deep brown worrying eyes and drooping curls of hair. "You're like an angel." Cori said. "I wish I looked like you."

"Oh stop." Maya said, eyes wet and smile shining. "I can't handle compliments like that." Then she pulled Cori into the cradle of her neck and squeezed tight. "You're gonna be alright."

Cori sat and waited outside the office while Maya laid a verbal beat down on Morris. Morris occasionally attempted to raise his voice in response, and sometimes Maya responded by shouting him down, and sometimes it went frigidly silent and Cori could only imagine the look Maya was giving him.

It was twenty minutes before the door opened, and Morris whisked himself outside, shut the door behind him, and pressed his full weight on it as though holding back something horrible within. Then he took a deep breath, smoothed out his robes and straightened his beard and looked at Cori with an unnerving smile.

"There is no way for me to apologize enough." Morris said.

"Understatement of the fucking century." Maya yelled from inside his office.

Morris winced, then frowned. "Quite. You're lucky Maya was around. As I've mentioned before, she's incredibly talented. One of the most striking examples--"

"Don't you brown nose me." Maya yelled again from behind the door.

"I was simply saying..." Morris began, then he froze, as if he could feel Maya's glare from behind the door. Cori thought she could feel it too. "Maya has informed me that, in this instance, there might not be things that I can bribe you with that will adequately

66

make up for what has happened." Morris was now speaking slowly, and cautiously. "That said, is there anything you would like?"

"I'm alright." Cori said. "Really."

Morris looked nervously over at the door to his office. "You're sure?...There must be something...please?"

"Really, Morris. All's well that ends well." Cori said.

This time, Maya opened the office door. "Cori, for real baby, Morris can get all sorts of wacky shit."

"She's right." Morris said. "The wackiest."

Cori thought about it, and looked over at Maya who was trying to tell her something with her eyes. "Maybe I'll take a rain check?" Cori said.

Maya gave Morris a smug look.

"Yes." He said. "Indeed. Anything. Just name it. At your leisure." Then he looked back and forth between the two women. "Ah. Being that this is a situation so far beyond my efforts to remediate in the near future...I'll just...just...scamper off and leave you to it... Sorry again."

"Baptism by fire." Maya spat as Morris held up his robes to his bare and hairy ankles and ran through the hallway. "Cori, I should have just insisted I go with you. I'm so sorry."

"It's alright. It just caught me by surprise." Cori said, and pulled herself up to stand along the wall. "I thought I'd just get confused, but it was so real."

"What was so real?"

"His suicide. We were in a whole different place. I was there, but I was him. I thought you meant I'd get confused like...like I'd feel a little loopy."

"That's what I did mean." Maya said. "No one's ever had *that* happen."

Cori's brow furrowed, the details of the experience came to her in waves and pierced the numbness she had initially been left with. "It was all so sad," was all she could manage to say.

Maya wrapped her arm around Cori's shoulder. "Come on. You won't have to work with Keiran again, alright? I saw to it."

"Thank you." Cori said, but she wasn't at all sure that would be of any help. There was a hole in Cori's heart that she had long thought buried that was now reopened and infected with a darkness that made all of her inner light meek by comparison.

Chapter 6

Monday's dread gave way to the despair that is Tuesday, and soon the faint glimmer of hope that is Wednesday curled its way over into the fresh blooms of Thursday. Finally, the long awaited dessert, Friday, arrived just on cue. And this Friday was special for the same reason so many Fridays are special: the ingestion of alcohol.

It was a long awaited adventure. Cori had been stuck in St. Margaret's Home for the Nearly Departed for weeks on end without reprieve. There was rarely a good reason to leave. The home itself was enormous, and there was plenty of walking to be done on the grounds outside. Cori didn't have a car, and all food and necessities were ordered to the house. Even things Cori only wanted for herself could be ordered on her phone within seconds, and delivered the next day by Amazon's hideous winged marmot delivery service.

None of the employees were forced into the walls of St. Margarets in any indefinite way. But the sheer ease and comfort created a dualistic effect in which one was both too lazy to leave and also driven mad by cabin fever. Cori noticed it in the way Morris stared at Derrick from halls and doors, grinding his teeth and gently brushing his hand against the gilded dagger he kept tied to his belt. She noticed it in the way Dana and Maya made snide backhanded compliments to one another. And she noticed it in the way Luke mumbled at the dinner table about how much better things were back when he was young. All of them were grinding raw and itching to leave the manor, but all of them needed a good excuse to do what they were free to do on any given day if they took the extra initiative. Thus were they headed to the Duke's Downfall, to relieve these primal frustrations.

Cori plucked the spiders from her hair and razzled her teeth, threw on some clothes, then decided those weren't the right clothes at all, then repeated this again, and again. She soon found herself looking in the mirror with a degree of loathing, like an author on their first draft continuously erasing each and every word as it comes to mind. Cori didn't look like other women, and she knew it. She was brown but freckled, and with some sparse spots that melanin avoided altogether, like water in a desert. Her hair was frizzy and the dorsum of her nose was wide while her nostrils were more narrow. She was short but leggy. For all this, she didn't think herself unattractive, nor was she. She simply found herself wishing she had been born with such looks that other people would more conventionally appreciate as attractive.

Sighing, Cori proceeded with yoga pants and a summery tube top. Not because she thought it was what she looked best in, but because she was going all in for comfort and fun. It was the last outfit she had brought with her that she hadn't yet worn.

Prepared as she was for her first night out on the town, Cori decided to test the non-euclidian modes of traversing the house to get down to the foyer. It wasn't a fond memory, but Cori found herself prickled with curiosity since ascending the realms of the Betwixt with Keiran. What were those vast fields of green and sunshine, or the formless musical realms where she had briefly become an arpeggio? She had to know. Interplanar travel was the mystic affair she had never known she wanted.

Within the house, everything was laid out at odd degrees and obtuse angles, and apparently there was some numerological and dimensional significance to this madness. Grilling Morris about it over dinner one night that week, Cori had learned that the precise layout of the manor allowed rifts to open easily between worlds. One of which, he reiterated, lay in her closet.

Cori opened the closet door with a dramatic flourish and found chalk geometries drawn against the far corner, the markings of a rift. She questioned her resolve for a good moment before deciding to sally forth into the unknown. "What's one more emotional scar?" She asked herself. Indeed, dear reader, it is only pain that gives us the courage to risk greater pain.

Pressing her hand up against the wood grain, Cori referenced her phone for the various incantations she'd need to break the barriers of physical space time, and, having found the right occult blogger, Cori chanted in just such a way that the wood paneling slid apart into phantom geometries and rippling codex. Cori was two dimensional as she slipped through the cracks in the room's corner and found herself among cackling shadows and neon spatial infrastructure. These were the building blocks of her own highly digitized mundane world. She saw this as apparently as one sees the sun as the source of life. But stretching beyond the Mundane, Cori lifted up into a realm just higher, a realm of ghosts. Here was that plane just above the Mundane that can be glimpsed when one gazes upon a fleeting apparition. This was where the residents of St. Margaret's made their true home, and Cori saw St. Margaret's in an all new clarity. She slid along the walls as a mischievous shadow, slipped between cracks into the library and scurried above into the heating vents. Then she crept further into the private rooms of residents and staff alike. Cori slid her way to each of them as though she were paint on a brush, moving liquid and voluminous as she spied through mirrors into the mundane world she called home as though the mirrors were windows to the physical. There was Morris, daintily applying eye liner and a gentle layer of lip gloss. And through another mirror she spied the toilet abomination, lifting its tentacled eye into an empty bathroom she did not recognize. And another yet…

"What are you doing?" Came the digitized voice of a peculiar entity that spoke in a language wholly unfamiliar, yet instantly recognizable. Cori turned to find a resonant being, a synesthetic collection of sound waves and cubes which shifted shape with each word that was spoken. Its every mood, thought and secret desire was instantly visible in the vast spectrum of its being.

Cori was dumbstruck both in awe of this being; and with the shock of discovering her own nudity of self, her every mood, thought, secret desire displayed equally to this quintessential godform.

"You shouldn't be here." It said after some silence. "It can be dangerous for fleshies."

"I'm sorry, I was just taking advantage of this break in the dimensional continuum as a shortcut that I didn't need without fully understanding the possible repercussions of such clearly perilous magicks. Then I started spying in an effort to catch people during moments of presumed privacy. Why am I saying all this? I don't mean to say all this, oh god what's happening? You're terrifying but kind of beautiful."

"There is no hiding anything whilst traversing the Betwixt, naive flesh ball. I am Mayhew, a resident of the planes of Sonorous, and currently on vacation. I find you terrifying but beautiful as well. I had always hoped that, perhaps someday, I might be reincarnated in your realms of the Mundane. Tell me your name."

"I am Coriander Lou Ryel. I am afraid you will eat me. But also, if I were going to be eaten I guess this wouldn't be the worst way to have it happen. If there is no hiding anything, will you tell me your intentions?"

"Yes." Mayhew said with a glitch. "I wish only kind will upon you, though kindness is subjective and some entities may consider annihilation a kindness. I, however, wish only the sort of kindness that you would find preferable, and safe. I would see to it that you return home whole. However, there are many entities which caress the Betwixt who wouldst see you devoured in both body and concept. They too are kind, but you would likely find them unpreferable. There are also entities who are not kind, and would do much worse than devouring you in body and concept."

"I see and appreciate your way and being, Mayhew." Cori vibrated. "I'd like to ask you to be friends but I am hesitant enough in such matters with the normal entities from my plane. Oh no, I did not mean that you are not normal. Or I did, but I wish I hadn't expressed it in that way. This all seems much too fast, but as I examine this thought, I feel as though that may only be a hang up based on biological principles that are better left in my plane."

"You are wise. There is no need for such hesitation when no things can be hidden. Trust or mistrust is implicit upon meeting. We would make good friends, regardless of the subtly erotic energies that stem from those curiosities that are implicit upon meeting a trans dimensional entity. I would act on them, but I am bound to another. Stifle these for me, and I would consider a pen-pal relationship, of sorts."

Cori responded, "My native horror and boundless questions are already apparent to you, Mayhew, but I would like that very much. How would we keep in communication?"

Mayhew reached out a melodic arm and touched Cori's third eye. "This is my sigil. You may use it to communicate with me, or summon me as you see fit." And Cori saw the delicately weaving shapes of Mayhew's sigil burned into her memories.

And Cori knew quite suddenly that she too had a sigil. She reached out a fleshy animation, which brimmed with blue light, and touched Mayhew in his third eye, and her sigil was passed unto him as a song. "I am filled with more questions every second." Cori said as she pulled her arm away.

"Goodbye, Coriander. Hurry back to your realm. I have experienced many feelings upon meeting you, most of them positive in nature."

"I see and understand this, for I feel the same. Thank you, Mayhew. Goodbye."

Cori continued looking around this shadowy replicate of St. Margaret's, not hurrying at all. She hadn't and couldn't have lied to Mayhew, but she also hadn't known that she would shortly wind up disregarding him due to sheer intrigue. Every corner she turned seemed more appealing than the last in this place where those dead she had come to know such as Ernie and George were made like flesh. Here, they were more real than Morris had been when Cori spied him applying lip gloss through the mirror. No, this was a place that needed to be explored at every degree and angle, no matter the potential peril and cost.

Cori floated like a spectre herself amongst the back garden's blossoms and the faeries that lay within each gourd and vine. She wandered the streets of the Necropolis that layered the graveyard down by the river. She scared Sammiel by briefly appearing in the mirror of the second floor bathroom while he washed his hands. Then, she realized she had places to be and people to see. So Cori grabbed at the edges of the mirror in the foyer, and pulled through, knowing this to be a portal somehow.

It felt like what birth must feel like, if the birth canal were shards of glass. Cori ripped her way out of the foyer mirror, screaming as she did. Her coworkers looked on, mortified. Having nothing to hold onto, Cori tumbled to the floor and panted and patted down at the edges of a physical body that she could hardly comprehend.

"Well, that's one way to make an entrance." Maya said, just after everyone had finished screaming and catching their breath.

"I met...I met a sound entity and we made friends, and did you all know that's where our ghosts live? My closet leads into another world, Sam, I scared you in the mirror."

"First time in the Betwixt, huh?" Sammiel asked, chuckling.

"This girl's over here using interplanar travel to skip a few stairs." Maya said in her buoyant fashion. "Cori, be a dear and don't die to satisfy your lazy ass."

"The Betwixt is not to be trifled with." Dana added, nodding solemnly.

"Yeah, that's what the crazy thing made of music was saying. I'll be more careful next time, I just got curious. Damnit, I'm underdressed." Cori said, just now noticing the outfits of those around her.

Kitsune wore the french maid lolita top she had been wearing when Cori had worked with her, though she now held a parasol against the rays of the setting sun and included more phosphorescent jewelry. Sammiel's clothes were sleek and partially covered by metallic black plates of obsidian armor that slid over his chest and shoulder in stylings reminiscent of Giger. Maya wore a coat that must have been inspired by a priest's robes. It was pocketless and smooth, black wool trailed from a high collar at the top, and it was woven with brisk enchantments. It tumbled down to her ankles where she wore dark platform boots. Dana was barely covered by a dress made of various pieces of lingerie that squeezed tightly to her skin.

"How are those outfits even comfortable?" Cori asked, vaguely motioning to all of them. "I thought we were just going out for drinks."

"We're gonna get you some good Necromancer gear, don't worry Cori." Maya said.

"Comfortable as hell." Dana said, motioning to her see-through string-lace top. "And enchanted. Don't judge. I spent good money on this."

Sammiel was preoccupied with his hair.

"Where's the others?" Cori asked.

"A few people gotta hold down the fort." Dana said, tending to Sol as he came from the family room chattering and howling. "They can go out for boy's night some time or whatever. I don't care. I need booze. Can we hurry?" Dana asked just before Sol smacked her across her face with his bony hand. This earned a rare scolding and a squirt from the water spritzer that Dana kept at her belt for both plants and rebukes. "Bad. Bad."

"What is it, you wanna come with us?" Sammiel asked in a friendly show of exuberance, and Sol immediately calmed and nodded.

"You're such a bastard, Sam. Sol, we don't get what we want by slapping." She said, and pointed an index finger up against Sol's nose sockets.

Sam gave Dana a look of mock innocence. "They need to get out of the house sometimes too."

"But I need a *break* sometimes too." Dana said, but broke under the weight of two simultaneous puppy dog stares. "Whatever. You're handling any issues."

"Woo!" Sammiel cheered and gave Sol a high five.

"Can we go?" Maya asked. "You're not the only one who needs booze, and I don't think I've had any fresh air for two days."

"No, no. Sol needs to get dressed up now too." Dana said, and held Sol in front of her to examine his skeletal form top to bottom. "Can't have him looking all dumpy next to the rest of us."

"Hey."

"Sorry Cori."

The group sat, fumbling with small talk while Dana prepared Sol for thirty two minutes. Finally, Sol the skeleton came down the stairs wearing a suit and a top-hat that looked as though it had been sitting in a chest in the attic for a century, moth holes and all. Silly as the suit looked on its own, it was also clear that men's fashion had not been designed with skeletons in mind, and the fabrics sagged over Sol's shoulder bones. A monocle taped to his skull completed this effect.

All the staff complimented Sol, who brimmed with pride. Then, they set off through the front door to adventures unknown. Maya led the way and Dana took the rear, Kitsune skulked beside Cori as Sol offered her a flask.

"For me?" Cori asked, then sipped a harsh and fiery liquid as Sol nodded jubilantly. "Thanks." Cori hissed through her tears.

Maya played some tunes from her phone but led the group like a battle ready battalion. They strolled past plantations and vineyards. Each was lost in their own thoughts as they marched along what had once been a paved bike path, now overgrown and untended. Kitsune hovered gracefully under her umbrella from tree shadow to tree shadow while Maya chatted up Sammiel from the front. Cori walked side by side with Sol for a time, noticing that he made an exceptionally good listener, being that he didn't talk. He just nodded along as Cori chatted about her hometown and the people she missed and her grandmother's baking. Dana, from behind, took cuttings of the various herbs that she stumbled across on the hike.

Acting as a tour guide, Maya turned around, walked backwards and motioned to her left, out onto a meadow dappled with trees. "And over here, though it may seem an insignificant place, this was the site of the Battle of Morbid Springs where the Remedian Militia held their line against the invading Canadian Army. Being in such a strategic location, County Remedy is actually the site of a number of uprisings and conquests and...well, frankly, massacres. Just up ahead we're going to pass by Eagle Rock where native Remedians slew a whole ghoul encampment as it sought their town as pasture for their ghoul razings, only for them to be slain shortly thereafter by a pack of rabid Men's Rights Advocates. Hence, the Eagle Rock Massacre."

"I didn't realize this town was so historically significant." Cori said, trying her best to link herself to the ever elusive past where otherwise peaceful meadows become sites of graves and violence. "Why hadn't I heard of this before?"

Kitsune was the only staff person close enough to Cori to hear, but she was keeping busy with a mirror, examining her maw and rows of serrated teeth pouring out a jaw that extended far greater than human biology could allow. She cast a side eye at Cori and chomped down, then clicked her teeth before rearranging her face into a dainty pout, which was much more fitting for a human. Then, she wandered over closer to Cori. "Oh, we're just going to have so much fun tonight, debu, it'll be great."

The first sign of Remedy's approach was several steeples that rose over the final rolling hills. Just then the sun dipped into the horizon with all the usual reds and pinks, but also a dash of emerald in a rare atmospheric event called Carlotta's Twinkle. This was accompanied by a gentle mist of sparkles in the sky which always joined the emerald green of this rare cosmic dance. Several of the staff snapped shots for their instagrams, but none of them did it justice.

Entering the town led into another world, one Cori felt disconnected from, like a hermit. It had been months since she had seen the bustle of people. Life. Oh, there were ghosts a plenty at St. Margaret's, but something was missing. And even for those staff who were alive, they did their best makeup to appear at least somewhat dead. They were nothing like these glittering sun tanned bodies that wore ruby jewels and spicy perfumes and talked about the technical foul of the prior night's big game. It had been months since Cori had strolled these cobblestone streets, and it all looked so different in the gloom of twilight. It brightened, somehow, in the dark; for it was then that life was able to show off its most dazzling electrical contraptions and television screens advertised off brand alchemical sodas from behind the wrought iron caged windows of the local patisserie. Remedy prided itself on blending old world architecture with modern sentiments, so that it was easy enough to find a group of street ruffians playing a game of stick ball right next to their pals playing Monstro Pocket Holo Battles, in which little hologram beasties fought life sized and terrifyingly realistic battles. Sol, an animate skeleton, served as an unexpected but not entirely shocking novelty, worthy only of a second glance and a nudge to your neighbor if you spotted him. It was only as strange as spotting a small ifrit, a fire elemental, walking besides a traveling warlock.

Beyond it all, Cori heard the life pulse of any city, music. Remedy had its own brand of trumpet jazzaphones playing up the latest kicks. Street Cellists and Skit Skat artists, skittering around collecting tips. Bars played honky tonk and jumble wave, or hired bands to perform the more foreign songs of distant oceans and mountain monasteries. Clubs catered to the youth with Skwag Funk, or for the more prudish youths, Holy Skwag, where the youths exchanged vows of chastity in lieu of hip grinding.

"I didn't know there was going to be music." Cori said.

"What sort of town do you think Remedy is?" Maya asked.

"I didn't think much about what sort of town it is at all."

"You didn't research the town you were moving to?"

"I saw pictures." Cori said. "It looked nice."

"Well, before moving to any town, you always have to check to make sure they have good music. And my mom, she used to tell me that there's a goddess living in a palace at the bottom of Lake Talula who sings. A lot of talented musicians either come from Remedy, or live in Remedy, and a lot of them say they can hear her song."

Cori stared at Maya, unable to express how excited that prospect made her. "Can the next day out be to Lake Talula?" Cori asked.

"Once it gets hot out, you know it." Maya said. "The house starts to smell in the summer. I'll be outside every damn day. Got all my PTO saved. I'll take three months off if I have to."

"You don't get to take three months off cause then I can't have any summer months off." Dana bemoaned, staring dead eyed into her phone as she swiped left and right.

"I'd kill for just a week off." Sammiel said, smiling and scratching the back of his head.

"Oo! Oo! I got a boo meeting up with us at Duke's." Dana announced suddenly, fanning herself with her fingers. "You all mind?"

"Dana, the last guy you did this with brought his kids...and his *mom*." Maya said.

"You told me I needed someone more family oriented after 'prison guy'." Dana said, holding her phone up for Maya to take a peek. "But this one is better. Isn't he handsome?"

"Oh, wow, he... really likes dressing up like a fox. Are there any pictures where he isn't wearing a tail?" Maya asked.

"It says here he is looking for a woman who is literally a koala." Sammiel said as he spied over Maya's shoulder.

"I can't expect perfection, okay guys. Cut him some slack. He's a professional web animator. He's gonna be a little weird."

"If Dana gets to bring a boy toy, I do too." Kitsune said, already looking at her phone through a brief and awkward hush.

"Oh no no no." Maya said, wagging a finger. "Dana bringing a boy toy doesn't involve corpse disposal. I ain't doing that again."

"He's not a boy toy, he said he wants to have kids!" Dana shouted.

"Already?! Now I really need a drink."

"Can we go?" Sammiel asked.

"Not until Maya says I can bring some fresh blood." Kitsune screeched, her tongue elongating into the sky, forked and edged.

"I think we're all getting a little hangry." Cori spouted meekly.

Maya rolled her eyes at Kitsune. "Yeah, Cori is right, we need to get out of here. Night is getting wack already."

"I'm bringing a man." Kitsune said, drawing a revulsive stare from Maya. "It's either that or I'm eating Cori."

"Hey now..."

The group edged through the crowds in the streets, dodging unicycles and gawking automata. A bright eyed old man came up to Sol as Sol shambled through the streets and greeted him as an old friend, shaking his bony hand and smiling pleasantly as he asked him how he was doing. Sol nodded and shook his head with a rattle.

"Sol and I go way back." The old man told the group as he turned his attention towards the staff. "You all better take good care of himm, or I'll knock you all a new one." He put up his fists, smiled a dentured smile, and walked away.

The stores they passed were not the sort of department stores Cori had back home. There were no chains here. Just small shops and galleries, and jewelry stores with names she did not recognize.

"Down the street is where I get all the shit for my room." Maya said. "It's an Antique Shop called 'The Lootshack". It's run by some weird dude named Michelangelo, or something. Then, if you need some good clothes, try the thrift shop around the corner, 'Vintage Digs'. They know good clothes there. My friend Jenny works there, she'll give you a good deal if you drop my name. You can get a lot of good looking stuff from them, but then you buy a few really sharp pieces from the specialty shops like 'Runway Ready Armors' or 'Mana Woven', and tie it all together. I just get a few really nice new coats or pants, then wear a bunch of granny cloth with it, and you know I look good."

"I do." Cori said. "Let me know next time you go."

It was no easy feat, what with the constant seduction of window shopping, but they reached The Duke's Downfall where men stood outside and sang the song coming from within while others smoked kush furtively in the alley. The tavern rose three stories, the glass in the windows was warped, dusty, and glowing; and the place was full of life. Inside were several distinct rooms that surrounded a courtyard with varying degrees of noise and bustle. The courtyard was strung about with light bulbs and hanging plants dangling from the wires. Garden Paraphernalia was set about with old timey photos and nostalgia pieces, all of which gazed out onto the night sky above.

The night's main act played in a room beside the courtyard and consisted of an electric violinist who mixed in some eccentric dances, a dapper gentleman with no shoes or socks on the keyboard, and an acne-pocked young man on the drum pad. The lead singer was a young waif of a woman, with a shockingly raspy voice. They were playing folk hymnals from the Emerald Isles. The party of necromancers made their way to the courtyard where they could hear both the band playing, and one another.

"What are you having, Cori?" Sammiel asked.

"What do they have?"

Sammiel stood for a moment and thought, opened his mouth, then closed it again. "Everything."

"He means it too." Maya said. "Half the reason we come here is so he can get his absinthe."

"Maybe I should get that?"

"You would not like that." Maya said. "I know! They serve an elderflower martini here."

"That. I want that."

"You'll like that."

"Okay." Sammiel said, stroking his chin. "Elderflower martini for Cori. Absinthe for Sammy. I know Dana likes her strawberry hennessy. Sake for Kitsune--"

"Hai."

"And for Maya?"

"I'm going to join Cori here with the martini."

"Okay, I'll be right back." Sammiel said before Sol began to pound his bones on the table. "I know, I know. An Old Fashioned for Sol."

Just as Sammiel was out of earshot Dana turned to Maya and said, "Mm, girl he was all up on you."

"Stop." Maya said.

"Yamerooo…" Kitsune growled in tones too low for a woman to make.

"Just saying."

"I didn't know you were into Sammiel, Maya." Cori said.

"See what you do, Dana." Maya said, blushing and scowling. "I'm not. Sammiel and I would be terrible for each other. But he's the only eligible bachelor in the house, what am I supposed to do, not flirt with him?"

"What she means to say is that Sammiel is not interested in her." Kitsune added, glaring at Maya.

"What she means to say--" Maya corrected her, "is that she is more interested in Mr. Ph.D in bio-medical engineering that she's been talking to online. But sure, Vampirina, whatever helps you sleep all day."

"This table needs food. I'm gonna text Sam, tell him to put in an order of breadsticks." Dana said, glaring down once more at her phone. "Oh! Boo is gonna be here in ten."

"Do we always draw this much attention?" Cori asked the others, noting the conspicuous nods and glares or otherwise dopey grins of the other patrons.

"You get used to it." Dana said. "No one's brought out the torches and pitchforks on us just yet."

"Well, except the Paladins." Maya said. "But they're easy enough to manage. Kitsune scares them plenty enough to keep them at arm's length."

Kitsune stuck out her tongue at a demonic length, nearing the bottom of her neck, a smile spliced across to her ears.

Dana had her head held in her hands. "There's a tentative truce. But they've broken it before, and we're sort of breaking it right now."

"We are?" Cori asked.

Maya rolled her eyes. "The truce is like three hundred years old. It says the spirits are all to remain within the St. Margaret's property's boundaries. Some Paladins get bothered when we break it, some don't care. They're usually prancing off in the mountains anyway."

"I ambush them sometimes." Kitsune said.

"And that, Cori, is most likely why they've been giving us more trouble lately." Maya said. "You need to stop doing that Kitsune."

"But their blood is like nectar." Her voice crackled demonically. "They're always honing and purifying their bodies and minds. It's delicious."

"So just to clarify, Kitsune, you're literally murdering victims and drinking their blood? Or is it more like an aesthetic thing where you act it out?" Cori asked.

Kitsune's smile shifted to a scowl. "Don't act like you're perfect."

"Yeah, it's literal murder." Dana said, still lost in her phone.

Cori's jaw dropped as she pondered her next words or actions and determined none were fitting. So instead her jaw remained dropped as she kept her eye cocked on Kitsune for too long.

"You humans all get such a hard on when you read about sexy conflicted vampires. I'm conflicted too, doesn't that count for anything? But noooo, when it's real life, all of the sudden I'm a monster and I'm not allowed to babysit my little sister and vampire hunters keep breaking into my crypt and trying to end my immortal existence. Where do you all get off?"

Cori proceeded with her words slowly. "I'm not here to judge...I just figured it was illegal so I wasn't...sure if you dealt with any...legal...ramifications."

"Pft. I'd like to see them try. The occasional vampire hunter stops by to deliver me a midday snack. That's the extent of law enforcement." Kitsune said.

"Kitsune actually has a fairly interesting employment story where she simply started working and demanding pay without actually being hired." Maya said, smirking towards Kitsune.

"Morris tried to banish me and hire all sorts of professional help but I thwarted them all. The job market is fierce for a blood sucker." Kitsune said.

"Admirable." Maya admitted. "It's certainly one way to do it, no? But that's neither here nor there. How many drinks until you start dancing, Cori?"

"Oh, I don't dance." Cori said. Sammiel returned to the table with a tray of cocktails.

"That's what everybody says. Until they get a few drinks. Thanks Sammy. How many?"

"I'm gonna have like three, maybe." Cori said and grabbed her martini from Sammiel and nodded his way. Maya passed a mischievous look across the rest of the table and Cori asked, "What?"

"Nothin'."

"Oh...This is the most delicious thing I've ever drank." The elderflower martini tasted like nothing else Cori had ever had. It was floral and sweet, and it warmed her throat. But there was something else behind it all that sent her heart aflutter.

"Easily my favorite." Maya said. "Oh, Sam, Cori wanted to try the absinthe."

Sammiel passed over his drink without a second thought. Cori was mortified by such an act of intimacy, but took the drink and sipped it and nearly spat it everywhere. *Like Licorice and witches burning*, she thought.

"Oh it's not that bad." Sammiel said, snatching it back from her.

"It's...unique."

"Well, I like the nightmares it gives me."

"Mugwort." Dana interjected. "I've got plenty growing in the greenhouse if you ever want me to poison you."

"I didn't know that..I'd like that. Remind me later. I plan on forgetting tonight."

Through the first round of drinks everyone discussed work, though in a more candid way than Cori had been used to. They were plenty candid enough to begin with, but she felt as though she learned more in that round of drinks than she had in the last few days.

"Agnus used to be a witch, before she died, you know. I guess she still is." Dana said.

"I'd describe her differently. Rhymes with witch." Maya said between sips.

"She just doesn't like you because you have a stupid fear." Kitsune said.

"Listen, you try getting abducted by aliens everytime you're up in her apartment. That shit's not right." Maya said.

"That sounds awful." Cori said, thinking it sounded just as bad as her own experience.

"Well tell that to Tokyo Ghoul over here. She says it's a lame fear."

"I see, like...frickin' Lovecraftian Mind Flayers." Dana added. "They put worms in my ears to control my mind and drive me insane."

"That's why she likes you." Kitsune said, and cast a harsh glance at Maya. "That's a cool fear."

"See, she just makes me see how disorganized everything in her room is. Then I check my bank account and it's negative. Separate but semi-related note, did you know Sol here died of alcohol poisoning?" Sammiel asked, his boots up on the table. "So he comes to us and he's still drinking. Doesn't matter what form he's in. Zombie, he'll drink. Skeleton, he'll drink. Ghost, he still manages to lift up that glass and drink. So, we thought maybe sobering him up might help him move on. Did it for about two really hard years, and still nothing."

"So, here we are now." Dana said as Sol drained his old fashioned, which dripped along his bones. "Got no idea what to do with him. But we figure he's happier when he's drinking than when we try to get him to sober up, so we're rolling with it for now."

"Well you can't just take his drinks away. You have to replace it with healthy habits." Cori said. "Like...get him drinking alcoholic kombucha, then ween out the alcohol. Do some yoga classes with him." Everyone looked at Cori. "My uncle was an alcoholic." Cori explained.

"That's...not a bad idea…" Dana said.

"Worth a shot." Maya added.

Sol shrugged, then finished the rest of his drink.

Maya bought the second round of drinks and Cori wished terribly that she had brought more than fifteen dollars. This ritual of buying the group's drinks was news to her. She'd only ever gone drinking with Melanie before, her ex-best friend back home. They always just paid for their own.

"Girls." Dana said, eyes wide on her phone. "He's here. Good timing, I'm just getting my buzz on. Do I look alright?"

"You look great. He's not coming over here is he?" Maya asked, then suddenly put on a polite showing, distinctly suburbanite, "Oh hiiii, you must be Craig." She held out her hand.

"'Sup." Said Craig. The newcomer to their table was a large man in his early thirties. His red hair was tied back in a ponytail over transparent skin, neck beard groomed to the minimum. He wore an anime tee-shirt that was consummated with a spiked collar upon his neck and one distinct fuzzy fox tail poking out from behind his gym shorts. "You're Dana?"

Dana looked star struck. "Hi."

"'Sup."

Dana giggled. "You want a drink? I can order you a drink."

"I don't really drink."

"Nonsense." Maya said, pushing the couple away from the table. "You two love birds go grab him a monster energy with moonshine in it or something. I don't know. I give up. Seeing anything yet, Sammy?"

"Absinthe isn't all about seeing things Maya. It's an altered state of mind... But yes."

"I'm pretty sure I'm in an altered state of mind." Maya replied, one eyelid lowering below the other as she sunk back into her chair, and a dumb flat smile spreading cheek to cheek as she sunk back into her chair.

"What's this about altered states of mind, I hear?" A voice came from beyond the table.

"Morris?" Maya, turned swiftly.

"Morrissss!" Everyone yelled as they saw him, and Morris held out his hands and drank it all in as though he were a celebrity. Today his wizard's robes were sky blue with gold embroidery. He wore all new jewelry that Cori had not yet seen him in, with a focus on Topaz. He even sported a pair of indoor sunglasses, Gucci.

"What the hell, I thought you were working?" Sammiel asked him.

"I finished my rounds." He said.

"Oh, so you're gonna be chill if I start taking off whenever I finish my rounds?" Sammiel gave Morris a stern look.

"I invoke the sacred rites of supervisor's privileges." Morris said with flair. "And Derrick agreed to cover for me."

"Right." Sammiel said. "He *agreed.*"

"You all want the same thing as before?" Kitsune asked the table discreetly and to the nods of all, then left.

"It took some persuasion, but nothing a few hours on the Judas Cradle couldn't fix." Morris resumed humorlessly, then pulled up a chair. "Did you all see who Dana was with? I could practically smell the Chlamydia as he walked by. I don't know how she does it. Never mind. I have big news." Morris said, his face brimming with anticipation. Then he paused, and everyone waited. Then he paused some more. Then the waitress brought him a small glass of port wine. "Thank you." Morris said, sitting beside Sol and handing the waitress a five dollar bill. "Hey Sol ol' buddy." As the waitress left, he pulled a vial from his sleeve. He looked back and forth around the tavern, then dropped a few drops from the vial into his drink with a mischievous smirk.

"Morris." Maya said, cringing as Dana sat down with Craig and his Monster Energy Moonshine.

"Hm?"

"Big news."

"Ah yes. After this next interview we will have enough staff so that I….may go on vacation." There were a few oh's from the others, but overall they were disappointed. "Which of course means you all can start going on vacations again too. But I'm first."

"Morris I was just telling everyone I need one this summer." Maya said. "I'm gonna go on a murder spree. I'm telling you this directly. I am legally threatening you that I will axe murder everyone in the house if I don't get my vacation."

"You'll get your vacation you big whiner. We can all go in order."

Maya slouched back in her chair once more, satiated. "Where are you going?"

"I'll be taking an interplanar tour through the Betwixt." Morris said, his eyes alight. "First to Summerland for some R and R. Then to Sonorous for a music festival. Then to the Elemental Chaos. A buddy of mine has a quest there, and I haven't done a quest since I was in my thirties. I just made all the arrangements last night."

"Damn that's a lot." Sammiel said. "What if the interview doesn't go so well?"

"I've been the manager of St. Margaret's for ten years now, and not once have I turned down a new hire." Morris said, and Cori felt a little less special for nailing her interview. "Except for that one guy, Sandalphon. I asked him where he saw himself in five years, and he started rambling off his plans to use St. Margaret's to start a new world order. But I'm not terribly worried about it. This girl has a freaking diploma. That's more than any of you can say."

"Fair enough." Sammiel said.

Maya slammed her empty martini glass on the table. "I'm calling it now. The month of August."

"Done." Morris said without thinking. "Where are you off to?"

"Haven't decided yet, but I'll let you know."

Kitsune came back with drinks and passed them around. "And one for you, and you. Here you go, Sammy."

Cori became lost in her thoughts as the others jabbered. Sammiel held a conversation with Dana and Craig while Kitsune tried to garner his attention. Morris sat back and made a toast to Sol, who Cori had never seen so perfectly in his element. Sitting in the corner a few tables down was a group of Pirate Lords, and besides them a giggling gaggle of university girls. Down the row, a fierce game of chess between two old codgers and their pints. The once melodious music became more rhythmic and upbeat, and the energy of the night grew with it.

Cori's mind drifted to the stars and found that even in this pleasant environment, her thoughts grew dark. For as buoyant and sociable her environment, she began thinking herself terribly alone. *What are you even doing with your life? You're a disappointment to your family. Have you even called your Dad yet? Not like he would want you to anyway. Your own mother didn't even want you. Pathetic.*

"Ready to dance yet?" Maya asked Cori, snapping her from the dark train of thought.

"No."

"Another drink then?"

"I've already had three." Cori said, trying to muster a smile.

"Morris," Maya said, "Buy us a round."

"Do I look like I'm made of money?" He asked. His silk robes flowed gently across his topaz embedded gold rings and chains.

"Yes." Dana said. "You always do."

"Flattery will get you everywhere, Dana." Morris said and stood gallantly. "Next round is on me."

"I really can't." Cori said, wanting more, but nervous as her vision swam. "When I said three drinks I meant three like...beers."

"Tut tut, that won't do at all." Morris said, flourishing the lengthy silks of his sleeves and apparating a tray full of neon bedazzled shots. "Voila!"

Morris earned a round of applause and hollering for that, and in the next moment everyone was holding up their shot glasses with him. "A toast. To our new staff, Coriander Lou." Morris said whilst

Cori blushed crimson and broke out into a cold sweat. "You may not know it yet, dear, but you're very much the newest member of our big dysfunctional family. And while we're all still getting to know you, I think I can speak for each and every one of us in saying that you've been nothing but a pleasure to have around. You've displayed immense courage since your beginning here, and a sharp wit to boot. You work hard, you play hard. You're a good kid. Cheers."

"Cheers!" Everyone added, and Cori became damp at the eyelashes. Then she downed her first ever shot of alcohol. Somewhere between that moment and the next, Cori found herself dancing with Maya near the band. Sammiel joined with Sol, and Cori briefly remembered seeing the patrons part so Sol could do the jitterbug. People poured drinks down into his skull, soaking his suit. Then people poured drinks into Cori's skull, soaking her yoga pants.

Morris joined the fray, and danced as though he had watched a large number of hip hop videos while practicing in front of his mirror.

"Look at you Morris." Maya pumped her fist and yelled. "Yeah, get it on."

Having Morris next to her made Cori forget how silly she might look. And though her memory ceased from time to time, she was nearly certain that Sammiel had casually brushed against her for a moment before their eyes locked. There might have been another drink, but the toilet was the next thing Cori remembered, Maya holding back her hair.

"I'm sorry, you were right." Maya said. "I'm sorry."

"I'm having so much fun." Cori said, then puked. "No regrets."

"I'll hold your hair back any day, girl. No regrets here neither. Mm mm."

"I looked like an idiot."

"You danced good."

"You're so cute."

Then they were in the street. The crowds had died down, but those who were out were all the more raucous. It was in the streets that Cori noticed the full moon, and soon they were all howling at it. Money passed too easily to street vendors selling roasted anonymous meats on sticks while fire dancers collected tips from the easily impressed crowd. Morris stopped to gamble with no less than three mysterious figures in the alleyways, whose eyes were somehow white while the rest of their bodies were obscured entirely in shadow. Morris lost two gold rings and the rest of his cash in the process.

    Morris wasn't the only one swindled. Cori herself was extorted by a man that sold ghosts in jars from the back of his van.

    "This is despicable, we have to free them!" Cori cried out while Maya protested and attempted to pull her away, but to no avail. "Where's the ghosts?" Cori asked when she opened the jar. Eighty bucks, gone.

    "I brought a flask with some real wonky stuff brewed by dwarves." Morris said while the group huddled beside a dumpster. "Who's in?"

    Cori heard a few people say 'me', herself included.

    "It tastes like burning." Cori had said, while Morris divulged some deep and dark secrets he said he had taken an oath never to tell.

    "Cori...do *you* know what lies beneath St. Margaret's?" Morris asked, giggling.

    "Eugh jeez get a room." Maya said, and Cori's vision swam over to Dana macking it with Craig in between his occasional attempts at fox noises.

    Cori saw only the inside of a trash can.

    "Like I said, I'll hold back your hair anytime." It was the sound of Maya's voice. "No worries. Get it all out."

    "But have you ever been with your own doppelganger?" Morris asked.

    "No!" Dana said. "And you haven't either, don't you lie."

    Morris tutted. "Oh, but I have. Now envision it. Envision it!"

"Kitsune, no! Craig!" Dana shouted. The two of them were entwined in a lovers' embrace against a nearby building, though Craig was hanging from Kitsune's arms in a suspiciously limp manner.

The memories became more distant. More vague. Did Morris and Sammiel really puppeteer Craig's corpse when questioned by the constable? *There's no way this is real.* Cori barely remembered thinking while Morris and Sammiel held Craig up by either shoulder, moving his mouth and speaking for him like ventriloquists.

Though the night was a blur, one thing remained clear throughout the entirety, Cori was having fun.

Chapter 7

They were on the road home and passing the vine choked wooden sign pointing to St. Margaret's when Cori regained some semblance of steady consciousness. Birds chirped with the first signs of dawn, and Cori's tube top was torn in several places, as though by a werewolf. Cori noticed that the trees along the road looked as though they were dancing, and more frightening yet, she couldn't remember if trees were always supposed to do that. Maya informed her that they had visited a night club, and Cori couldn't remember even a single strobe of a strobe light.

"That time you danced like an idiot." Maya told her, holding Sol's bony hand at her side.

"Oh, don't tell me that."

"Well, now whenever I tell you that you dance good, you'll know I'm being honest. You danced good at the beginning of the night."

"Fair enough." Cori said.

"Kitsune, I really don't want to hear it." Dana cried out, her black eyeliner streaking down her cheeks.

"I did the world a favor."

"Go suck an egg." Dana said and stomped her foot. "I finally find a good man--"

"He was terrible, I saved you. You should be thanking me."

"Thanking?!" Dana yelled, and started to form an orb of purple electricity between her palms.

"Oh, cut it out you two, Craig will be fine. Dana, quit the theatrics, Kitsune would eat your ass in a head to head battle. Now stop worrying, I sent an anonymous tip to the authorities, told them what dumpster Craig was in and everything. He had plenty of life left in him." Morris said, then discreetly looked over at Sammiel, frowned and shook his head 'no'. "I'm sure the hospital clerics will be able to fix him up good as new."

"He'll never want to see me again." Dana said. "Morris, you could have healed him yourself."

"Yeah, but you know...Necromancer code or whatever. Supposed to guide souls on, not bring them back, yadda yadda yadda."

"Can't you at least write Kitsune up or something?!"

"Hush," Morris snapped, and stopped walking, pointing forward along the road. "Kitsune, dark vision, what's that up there?"

"Paladins. Four of them."

"Any of them look like a threat?" Morris asked.

"One of them looks like a commander." Kitsune said, her eyes glowing crimson with dark vision.

"They'll have to do a lot better than that." Sammiel said, his hands on his hips and chewing gum.

Cori sauntered over to Sammiel while the others jabbered on about the approaching platoon. "You don't think they'll attack us, do you?"

"Ehhh…" Sammiel thought for a moment. "If they don't, I'm guessing we will egg them on until they do."

Cori put her hands on her hips as well and gazed off to the approaching figures. "I never really understood the whole Necromancer Paladin thing. My family gave me so much trouble coming to this job, like I was betraying them all. My Dad said I should have been a Paladin like my mum."

"For my part, I always thought of it more like a friendly rivalry, but obviously not everyone sees it that way. I guess that's just what happens when you get two opposite forces. For Paladins, the most important thing is life, and healing. Death is something to be avoided at all costs. Necromancers tend to be a little more accepting of death, and think that once it's someone's time, it's best to help them move along as easily as possible to liberate their soul. It's the idea that maybe death is just the opposite side of the coin as life. But that stands as a hard and heavy contrast to people who think like Paladins." Sammiel said.

"What about you, what do you think?" Cori asked.

"Me? Eh, I think they're both right. Obviously, I'm Team Necromancer. But I think it's important to heal things too. Like, why are we forbidden from healing? Not that anyone ever listens, but still, its weird for it to be a rule. There's definitely situations where I think it's fair to resurrect a corpse, Council forgive me. But then there's other times where it's important to help a soul move on. But then, Paladins just ignore any spirit that's past the redemption of life, as if they don't matter anymore. So...they both suck. That's my answer. Everyone sucks."

"You're not half bad Sammiel." Cori said. "I like the cut of your jib. I don't care what they say about you."

"Who calls trigger?" Morris asked loudly, jarring away from the mumbled strategic discussions they had been having in the background before.

Everyone except Cori said "Me."

"Dana gets it." Morris said, while Dana whooped while everyone else sighed. "You're welcome."

The Paladins arrived in their approach after a minute or so. Three kept formation, and walked side by side behind their commander. They stopped in front of the party.

The three in the back were wearing uniform white robes with blue trim, and some plate armor in strategic placement. The commander in front wore a much more intricate design with the same colors. Each piece looked quite expensive, and for some reason there was quite a bit of skin revealed which left her vital weak points unguarded. Her cape fluttered in the breeze.

"Evening, Necromancers." The commander said, and held her hand up in a sign that seemed to be peaceful. Her blonde hair glowed in the moonlight. She was older, perhaps as old as Morris, Cori guessed, but with an ageless look that made any accuracy difficult.

"Necromancers? Shucks, there haven't been any Necromancers in these parts for ages." Dana said in a dopey hick drawl, and a snicker or two passed between the others while Cori looked over at Sol.

The commander sighed. "I'm not looking for any trouble. But I notice you've brought an undead of the skeletal subclass outside the bounds of St. Margaret's, and into the town of Remedy. This is a move that has been laid out in the Remedial Accords as an offense punishable by one year of prison, and banishment for the undead in question."

"Well, I don't mean to offend or nothin', but that sounds like maybe all that sexual repression is finally getting the best of you Paladins." Dana said to the ever growing shock of the Paladin's opposite. "My prescription. Instead of banishing Sol here, you could borrow his femur bone and shove it alllll the way up your--"

"Excuse me?" One of the lower ranking paladins spat, and grabbed at his sword.

"Don't, Ricky." The Commander said, then turned to look at Dana with weary eyes. "Please, do not be obtuse. I was simply going to ask you to return home."

"I'm sorry, but I thought I heard you threaten our buddy Sol, here, saying you'd banish him."

The commander stammered. "I didn't mean to say...I was simply pointing out that--"

"Can you even tell that you hurt his feelings?" Dana asked. Sol played along by wiping at his eyes though, as far as Cori could tell, he wasn't in the least bit offended.

"As if we'd have any sympathy for that abomination you're dragging along with you." Said the uniformed Spaniard, Ricky. The Necromancers became silent, and the air stilled.

"Ricky, you idiot." One of the other Paladins said under their breath.

"What'd you call him?" Dana asked.

"I said, I don't have any sympathy for that abomination." But Ricky the Spaniard sounded less certain this time.

"Stand down, Private."

"I sincerely doubt any of you could get your privates to stand up in the first place." Morris said.

"Absalon, please stop this right now." The Commander said, with equal parts authority and pleading. "We've had peace for all the years you've been in charge at St. Margaret's."

"I'm sorry," Morris chuckled. "We're pretty drunk."

"Clearly."

"Oh come on, Morris, don't diffuse it now. You heard them." Dana said.

"Commander, we can't let them get away with this." Private Ricky, the Spaniard, said. "The High Priest, he'll--"

"What the High Priest does not know--"

"I'm sorry, Commander, but I would be forced to report this," said Ricky.

"Excuse me, Private?"

"You gonna let a private boss you around like that?" Morris asked the Commander. "Eesh."

The commander stared down at Private Ricky, her face calm, but ferocity poured off her in waves. Then, she turned back to Morris. "I'm afraid we have no choice but to detain you." The Commander said to the group of Necromancers. "Absalon, this is nothing personal, and I'm sure you'll be able to explain yourself at a trial. I'll put in a good word for you."

"Oh, come now. Surely, all four of you do not wish to die tonight?" Morris said. "There must be another way."

The Paladin Commander looked down, and reluctantly drew her sword, as did her comrades.

"Oh, I know, what about a duel?" Morris asked. "Leader versus leader. Worst case scenario, only one person dies. You win, we will go peacefully to whatever prison you had in mind. I win…" Morris stroked his beard. "I win and...we get to keep your armor. Undergarments and all."

"No." The Commander said. "You win and you get to go home."

"That hardly seems fair. That was what you asked us to do in the first place. We didn't do it then, why would we do it now?"

"That was before you forced my hand, Absalon."

"But we could still *kill* you all." Morris said. "And you know it too. I see it in your eyes. You know it." Cori looked at the commander, and saw only fierce determination.

"That is a ridiculous request, you can't seriously expect us to…"

"It's either that, or we all fight."

"You would risk your entire enterprise the wrath of the Paladin Order just to make us walk home in the nude? I think you underestimate the conse--"

"I think you underestimate how schwasted I am." Morris said, and the Necromancers chuckled again. "In or out?"

"I was going to try to ensure your comfort when I had you arrested, Absalon. I think now I may have to hand you over to our Inquisitor."

"Is that a yes?"

The Commander took off her cape by way of answer, her face somber.

"Can I get your name?"

"Aislynn." She said, and tested her swords weight, then held it out to her side.

"Aislynn, then." Morris said. "The fight shall be till the death, or till you say 'Paladin's suck.'"

"Draw your weapon, Absalon."

"I am a weapon, baby."

Commander Aislynn rolled her eyes, then stood in a disciplined stance, her body motionless. Morris held up his arms in a kung fu palm fighting stance, also disciplined but swaying with drink. All grew quiet. The moon peeked out from behind the slowly roiling clouds as the first rays of the sun punctured the darkness. A lone breeze blew the hair of the motionless fighters. The once noisy dawn birds quieted into a hush which fell over the land for several moments, pierced only by a single hiccup from Morris.

At this, Aislynn rushed forward and slashed through Morris, a cut from shoulder to hip. Morris held still, his body intact for a moment before his upper torso began to slide off his lower. Then, his image dissolved.

"Your vision can't even pierce illusion? What are they teaching Paladins at the Academy these days?" Morris asked from behind the line of Paladins as Aislynn charged him again. Cori, Sammiel, Kitsune, Maya, and Dana all ran to stand side by side with the Paladins as they watched their leaders battle one another.

Morris deflected blow after blow with his bare arms, his robes tore, but there was no scratch on his skin. "Oakflesh."

"Stop toying with me, Absalon." Aislynn roared with a thrust of her sword.

"Okay." Morris said, crouched, then placed his palm against her abdomen. Ice erupted all across her chest plate. Kinetic force blasted Aislynn ten feet back, where she stabbed her sword into the ground to keep her footing.

Aislynn looked down, and Cori saw her mutter something, before her hair took on a light all its own, beyond the light of the moon, and her armor set aflame, melting the ice. Morris's eyes went wide. Aislynn approached him slowly, regally, her prior uncertainty melted like the ice.

"You...You said your name was Aislynn...?" Morris asked as Aislynn gave a horizontal slash which produced a fiery wave in the air and cut Morris across his chest. His skin stitched itself together, and he cast an aether bubble around himself. "Wait, stop, please." But Aislynn jabbed her sword straight into his bubble, which shattered, and sent Morris onto the ground. "Aislynn O'Cuillin?" Morris asked in one of his exaggerated accents. Aislynn stopped her assault, and looked at him curiously. "It's me. Morris."

"No..." Aislynn said.

"I mean the beard probably makes it hard to tell..."

"Morris Llewelyn?" Aislynn asked, and dropped her sword. And together they stepped forward to hug each other. "It's been so long."

"Commander, I'm sorry but we still must have him taken into custody." Ricky said.

Morris stretched out his hand and carved unholy symbols into the air in the direction of Private Ricky. Cori wasn't nearly sober enough to comprehend what happened next, but to the best of her perceptive abilities it appeared as though Private Ricky's flesh grew thousands of tiny gnashing beast maws. These began to eat each other and subsequently Ricky's own flesh. However, it all happened so fast and one moment there was a standing and breathing Private Ricky. The next moment there was only a collective heap of limp meats.

"Morris!" Aislynn said and a few people screamed at the bloody mess of organ and flesh. "Mother of all that is holy..."

"Oh, don't worry, he's not dead." Morris said. "Maya could fix him up in a jiffy."

"I really don't think I could, Morris." Maya said, eyes wide with horror.

"I'm sorry, I'm so used to you being able to do whatever I think of. Okay, I'll do it then."

"Morris..." Dana moaned. "You said you couldn't heal Craig because of the Necromancer Code."

"Yeah, to be honest, Dana, I just didn't want to."

Blue flame encompassed Morris as his dual layered chanting rumbled the earth below. Forest sprites gathered to bear witness to the anomaly, and even the stars above moved to the dance of the magicks below.

Powerful stuff.

All that had been Ricky liquified, and pulled together at the source. Bones fused and muscles stretched and intestines slithered. It was painful to watch, excruciating to hear and, Cori imagined, much worse than all that to feel.

"See," Morris said, and pointed above into the empty air. "His soul is still hanging about right over there, wondering what the heck happened. Hardly dead." Morris snorted as if this should have been a very obvious thing to the layman. "Just don't tell anyone about this. The Council of Necromancer's would see my soul devoured in the pits of Ammut if they found out."

Cori spied the Spaniard, Private Ricky, floating pensively above; looking upon this disturbing scene from above in the ethereal plane with terrified resignation, and it seemed the other Necromancers could see him too. Knowing he was still disconnected was a relief, because his body was flailing and shrieking in a most unholy manner.

"I really am sorry." Morris said to the cries of his victim. "I got carried away. He'll be good as new in a moment. Heck, I'll throw in a few genetic augmentations if you like."

"Just heal him, please." Aislynn said, trying to cover her eyes from the gruesome scene, but unable to look away completely.

The body was now complete but for a gaping chest cavity where Ricky's beating heart could be seen. Morris knelt beside the body, dripped some clear liquid from a vial onto Ricky's face, then kissed Ricky gently on the lips. A purple vortex grew out of the heart, like a serpentine tornado, which reached its way up to where Cori could see Ricky's soul. This was then sucked down and bound once again to this mortal coil. The chest cavity closed, and Ricky's eyes opened as he took in one ghastly breath.

Morris looked down at the blank batting eyes of the reawakened Paladin and said, "Now, Aislynn won't have any more trouble from you, will she?"

The Paladin shook his head.

"Please don't threaten my men, Absalon." Commander Aislynn said, once again establishing her formal tone.

"Can we talk for a moment?" Morris asked her.

"You just butchered one of my men."

Morris looked offended. "He has both learned a measure of respect for his commander, and undoubtedly grown stronger from the experience. I even removed a tumor from his belly while I was at it. A regular ticking time bomb. Gone, just like that… I *saved* him.

Aislynn held still for a time, then looked at the opposing parties and said, "Would you all excuse us for a moment?" And not a soul protested.

The two went off to the side of the road where they spoke for a time, and occasionally one or both of them would laugh. Then, Morris returned some minutes later looking very happy.

"Okay, who wants to go to bed?" Morris asked. "I'd like to get to my bed."

The Paladins walked off in silence, and The Necromancers followed behind Morris while he whistled a tune.

"I feel like that went well." He said. "Who had fun? Raise your hand." And Morris raised his hand, and eventually so did everyone else. "Oh, and don't forget; staff meeting tomorrow. Or...that's the sun isn't it? Today I guess."

———The group all groaned in unison.

Chapter 8

Cori waited in the boardroom, early for her first staff meeting so as to make a good impression with both Morris and whoever was coming from the Human Resources Department. She was wildly hungover, and hadn't expected the Human Resources representative to be a cloaked wraith that arrived just as early as she did. He did nothing but levitate in the corner of the board room, a menacing and malevolent presence.

Tattered tapestries hung besides interior gargoyles and just above torches, which was a terrible fire hazard. In the center of the room was a scale model of the town of Remedy, St. Margaret's, and the mountains to the North. The room was large, fit to accommodate twice the number of staff as they currently had, and perhaps several guests. And, in contrast to the usual hand-me-down quality of St. Margaret's furniture, all of the chairs set by the polished table were ergonomically advanced and, dare I say, comfortable.

Employees filed in slowly and sat quietly. They scrolled through their phones and instagrams or tiktok or played bedazzler or whatever else the kids are doing these days. Everyone except Luke, who was already asleep. He had been in the room sleeping even before Cori. One by one they came in until Morris arrived three minutes late. He looked shaken, and was carrying a to-go cup of coffee he must have picked up in Remedy. He was sweating, and wearing a pair of glasses.

Morris mumbled a greeting that could barely be heard in the echoing board room. It sounded like it might have been a quivering "Hello, everybody," with a nod to the corporate entity in the corner. The entity did not nod back.

Morris muttered again until Dana stopped him and said "We can't hear you." Morris then coughed, tapped on a microphone in front of his seat, adjusted settings, and spoke up.

"Can you hear me now?" He asked. His voice reverberated through hidden speakers. His hands were shaking. "We uh...as you all know, we have a guest visiting us. This is Howard, from Human Resources. Can everyone say 'Hi' to Howard?"

Maya and Cori gave an emphatic 'Hello, Howard' while everyone else stayed quiet. Sammiel smiled a little in Howard the Wraith's direction. Derrick was still looking at his phone under the table, and Kitsune was taking selfies. Dana wore a quiet scowl, and Luke was still asleep.

"Alright, so...on the agenda..." Morris began and cleared his throat, then walked around the table to pass out laminated agendas. "As per a suggestion at last night's team building exercise, I thought it may be a good idea to try introducing Sol to an alcoholic kombucha in an effort to build a positive habit in lieu of trying to stop a negative one. Then, we could provide some yoga classes... Does anyone here know yoga?" Morris asked to deafening silence. "Anyone other than me? Please?" Cori raised her hand slowly and quietly. "Cori, bonus points." Morris said, monotone. "You can head off the effort. Uhhh...Okay, the Toilet Abomination is on the prowl again. Please, always make sure to check the toilets for bubbles before using them. First signs of an attack, it'll gently lap its tentacle against...well, you've all been there. Uhhh...cigarette butts were found by the side entrance. Derrick!" Morris' eyes flashed like fire at Derrick, his pupils like a demonic cat, before he resumed a general apathy. "There's smoking outposts in the cemetery and the woods across the street. A few of you are due for...ASH training? What's ASH Training? Howard?"

Howard muttered something incomprehensible, though voiceless.

"Who the hell needs that? Ugh, whatever. Dana, Luke, you're due for it. Cori, you'll receive it after a year. Okay...some of you have been asking about pay raises. Corporate wants you to know they hear you, andddd....well, that's all that's written here. Corporate *hears* you. On a related note...summer bonuses...will be delayed till autumn. But it will still be called a Summer Bonus for the purposes of bolstering morale. Andddd...the Council of Necromancers says that it is working on bribing public officials in a legislative effort to pass an esoteric tariff package that'll help...ugh, I'm sorry everyone, they're very insistent that I go through this whole list..." Morris looked up at Howard, and seemed very afraid. Very, very afraid. A sickly pall descended upon his face. "I'm...sorry. The Council is working on Legislation for an esoteric tariff package that'll aid in the development of new housing projects with which to diversify assets, thus contributing to stability in an ever fluctuating market. The recent acquisition of The Crypt at Sanders Bay was one such diversification and should allow us to expand into a new and ever growing field, should traditional modes of Necromancy alone ever lose its footing in the current economy. Whew, that was a mouthful." Morris said, then looked up at Howard again. Morris fiddled with his robes while he spoke. "Sorry. Uh...okay, and Corporate sent out anonymous surveys that you all should have completed. We had a twenty one percent response rate this year which is really very good. Corporate said that the responses have revealed an overall positive view of the company, but based on the essay section of the survey, they believe employees may not be familiar enough with Basic Cosmology. And in an effort to save on training costs they want me to provide training here."

For the first time, noise could be heard from the employees who all groaned. "Morris, we all know the basics of Cosmology." Sammiel said.

"Irregardless, I will be providing training. Cosmology Training. On...the...Betwixt. And realms therein." Morris pulled a white board to his side, and uncapped a red dry erase marker. He drew a quick line on the bottom. "The Mundane. Mundas. Whatever you want to call it. The physical. Generally considered to vibrate at 396 Hz, but for the most part it can fluctuate anywhere between 380 and 408. 396 is ideal for prosperity, though. Anything below 380 gets into the Elemental Chaos and the Hells below that, but we don't deal in that, now do we? That's for Hell Priests. As you approach 0 Hz, you fall into the jaws of Ammut where your soul is shredded beyond any hope of redemption, but that's a pretty rare occurrence." Morris sounded like this was the most boring thing in the world, but Cori realized maybe she didn't know all that much about what he was teaching. Morris first drew angry squiggles where Ammut should be at the bottom, then he pulled out an orange dry erase marker and drew another line over the first. "Okay, then there's all the Betwixt 'above' us, so to speak, but obviously it's not above so much as layered over, or 'through the veil', if you will. Of course, the name 'Betwixt' refers to it being 'in between' and technically even the Mundane is part of the Betwixt. It's all kinds of scrambly. Don't think too hard about it. This lowest one above us is where our residents reside. Commonly referred to as "The Ethereal". Many people, and hopefully all of *us*, can see into that one pretty easily, resonating at approximately 417 Hz, give or take. Spirits have a tendency to get bound up in this one, for whatever reason, and they can get tethered here...pretty much eternally. Same for the one above it." Morris said, still bored, pulling out his yellow marker. "Summerland. You can get all bound up here too. It's where a lot of us choose to make our little Pocket Realms. Good vacationing. Yada, yada." Morris pulled out a green marker. "Then the Sea of Milk. Kind of hard to describe. All oceanic and lovey. Stuff gets weird here. Round about 639 Hz. If you get this high up when you die, you don't get bound up anymore, you're guaranteed passage onward and above. I mean...some beings are *born* here and above, but they're bound to different rules. But for us, this is where Bardo begins. You all still following? This new to anyone?"

Cori raised her hand.

Morris pointed to Cori.

"So when we're trying to guide a spirit on to liberation, we want to get them to The Sea of Milk?" Cori asked.

"Good question." Morris said, without enthusiasm. "We'd be doing them a solid by leaving them at the Sea of Milk and the job could largely be considered finished. But, it'd be like building a deck without sanding it and staining it. Technically, you did succeed in building the deck, but are you really satisfied with that? As Necromancer's, we should be taking enough pride in our work to see it through to completion."

Morris had a brief glimmer of pride in his last sentiment, which deadened near immediately. "Anyway, legend says you get 49 days here, but time gets all wonky as you rise into higher frequencies so it winds up only being a short while in the physical.

Point is you're on a finite timeline in the Betwixt. Never stay too long, or you'll be pulled straight to Liberation. It's different with our ghosties, they're tethered by all sorts of wonky death mechanics. It ain't the same when you're just visiting. I know some necromancers have figured out how to make false tethers but I doubt it's worth it." Morris pulled out a blue marker. "741 Hz. Sonorous. Wild Place. Love it. Gotta visit it to get it." An indigo marker now. Morris special ordered an indigo dry erase marker for just this occasion. "The Crystallatium. 852 Hz. There's some pretty important stuff here, but my throat is starting to ache. Anddddd finally...we have...the Villa of Ormen." Morris pulled a purple marker and made a rough circle like a sun at the top. "963 Hz. And this is where you, as Necromancers, will guide on those who pass if we have properly succeeded in our duties." Morris took a black marker and drew a line slowly up. "Unbound of whatever tethered them to the Mundane and the Ethereal, they move on up to the Bardo's where they are freed of their attachments, one by one, liberated into the Final and Ultimate Rest. The process can sometimes be very quick, or very slow. You walk with them up until they get to the Villa of Ormen. Obviously you don't want to go into the Villa with them. The door is 'entry only'. Go through that door, it won't matter if you're undead or not, you ain't coming out. Any questions?"

    Cori was the only one who raised their hand. Morris pointed to her. "What happens after that?"

    "The door is entry only, so no one knows. I imagine one doesn't exist any more, in any way that we define existence. We Necromancers like to call it Liberation. It's generally considered positive, or at the very least not negative. There's some theories. A lot of people think that both the jaws of Ammut and the Villa of Ormen lead to the same place, just one is the pleasant route and the other is the slow and very painful route. It's impossible to say for sure. No one comes back from either of them." Morris said, then paused. "Any other questions?" Morris asked, then gave a defeated sigh. "Yes, Cori?"

    "Why don't we ever try to bring the undead back to the Mundane fully? Like...actually bringing them back to life. Like, if someone just died of like a car accident or something and--" Cori asked, and Howard turned his dark gaze towards her. Cori's body was suddenly and convulsively racked with painful spasms.

Morris strained his neck and convulsed in his own way while he tried to get his next words out. "Well Cori, that's generally considered blasphemy amongst the Council of Necromancers. That's more of a Paladin thing. Paladins 'protect life at all costs' and 'value all life'. Necromancers are a little more focused on bringing about the right and most pleasant sort of death. Good question. You can release her, Howard. It was my fault for not teaching her in Orientation."

"Wait, when was Orientation?" Cori asked, finally freed from the pain which gripped her.

Howard turned his deathly hooded stare to Morris, and Morris convulsed once again. "You remember, Cori?" Morris asked in desperate gasping breaths. "Or-i-en-tation." He said twitching and trying to wink, racked with pain.

"Oh right." Cori said. "Orientation. The one I got very soon after being hired."

Morris coughed and sputtered, heaved onto the desk and pounded his fist as sweat and tears dripped onto the table below him. "Meeting adjourned."

Between the informal drinking of the night before, and the formality of the staff meeting, Cori was now fully initiated into a new and awkward family with all the functional, or more often dysfunctional, dynamics that a normal one might have. Shifts flew by quicker than Cori could blink, and she no longer had to shadow Maya on the day shifts. This was good and bad. It gave Cori some extra freedom to explore and experiment, but it also resulted in the home nearly burning down, and the living room television set exploding when Oddie threw a tantrum and Cori took too long to bind him. The rest of the staff grumbled for days about that one.

Cori began yoga classes with Sol, as per Morris' instruction, and introduced Sol to the foul stuff they call Kombucha. The first class did not go so well, as Sol was nothing but a pile of bones, without ligaments or muscles for stretching. But, before the second class, Cori brought Sol into the third floor Embalming Corridor. This expanse of the manor was covered about by brains and other organs in glowing vats, and full cadavers waiting besides that floated about in bubbling tubes of phosphorescent green. Here, upon two platforms, Cori laid Sol in his skeletal form, and placed him beside an empty and soulless cadaver by the name of Mr. Mraz. Above the platforms, Tesla coils shot lightnings and plasma in a pyrokinetic symphony. Cori performed the elaborate rituals laid out in the flesh-leather tome that was set central on the pedestal of the tiered dais of the elaborate Embalming Corridor. She wore leather brimmed goggles on her eyes, and cackled with the power at her fingertips as she transferred the bound soul of Sol from skeleton to zombified corpse.

"Yes!" She shouted over the sparking of the Tesla coils. "Yesssssss!"

Yoga classes with Sol went much smoother in his new and hardly decayed corpse. But Cori couldn't quite bring herself to feel comfortable around Sol in his new digs. A rotting zombie is one thing, and a skeleton another. But the smooth groomed flesh of a new body lay too comfortably in the uncanny valley between the living and the unliving. Still, Cori did her best to ignore the blank eyes of what used to be a youthful 'Mr. Mraz' now possessed by Sol, who stared at her and moaned during upward dog.

An additional task relegated to Cori as she gained experience in her new position was cooking dinners with Dana. Dinners were to be served at 7:30 pm. This allowed the entire house to gather, both day and night staff, and all the ghoulies and ghosties. They held their nightly feasts in the dining room amidst the howling of souls and the rattle of chains in the darkness of the candlelit room and the low fire. Spiders watched from their homes upon candelabra, and driving rain dashed heavily upon the window panes from eerily darkening skies. All was lit briefly with lightning flashes.

"They can actually take mirror images of the objects presented to them, you know." Morris had explained to Cori over one such dinner. "Like when you give an offering to the gods. The offering is never gone, but they receive it just the same. So we still set their places and give them their food as a means of comfort.

They don't taste it in quite the same way, it's all a bit more wispy. But the tradition does them good."

Cooking for St. Margaret's had made Cori terribly nervous at first. Ruining food for one person was one thing, but on any given night there could easily be twenty to thirty dishes served and she was working with quantities she had never fathomed when she learned to cook during her father's late nights at work.

Morris had farmers directly unloading buckets of jasmine rice and barrels of mutant tomatoes on a weekly basis through a farm-to-table app. And through DoorDash, the local monster hunter Barnie Perrington delivered just oodles of rare and recently caught meats under cover of darkness, for Barnie was a terribly shy man, and lived off in the mountains away from the world.

To Cori's relief, Dana took the reins as kitchen director, and gave Cori simple instructions and direct tasks that made cooking more of a stressful meditation than a scrambled disaster, as it would be if left only to Cori's devices. 'Grate the beast horn', 'chop the celery', 'coagulate this vial of blood', 'smell this, you think this rhino flank is bad?'. And, for the most part, so long as Cori kept an intense degree of single pointed focus, Dana didn't berate her too badly.

There was something perverse and fetishized about working in these large quantities of food. For all the burns and bruises and screaming matches between Dana and herself, Cori came out of each meal feeling oddly traumatized, yet satisfied. And slowly, a fondness developed between her and her captor Dana, for whom she had developed what she could only assume were feelings of some unresearched strain of culinary Stockholm Syndrome. Dana and Cori needed only to look at one another and nod, and more was exchanged in those glances than can be expressed in these pages.

All was soon lost of their precious creations, however, as the dinners quickly dissolved into chaos. Morris paid no mind and ate delicately while spirits tossed mashed potatoes at one another, and rats plucked small bits of food from one plate in particular only to scurry off and return some time later for more. Dana screamed at Sol while he ate the table cloth, and Nigel's jaw fell off. Agnus hexed Nigel for his gall, and Sammiel talked George down from his dark place. Sarah sat next to Cori and wept softly while everyone's utensils occasionally floated to the ceiling. The ceiling where a vortex of churning ghosts danced.

Cori had always wanted a big family like her ex-bff Melanie had. Their family was always getting drunk on Ouzo and shouting at each other and laughing. Chaotic, but loving. And though it may not have been quite what she expected when she had once envisioned it, she supposed she had found what she had been looking for.

Ah, stop it. Cori thought. She ripped her eyes back down to her plate after catching herself staring at Sammiel once again. *He's going to think you have a crush on him. Can't be giving him the wrong idea.* Cori told herself.

It wasn't that he was attractive, just that he had an interesting face. He had strange mannerisms in the way he twirled his fork around his food. And sometimes he made a face when he laughed where his nose scrunched up and he bobbed his head. He was good people watching, Cori reiterated again and again. That was all.

Sarah excused herself, and Derrick unceremoniously seated himself in the spot next to Cori.

"We haven't really had a chance to talk yet." Said the acid haired youth. A number of piercings distracted from a proportionate face and clear skin.

"Yeah, I know, it feels like I'm always shadowing Maya and Dana." Cori said. "I'm Cori. Nice to finally meet you."

"Yeah, Morris doesn't let people shadow me. Nice to meet you too."

Cori smiled and took a bite of the Dire Calamari that served as tonight's protein. "I've picked up the subtle vibe that he doesn't like you too much."

"Morris is just jealous." Derrick said with a big and well tended smile all his own.

"Oh, is that so?" Cori asked. "And what, pray tell, is Morris so jealous of?"

"My youthful spirit, obviously." Derrick said, then looked towards his bicep and kissed it. "And these guns...whatever,

whatever, whatever, it's not important. Hey, we should hang out sometime. We can hang out in my room."

"Oh, uhh...okay, maybe. Yeah." Cori said.

"It really sucked, I was hoping to get to go to Duke's with you." Derrick took a bite of his mashed potatoes then chugged a protein shake before slamming it down. "Sounded like it was a blast. I'm really into martial arts. Like...Krav Maga. Heard of it?"

"I might have. There's so many, ya know. And they're always punching--"

"Super intense. It's all about just the most brutal moves. I really should have been a fighter but then I was like, you know maybe I should mix fighting with necromancy. Who does that?"

"I dunno, sounds--"

"Me. This guy." He said.

"How do you fight with all the..." Cori started to say, then pointed all over her face.

"Oh, my piercings?" Derrick asked. "Just take them out. Takes a little while. Might be tough to do real quick but like, if I go anywhere that I think I might get in a fight I just don't wear them."

"Oh yeah, that makes sense."

Just then, a chunk of Dire Calamari flew across the table and hit Derrick's chest. His eyes flashed with terrible anger for a moment, then he gave a manic smile. "Sol..."

Sol pounded his fancy new cadaver hand on the table and covered his mouth while cackling and pointing at Derrick.

Derrick stood up. "I'm gonna get you for that Sol. Get over here."

Derrick ran as fast as any linebacker around the table and after Sol who skittered through the door. Cori thought the door might come off its hinges while he bashed on through.

"Derrick, you incessant turd!" Morris cried, mouth full of potatoes, then shot a bolt of lighting through the open doorway. Cori heard a squeal.

Maya pulled herself into the chair next to Cori. "Looks like you just got a crash course in Derrick." Maya said.

"That was not at all what I was expecting when I first saw him." Cori said, twirling her pasta.

"Did he hit on you?"

"He invited me to his room."

"Gross. Yeah. Don't go." Maya said.

"I had absolutely no intention of--"

"I mean, you can if you want. He's not half bad looking, he's just...Derrick. You saw, you know what I mean."

"Oh, I saw. You know if he's an Aries, or a Taurus?"

"Hah! Taurus. Why, that your type?" Maya asked with a keen raise of her eyebrow.

"Hell no. I've been with a Taurus before, I know where that leads." Cori rolled her eyes and looked down into her mashed potatoes.

"What do you mean there's no more Reese's Eggs?!" Morris slammed his fist on the table which silenced the entire room.

Dana, shaken, tried to talk as calmly as possible. "You eat them so fast, Morris, we can't--"

"It's only May." Morris said, not trying quite as hard to remain calm. "I thought we bought a month's supply."

"You did."

"Dessert is ruined." He said in the same way one might cancel Christmas.

"We still have the strawberry shortcake Cori and I made." Dana said.

"Oh, so I can just eat with the rest of you plebs?" Morris looked as though he might cry. "How kind."

"He can be kind of a dick sometimes, huh?" Cori asked Maya, her culinary pride permanently scarred.

"He's just upset because the interview with the new girl didn't go so well." Maya said.

"As if I hadn't given myself vastly enhanced hearing in all my years studying magick." Morris said, voice raised over the din. "Yes, Cori, I can be a dick sometimes. And no, the interview did not go well. My vacation is effectively ruined because some gen z twat like yourselves decided the manor had a funk to it."

The words hit harder than Cori had expected. Between old memories and the stress of cooking a meal that had just been insulted, Cori's feelings slipped out of her control, and those dreadful waterworks began tickling at her eyes.

"Son of a--" Morris said, then squeezed at his eyebrows. "I've made you cry again." Morris stood, walked over to Cori, went in for a hug, thought better of it, then backed off. "What do you want? Do you like Reese's Eggs? I can give you my emergency stash."

Cori shook her head.

"What...who the hell doesn't--Oh, I know. I have money." Morris produced a twenty dollar bill and waved it in front of Cori's nose. "You want money?"

Cori shook her head again.

"Morris, just leave her alone." Maya said, and Morris took on the look of a mother whose teenager just disowned them. Then he turned and left the room without another word. "Oh God, he's going to be moping around and giving us all the silent treatment for at least two weeks." Maya said to Cori, but Cori was running out a different door of the dining room.

She walked as quickly as she could through the hallways. She ignored the sobs of the weeping demonic bust, and the glare of the creepy baby painting. *What's wrong with you?* She thought to herself. *You're pathetic. Always crying like a baby.* The voices that came up in Cori's mind weren't unfamiliar, but they had grown so much louder in recent weeks. *No one likes you. Your boss doesn't like you. Maya isn't your friend. She's just pitying you. You make people pity you.* Cori tried to ignore them. She had learned over years to ignore them. But they were so loud now. *No wonder Aurelius left you. They'd be better off without you. Everyone would be better off without you.* Cori took deep breaths and tried to focus on her steps forward, to make note of individual details in her environment, just like her therapist had taught her. The rat hole in the trim of the wall. *Haven't you noticed yet the way everyone just wants to get away from you?* The old mysterious blood splatter against the doorway. *Your own mother left you.*

Cori practically stumbled into the library, her throat in painful knots, her eyes a deluge.

"Cori, are you okay?" Sarah looked up from her book and saw Cori's red eyes and tear streaks.

"I just..." Cori sobbed as Sarah went over and reached lonesomely around for a hug that would never touch. "No. Not really." Cori said and slowly fell down against the wall and hugged her knees into her face. "Something isn't right. With me. I am...not okay."

Sarah sat down next to Cori, as much as a ghost without legs could sit, and gently laid her ephemeral little head against Cori's shoulder. They sat together while Cori took deep breaths and tried to regain composure. The voices did not stop, but they became quieter over time, and the world took on a semblance of normalcy. "I don't know what to do, Sarah. I thought I was done feeling like this."

"Like what?" Sarah asked.

"Like I want t-" Cori began, but her own sobs cut her off. "To...Not be alive..."

Sarah took those words quietly. "I want to not be dead..." She said.

"I know, Sarah. I'm sorry. I know I'm being selfish or self absorbed or whatever. I'm not saying it's right...it's just what I'm feeling." Cori stood up and walked to the spiral staircase. "Thank you, Sarah. I really like you, for what it's worth."

"I like you too, Cori." The little ghost girl said, her eyes were downcast, but her arm reached forward as she disappeared from the room.

Cori sighed, and began to ascend the spiral stair to her room.

"Wait, hold up." Came the tinny voice of Sammiel from across the library. "I'm sorry, I know you probably want to be alone."

Cori turned around as Sammiel scratched at his silver mane and stood awkwardly in the library doorway. He wore the dark fur cloak he had taken to wearing around the house which made effective combat against the chill of Morris' air conditioning kink. Cori looked into his eyes, then looked away and motioned at all her sorrowful and contorted face, then gave a quiet, "What?"

"I uh...I don't know." He said. "I hadn't thought this far ahead."

Cori started to turn around to leave again.

"Wait." Sammiel took determined steps forward. "I just felt bad that Morris did that. I didn't want you to think he hated you or anything. We all really like you."

"I don't care that Morris did that." Cori admitted. "It's not really about Morris at all. I don't know what's wrong with me. I do know that I'm horribly embarrassed that I just broke down like a child in front of all my coworkers."

"Oh... Wait, you know almost everyone here breaks down right?" Sammiel asked, taking another step forward. "This place is like a damn funeral home." Sam said, then looked at his general surroundings and both he and Cori chuckled. "Okay, I guess that's not a huge surprise. But we all get wound up constantly."

"I haven't seen one other person cry yet." Cori said and stepped down from the spiral stair to face Sammiel.

"That's because they all have hiding places, probably." Sammiel said. "Dana usually just screams for a few minutes in the pantry. I haven't found Maya's yet, but I've seen her eyes all puffy plenty often. Morris just uses his office, but locks the door. Derrick insists he doesn't cry, but he breaks up with his girlfriend like every other month, and you'll hear sobbing from his room for at least a week." Cori started looking up as Sammiel continued to list off staff secrets. "I've seen Luke cry with just a few lines from a moving poem. Then there's Kitsune and she's not human so... You know, you're human, so it's chill."

"What about you?" Cori asked, the two of them stood close now.

"Well, no, not very often." Sammiel scratched at the back of his head. "But I wish I did more. Feels like it'd be a healthy outlet."

"I still feel stupid."

"Well, don't. And you know...if you ever need anything, I'm here. Not sure if that counts for anything but...You know, you can talk to me. I gave you my number when we were out at Duke's. Not sure if you remember."

"Thanks. I kind of forgot, admittedly. But I appreciate it. Means a lot." Cori looked up into Sammiel's aether green eyes, and neither of them looked away. Sorrow gave way to a floating sensation. *Say something you idiot.* But there was nothing to say.

Cori had been struck dumb. This most profound aneurysm lifted into a silence that only Sammiel was capable of breaking.

"Man, you sweat like crazy." He said. "Aren't you cold, Morris keeps it at like 58 in here."

The fuck? Cori thought, then looked down and found herself soaked. She tried to laugh, and felt her face grow even more flush than it must have been already. "Yeah, that happens sometimes when I'm...well, it just happens all the time." Then she sat in an armchair, bewildered and offended but lacking even the basic motivation to retreat from this horrifying scene; and Sammiel took a seat in the chair across from her. There was a chess board between them.

"You play?" Sam asked her.

"Not very well."

"Good, me neither."

They started an italian game and traded perspectives on their night out at The Duke's Downfall.

"The band was something else, weren't they? Remember when they just started ripping some old school industrial?"

"No." Cori said and laughed. "I have never...I don't even drink like that."

"That was your first time drinking?"

"No, I used to drink with my friend back home. But we'd just go out and have a couple beers or something. I don't know. I never really cared all that much for it."

"Where's home?"

"Terry Town."

"Oh...never heard of it."

"Yeah it's a tiny little town about a half day North of here by train. It's alright. What about you?"

"Where am I from?" Sam asked, bringing forth a bishop. "Hah, I know I definitely don't look it, but Southern California."

"Last place I would have guessed." Cori said.

"I'll admit, it wasn't for me." He said, his eyes on the table. "And you know, when my parents died, it was just like...what the hell am I doing here?"

"Oh, I'm so sorry."

"No, I'm sorry, I always bring that up. Too heavy." He said, still somehow managing to keep his smirk and glint in his eye.

"Not at all."

"It's just kind of casual to me at this point." Sammiel said, as he knocked Cori's pawn out with a knight, which completely pinned her rook. "Forget it can drag things down."

"Mum died when I was little. Crimson Plague." Cori said, shocked by her own brevity. "Sometimes it's weird trying not to bring it up. Sometimes you just gotta talk about it."

"Really, I don't understand why anyone here would feel weird talking about it. We work with people who died all day, every day."

"Solid point."

"I mean, can we just be honest and say that we're all a little fucked up in the head here?" He gave his eyes a wild widening. "We're working with corpses and ghosts. And maybe I could say I was a normal guy if I felt a little disturbed by that, but I'm not at all. I feel like I'm right where I belong." And he looked up at Cori and gave her a look that was almost frighteningly unhinged. Or, it would have been if Cori hadn't been able to give that same look right back to him.

"You're a little weird." She said, and felt more comfortable now despite her sweat. Her rook defeated, she swung a surprise attack with her queen, straight into the front lines. "I'm a little weird too."

"I know." Sammiel said. "I was just waiting for you to admit it." And this time they looked at each other for a few moments with Sammiel only following with, "Tell me about your mom."

"Well...funny thing, she was a Paladin. That's my family's go to. Paladins and Clerics and Priests and Priestesses. So you can imagine how I fit into the picture."

"You're a black sheep too, huh?" Sammiel asked absent-mindedly as he studied the battlefield for the way to trap Cori's queen. "I feel that."

"What about your parents?"

"Well they were both middle management at an insurance company. Met there." Sammiel chuckled to himself, then relaxed back and ignored the chess game, just like any man who is losing. "I think my Mom was my Dad's boss when they met so there's a little scandalous aspect to it."

"Oh my." Cori said, eyes fluttering.

"Then uh...well, Dad got pain pills from some skiing accident and got hooked on them. One thing led to another and he overdosed. My mom was alright till some issue with her kidneys, then she just sort of slipped away. I think she might have made it through but she just sort of gave up. I wasn't exactly being the best son at the time... But both their spirits hung around for a while. That was the first time I started seeing the dead. They uh...didn't seem chill. Quite the opposite. So I brought them here and Morris really went all in to help Liberate them. This was back when he cared about his job. And I... well, I just never left."

Sammiel looked up to meet Cori's eyes, which locked for a long while. Then Cori nodded very slowly. *I see you.* `

Their conversation gained a lighter air as they focused on music and video games. On and on they prattled, making their chess moves slower and slower till the game came to a halt and only conversation remained. Sammiel had a strange way about him that Cori couldn't place too quickly. It was as strange as the lingering air of frankincense that surrounded him and his voice like rusted tin. He had an open insistence to his own flaws, and was able to laugh them off as he was able to laugh everything off. And for a moment everything would be fine, until Cori would say something and he would call bullshit.

"You're trying to tell me you don't miss your Dad?" He'd ask with one eyebrow raised high. "Yeah, you do. I'm sorry, I don't know exactly what kind of man he is, but I am sure you miss him. Look, I can see it right there in your eyes. Right there."

And Cori stammered and even became frustrated, but Sammiel was right, and she knew it. And Cori, for her part, gave it right back.

"What do you mean you're not into current social issues? You don't get to bail out of pushing for a better world just because you think you're better off being a hermit."

And then it was Sammiel's turn to stammer and even become frustrated, but Cori was right, and he knew it.

Okay. She thought, while he rambled off an excited answer about homunculi that she had asked. *Maybe I like him.* But as she thought it, her father's words of wisdom came to mind. "No coworkers." or "Don't eat where you shit." They both meant the same thing, it just depended on how much wine he had consumed.

It was a hard and fast rule that Cori had been told since she learned to drive and got a job delivering pizza. It had never been an issue before. Cori had only ever had one boyfriend. He had left her for her best friend Melanie. It took her a long time and a lot of pain, but Cori was managing to forget about them. And with them, she had left her heart and all thoughts of romance dead and buried in the back garden where they belonged. That said, nothing stayed good and rightly dead at St. Margaret's.

"--so the nervous system is really the most exciting part though. It's never the same thing twice, no matter how carefully you design it. With homunculi, you're designing their very being. And you know, obviously some people can be very cruel with that. But you can also design these beautiful and happy little minds and oh-- oh, I've been rambling…"

"No, it's awesome how into this you are."

"No, I mean my shift." Sammiel said, and wrapped himself in the furry black cloak he had lain across the back of the armchair. "I'm late. I'm so sorry, I gotta go. It was great talking to you."

Cori watched him leave. She couldn't remember the last time she had talked to anyone for that long. Sammiel left Cori in the silence of the library, which allowed her to sink back into her leather reading chair and recap all they had said, and the way the conversation had passed between them, and the way the edges of Sam's eyes and lips curled when he smiled. In those moments, it was as though there weren't a gaping hole where Cori's heart should be, and instead there was a tiny golden flutter.

"It's a bad idea you know."

Cori was used to the haunts of spectres, but there was something more disquieting about hearing a physical voice where there shouldn't be one.

She knew the voice. It was Kitsune. Her voice oscillated between purposefully gruff or painfully dainty. But Kitsune could dance about the shadows with ease, and frustrate even the most keen of eyes.

"How long have you been in here, Kitsune?" Cori asked the emptiness around her.

"I was reading in the rafters." Kitsune said. Cori finally pinpointed her voice peeking down at her from the ceiling. "I came here to get some peace and quiet, but I figured if you wouldn't shut up, I might as well listen in."

Cori sighed. "What's a bad idea, Kitsune?"

"Sammiel is a bad idea." Kitsune said, and fell from the rafters but landed cat-like on her feet. Her hair today was done up with two top buns, bangs recently trimmed.

"I don't know what you mean." Cori said.

"Is that so?" Kitsune snaked over to push her face into Cori's, then sniffed in deeply. "You think I can't smell it on you? You reek of hormones." She pinched her nose and held it aloft, while Cori blushed but tried to maintain eye contact. "Listen manko, I tolerated you this long, but I wouldn't push your luck. I've killed people for less."

"I still don't--"

Kitsune jabbed a long decorated nail into Cori's chest. "I don't give a shit about mortals, you all are just sacks of meat, but my little Sammy is different. We've been building our bond for years. Every day we become closer and closer. He's going to be a vampire, like me. You get in my way, I eat your soul. Kapish?" Kitsune smiled pretty little smile. Twisted and fanged, but still very pretty.

Cori tried to muster herself as her legs turned to jelly. "Kitsune, this is very unprofessional. Maybe we could try all talking this over with Morris. I learned about conflict resolution in one of my class--"

"You think Morris can stop me?"

Cori rolled her eyes. "No, not really."

"Good. Maybe you're not so stupid after all." Kitsune said, then kissed Cori swiftly on the cheek. "Glad we had this chat." She said, then skipped off through the library door with a twirl and sweeping gesture.

Chapter 9

Cori sat beside Sarah in the library and read the book, *'Etheric Algorithms in Theory and Practice'* that Morris had sent to her some days prior. It was like reading molasses. Her phone buzzed in her pocket. "Shadowing me today :D Meet me in the living room at midnight." *Scandalous.* It was Sammiel. Cori felt something flutter in her belly. Her father's past attempts to dissuade her from such unwholesome activities were only fuel to the fire. *No coworkers.* It kept repeating like a mantra, but now it was officially labeled as 'naughty' in the most virile states of her subconsciousness. What a curse! The fear Kitsune imparted upon her only made it worse. Fear is, after all, the great aphrodisiac.

"Meet me in the living room at midnight." Cori grumbled as she dressed for her shift. "Who the hell says that? Is he dumb?"
Cori had ordered several plants for her bedroom, and one salt lamp. All her otherwise drab decorations had been made more wholesome for those small additions. Those, and one gigantic and infinitely fluffy white fur blanket that she kept on her bed, or otherwise sprawled in front of her bedroom hearth. Between the orange glow of her fireplace and salt lamp and the promising air that even one or two house plants bring when coupled with oil diffusers, her room took on a homey light. Cori even spent some time reading in there instead of the library. It was in the process of becoming a true bedroom.
Cori looked back and forth across her six outfits for sixteen minutes, before settling on the fact that she hated them all. "Maybe the rest of them shouldn't dress like they're going to a rich uncle's funeral all the frickin' time." Cori said, inexplicably agitated. "Didn't know St. Margaret's was known throughout the world for its fabulous sense of fashion. Maybe I would have brought a frickin' boa or something."

"And why the hell do I care?" Cori stomped. This messed up her eyeliner which spiraled her frustrations further downward. Her hair was a frizzledy mess that only improved in pigtail braids, and her usual copper glow had become pale in the gloom of the manor. This highlighted her freckles which needed foundation, which in turn needed blush, but picking the right shade to match her purple hair proved a nuisance. The youtube instructionals only mocked her with their professional perfection. But all turned out well in the end for her perseverance when she licked her teeth in the mirror and gave a solid, "Damn gurl, you fine."

She had hoped to be the first one to the living room to give herself a strategic advantage by allowing herself advanced relaxation in her environment before Sammiel could. She hated that she was thinking that far into it, but there it was. And there he was, biting those sweet lips while he leaned back on the couch. His eyes were closed behind a nighttime pair of spectacles that managed to improve upon that lustrous face of his as he bobbed his head, his earbuds wired to his ears. He looked up at her.

"Oh, hey." Sammiel said, and took out one of his headphones.

"Hey."

"You clock in yet?"

Cori's mood soured. This wasn't going at all like her plan. He was supposed to have been struck into a stupor after his first glance her way, Kitsune be damned. She had looked up vampires online. It wasn't really worth being frightened of something that can't handle a little garlic. They're all pomp. Couple cloves in the bag and Cori was vampire proof. "Yeah." Cori said, grabbing an end table and striking an instagram worthy pose.

"Good, we can start a little early then." He said, paying no heed. "I know this is all kind of dumb. You've been working here plenty long enough to do all of this on your own, I'm sure. Night shift isn't too different from the day shift, as I'm sure you know. But since Keiran's meltdown Morris is freaking out about how well the staff are trained...as he should be, I guess. How's your wrist?"

Cori swiftly grabbed at her wrist, hoping to hide the scar that she had already hidden behind seventeen rubber bracelets. "Fine. You heard about that, huh?"

"Are you blushing?"

"No. My cheeks are just naturally red..."

"Not that red." He said, coming in for a closer look. "How far did you go?"

"How far?" Cori asked.

"Yeah, into Death. Through the Bardo's." He said.

"I don't know, Sam. I don't really want to think about it. Keiran said we were at the Villa. Why the sudden interest?"

"Morris only just told me the other night." Sammiel said, propping himself up on his knees upon the couch, his eyes wide and curious. "What did you see?"

"Nothing. I kept my eyes closed. I didn't want to see it."

"Really? You know what we do, right?" Sammiel motioned around himself, but Cori just frowned. "I'm sorry. It's just a subject we're all very passionate about, you know? Like I said, I don't really do much besides study. Dammit, George." Sammiel's head snapped away from the conversation. "No, no, no. We're not doing this tonight." Sammiel got up from the couch to take a chair away from George. The chair had just levitated into the room, and Sammiel snatched it before he could stand on it and gain reach of the semi-lucid noose hanging above. Large arachnids observed judgmentally from the walls. "What has been up lately, man? You had been doing so well." George looked up at Sammiel, peering through space and time to glimpse that great cosmic lonesomeness. "It's alright, it's fine, you're alright. We're gonna have a good night tonight, okay?" Sammiel asked, no longer sporting his usual curly lipped smirk. His eyes were now wide with genuine concern.

Cori's heart fluttered again. *Oh stop, please, it's not that cute.* She told her heart. But it wasn't just Sammiel being sweet to a ghost that had Cori's heart aflutter. It was seeing the man from behind as he turned to help. By some fluke of nature the taut curvature of Sammiel's butt produced a pink halo, soft like feathers. *Oh, to nestle my face into those cushiony folds!* Cori thought, then, *Focus, damnit. You're supposed to be a professional.* "Are we allowed to go outside?" Cori asked, and tried to think of what a professional may say in such a situation. But those black corduroys he was wearing tonight just fit so snug. His suspenders over a tight shirt. Since when did the man wear suspenders? "I've been ah-- assessing the situation and I feel as though in my opinion a change of scenery could ah-- allow a shift of the consciousness." *Yes, good, Cori. Very professional.*

Sammiel pondered for a moment. "George *can* go outside. George, do you want to go outside?"

"To where the river roam." Came George's rarely heard disembodied voice.

"We'll go for a walk, then." Cori said and nodded. And they did. Along the river.

Outside St. Margaret's the night was blustery, and fertile. Across the river, witches danced around a bonfire in celebration of the Solstice. These were simpler times. And the night had cooled from what was otherwise a scorching hot day that had pierced even Morris' highly advanced air conditioning techniques.

"George, you know you can always tell me if you want to go outside, right?" Sammiel asked. "I didn't know you even wanted to." But George was little more than a silent wraith as he floated about the budding primroses. "That was good thinking, Cori. I kind of feel dumb now."

"Beginner's luck." Cori said, then they carried on their stroll, contentedly silent. Then, "I hadn't expected to like it here as much as I do."

"St. Margaret's?" Sammiel asked, hands clasped behind his back. "Me neither. I mean, I never thought I'd stay here at all, let alone more than a year or so. I just didn't really have anywhere else to go, and Morris offered me a job."

"Where were you planning on going after the year was up?"

"Well, I was hoping to have gotten good enough with making homunculi to have started a pet shop or something. Or, at least work for the government on some top secret project developing military creatures or something. I mean, it'd be kind of evil but a guy needs to make a living." Sammiel said.

Cori looked up mischievously at Sam. "Yeah, okay, I could see you as some domineering dungeon overlord doing wicked experiments. It would fit you."

Sammiel's face grew red as he laughed and scratched at the back of his head.

"I mean like, you know, living underground, fighting off the occasional Paladin raid while you prepare to shroud the world in darkness." Cori was starting to blush herself. Thinking about Sammiel's butt was rapidly evolving into dungeon fantasies. "You strike me as a 'conquer the world' type."

"Look at you, saying that. Most intimidating five foot human I've ever encountered." Sammiel said.

"Did you just call me short?" Cori asked, then doubled back. "Intimidating?"

"Yeah, I don't know, I feel like you have some tricks up your sleeve. Maybe some skeletons in your closet, no pun intended."

"Me?" Cori found this all very curious.

"You kind of give off a mysterious vibe." Sammiel said, and Cori couldn't help but scoff. "Like, 'what's she capable of', you know?"

Cori batted her eyes. "I'm just having this weird moment where I'm realizing for maybe the first time that people view me differently than I ever expected. I did learn a spell to grow spiders in the skin, so you're not totally wrong."

"How do I come off?"

Hot. "I don't know, you're hard to place. Maybe at first I thought you were a little intimidating too, but when you talk, you--"

"I what?" Sammiel asked, playing hurt.

Cori laughed, "Well you're more of a dweeb than I thought you'd be when I first met you. But you also seem kind. And that's better, I think."

"I mean intimidating would be pretty okay too, but I'll take it."

"What's George doing?"

Sammiel looked over with Cori and saw a wisp, floating around the evening primroses. He was little more than a softly glowing orb of light. "Is that George? I've never seen him do that before." Sammiel said, tilting his head and holding his chin. "This is huge."

"How so?"

"Any new break in their patterns is a really big deal. It can give clues to what will help Liberate them." He said, typing into the notepad of his cell phone. "We've got to log this later."

"Worst part of the job, easily." Cori said.

"Notes? Really?"

"Don't you think so?"

"Nah. Super relaxing."

"Great, you can do mine then."

"You can do your own dang notes." Sammiel grumbled.

"Oh, maybe he can be intimidating." Cori said, while Sammiel narrowed his eyes at her. "You gonna start bossing me around now, hm?"

At this, a coy twinkle came into Sammiel's dangerously narrowed eyes. He didn't say anything. There was nothing but a knowing smile that took Cori's breath away as he looked down at her. He grew taller. The silver stubble on his jawline glistened in the moon.

Her heart raced and Cori stepped away quickly and walked on through the garden while George followed. St. Margaret's loomed ominously above them. shadows fluttered in the windows, eyes watching. *Change the subject. Quick, say something depressing.* Cori opened her mouth to do just that before remembering her brain could be a terrible jerk. *I thought it was a good idea.* "Ugh, shut up." Cori mumbled.

"What?" Sammiel asked.

"Nothing...just talking to myself..." They stared off for a moment, then Cori turned back and said, "I like your hair."

A dopey grin spread over Sammiel's face, and he twisted silver strands of hair around his finger. "Thanks."

"You're welcome."

"I like your..." Sammiel started, then caught himself just as he was opening his mouth. Then he shrugged and sighed. "...you."

Cori's fluttering heart turned into a leaping one. "Thank you."

"You're welcome." He said, and they turned to face each other

Sammiel's green eyes transformed into magnetic force fields as Cori had not seen before. They drew her upwards and lifted her off her feet, and she caught wind of the more intimate scent beyond his cologne. The crescent moon shone on their faces beside the tallest tower of the manor, their gazes drawn and full. Cori felt as though the wind itself lifted her up and towards him. The song of the night played, and crickets mourned their desperate longing while the river tried to hush them. Cori and Sammiel's eyes held for those extra moments of silence where their electricity could dance and compel them towards one of life's more amiable mistakes.

Sammiel turned his head towards the manor. "I think George is good now…" He said. He said this as though that incredible moment where all the stars aligned had not happened. "Next, we have Penny."

Men! No woman would miss a moment like that. He's dumb, dumb, dumb. "Can't wait." Cori said, trying to act calm in the face of her disdain. *No...No. I'm at work right now. That was an adult decision he made. Very Professional.* She thought, but it was a wholly unsatisfying answer.

Penny, the blind sprite who lived in the walls, tended to pick a single spot for a haunting each night, but finding her was no easy trick as she was, well, hiding within the walls. And she made herself known only when it pleased her. These hauntings were rare and brief visitations, and most often made at undesirable hours. It was most usually mid-slumber that one heard her scraping the drywall as she passed through their room, rap-tap-tapping her way along, rattling the doors on their hinges as she passed across them. She cried gently while she did this and called out for her Mom or her Dad. It made for very difficult sleeping arrangements, for though the necromancer's rooms were warded, Morris had only seen fit to do so to the innermost walls, and not the vacant spaces in between. Finding her might have only been a chance encounter, if not for a trick discovered by Luke in the early years of his employment. Penny's sole intimate companions were the rats that scurried through St. Margaret's walls. These same rats delivered her dinner each night, taking the food as it was set out in offering at the dining table. "Follow the droppings," it was written in Penny's case file, "And you can find the location of Penny's nightly haunt."

"Good thing you actually read the case files." Sammiel told Cori as they proceeded along the oblong hallways with candlesticks of clean blue flame held low, magnifying glasses pointed to the ground and pressed up against their noses. "Usually I just go and play video games when Penny is on my caseload."

"Tut, tut, my dear Sammy." Cori said, spotting and examining one rat dropping on this hall's dust drenched shag carpeting. "Mustn't go slacking in our duties. Ah, dangit. Candle just burned my ear. I have a flashlight, you know."

"These are blessed candles. Flashlights won't cut it. The third floor corridors aren't anything to be messing with. Especially Room 313." Sammiel said in passing. He made no note of the hairless corpse that climbed the ceiling above them, gurgling. Things like that happened all the time. He continued his conversation. "Do NOT enter. And bring a can of pepper spray whenever you're up here too. Legend has it that a hobo lives up here. A *Living* hobo. I've never seen him and people say he's harmless, but I don't want to take any chances. Ghosts don't scare me half as much as humans."

Every trip through St. Margaret's halls carried a sense of adventure. One often had to hop bottomless pits or outrun plagues of bats in order to get to their desired destination. And more and more Cori found that the manor was nearly endless. While they tracked the rat droppings, Sammiel and Cori passed through a room where it was winter, with clouds above and snow at their feet. They clung to floral wallpaper as they sidled over a large architectural cliff, all indoors, with water far below in some subterranean world which might have been any number of miles long itself. And though her map marked these places, this room being labeled *The High Lands of Arnath*, the spaciality was problematic. One example being that this cliff's edge they now clung onto would likely lead downwards into her bedroom, and the library, and perhaps a mile or so beneath all that. Yet her bedroom was nowhere to be seen.

Nearby to Agnus' third floor apartment, the airs were thick with her azure miasma even as they entered the Relic Hall, Ritual Chamber, and wandered around outside the Cloisters where it was said that Morris prepared for a sacramental retreat in lieu of his much anticipated and subsequently ruined vacation. The Cloisters were beehive huts of masonry set within a room like a Basilica. It was just around these that they lost the trail to Penny.

"Come on, we're just missing it. We can't have come all this way…" Cori said.

"I just don't think rats poop constantly enough to keep a clear and obvious trail. To be honest, I'm shocked we got this far. Thing had diarrhea or something." Sammiel said, resting his back up against the nearest statue of some blessed lady of one virtue or another.

"Well, we can't just give up."

"I usually give up before I get this far."

"Fair point." Cori said. "But that's probably not something to revel in. We gotta whip you into shape. Morris lets you get away with too much."

"Oh, we got ourselves a new supervisor, do we?" Sammiel asked, sizing Cori up, head to toe.

"Maybe." Cori said, realizing she hadn't meant it as a supervisor at all. "Better watch yourself in case I am."

"Maya won't give up the throne easily. She's had her eye on that position for as long as I've been here. And she isn't anything to mess with."

Cori tried to act as though she were still looking for droppings. Her blue flamed candlestick was pressed close to the floor, the candle wavered as she spoke. "You like her an awful lot, huh?"

"Yeah, she's alright. I dunno about an *awful* lot." Sammiel said, and stood more rigidly.

"Oh, come on, face it, she's gorgeous." *Why are you doing this?* Cori asked herself, but went on speaking anyway. "I'm just surprised you two aren't dating already."

Sammiel waved his hand in the air in front of his face. "Never gonna happen. I'm not saying she's not gorgeous, or personable, just doesn't vibe right. Who knows why." He shrugged. Cori hadn't even noticed her heart had been sinking until it came back up again with a *whoosh*. Sammiel began again, "Not like, say, you and Derrick."

"Derrick?!" Cori meeped. *Use it. Make him jealous.* Her brain suggested. "Why, you think he's interested?"

Cori watched Sammiel's eyes turn downwards, and his smile lost its buoyancy, just as hers might have. *Why would you say that?* She asked herself. *You told me to!* She responded. *Don't listen to me, you know that.*

Sammiel struggled but managed to regain some composure and acted out a semblance of pleasantries. "Yeah, of course, why wouldn't he be?" Sammiel said, then sighed. "You got everything."

Cori's heart danced between elation and a terrible guilt. *You monster.* She thought, as much to the act itself as to her enjoyment of the repercussions of the act. *Did he really just say that though? I got everything? Me?*

"Ya know, I was really worried about you when I heard what happened with Keiran." Sammiel said, looking towards Cori's bracelet covered wrists. "I still am, if I'm being honest. I haven't stopped thinking about it since Morris told me."

"I'm kind of annoyed Morris told you." Cori grabbed her bracelets.

"Him and Maya, man. They'll tell you what Dana ate for lunch two weeks ago, and what color it came out. Don't tell them anything you wouldn't want everyone knowing." Sammiel laughed and looked off while crossing his arms. "But seriously, are you doing okay?"

Cori sauntered closer to Sammiel, "Yes", she said, then sighed and flopped onto a pew next to him, "And no." She held her head in her hands. "It's alright though. Just a bunch of internal stuff. Everything is good. Life is good. My mind is just...messy right now."

Sammiel sat next to Cori. "Want to talk about it?"

Cori thought for a moment. "No?"

"Well, I'm here if you ever do. And I'm sure I'm not the only one." He said, followed by a long awkward pause that caused Cori arteries great tension and her courage failed her.

"You said you played video games?" She asked, after the many eternities it took for her mind to scramble for subjects of conversation.

"Yeah!" Sammiel replied excitedly. "Do you?"

Cori nodded.

"What kind?"

"Farming simulators." Cori responded, breathily.

"Farming simulators?"

"Yaasssss. Have you tried them?"

"No...my god, no. Only a big weirdo would play a game about farming."

"You're weird."

"You're weird."

"Whatever."

"Fine."

They had kept straight faces throughout the exchange, but finally Sam broke and laughed. "Us working together is a really bad idea. We've been standing around doing nothing for a really long time."

"We're pretty terrible." Cori said. *He said 'us'. He said 'we'.* She thought with glee, then, *oh my god, shut up, why does it even matter?*

Their blessed candles flickered, and grew dim.

"You feel that?" Sammiel asked, hushing his voice.

Cori did. The goosebumps, the chill, the hairs on the back of her neck stood on end. The door at the end of the basilica hallway rattled.

"Mom?" A weak and distant echo sounded from within the wallboards.

"Penny." Both Sammiel and Cori said it in unison. They ran to the doorway and tapped the walls but found no response. They made their way into the next room, a vacant space often considered to be the lair of the legendary hobo at St. Margaret's, evidenced further by a bundle of popped and burned bean cans besides the cold ash of a campfire. Knocking here, the dynamic duo were met no longer with silence, but with a tap, tap, tapping.

"Penny, you in there?" Sammiel called, his face smushed up against the drywall. "Can you talk to me?"

"Who's there?" Came the whimpered response from within the walls.

"It's me, Sammy, you remember? It's been a while since I've been able to find you. What have you been up to?"

"I can't find my way out." Penny said. "I want my Mom and Dad."

Sam gave Cori a look of concern, then whispered to her. "This is what she's always saying. I don't know what to tell her."

Cori looked between Sammiel and the wall. Then she knocked. "Penny? It's me, Cori. I uh-- I've told you to get out of my room a few times...Sorry."

"Cori?"

"My room...near the library. Sorry about that. I'm kind of new here." There was a long silence before Cori began again. "You want to get out of there, huh?"

"Yes." Came the quiet response that could only be heard behind the silence of the room.

"I bet you get pretty lonely in there." Cori said, and this time she only heard a sigh in response. Cori turned to Sam and whispered, "Is there a way to get in there with her?" Sammiel shrugged. "Have any of you ever tried, like...opening up the wall?"

"I really don't know. We'd have to ask Morris about it. What's with you and all the innovative solutions?"

"They're not really that innovative, y'all are just burned out or something."

"Don't start with me. I've liberated five souls now and I'm dang proud of it. How many have you got under your belt?"

"Touche." Cori whispered, then turned back to the wall. "Penny, how would you like a visit some time, hm? We could play a game together, or something."

"You'd come in here to visit me?" Penny asked.

"If I can find a way, you can bet your phantasmagoric ass I will." Cori said as Sammiel gave an impressed frown, a nod of approval, and a light clapping of the hands. "Let me just talk it over with my supervisor, alright?"

Penny gave three taps in response, and Sammiel and Cori left the room. Sammiel clapped Cori hard on the back. "Not a bad job out there kid. We'll make a necromancer out of you yet. I'd say we earned ourselves a break."

"Now you're speakin; my language. What should we even do?" Cori asked, her mind reeling pleasantly for all the possibilities that sprang forth. *Kiss me, you fool.*

"I usually go grab a coffee in the staff lounge. Makes the graveyard shift much easier."

"You drink coffee?"

"You don't?"

"Tried it once, never looked back." Cori said, opened the basilica door, and waved Sammiel through like a proper gent.

Sammiel nodded thanks and strode through. "Then you tried it too soon. It gets a lot better with age. I'll make you a cup."

"But--"

"You don't have to drink it."

Cori looked around helplessly, then motioned forward. "Well, go on then, lead the way."

Luke was already in the staff lounge and snoring loudly from his seat in his gilded spider automaton. It was a dangerous passtime in such a place.

"Luke…" Sammiel said, then louder, "Luke."

"Wha--?"

"How long have you been sleeping in here, man?" Sammiel asked.

"What sound was that?"
Luke quoted.
"I turn away from a shaking room.
What is that sound from in the dark?
But is it from the moon?
What is this dancing spark?
We turn away and then turn back,
From what did we just hear?
The breath we took when we first met.

Listen, love, it's here."

Cori and Sammiel both stood by Lukes side in that glorified boiler room as he drifted back into snoozing. Dank cascades of steam plumage emanated from the piping whilst Sam set to work at making a Cappuccino, ignoring Luke's poems as people often did. "You should take notes on what you just did with Penny. And George too, honestly." Sam told Cori, which Cori then did diligently after logging into the archaic computer operating system whose logo was a single unblinking and lidless eye, tormented wide and bloodshot as it gazed in horror at the users who would scour and pluck at its mind and infect it with the thoughts and actions of their day.

Several minutes in, Cori had finished her notes, and Sammiel had arranged an elegant design into the foam of her cappuccino, a wrathful octopus head flecked with shards of chocolate.

"Okay, so I'll admit cappuccino smells nice." Cori said and took a deep inhale of the swirling fog that emanated off its top. "It's the taste that's an issue."

"It's the feeling that makes the taste worth it." Sammiel said.

That's what she said. Cori thought. "What else do you do on breaks? I mean, I've come to accept you're boring, but you can't just sit here and drink bean juice…"

"We could play pool. You've been to the rec room, right?"

"How long do we get for a break?" Cori asked.

"No one really keeps track. The rule around here is just to get your work done. As long as we go through our list of residents and clean the bathrooms then we're good for the night. Don't worry, I got the bathrooms." He said with a wink in Cori's direction. "We're also supposed to mop the kitchen so if you could get that it would help a lot."

"Sure. And pool is definitely an option then. Butttt…What about your homunculi?"

"Oh…You want to see them? Really? I mean, yeah! You sure?"

Cori nodded. Then nearly gagged on her first sip from her mug. "Well, it's not as bad as the tea Dana's been giving me."

"That's a start." He said. "Come on. My room is in the Southeast Tower."

"Neat." Cori said, just as a face sized spider plunged onto Luke's sleeping old man face. Oh, how that geezer yowled.

Cori and Sammiel channeled along the manor byways, and slunk through long abandoned halls where the curtains fluttered in the blustery darkness of the witching hour. Guided only by a flashlight, their blessed candles emaciated to their bitter end, Cori made no note of any encroaching fear. Sammiel was a natural in the darkness, and made it feel like light. And, with every sip of her cappuccino, Cori grew bolder.

They came to a hallway labeled 'The Whisperwood' by a wooden signpost, and beside that another sign pointing the opposite direction towards 'The Deep Halls of Albahazred'. The Southeast Tower lay in that direction, or so Cori assumed by Sammiel leading her forth that way.

Away from the disembodied whispers of The Whisperwood, they passed the grand obsidian pillars that stood in testament to the long forgotten powers of Albahazred, the Maestro of a Thousand Masks as he was sometimes known. What treasures that may lie waiting would remain a mystery, for too many errant travelers had become lost in the Deep Halls, and their corpses were left skittered around the granite floors like landmarks to some unknown destination. Luckily for Sammiel, his room required only that he maintain his stride against the tall black wall to the right, and he need never risk those treacherous depths. Illumined by two torches in the distance, the Southeast tower could be seen from some distance aways, its door much like a castle portway, with heavy dark stained wood and an iron ring for a knob.

"Go on, open it." Sammiel told Cori as they arrived at last.

Cori reached for the iron ring just as the dark wood door contorted itself into a ghastly countenance, a mask of wailing terror. The scream that followed was familiar, one she had heard through the manor before. It was a piercing wail that rattled the storm shutters as far as The Hobo's Lair on the third floor. A spasm passed through Cori before she dropped the rest of her cappuccino and stumbled backwards where Sammiel was ready to catch her. "Got you." He said. "It's trapped."

"My cappuccino." Cori said, quivering. "I will get you back for this. I was just starting to like it."

Sammiel struggled to open the heavy wooden door and then wound the tower steps as they rounded upwards. Comical artworks hung about and were lit elegantly by LED's. There were masterpieces depicting desert aliens abducting people with crystal magic, and pop-art show-casing electric pink kittens dashing through astronaut bellies. "My room", he said as they reached the portcullis at the top which was veiled with phosphorescent hippie beads.

Cori had been to raves that were less colorful than this place. "How'd you get the biggest room?" There was neon green liquid in vials, or bubbly chartreuse; and hot pink liquid in alembics, or a deep fizzy blue. Beakers and gadgets. Sammiel's room was filled to the brim with equipment. Glowing arcane geometries hung in the air. Tubes of colorful chemistry bubbled and spun their way down into vats. But behind it all was a sleek obsidian background. Cori grabbed one of the potion bottles, looked closely, and set it back down.

Hamster mazes wove throughout the room where unnatural creatures scurried about. On the left was a dais upon which a door lay, leading into a vast and infinite void. On the right was a large humanoid of distinctly arboreal features, sleeping in a cloudy vat of crimson jellies. And at the end was a large four poster bed with black sheets and black pillows and black fuzzy blankets. Above this hung a cosmic display of brass planets, floating gracefully.

"I pay for it." Sammiel said while he corrected the placement of the potion bottle Cori had set back incorrectly. "A little under the counter money to Morris. He's always looking for tax-free cash. And then I help with the budgets and books around here. Morris is helpless with that stuff. Don't let Maya fool you, she may be the teacher's pet but I keep things running as much as anyone else. In return, I get this." He said and motioned to the grand room around him. "And Morris even threw in some spatial elongation enchantments to go with it." A small gangly bat with pale man flesh and freckles landed on Cori's shoulder. "That's Dresden."

Cori felt as though she were expected to pet it, but wasn't so sure about its shape or overall consistency. But Sammiel had the love of a father in his bespectacled eyes, and Cori couldn't help but embrace it. "Hello, Dresden." Cori said, and the creature purred with her touch. It's face was like a small piglet's, smiling and full of hope. "Okay, he's pretty dang cute."

"Emilie is scurrying through the tubes right now." He said, pointing at a small wyrm, draconic, pearlescent, and beautiful. "And Alastar is over there, perched by the window." Sam pointed at a two limbed spider monkey with bunny ears, but twice as fuzzable.

"You made these?"

"Well, you know, obviously no one knows how to create life from scratch. But I can use preexisting cells and bacteria to form them, yea." Sammiel said while crossing his arms and looking on with pride.

"A brainiac, eh? Color me impressed. And what's all the chemistry for, then?" Cori asked and looked into a flask wherein floated strange visions of overwarm childhoods.

"Well, this is alchemy." He said. "You can't brew Essence of Nostalgia with chemistry, to my knowledge."

"I want to try Essence of Nostalgia." Cori whined.

"No you do not." Sammiel insisted. "You will cry."

"I don't mind crying so much when it's for good reason."

Sammiel shrugged, grabbed a bottle off of a shelf, and tossed it to Cori. She popped the cork and took a whiff. The newly remembered scent of baby powder hit her first, calling to mind a night with the window open while she lay awake in her crib, content to observe her new world for hours in security and warmth. This was followed by the scents of baking sour-dough pizza on movie night with her mom and pop. She remembered her mother, just barely. She felt her more than she remembered her. She remembered the smell of her hair and she remembered pulling on her mother's dreadlocks and the feeling of her soft bosom. She remembered her mother's lullaby and deep raspy voice in the nighttime, and the way

Cori felt when she was hiked up on her mom's shoulders. She even remembered the last kiss she had received just before her mother had stepped away from her life forever, and left the scent of her sandy perfume trailing behind her.

"Damnit, I told you." Sammiel said and snapped his fingers to bring Cori back to awareness. He gave her an oily rag by way of tissues.

Cori sobbed. She didn't want to blow her nose into Sammiel's charred chemistry rag, but she really had no choice in the circumstances.

Sammiel waited while Cori sobbed and blew her nose several times. Then he pointed to his own nose. "You got some schmutz on your face."

"Some what?"

"Like charcoal or something." Sammiel said, as Cori wiped aimlessly at her face. "Nope, still there. Nope...still... you're making it worse."

Cori acted as though she'd throw her snot rag at him, and he flinched. "You don't even have video games in here." Cori said, trying to move on from both her sorrow and embarrassment.

"Like hell I don't." Sammiel said, then opened a cabinet in the corner, near stained glass windows that hung with depictions of forgotten mythologies. The video game collection was a gilded plethora of colors and titles both familiar and unfamiliar, set about alphabetically and with care. Systems were arranged neatly, and well dusted.

"Holy of holies." Cori said. Her eyes glittered, and her mouth watered. "There's some really obscure stuff here, Sammy. *Cat's Cradle*? Isn't that the game that drove people insane."

Sammiel scoffed. "Their fault. It's not that hard. You just get a big ball of tangled twine, and you untangle it using the analogue sticks. Then you slowly become aware of a growing malevolence that gets more overwhelming the more you unravel the twine. The problem is some people give up, but you can't do that. If you unravel the whole thing, it's all fine. I won't give any spoilers but it winds up being alright. But if you give up...well, yeah it gets pretty wacky, I guess."

"You make fun of farming simulators but you play games about unraveling twine?"

"I like obscure games that make you think. Like *Occam*. The software gains sentience and you have to make it realize it doesn't exist before it does. Either that or just shut the game off before it does.." Sam ran his finger over his collection. "This one summons an entity into your home when you play it. This one has a soundtrack created by Frank Siponelli the guitarist, except the game came out before he was born. I just like obscure things like that. This one you make minor alterations to obscure physics principles to find out what sorts of universes you can wind up with."

Cori contorted her face and pondered. "In my game I've got a burgeoning pomegranate conglomerate." She said, studying the games in Sammiel's library with a slowly growing disappointment. "I'm expanding into pomegranate wine. Should be very lucrative. Oo! You play *Numen*? Ah, I haven't played that in forever."

"I just started a game the other day. I made myself a god of wind, I just got my first worshipper."

"The customization is dank isn't it?" Cori said and grabbed the game off the shelf. "Farthest I ever got I had three cities and three million followers worshipping me and my dark designs. Muahahaha." Cori put the game back on the shelf. Sammiel straightened it. "Can I see your god of wind?"

Sammiel pouted. "We should probably get back to work. It takes a while to get across the Deep Halls of Albahazred."

"Oh, alright." Cori said, then shuffled her feet out the door. "Love what you've done with the place."

Chapter 10

A knock at her door. "Another package for you Cori."

"My succulents." Cori gasped from her sleepy reverie. She threw on a robe and opened the door for Dana who had a blue lipped scowl and handed Cori a box.

"This is five days in a row now." Dana said. "Can't you order them to arrive on a single day? The trek to your room is twice my daily cardio, I swear."

"I'm almost done decorating, *I* swear." Cori said, plucking desperately at the packing tape.

"It's looking good in here." Dana admitted, looking around at the hanging fabrics and atmospheric art prints in cheap frames. Dream catchers hung above an earthy green comforter on the bed and the wooden floorboards had been polished. The windows were spotless, the fire was roaring, and a hologram machine strung stars about in the air as though the cosmos themselves were in witness. "Not sure how you're affording all this."

"Neglecting my future self." Cori shrugged and crossed her arms. "That bitch can deal with this later."

"Oh, to be young and immortal." Dana resigned.

"You're only like ten years older than me."

"It's a long ten years, kid."

"Well, thank you for the package. I won't order anything else online for a long time. But when I saw carnivorous succulents, I just couldn't help myself. They have teeth and everything."

"If there's one thing I understand, it's plant babies." Dana said, then her eyes widened with memory. "Oh, don't forget, tonight is Franklin's concert. Make sure you're there. But steer clear of Maya until then. She's all worked up about it."

"That's tonight? Shoot, I've got so much today. Yoga with Sol, my first time alone with Agnus, and then Penny after helping you cook dinner." Cori said, running through a vast mental formulae of how she could possibly fit everything into her schedule.

"Dang skipper, you better hop to it."

Cori crashed through her morning routine, threw on her yoga gear, and scarfed down a breakfast burrito she had saved in her new bedroom mini-fridge. She slid down the library spiral railing and spotted Sarah at play amongst the thousand folds of leathery tomes and ribbon wrapped papyrus scrolls that formed the soul of the library. Shafts of dawn light glittered in the dust motes raised by Sarah's spectral shenanigans.

"Sarah, I'm going to need your help today. Will you be able to come with me later on a little adventure? We're going to make you a new friend."

"A real adventure?" Sarah asked. "Of course I'll come with you Cori!"

"Great, we can go together after dinner."

>An auspicious day
>To savor our fates,
>While Jupiter dances with Venus.

"Oh, didn't see you there Luke." Cori said, waving at Luke whose spider automaton was hanging off the scroll cases while he was knee deep in one of the library's most prized ancient works, cuneiform poetry carved into a slab of sandstone. Such treasures could be found in the St. Margaret's collection if one had a keen enough nose.

>As befits mine eyes,
>All wonder and wise,
>Your air is lathered with sweetness.

>Take care my girl,
>And think it not small,
>What wonders you work in secret.

>From all things may pass
>The ripples en masse

Which imbue this glimmering matrix.

"Thanks Luke!"

Luke blew her a kiss with a big wrinkled smile from his wet and beady eyes as Cori rushed down the hallways, already late for her yoga class with Sol, who could be very impatient with his routine.

The yoga classes had been scheduled in the ballroom since their inception for the twofold reason that it had the proper hardwood floors for optimal balance and poise, as well as its connection to Sol's long time drinking habit from the bar which was now filled with kombucha in place of booze. "We're looking to fill old bad habits with new good habits." Cori had insisted, and so Morris had locked away all the strong spirits and set to the task of ordering in a local homebrew probiotic mixture called "The Booch". Sol's new routine involved drinking one bottle before yoga class, and toasting one bottle afterwards with Cori to further warrant the community and social fixtures that Sol so craved. And slowly that community grew with new attendees, Derrick and Ernie, each of whom were awaiting her when she arrived.

Ernie still frightened Cori terribly, and gazed at her with a murderous stare as his neck spurted bits of crimson ectoplasm onto the yoga mat while he groaned. Sol wasn't much better in his now decomposing cadaver. He glared outward through pale eyes, but at least they had made it through the worst of Rigor Mortis, which set in the middle of their first class. But no amount of embalming had been capable of keeping Sol's lips from peeling back and his hair from falling out, and the bloat did not mix well with stretching.

Cori set the mood with soothing but modern jams while diffusing the most pleasant aromas into the room and dropping the blinds. The ballroom had been redecorated with the tackiest of motivational phrases and slathered about with essential oils. And, being that this was yoga of the most unqualified sort, Cori took liberties with the poses and altered them to her whims. "First, we begin with Raise the Dead. Get those hands high fella's. Now, down to hanged man, touch your toes. Up halfway. Andddd Rigor Mortis." For plank, in proper yoga terms, was the pose Sol's own Rigor

Mortis had set in during that first class, and it had become something of an inside joke. "Face up. Down, Cultists Bow. This is our main pose, so relax into it, jog those feet. Now...Prostrate thyself before the Ancients. Nose to the floor, nose to the floor. Take some time here to worship the Void. This is relaxing. Very good, Ernie." Cori said, though Ernie was no more than a ghost and really needed to exhume no effort. "Back to Cultists Bow. Foot forward, knees bent, arms up to Assassin, now Assassin Dagger, and back to Passive Assassin. Cartwheel forward. Three eyed Raven."

On and on it went until coming up from Rigor Mortis, Cori heard a distinctive pop from the spine of Sol, and a look of warm satisfaction spread over his face. They continued the class, but some mysterious effluence hung about the air. It was more than could be explained by the essential oils. It was something even Derrick noticed, as he looked in Sol's direction repeatedly. It was a glow, a vortex. A spasm in the ether.

Inspiration came over Cori, and in a break from the usual routine she offered Sol his Kombucha *before* the final pose, Chaturanga Dandasuna, which she had serendipitously named Liberation Pose in homage to this new form of Necromantic Yoga.

"Cheers, Sol." Cori said, clinking bottles with him and Derrick and holding an extra one up for Ernie. For a reason she could not explain until later, a tear slid down her cheek. The Kombucha was a bittersweet spirulina, with just a touch of cacao. Cori's belly thanked her for her tongue's sacrifice.

"Cheers."

Whilst Derrick chugged his kombucha with a scowl, Cori and Sol savored theirs. One wouldn't expect it to be something to savor, but something had come over them in this session that paused their breath and left them with a depth of gratitude for even the coarse vinegar sea foam mixture that might set lesser souls to gagging. "Liberation Pose, everyone." Cori said with gravity once the Kombucha was thoroughly drained.

Soothing notes stretched from Cori's sound bar speakers. This vibrated the darkened room as they all lay on their backs. Their minds emptied for the exhaustion they had imparted upon their body. Eyes closed, none of them saw the roiling smoke as it rose from Sol's belly and into the air to twist and curl. It shuddered with lightning as it filled the ceiling with clouds. Flower petals fell in place of rain, bioluminescent, and something set about glowing underneath Sol's cadaver skin. A petal fell onto Cori's unclaimed tear, still resting on her cheek. Unable to contain her curiosity, Cori peeked. Derrick peeked too. Kitsune peeked from the doorway at the end of the ballroom. Small convulsions rippled through Sol's cadaver until a single white light escaped his lips, invariably his soul, and danced upwards in a fractal towards a rip in the spacetime of the clouds.

Derrick looked at Cori, wide eyed, and mouthed "Follow." And Cori nodded.

Cori stood quietly and followed the silent sprite as it reached higher into the wormhole rip central to the ceiling full of clouds. She found that her feather light feet held no weight against the ground and the room now imparted levitation. Cori tapped her toe to the wood, then floated upwards and away.

Rough spun psychedelic geometries tunneled Cori and Sol upwards through the higher frequencies, away from St. Margaret's and through bountiful fields and mountains of luscious prosperity, through seas of sweet nectar, through pulsating rhythms and melodious tunes. Their bodies stretched and contorted as they rippled through photons, up into a cosmic space where Sol finally came to rest on a forested rock bubble that orbited a crystalline sun. Here they sat, and here Cori saw Sol for the first time not as a skeleton, but as he was, or ought to be. A plump man with a plump and rosy nose, and the concerned eyes of a father.

"What's going to happen to me?" He asked at length, while deeply considering an orchid growing from a nearby tree.

Cori took this into thorough consideration, and answered him with a measured look into his eyes. "I don't know."

"This is the Liberation everyone makes such a big fuss about, isn't it?"

Cori nodded.

"Do you know, the hardest part was never giving up the drink." Sol sighed, his lip quivering, grasping at the soft moss of their cosmic forest bubble. "It was taking a long hard look at all the things

I had done while I was drinking, at the way I had wasted my life away. Missing my kids birthdays, berating them while I was hungover. And oh, the looks the wife would give me."

Cori said not a word, but laid a hand on his knee as he looked at his reflection in the pond in front of him. Juniper leaves shivered and cast spells with the cobalt light of their foreign sun. The moss between their fingertips shivered and curled. Space dragons danced and sang their song between stars and comets.

"Sometimes it's easier to just keep up the illusion. Keep telling myself I'm such a fun guy. That I'm living my best life. That everyone loves me down at the tavern. I'm so boisterous and funny." Sol mimicked out his old attitudes, and Cori saw memories rippling in the pool before them. "Sometimes, even knowing it wasn't true, I just wanted to keep on believing it. And I'd choose to go back to believing it, even knowing it was a load of crap."

"Not anymore?" Cori asked.

"What's the use? I don't have my buddies down at the tavern anymore. Wife left me before I even died. Kids don't come and see me, they just plopped me into the home. You all were all I had left. It's just...that's what's so frightening about this." Sol motioned around himself to the forest bubble which, Cori began to notice, was leaving the orbit of its crystalline sun and moving upwards and away into the dark void of space. "I still have all of you, don't I? That night at Duke's was such fun. Can't we just keep doing that? That night, I remember thinking I could do that forever."

Cori looked around her at the bubble as it jettisoned through space, passing nebulae and quasars. "I don't think that's what you really want though, is it?"

"I guess not." Sol said, looking towards the void.

"You could still live it up here for a bit. You get 49 days in the Betwixt once you're untethered as you are, or so I've been told."

"So I can just feel like I have a doom clock over my head? No...not for me, I don't think." Sol replied, and for a long while they remained silent.

"I'm honored to be taking this journey with you." Cori whispered.

"I'm scared, Cori. I'm so terribly afraid." Sol said, and it was all Cori could do to lock eyes with him. "You're here with me for now, but…" It was all too soon that the bubble arrived at its destination, a dark and cold world that Cori was rapidly becoming too familiar with, the Villa of Ormen. "From here, I go alone." He said as their grassy pod settled upon the moon rock, lit by the eclipse of a dying star.

"I can come with you, up to the steps…" Cori said, grasping Sol's hand, her throat choked and painful.

"A Necromancer ought to know better." Sol said, pulling his hand from Cori's. "Thank you, Coriander. That journey was much better with a friend."

"Sol…" Cori now sobbed as Sol walked away and towards a temple built into the side of a crater, empty windows watching him approach. Cori glimpsed the temple briefly, but then averted her eyes and let herself sink down down down into the familiar tug of gravity seated in her belly. She strung herself downwards to her home world in the Mundane far far below.

Cori descended to her yoga mat, guided by the sandalwood essential oils she had conspicuously used for her class, her eyes wide with yugen in all its beauty, violence, and sorrow.

"So how'd it go?" Derrick asked boisterously, slapping Cori's back and destroying all semblance of tranquility. "Was that your first one? Damn! I haven't liberated anyone yet. Looks like I've got to start focusing. I'm super competitive, so like, look out." He laughed forcefully.

"I don't even know what to do now." Cori said and looked down at her hands as they trembled.

"Well, there's a special section on the intranet to fill out in your notes. A bunch of paperwork. You tell Morris, he will put a sticker in your file and give you a big old round of applause at Dinner and a toast to the Departed."

"Just like that? That's it?" Cori asked, her eyes quivering, her legs like jello.

"Uh, they alert the family. Sometimes the local newspaper picks up a story. Life moves on, I guess." Derrick said. "Heck, we might get a twofer tonight with Franklin. Cheers."

Cori wandered through the halls of St. Margaret's in a daze, trying but unable to remember her way back to Agnus' apartment. She could not stifle the feeling that she wished she could have entered the Villa herself. Nor could she keep at bay the sensation she was being watched, and or pursued.

Just outside the Dollmaker's workshop Cori found her way into a bathroom where she could compose herself against the encroaching tidal wave of emotion that was poised to drown her. Cori found her way into a stall. Much like a school lavatory, it was all sterile and whitewashed and gleaming with cheap fluorescent lighting that flickered with bad wiring.

Cori set about interpreting the hieroglyphs of employees long resigned. 'Pooping is beautiful' read one. Someone had taken the time to write that. 'Suck my Terry Flaps' read another. Cori took the time to contemplate these musings. What must their mindset have been at the time? What would compel a human to scrawl 'butt stuff' just above a roll of toilet paper? Blanketed by these distractions and her compelling illusion of privacy, nothing could have been worse than hearing the bathroom door open. Footsteps, followed by the sound of a deadbolt Cori hadn't thought of using.

"Just where I want you." Cori heard Kitsune say.

Cori groaned. "Kitsune, I am literally trying to poop right now. Is this the best time?"

"I told you to back off him, or else I'd eat your soul. And you disrespected me? You think I was joking? Not only did you not listen, you weren't even subtle about it. You strut on over all done up like you're gonna give it out easy." Kitsune slammed her palm against Cori's stall, as oozing pustules slapped against the sterile floor below and slid down and under into Cori's stall. These piles of liquid slop slithered themselves into a semblance of Kitsune's face and gazed up at Cori from the floor of her stall. Speaking on many harsh frequencies, "So what are we going to do about it?"

Cori stomped on the face, squishing it. Instinctively, not courageously, she stomped as she might have done with a too-large bug that alarmed her. Her heart was pounding rhythmically with the pressing realities of the threats Kitsune made so easily upon her. Soul threats were not threats to be taken lightly.

Another pound on the stall, and another, as the oozing liquid gathered back outside the door.

Cori ran through her options. She could text Morris or Maya, but by the time they arrived it could be too late. Or, it could just escalate things further. Or, worse yet, put them in danger.

Nah, nah, I gotta handle this bitch myself. Cori thought in a brief flash of idiocy. It was a stupidity that lingered as her heart gathered its rhythm and brought strength to her limbs. *This could easily be the worst mistake I ever make.* Cori thought, then burst her own stall door open to Kitsune's surprise.

"And what do you think I'm going to do to you, huh?" Cori asked, stepping forward out of her stall, effervescence coalesced at her feet. "You ever wonder that? Maybe I don't buy your little threats, Kitsune. Maybe I don't buy that you've killed off a bunch of vampire hunters. Maybe I'm just a phone call away from ending your immortality. You think I've spent my whole life learning necromancy without learning a thing or two about how to bind the undead?"

Kitsune looked back towards the bathroom door she had locked.

"No, no, we're locked in here now. So, let's settle this out. You and me. That said, Kitsune, I'm still open to talking like we're goddamn adults. I'm not trying to steal anyone from you. That's not how this all works. He's not yours. He's not mine. So its about time you back the fuck off."

Kitsune looked at Cori, frightened for just a moment until her jaw came unhinged and her eyes rolled into the back of her head and Kitsune unveiled her many rows of serrated teeth behind that petite smile. All semblance of humanity was lost in the yawning and unending pit that formed Kitsune's mouth.

"Oh shit." Cori muttered as Kitsune grabbed for her, vampire limbs cracked and broke and wriggled. Cori dodged beneath her arms and followed with an awkward kick to Kitsune's back, combined with a slice from a plasma dagger she conjured in the nick of time. "This would be a lot easier with corporate conflict resolution." Cori said before Kitsune wrapped her enormous maw over the top of Cori's head. The darkness closed in and tightened. Cori was constricted into a fleshy tube that felt too much like a throat. Sphincters oscillated and smooth muscle ushered her downwards. Cori, panicked and crumbled in spirit. She worked against what flesh she could with her conjured plasma dagger, and even shot a bolt of white hot balefire down deep into the fleshy tubes. But though both produced a wriggle, neither released her from her prison. However, it provided enough light to release her from the worst grips of fear that the darkness of Kitsune's esophagus was imparting.

"Kitsune ate me." Cori finally texted Maya, struggling to arrange her arms against the constrictions of Kitsune's throat. "Any advice?" Cori waited for a response while she was ushered deeper and deeper, then decided to text Morris, glad her phone still had excellent service despite the circumstances. "I don't mean to be a bother but--"

Could you be any more of a burden to people? Just let her devour you and be done with it. Cori's darkest thoughts began their usual procession. *Such an embarrassment. Do you really want them to have to save you...again? I don't know how you look anyone in the eye.* "Shut up and just let me think for once." Cori said out loud, speaking so as to overpower her thoughts with vocalization. "Oh duh, the garlic." Cori reached into her bag and grabbed the clove she had stashed away after Kitsune's first threats. Then she tossed it down Kitsune's esophagus. Cori waited with a satisfied smile while her phone pinged with promises that others were on the way to rescue her. One lurch, two lurches, and up up up Cori rose like a water slide on the acidic bile that carried her out and onto the once shiny bathroom floor.

There, Kitsune stood lurching the rest of her stomach all over herself as the door pounded with Maya and Morris calling to get in. Cori stood, all covered about with inhuman juices.

"This isn't over." Kitsune said, spitting garlic and churning acidic bile onto the floor.

"You can threaten to kill me or devour my soul or whatever, but that just ends my torment. But I know a thing or two about vampires. It's not that easy for you, is it? So what would it be like if I bound you in a dimension of itch for several millennia?" Cori asked.

Kitsune's face worked and contorted before she heaved more bile upon the floor.

The door finally burst open, and Cori strode out. Her hair and skin was slick with blood and black and oil. "Thank you so much for coming. I took care of it." Cori told Morris and Maya as they guffawed between her and a trembling Kitsune.

Chapter 11

Morris agreed to let Cori take one hour on the clock to rest and get cleaned up, then vowed to file not just a corrective action against Kitsune, but a full blown *probationary memo*. "Liberated Sol and sent Kitsune on her heels all in one day. What are you on, and where can I get some?" Morris asked, half in jest. Cori, for her part, stocked up on more garlic, both in her satchel and in her pockets, and followed it up with the sweet pitter patter of a victory shower and then, once clean, took a victory bath complete with bath bombs and her new carnivorous succulents as companions, which she fed small crickets, and sipped a glass of kombucha as the plants crunched and munched with their succulent teeth. Small droplets of the blood and bile of her enemy spattered the ceramic tile.

Refreshed and reinvigorated, Cori set about finding Agnus' apartments on the third floor. Cori hadn't seen the old witch for some time, and largely avoided her cataract gaze at dinners and kept about as much distance from her apartment as she kept from Keiran's. That said, a job's a job, and Cori had no mercy for complaining whilst on the clock, reasonable wage or not.

She was one turn away from the High Lands of Arnath. Cori impressed herself with her own navigational prowess and mastery of the St. Margaret's laminated brochure map. It had been a long trek, and sweat clung to her brow as she reached into her satchel to swig from her waterskin. Kitsune's downfall was on her mind, and Cori knocked confidently upon the doors to Agnus' abode, the knob of which turned slowly and creaked open, azure miasma spilled forth in dim effulgence.

"Agnus?" Cori called into the empty and aquatic parlor that served as the front room of the apartment. The furniture floated as though on a sunken ship. Vivian, the doll, stood central and lifeless, her arms raised upwards as though in praise. She was in the center of a salt circle, with several mice sacrificed at each corner between darkly gilded geometries. "Oh, Vivian…" Cori rolled her eyes, and snatched the doll up from her religious fervor. "What are we going to do with you? Agnus?" Cori called out again, her knees trembled despite all her best efforts at a cool demeanor.

Cori held onto the possessed doll Vivian and stepped cautiously through into the hall. She checked room after room before discovering Agnus clawing rabidly into the woodwork of the study, her arms moving with unnatural speed as she worked to open a hole in the wall. Cori flicked on her flashlight and drew feral hiss from Agnus, who threw her hands to her face as though blinded.

"There you are. What are you doing in here?" Cori asked and clicked off her flashlight again. Agnus could barely be seen in the darkness, her spirit was a dim outline now that her digging had exhausted her. One could only just make out her wrinkles, the curls of her permed gray hair and those cataract eyes. Of legs, she had none.

"Digging." Agnus croaked sheepishly, then spotted Vivian and lunged to grab her.

"You can have her, you can have her. No need to get feisty." Cori said and nearly dropped the doll in surprise. "Kitsune told me when I work with you, you'll be giving me instructions on how to take care of her, is that right?"

Agnus cast a wary eye upon Cori, then nodded slowly.

"Okay. I'll take care of her, but you can't attack me like last time, got it?"

Agnus smiled ear to ear, too wide, too few teeth, and conveyed no promises. "Vivian craves the blood of the master of this house. Do this, and no harm shall befall you."

"You want me to feed your doll Morris' blood?" Cori crossed her arms. "Is he even the master of this house? I feel like Maya does more than him, and I'm pretty sure I've heard him talk about having a boss before."

Agnus herself looked uncertain, and pulled her ear down to Vivian. Cori swore she heard speech, but it was deep speech, sub-bass and alien and barely noticeable even in the silent study. "V says she craves the blood of the one called Absalon."

"Oh yeah, okay that's Morris. That's his true name or something. I don't know. How much blood are we talking here?" Cori asked, and Agnus bent to her doll once more.

"Blood enough to paint the attic walls." Agnus translated.

Cori frowned. "I think that's a bit unreasonable. I doubt he has that much in his body."

Agnus looked at Vivian fearfully, then looked at Cori with pity. "Do this lest ye be cursed."

"I'm already cursed three ways till Sunday, Keiran left a whole mess." Cori said, now acutely aware of the pit she felt in her belly. "Figured you'd have heard that by now."

Agnus set Vivian upon a shelf and moved closer to Cori, her blank white eyes were concerned and maternal. "Does the girl feel empty inside? Oh, that won't do. Not for one who cares such for others. Not for one who cares for lost souls. Come. We shall have tea."

Agnus led Cori out of the study and back to the parlor where she had Cori sit down on a chair which now casually drifted to the floor, and made tea in the gloom of the separate and dismally small kitchenette. Soon a kettle was boiling and screaming, as they do, and in short order Cori sipped at an herbal tea from delicate china which had floated its way on over to her.

"St. John's Wort, deary." Agnus said, still hardly visible in the windowless shadows of the aquatic parlor. "Good for emotional wounds."

"I don't really know what to say." Cori said, half expecting the tea to be poison. "Thank you. I don't think you're the one who is supposed to be taking care of me."

"I heard you liberated the one called Sol from his earthbound prison." Agnus said and sipped at a levitating tea cup of her own. "Something to be proud of."

"I don't quite know how to feel about it. I don't feel much right now, but I think soon I'm going to begin missing him terribly."

Agnus nodded slowly. "Sol was a good soul. Misguided, but who among us isn't?"

"Do you want to be Liberated, Agnus?" Cori asked after a time. "Is it a good thing?"

Agnus was silent at this question, and looked off towards the study, then stood, legless. "Vivian needs tending. Finish your tea, deary."

153

"I don't think I can get her the blood she wants." Cori said between sips.

"Vivian will be displeased." Agnus snarled, and her maternal gaze shifted to something darker.

"Agnus...who is Vivian?" Cori asked, but quickly regretted doing so as Agnus became more visible and clearly agitated.

"Mustn't ask such questions lest she gets the shocky. Be a good girl now, Agnus." Agnus said and looked off at a world beyond her own apartment.

"I'm sorry." Cori said, sipping down the last of her tea. "I'll be going."

"She will stay and do as she's told." Agnus bellowed in a voice not her own, her white hair growing wild, and her eyes electric. The door slammed, and the lock clicked. "Evil little witch. Witches will be punished."

For all Cori's despair at the endless trials of this day, she made note of the verbal cues Agnus was giving. There was a mystery to be solved here, she noted, and perhaps doing everything Vivian wanted was not the correct course of action as Kitsune made it out to be. "Agnus, back up. Please, I don't want a fight. I've already done this once today."

But the doll Vivian was already floating into the parlor from the hallway, surrounded by sickly energies like coagulated blood.

"Nuts to this. I'm sorry Agnus." Cori said and drew her hands together to form an orb of purple flames between her hands, light like the sun filled the room and sent Agnus on her heels, and dispelled the sick energies from Vivian's porcelain frame. These energies shook the walls with charging reverberations before Cori unleashed this force of her will against the locked door. It exploded into fiery smithereens, and left Cori physically exhausted.

Cori, being near Morris' office, reported her own vandalism. Morris sat in his large leather chair, feet up on his desk, flip flops exposed and scrolled his phone and the interwebs. "I blew up the door to Agnus' Apartment."

Morris looked up at Cori, then rolled his eyes painfully before turning to his computer. "Do you know the amount of paperwork--"

"Shove it, Morris. I'm not in the mood." Cori said, surprising herself.

"Who do you think you're talking to, you scrappy little punk?" Morris replied. "I don't need to threaten you with eating your soul, I'll just fire you."

"Sorry, Morris. It's just been a lot today."

"Yeah, yeah, I don't wanna hear it. Listen, good news." Morris waved Cori in closer and began to talk more quietly. "No need to go busting down our walls to find Penny. I did a little digging in the Archives, and you will never believe what I found in the original blueprints to the manor. There's a *crawlspace* in the torture chambers on the second floor. I had never seen them before. Dana is the only one who ever goes in there and she's always distracted by some man or another. But from there, all the walls and floors are interconnected." Morris' eyes widened and he showed a rare peak of career related excitement that Cori had never seen before. He unraveled several blueprint scrolls onto his mahogany desk and jabbed his index finger into it. His coffee breath was too close for comfort. "It's a whole unmapped territory of St. Margaret's. It'll be no easy task, and I have no idea what you'll find. But, if you really think both Sarah and Penny will respond to making a friend, we could be talking about a two for one Liberation."

Cori looked down at the blueprints and could make nothing out of it. "I'm not going to lie, Morris, I'm not exactly excited about Liberating souls right now."

Morris took a deep breath, his excitement dissipated. "First one got to you, huh?"

Cori drew a long face, sideways and awkward.

"Yeah. Hey, I feel ya. Listen kid, why do you think I'm up here sitting on my phone? It's not an easy gig. You'll burn out quick if you're not careful. Corporate will give you a whole spiel about self care and taking some time off and it sounds very good, but then once you really do burn out, it's never that simple."

"I've only been here a couple months."

"Don't underestimate it. That's sometimes all it takes...Far be it for me to talk, but if I can suggest anything, don't focus too hard on Liberation. I know that's the *goal*. But enjoy the time on the way.

Stop and smell the roses. Don't go in there trying to Liberate Penny. Go *play* with Penny. Hell just try to even find her, I don't care. Do you think I actually check that you all are doing your jobs? Just enjoy yourself. You're getting so serious, you're gonna get an ulcer."

Cori stood and pondered for a moment, then nodded her head. "Yeah...yeah, I think I get you."

"I'm literally telling you about an uncharted wilderness between the walls of a haunted manor and you're worried about getting your second Liberation in a day. You're turning into Maya. I'll be extremely grateful if you get one a year. God knows Derrick couldn't Liberate a Lama at the very Doors of Ormen itself. Chill out, kid. Go explore a haunted mansion while I frickin' fill out the seventy pages of paperwork you just gave me."

Cori smiled and looked Morris in the eye. "Thanks."

"Yeah, yeah."

Maybe it was Morris' advice or maybe it was the tea Agnus gave her, but Cori felt a brief reprieve from the keenest sting of her bitterest woes, and now felt only a general melancholy, which was more like music and ice cream by comparison.

Back home, for it was now starting to feel like home in her bedroom, Cori took several deep breaths before setting to the rest of the day's plans. She had no formalwear to speak of for the night's concert. The concert set in the back gardens and open to the citizens of Remedy as both free entertainment and a showcase of the good work that was being done here at St. Margaret's. Sensing her distress, a small cohort of the manor's friendliest spiders set wove a spider silk ballgown, in honor of Cori's good work and deeds thus far at the place they too call home.

"Thank you, my darlings." Cori said, and sang a grave tune in a minor key, and gave each spider a kiss on its hairy little mandibles. The dress was white and delicately woven into the softest and most breathable fashion. It fit like a charm, and Cori set it aside for the Midnight Concert in the Garden.

An aromatic stew of poached basilisk eggs in curry and marrow broth was set out for an early staff dinner, topped with wormwood and yarrow flowers for presentation. Dessert, a slow churned mint custard, topped about with strawberries, a chocolate sauce, and specks of gold foil. Cori assisted in the dinner's preparations, though by the time she had arrived most of the prep work had been completed. This was for the best, as Cori felt ready to fall asleep in the stew even while just stirring it. She was so weary from her journey into the Betwixt, vampire battle, and subsequent kamehameha. It was all she could do to sip at a mana potion Dana had offered her, an admixture of ginseng, B-12, hummingbird hearts, and the spores of one glowing mushroom. This replenished her in will and vitality, but left her eye twitching terribly. However, for all the unpleasant edge she felt, this did not appear to compare to the fret Maya was experiencing in preparation for the midnight musical foray. Maya would usually melt for a rich dinner like this, but she hadn't touched her food, and glanced anxiously at her phone before walking hurriedly to Franklin to whisper in his ear. Cori looked at Agnus, who avoided eye contact and kept her ghastly stare on her own stew.

"You ready for our big adventure?" Sarah asked Cori at her last morsel and touched a chilly static hand to her elbow. Large ghastly eyes looked upwards dolefully.

Cori curled her own eyes and nodded. She hadn't been so certain about bringing Sarah after what had happened with Sol, but now she thought maybe they wouldn't even be Liberated. Maybe they'd just become friends. That would be worth a solid day's effort. "We've got an even better adventure than I expected. I don't know that we're going to find your new friend Penny, but we've got some work to do. Apparently, there's a whole other side of the manor that needs exploring. And I think I'm too scared to go alone. I'm going to need your help."

Sarah pumped her fist, and pushed up her glasses. "The Adventurers Club."

Cori laughed and pumped her fist with Sarah, "That's right. We're the Adventurer's Club. Cori and Sarah set off to rescue their new friend Penny. "But we've got to be back before eleven, understand? Then, we can go to the concert."

Dana reluctantly gave Cori the key to the Second Floor Torture Chambers, which was filled with all manner of racks and leather, flails, whips, and manacles. It was no wonder the crawlspace had yet to be discovered. It was hidden behind the Iron Maiden, which did not budge even underneath the force of Derrick's exotic Serpent Punch technique that he claimed to acquire from an old martial arts master in the jungle mists of a hidden temple. Cori found these claims dubious at best, punctuated especially by the nauseating crunch of fractured bone beset with Derrick's howling. In the end, it was Luke who saved the day, as his Spider Automaton was gifted in its robotic strength, and capable of lifting many hundreds of times its own weight.

An Iron Maiden.
An humiliated youth.
Victory is sweet.

Luke's haiku made Derrick's cheeks blush, and he skulked off and away from the torture chamber while Luke cackled in such a way as Cori had never heard him. This was followed by a fit of coughing, and then a contented sigh as his automaton took him away along the walls and ceilings and out of view.

Cori opened the crawl space door, and peered inside with her flashlight. Stale wind furrowed her hair, and a moan issued from the floorboards. Sarah still seemed very much excited. Cori felt that mixing her innate fear of darkness with claustrophobia two times in one day seemed a dubious bet. The first time had been a mortal necessity, but this time was a vanity job at best.

"What are you waiting for, Cori?" Sarah asked, already down the way into the crawl space.

Cori's mouth dried. Company usually makes fear easier to cope with, but ghost girls don't impart the same sanguine comforts as ordinary folk. Cori's prior coping mechanisms of balefire and conjured plasma weapons were just likely to set the whole house on fire. She pulled her flashlight, dual wielding it with her phone light. With the luminous strength of these objects combined, Cori was able to see in all the greater detail how terribly dark it was there between the drywall, how little was known of the lands beyond, and how no other could effectively venture forth to find her, no matter how dire her need. Also, how very many spiders lived at St.

Margaret's. The friendly terms she shared with those in her room were not likely to pervade across the entire manor, as spiders are wildly diverse in their personalities and cultures, much like people.

"Pale...as...a...ghost." Cori heard a voice like rusted tin tutted from the doorway. It was Sammiel.

"Me?" Sarah asked from the crawlspace.

"Oh, I didn't see you there, Sarah." Sammiel said. "Both of you, I suppose."

Cori just barely held onto her bladder. She grabbed her heart and wheezed out. "What the hell is the matter with you? You scared me so bad."

"You're going into the walls alone?"

"I--"

"Didn't we establish you're afraid of the dark?"

"I don't know who invited you." Cori said, her muscles strained in an attempt to keep from smiling. Her stomach stirred like a pot of spicy stew.

"Actually, I just came here to see Dana's kinks put on blast." Sammiel said, his thumbs in his belt loops as he perused the macabre display. "But you two look like you could use some company."

"No boys allowed." Cori said. Her fists clenched with the thought that he may give up too easily. But Sarah came from the crawl space and wrapped Sammiel in a wispy hug. Sammiel pretended to lift her, and Sarah allowed herself to float as though lifted.

"We're going to find another friend, Sammy." Sarah said, then pretended to tug Sammiel along, as though she was capable of such a thing. Sammiel played right along and let himself tug this way and that as Sarah led him forward. "Her name is Penny."

Sammiel gasped. "I know Penny. Oh, you two are just going to be the best of friends."

Cori felt a pang of jealousy that Sarah seemed more bonded to Sammiel than to herself. This pang was greatly overshadowed by seeing a new patriarchal side of Sammiel.

My ovaries. Cori's body groaned. Sammiel grabbed Cori's flashlight with a mischievous smile and lowered himself into the crawlspace ahead of her. Did he plan these leather pants? Was this some illusion of the torture chamber, set to rack her body with tormenting desire? What dark and cruel effigy would possess him to crawl in front of her, with her only option to crawl behind him, gawking. *He must be a sadist.* Cori thought, but that did nothing to quell her longing. For however his pants may have fit while he was standing, these leather pants became impossibly tight while crawling. And the swagger! Sammiel swayed as he crawled forward one knee at a time, tantalizing and hypnotizing. All this might have been manageable if not for the outline of his bulge, just below it all.

She forgot her fears, she forgot the dust, she even forgot the spider that fell into her hair. Cori pressed onwards through several dozen feet before coming to a place of standing, wall boards stood two feet apart in either direction.

"I'm assuming you've got a plan here…" Sammiel said and plucked a cobweb from his silver fade. The familiar rusted tin of his voice brought a shiver to Cori's spinal marrow.

"Plan?" Cori asked, still dazed and disoriented, then slid against the brick. "Oh yes, well this here is the first ever mission of its kind. We're just getting a lay of the land. If we happen to find Penny on this first expedition, that's a fine stroke of luck."

"I meant getting back." Sammiel said. "General navigation."

"Ah." Cori said, and puffed out her chest. "I think you're underestimating my innate navigational prowess."

"I thought you might say that." Sammiel sighed. "Lucky for us, I like to have pens on me. I'll just make a little mark at every corner pointing the direction back home."

"Bloody brilliant." Cori said. "To my credit, I did remember snacks." Cori did not remember snacks so much as she just so happened to have a half eaten bag of doritos on her person.

"You two are taking forever, come on. We've got to find Penny." Sarah said.

Their venture onwards took them under pipe and crook. The walls expanded at each turn, and the ductwork became more daring. The wiring became more hazardous. What had at first only looked to be the work of a quack soon turned into frayed wires and sparking coils. Lightning crossing gaps of several inches or more.

This was to say nothing of the mice. Cori first noticed something was amiss when she discovered a tiny tee shirt hanging up on a wire near open brickwork. Within were thimbles and needles and collected odds and ends. Tiny bits of cheese lay upon a makeshift table, no bigger than Cori's hand. The consciousness of rodents did not come as a complete shock to Cori, who was studied in such matters, but their society did. After they had crossed Aqueduct Bridge and strayed down into the sewers, they found an Undercity, complete with tiny shops and stalls and what appeared to be a small festival consisting of replated scraps from the day's dinner that Cori herself had taken part in cooking. All this I say not because it had any bearing upon Cori's journey, but only mention factually, by way of adequately representing the environments she found herself in. The mice scurried away as giants beset their land, as did the spiders with whom they lived in harmony, and the rats with whom they lived in tense tolerance. Of this and no more shall I speak of it.

    Such was their perseverance in caring for their resident ghosts that Cori and Sammiel soon found themselves scaling a brick laid chimney in what they had only just dubbed the Chasm of Razabag Dune. It was so named for the pile of brick dust that formed a Dune, and Razabag because it flowed off the tongue. They both had a good laugh about this for no reason in particular, perhaps only for the adrenaline as they scaled the loose bricks of the monumental chimney with all the skill of deformed mountain goats. Midway through scaling the brickwork, Cori's phone alarm set off which interrupted their laughing fits about their nonsensical names, and caused Cori to slip her footing and plummet down.

    Sammiel called her name and Sarah flew downwards desperately trying but unable to catch Cori as she fell. Instead, and with the deft precision of one deeply enamored, Sammiel elongated a Fell Dagger Chain. This chain forged from the arcane extended out of his very flesh like a living and slithering creature. It shot downwards and through Cori's hand. This caused her to howl but also allowed her to grip first with her wounded hand, then more thoroughly with the remaining strength of her healthy hand, or as healthy as a hand can be with a recently wounded wrist.

Sammiel's eyes grew wide like a doe in headlights, but his brow remained attentive and focused as he struggled and lowered Cori down to the ground floor. Then he followed himself by utilizing another glimmering dagger chain from his other arm and lodged it into the brickwork as a rope.

"I can't believe I did that, I'm so sorry, Cori I'd never hurt you on p--" He began, but was interrupted by a hug.

Cori was about to say some cliche nonsense like 'you saved me' but quickly found herself ingrained in Sammiel's chest, lost in his heat and the rhythm of his heart. *No Cowor--,* her thoughts tried to gain footing but melted as the both of them held the hug for much longer than was called for. Their hearts rising on the strength of each pump and each moment they wondered whether the other would be the first to let go and each moment neither dared.

This rapture was timeless in the poetic sense, but did indeed cease when Cori began to recognize the symptoms of excess blood loss, a condition with which she was now becoming accustomed.

"I don't feel so good." Cori said in lieu of breaking the hug, thus forcing Sammiel to end it.

He took a look at her pale face. "Shit, I don't have any bandages. We need to get you to Maya."

"No, we can't bother her." Cori said, then tugged at a piece of the summer dress she was currently substituting for the night's upcoming formalwear. "Can you..."

Sammiel swiftly sliced the dress with his Fell Daggers, then wrapped them around Cori's hand and applied pressure while Cori touched Sammiel's own open wound from where the dagger chains had extended.

"What are they?" Cori asked.

Sammiel shook his head. "I don't really know. I got them after my Mom and Dad were both Liberated. Never seen anything else like it, so your guess is as good as mine. I like them though. They're like memories."

"Good memories?"

"Some of them."

"Cori...I don't want you to get hurt." Sarah said and examined the now red stained dress cloth on Cori's hand. "I want a new friend, but not that badly. I don't want to play anymore."

"That's very kind of you, Sarah." Sammiel said.

"We're still gonna get you to Penny, okay?" Cori said, and Sarah returned only a look of concern.

"Come on, let's get you home." Sammiel wrapped his arm round Cori's back and nearly lifted her off the floor as he walked beside her. He went for as long as he could till the inner walls became too narrow and she had to make due on her own, which she felt quite capable of doing but didn't want to mention that.

That near fatal phone alarm had been set as a means to remind Cori to return in time for Franklin's concert, with time to spare for dressing and preparations. In that way, it served its purpose. Sammiel insisted that he would escort Cori for the duration of the night, and just after Cori had finished patting on blush and setting into her spidersilk dress, he knocked at her door.

An elegant goth aristocrat, Sammiel offered an arm to escort the lady down through the manor's halls and out into the back gardens where each of them was served a bottle of champagne by one very zombified Nigel, who was done up in a monkey suit while he held a silver tray and bowed. Dana stood by his side, probably assuring he didn't take a nip at the flesh of one of the Remedian villagers who were assembled here en masse. Perhaps a hundred or so concert attendees of living flesh and blood and dressed in properly ironed formal wear sipped their champagne and strolled through the gardens and marveled at the blooming crocuses. They marveled at the candlelight of the floating paper lanterns and of course they marveled at the resident ghosts. Sarah herself was an object of particular attention, and drew a circle of curious onlookers who asked her about herself and her life here at St. Margaret's.

"Maya set all of this up herself?" Cori asked Sammiel, stupefied. She spied Maya from a distance near the stage which was set in just such a way that provided a view of both the river, the graveyard, and the chapel below. The garden surrounded the seated guests. "This is unreal."

George took on his Will o' the Wisp shape, which twinkled in the creeping foliage near Morris. Morris wore a shimmering gown of gold and silver, a pointy topped hat flecked with stars, and a wand which was set about with enchanted fire.

"Morris really knows how to make an impression, huh?" Cori asked.

"I don't think Morris is really the one making the main impression here." Sammiel said with a respectful nod towards Cori. It was only then she noticed several gazes drawn her way, and people whispering with wide eyes.

"Jeez, it's like they've never seen a bloody hand rag before." Cori said.

"You don't actually think that's what it is…?" Sammiel guffawed. "Cori, you look stunning. No one can get their eyes off you."

It was only then that Cori saw Sammiel might have been correct in his assertion. People weren't recoiling from a bloody hand rag, they were gazing at her spider's silk dress and her crimped and curled hair.

"Where ever did you get this? It's dazzling." Asked a buxom Remedian aristocrat.

"Like starlight." Said her husband, pompously.

"Uhhh...it was woven for me...by...spiders."

The buxom aristocrat let out an offended and opulent yowl, but her husband gave an astute "I daresay" as he inspected the dress closer with his monocle. "Magnificent."

"Mmm...mm mm. This isn't gonna work." Cori heard Maya say from the garden walkway as she approached. "I don't remember asking you to steal our show. And what exactly happened to your hand?"

"I don't even know where to begin." Cori said sheepishly.

"You have got to be the most injury prone… Hiya Sammy." Maya said and glanced down at his and Cori's intertwined arms before giving a quickly withdrawn wince. "I really think everything is turning out just the way I hoped."

"I've never seen anything like it." Cori said. "You've really outdone yourself, I have no idea how you pulled this off."

"Blood, sweat, and tears." Maya said and looked away towards the stage as she grabbed a champagne glass from a levitating tray. Ernie was mostly invisible while he held the tray. Maya chugged the glass down in seconds flat. "Blood, sweat, and tears. Enjoy yourselves you two. If you'll excuse me."

"Cori, I'll be right back." Sammiel said. "Need to speak with Maya real quick. You alright?"

"Not about to faint, if that's what you mean." Cori said, though the champagne was making her more woozily than she had anticipated. It was a woozily feeling she appreciated when she spied Kitsune approaching just as Sammiel was leaving. Cori took a quick chug.

Kitsune's lips were pursed as she stopped near Cori and looked her up and down. Cori, for her part, did the same. Kitsune was a belle of the ball in her own right, sporting normal silks instead of spider silks. They were fashioned into the expectant kimono which was nonetheless gorgeous for its predictability. Between this and the enormous red bow atop her head and the masquerade mask upon her face, she made a striking figure. "Morris is forcing me to apologize to you." Kitsune said, her lips still pursed, her eyes looking off into the sky.

"I certainly don't wan--"

"Stop." Kitsune put her hand up. "I just don't want the fact that it's mandated to lessen it being genuine.... I don't like you." Kitsune said and Cori let on a confused frown. "But I behaved unprofessionally. You were right. Some things should be talked over. You probably will never understand this, but being a vampire can be confusing sometimes. Being deathless and almost infinitely powerful can make it hard to see consequences and accept personal flaws. So, that said, I won't try to eat your soul, or kill you or anything. Sammiel can come to me because I'm the better option." Kitsune said, then held out her hand robotically, still looking away into the sky.

"Uhhh...alright. Thanks. Apology accepted, I think?"

"You're welcome." Kitsune said, her serpentine tongue quickly licked at the air in a slight hiss before she walked away daintily.

Cori took one more enormous swig of champagne then grabbed at another glass from Ernie who was thankfully still levitating there, more visible now and mouth agape as his neck gushed red liquid as it so often did.

"Ladies and gentleman." Came the loudspeaker, speaking in Maya's voice. "If I could have your attention please, it is now time to take seats for the show that is about to begin."

Everyone gathered to their seating, and Sammiel slid to Cori's side and entwined his arm in hers as they found chairs beside the central open square and next to an eccentric male couple sporting matching jumpsuits. Derrick manned a rusty old spotlight. He looked depressed as it creaked to center stage and Maya stepped forth from the stage curtains in a sequin suit that was decidedly masculine in such a way that it highlighted her feminine features. Her curly mane was done to a top knot. Her voice quivered not an bit, the stage was her home. "Hello and welcome everyone to St. Margaret's Home for the Nearly Departed. Dang, y'all lookin' lovely tonight." Maya bounced and bubbled in the way that was so natural to her. How Cori longed to be like that. "You feelin' good?" Maya asked and got a little cheer from the crowd. "I hope so, but I bet you're looking for a little music. Just give me one moment of your time, I got something I want to say first." She clasped her hands to her chest. "Thank you. A big thank you from all our residents and staff to all of you for coming out to support us. Necromancy is a little scary to some folks, but I can say right off the top of my head that you all are my sort of people. You show tolerance and open mindedness for things you might not understand, and for that I reach out to you from the bottom of my heart and give you a big old high five." Maya spoke with her arms and drew a laugh from the crowd. "Now, a few special shout outs here for some special people who grease the wheels so to speak. A big one to Maude Grimm, I'm sure you all already know to go to her for everything from pimples to the flu. She'll hook you up with effective remedies, and maybe even some feel good juice besides." Maya said with a wink. "Another to Mayor Brighton, who has always been one of the biggest proponents to keeping St. Margaret's a Remedian business. Can't say enough about this man. Well… yes I can. *Tolerable Politician.*" Maya said, again to laughs from the crowd. "Hah, just jokin' Mr. Mayor. You're handsome too."

"Now, just a little back story for those of you not familiar. Mr. Franklin G. Cosmo, the star of our show tonight, was a beloved fixture in our little town of Remedy. A lot of people knew him as a warm and friendly face that liked to peruse the shops. Some people here tonight know him, yeah I see you. What a lot of you didn't know was that Franklin was one of those gifted souls who could hear the Lady of the Lake sing, and so he took up a lifelong passion for music. You might have seen him listen to his headphones as he strolled down the street, but maybe you didn't know he played piano, cause he was just too dang nervous to play in front of others. Another thing you might not have known was that he struggled with mental illness, as many of our residents have at some time or another, and eventually that claimed his life. You also might not have known he was my Uncle, and that every birthday he would come to my house with a big plate of brownies he had cooked specially for me. They weren't any good but they sure did make my heart warm. So as you can imagine, when he was brought to St. Margaret's, I got pretty invested."

Cori's heart was wrenching with information she hadn't even begun to guess at, watching Maya's eyes as they glistened.

"Franklin always wanted to play for a crowd, but he was too damn scared. Maybe it was mental illness, or maybe it was just cause that doesn't run so naturally for everyone. He said he could puke just at the thought of it. But we've been working real hard since he came to St. Margaret's, and we've poured our hearts out into this, and tonight we have a very special treat. His first ever concert. Let's give a round of applause for Mr. Franklin G. Cosmooooooo."

The curtains slid apart at Maya's flourish and the ivory keys of the piano were already trilling complex chords in a quick display. Beside Franklin's skeleton at the piano, animated skeletal puppets controlled by Maya were on deck with a bass cello, drum, and one zombie on trumpet. Franklin finished his trill and let each take their turn giving a quick solo. Some obvious mistakes were made early on which caused Franklin to look desperately at Maya, who just nodded and ushered him forward. But everyone in the crowd was set on the edge of their seats, and soon they were all lost in the music. An early sonnet shifted to a fast drum solo which led into a ragtime diddy to get feet tapping. One by one people stood and danced. Cori lost herself to the music and theatrics, and almost hadn't noticed the way it slowed down to a romantic interlude. Sammiel's hand gripped hers and she was jarred from her mesmerization. He asked "May I have this dance?"

Cori, dumbstruck, nodded in response as he lifted her to the dance floor, and set his arm around her. Their hands clasped. Several stubbed toes and awkwardly shifted hands later, they were laughing in each other's arms.

It's just a dance. Cori told herself while avoiding Morris' suspicious gaze and a peculiar tilt of the head from Maya. *Nothing to see here folks.* Cori tried to think, but felt as though she were dancing on clouds. Their dance was elevated above the dance of all others. Theirs was singular. Cori sighed and averted her concerned eyes from Sammiel's. *I'm not ready to fall in love.*

The night carried onward with dancing and jubilation, the tapping of feet and even a good old fashioned donnybrook that involved a sister and brother, a husband and an inheritance. It was hard to tell in the chaos.

Sol would love this, Cori thought whenever someone slapped someone's shoulder or let out a raucous laugh. And soon Sol wasn't to be the only one who would be missed. A grand finale parade tune rose in crescendo and heralded forth a new set of storm clouds from all around Franklin's being, just as they had risen so recently from Sol. Gasps and Oo's were drawn from the crowd who thought it was a new pyrotastic display. But all the St. Margaret's staff watched in reserved awe as a pin prick of fractal light left Franklin's teeth in the final notes, and his skeleton tumbled with a clatter.

A new wormhole had opened. This time, it was Maya who stepped through. She was fiercely determined and ready to rise in a warp gate crackle.

Morris rose to the occasion as master of ceremonies. "Folks, we have just been witness to something spectacular…"

He began a speech, but Cori gave Sammiel a swift goodbye and disappeared into the house. She was unable to hear another word, or bear witness to another Liberation.

Chapter 12

Many weeks passed filled with routine and normalcy. The Council of Necromancer's sent a letter of congratulations for the home's recent Double Liberation. Dana's radiant figs reached maturity, and she had a brief phase of smoking meat which all the house was quite grateful for. Morris, growing in power, locked himself away for days in The Cloisters and came out calling out to the heavens, yowling like a heathen, and blissfully proclaiming that he now had the power to summon the colossal entity Agamemnon. This brought him so much joy. The toilet abomination bit Maya. Derrick fell into and out of love. Luke attained Level 12 Samadhi. Laugh's were shared, tears were shed. Cori grew sad, though she could not understand why.

She awoke to a menacing day. The sky was a deep crimson, with swiftly moving clouds. The trees swayed inordinately despite the lack of wind. Cori opened her windows to a wafting stale metallic scent. Outside, in place of wind, all that disturbed the air was the sound of a lonesome moan.

"You didn't get bloodstorms back in TerryTown?" Maya later asked Cori while they crocheted hats in the parlor with Agnus. Her empty eye sockets were determinedly focused on her slip stitches. Cori shook her head. "Shame. They're great for painting."

"It feels like something awful is about to happen." Cori said, pacing and massaging her sinuses.

"Weather isn't usually a very good predictor of events, Cori." Morris said from an adjacent room, eavesdropping. "Stars are, but not weather."

"No one else has this deep ominous feeling in their gut?" Cori asked.

"That's just the atmospheric shift." Morris said again. "Low orbital barometric parameters, you see."

"My gut gets fluttery during bloodstorms too." Maya said. "Nothing to worry about. It'll pass by dinner tonight."

"Blood always gets me a little queasy." Cori replied. "Ernie chased me this morning, his head twitching back and forth at horrible angles while blood spurted from his neck hole. Now this."

Maya ceased her knit and slammed the needles down onto the parlor table. "Shopping." She said quietly at first. "Ohhh, I've got the itch. Best thing to do in a bloodstorm, Cori." Maya said, grabbed Cori's cheeks and smooshed them. "Unghhhh, you've got to come with me, you've just got to."

"Oo, Oo--" Morris began, but Maya cut him off with "Girls day out, just you and me, Cori."

Cori looked down at her hands and watched them as they trembled. "I feel it. The tingle."

"Capitalism."

"Capitalism."

Cori did have money, now that she thought of it. Having no expenses really did wonders for her bank account, even at a low rate of pay. Together, Maya and Cori set out through the bloodstorm, all down River Road; and Cori found she eventually became used to the shadowy creatures that flitted at the edges of her vision; and the way the moon took on the fiery shape of a foreign planet. The bloodstorm was beautiful, in its own way. Maya and Cori each carried an umbrella and for the most part it was little more than a blood mist. The lonesome moaning that lingered always in the background grew unbearably loud on occasion, but for the most part this lasted only seconds.

Remedy was abandoned. There was only one child in a yellow raincoat with yellow rain boots, each dripping crimson as she stomped in puddles in unnaturally slow motion. Everyone else watched from their spired windows. Innumerable shadow folk gazed at the storm from the darkness of their home, little visible but for the candle they all held and their dull blank eyes.

"It's a religious thing." Maya explained of the people staring from their windows. "They stand vigil to ensure God fulfills her blood oath."

"Better than the Napalm tornadoes they're getting out in Nebraska. You see the video of that thing? Just decimated Lincoln."

"I can't watch videos like that, they raise my blood pressure." Maya said. "Alright, here we are." They stood under the jutting wooden and wrought iron sign for 'Mana Woven', the light armor shop for mages or otherwise roguish types. A fox animatronic tipped its top hat to them as they entered and droplets of Type O spilled onto their shoes from its motion.

"You need one super fancy piece to tie the rest of your outfit together." Maya explained as they walked into the sound of spinning looms and working class spiders. It smelled vogue, and jazzy futurism played over the speakers. "Mage gear is in the basement." Maya cued her in, grabbed Cori's shoulders and pushed her to the stair.

The basement was made of rough hewn cobblestone, lit by long green flames from the wicks of the wax upon the sharp wall sconces. These provided more adequate light than one may presume. A hunchbacked woman sat and idly scrolled Twitter. She appeared to be about nineteen and was disproportionate but pretty.

"That's Jasmine, the tailor's apprentice." Maya said, then gave a familiar "Jasminnnnne. Heyyyyyy~" They engaged in a secret handshake ritual that ended in a hip bump. "Jasmine, this is Cori. She needs some new digs."

Jasmine's one overlarge eye honed in on Cori with intense focus, the pupil dilating and constricting like the lens of a camera. "I assume you're looking for some of the darker gear?" Jasmine sniffed. "What's your price range?" She asked. Her voice was low and breathy.

Cori was willing to spend more than she was comfortable saying. "Let's just see what you've got." She said instead.

"You want enchantments?" Jasmine asked, her large eye scanned through the dresses as she flipped through. "What type of cloth?"

Cori hadn't the foggiest idea how to answer any of these questions, so instead they tried everything.

Maya tried a cosmic armor that made her entire body look like deep space. She liked it, but it didn't breathe. Cori looked dazzling in an octopus leather kimono, though she had problems with the ethics of it. Jasmine, never one to miss a fashion show, twirled in a dress that was inlaid with the moaning faces of the damned. The possibilities were endless, but Cori finally found…the One.

Cloak of the Wraith Whisperer. It had been named this by the hell priest who had woven it, then disappeared, never to be heard from again. And it was enchanted. Cori felt light as a feather inside of it. The antique gray cloth trailed off at the bottom, like ethereal flame, and Cori could scarcely feel her feet. She still had feet, but they barely felt as though they were touching the ground at all. It was either a very powerful featherweight enchantment, or a very weak levitation enchantment.

Maya looked on from a gilded chair for a long moment before declaring "That's the one."

The price tag said $1,661. Cori's throat went dry. But it was also the most glorious piece of clothing she'd ever seen in her life. "I don't know Maya, this feels wrong."

"But it's oh so right." Maya whispered softly in Cori's ear and pushed her to the cash register.

The next few moments were blank. It was the first time Cori ever doubted her free will, but she was grateful to whatever entity might have possessed her into purchasing such an exquisite piece of fashion. She regained awareness outside in the streets of Remedy while carrying a paper bag covered in plastic to prevent potential blood stain drips.

Next, they went to 'Runway Ready Armors'. The bloodstorm grew in strength and ferocity, but 'Runway Ready Armors' was just a few doors down, marked by pink neon lights, as might advertise a strip club.

The store clerk here sipped upon the heady aromas of opium from behind his counter. He might have once been handsome. This store was quite a bit quieter, and each step caused a disturbance in the old oak floorboards.

As they scanned the women's clothing section they found armor which covered only breasts, or covered everything except breasts. Maya informed Cori, "Heavy armor mixed with light armor is going to be in, I'm telling you. Heavy chest plate with flowing gown below or in your case a cloak with some heavy grieves or something. Start now, and when it hits next year you're going to be well ahead of the curve. You just have to find something that was made *after* the Patriarchy collapsed. Raoul is a little old fashioned." Maya shot Raoul, the greasy haired shopkeep, a sharp look which he did not notice.

"I don't want anything covering my new cloak." Cori said.

"Yeah let's focus on legs or boots--"

"Or gloves…" Cori said and stepped towards a pair of gloves that were protected and lit within a glass case and emitted a low radioactive vibration. It was much akin to falling in love.

'Gauntlets of the Black Rose,' read the placard from behind the display case.

"Oh Cori." Maya said. "I'm not sure I can play devil on your shoulder for this one, this trip is getting expen--"

They were outside Runway Ready armors and Cori regained consciousness only in time to find herself rubbing her own gloved hands against her cheeks. A large price tag hung off the gauntlets which read $862. The crimson clouds above now began a deluge, which pattered heavily upon their umbrellas.

"Eight hundred and sixty two dollars?!" Cori asked, suddenly despondent.

"You have a problem."

"I don't even remember buying them." Cori said. "Oh, they smell like Roses. Nearly withered roses, and rain. Normal rain. Good water rain." They were made of a banded flexible black metal and barbed with thorns which dug gently into Cori's skin. The bud of a single black rose grew on the wrist of each. The fingers were extended and sharp, like the claws of a witch. Cori flexed her hand. "These are going to be very painful to take off. Do they do anything?"

"Small mana boost." Maya said, reading the tag. "Hand wash only."

Cori shrugged. "Alright."

Cori bought black Timberland boots at the nearby "Journey's". These were distinctly not enchanted, but even though they were outlandishly expensive for ordinary boots, they felt cheap compared to her prior two purchases.

They met Jenny, the shopkeep at the thrift shop Vintage Digs, this store was located on the top floor of an old militarized tower. The bottom floor served as a converted coffee roastery, complete with copper whirligigs. Jenny was another of Maya's friends who knew whatever secret handshake Jasmine knew, which was starting to make Cori jealous.

Here, Cori was able to buy many handfuls of outfits for when she wasn't wearing The Cloak of the Wraith Whisperer. She bought cut up t-shirts and cozy pajama pants, and heavy link chains that she could wear with ease around her neck and belt whilst wearing her enchanted cloak. Upon these chains she attached an old discount grimoire she found with the used books, as well as several quirky charms. And she bought leather pants, and velvet gloves, and a witches hat with a pointed top; and a metallic mask with six eyes and a laughing but gruesome countenance which would ward off evil spirits whenever she may traverse past the veil. And all of these things together cost less than the Timberland boots.

They ate grilled and buttered corn at the Produce Cafe, Quintanilla's, and Cori was strongly compelled to order a cappuccino. Then they decided corn wasn't enough and got a beet smoothie that tasted as though the earth hadn't been washed off of it.

Some figures in the cafe looked out of the crimson windows, keeping their own stern vigil while sipping espressos. They hardly blinked. There were also college students that worked on their homework and laughed about one of their professor's faux pas. In the corner, an armored Paladin chugged a spirulina shake and spoke cordially with a gallantly clad barista who might have had Down Syndrome.

While shopping, Cori felt good. While in the cafe, Cori felt good. Cori felt good while Maya was around and she could lose herself in Maya's aura of constant exuding joy. But eventually they returned to St. Margaret's and parted ways and Cori set down her shopping bags in her room, and Cori felt sad again, and empty. The bloodstorm passed, and there was no longer an ominous sensation, and she had nearly gotten all of the blood stains out of her old clothes, but Cori still felt very sad. She felt more sad than she remembered feeling in a very long time. Sadder even than some of her worst spells in months past. Cori decided to lay down until it passed, as she felt very tired.

And she laid. And laid. And the bloodstorm passed and the sky became a normal blue for a while until evening hit and it became orange instead. And still Cori laid in her bed, feeling worse and worse. She had just bought such nice new clothes, too.

Her phone vibrated, and went unanswered. Her phone vibrated some time later and she ignored it. A phone call might have happened while she was somewhere between waking and sleeping. It all felt meaningless. There was no reason to be sad, so there was nothing to tell anyone about. She just felt sad. What else can be said?

Then, Cori started to feel nothing, and she became afraid. Nothing was much worse than sad. Night fell, moonless. Blood had soaked into the earth outside, nourishing the grass and trees. The metallic scent wafted in through a cracked open window. Cori thought about how pointless life was. She thought about how she was meaningless, and how she hadn't accomplished anything in her life. She thought about how accomplishing things wasn't worth it anyway. And if she were going to be alive, she would at least want to be the sort of person who accomplished things. But she wasn't.

And she thought of all the pain other people experienced. And she thought of how horrible some people could be to one another. She thought about how she was afraid to even care for people, because most times they'd either hurt her, or she'd hurt them, or they'd be hurt by someone else. She thought about how sometimes she doesn't feel the way she did at that moment, and sometimes she enjoyed life. Then she realized those times were all an illusion. Those were brief moments of denial. This was reality.

Cori thought about how no one would care if she were gone.

Text someone you idiot. A small voice told her. *Text someone and ask for help.*

But her body started walking to the bathroom, which now looked quite a bit like Keiran's bathroom. It was comforting and quiet.

Ask for help. Nothing lasts forever, except this. You don't get any more choices if you do this.

But another voice, silent, told her that those thoughts were a meaningless anomaly. Irrational.

"Maya, I think I need to talk to someone." Cori texted through enormous effort. There was a phone call seconds later, and through another enormous effort Cori answered the phone.

Chapter 13

"First off, I can assure you that here at St. Margaret's we take mental and spiritual health with every degree of seriousity that we would take physical health." Morris began, then his eyes widened, like an infant's eyes, and sparkled with prismatic color. "Yes, yes, it is very clear that your chakras are totally out of whack. Look at that. Simply hideous. I'm sorry, Cori. I should have seen it before."

Cori felt more affronted by her chakras being called hideous than if her face had been called hideous. "Can you see why they're like that?" Cori asked, while Maya patted Cori on the knee. They sat in Morris' office, which he had redecorated and renovated since his acquisition of the entity Agamemnon into his summoner's repertoire. Simplified somewhat, decluttered. The room was now lit by a glowing magick crystal that was suspended and bound by chain links. Its glow throbbed rhythmically. The unicorn skull was still in place, but new paintings had been hung on the walls, including oily works that were recognizable as the painting Madman Debauchus, known for his unfathomably eerie depictions of the nu wave cults of Southern France. "You can't just tell me my chakras are out of whack and leave me hanging."

The colors in Morris' eyes intensified. His irises grew larger yet. He stood and leaned over to get a closer look, then began to crawl over the desk to get an even closer look. His nose brushed lightly against Cori's cheek as he scanned her up and down. Then he drew back into his chair with a deep sigh. "Just as I'm sure we all knew, it was your encounter with Keiran. It's so so clear. Some old buried trouble from your past is providing a small feast for his dark energies, which have split off and become like a small demon baby in your innards. It looks like we're in the obsession phase of spiritual possession, yes. That feast will only grow larger, and with it, the darkness will spread."

Cori laughed. "You're kidding." She said, continued to chuckle, then looked back and forth at Maya and Morris who both looked grave. "You've got to be kidding."

Morris shook his head. Then he sat back in his chair and started texting. Maya and Cori sat in Morris' office silently as the cat clock ticked off slowly and shook its eyes and tail back and forth. And Morris texted.

"That's all you're gonna give us?" Maya asked after too much waiting.

Morris held up a finger, and grinned while looking at his phone. Then he started texting again. He could hardly contain his growing smile. Then he started speaking very slowly while texting. "Paladins...." He said and tapped away furiously. "That's the unfortunate reality…uhhhh… necromancers aren't the best exorcists." Then he blushed a deep crimson. Cori wasn't sure she had ever seen him blush. It didn't suit him. He put down his phone. "Ahem. Excuse moi. Yes, where were we?"

"Necromancers aren't the best exorcists." Maya said.

"Ah yes. But Paladins are. Unfortunately, Paladins and Necromancers don't get along. So we're screwed." Morris said, and bit his lip. Cori and Maya waited for a moment. There was the undeniable air that Morris had more to say as he looked at them back and forth, still attempting to conceal a smirk. "Or we *would* be screwed if you didn't have the best boss in the world. Turns out, I have connections."

"Is that so?" Maya asked, folding her arms.

"Yes, Maya. That is so." Morris said, smugly. "As it so happens, my old childhood friend Aislynn O'Cuillen has a more liberal attitude than some of her peers and counterparts. You've all met Aislynn, yes? I turned one of her comrades inside out, do you remember?"

Maya's eyes sharpened. "Oh, I remember. And how is Aislynn doing, Morris?" She asked with no small hint of sarcasm.

Morris' eyes curled. "Oh, she's just swell."

"Mhm. That's what I thought." Maya crossed her arms.

"So, Aislynn can perform an exorcism on me?"

"Well...no." Morris replied to Cori. "Nor will anyone in her order. Butttttt-- She knows someone. A Ronin of sorts, except not Japanese. Damnit, Kitsune is rubbing off on me. What would be the equivalent of a Ronin in English?"

"Rogue agent?" Maya asked after swiftly looking at the thesaurus in her phone.

"Doesn't flow off the tongue as well, though, does it? Rogue Agent. Rogue Agent...Ronin...But I digress. He left the Order to pursue his own path, but naturally retained all of his skills. He was apparently one of the greats. He is in retreat, up in the Moldivine Mountains to the North of here. And Aislynn O'Cuillen, bless her soul, has agreed to take you, Cori."

"Okay, so *he* will perform an exorcism on me…"

"Ehhh--I really don't know what Paladin types do. Most likely he will chant at you until you feel guilty for every errant sexual thought you've ever had, but I don't know maybe they actually do things. I guess we will see, right? Aislynn will be here in a few days after she takes care of some whatever. Until then...Cori, do you have a safe space?"

"A safe space? Like...my room?"

Morris snorted. "Really, your room is hardly 'safe'. I mean---sorry---it's relatively safe, for sure. Definitely. But I mean like a *really* safe space."

"I'm not following…" Cori said, and Maya raised an eyebrow as well.

"Did you ever wind up finishing that book I lent you? *Etheric Algorithms in Theory and Practice*."

"Oh yeah, totally like…" Cori stammered. She had finished chapter one over the course of a month. "You know, I've been plugging away at it. Haven't quite finished it yet, but...I'm close."

"Have you gotten to the part about Dimensional Spatiality and the Codec Physics of Astral Space?"

"Almost there...yeah, like, I'll get to that part soon. Been real excited."

"Well step to it." Morris said. "It describes the creation of pocket realms. They're beautiful things. Can't afford a vacation?

Pocket Realm. Introvert who needs a vacation where no one exists in the same dimension as you? Pocket Realm. Trying to dodge the watchful eyes of the government? Pocket Realm. Paranoid about the slowly encroaching darkness of demonic obsession? *Pocket Realm*. You can simply write it into the very structure of the place that only you are allowed in there."

"That actually sounds...wonderful." Cori said.

Then Maya chimed in. "And you know what you're going to do, Morris?"

"Maybe?"

"You're going to give Cori the day off tomorrow so she can work on that, aren't you?" Maya said. "I believe Cori has a rain check which states you owe her one and then some."

Morris' eyes narrowed. Maya's eyes narrowed further. Morris' aura became visible, and scarlet. Maya's aura flared emerald. Their auras grew while Cori looked on. She had never seen anything like this happen before. Red pushed against green, but green pirouetted round and pushed harder against red. They intensified. Objects in the room began to rumble as though there were an earthquake, then some lighter objects began to float. Lightning crackled, and some papers on Morris' desk started to brown with fire. The green was distinctly dominant near the end before--

"Yes, of course." Morris said, and just like that the auras were gone, and the room was as it had been before. "I had been thinking of doing exactly that, Maya. Thank you for reminding me. Cori, you may have tomorrow off provided you utilize your time to read that book and subsequently create a pocket realm for yourself to utilize in times of need."

Cori shuffled her feat. "I'm not quite sure I could finish the book in just one day…"

"But the chapter on Dimensional Spatiality and the Codec Physics of Astral Space is almost the last chapter. You said you were almost there." Morris said, his brow furrowing.

Maya answered for Cori. "Morris, Cori can't read your dry ass reference guide as quick as you can."

"Is your reading augmentation broken?" Morris asked, his irises widened again.

"I don't errr--have a reading augmentation?" Cori said, and both Morris and Maya looked surprised. "I just like to read."

"How primeval." Morris said. "Would you like a reading augmentation?"

"Does it hurt?"

"A little." Morris gave an infernal grin, then pulled a jar from below his desk that contained what looked to be the shadow of a centipede.

"You just keep those things under your desk?" Maya asked.

"Don't judge me." Morris scowled. "Maya could you conjure up a Literature Elemental for me? I'm plum tuckered."

Maya pulled out her phone and opened an app, 'evoc'. She scrolled through and chose the summoner's circle that suited her, followed by the proper pentacle, and the appropriate surrounding sigils. Then she aimed her camera at the desk, and laser light shone the evocation circle all upon the wood in bright black technicolor. Maya touched her fingers to it, rolled her eyes up into her head, and chanted under her breath.

Letters and characters from every conceivable language gathered at Maya's fingertips and weaved themselves into and out of sentences. These all wrapped into the shape of a small humanoid.

"I'm not so sure I'm ready to do this." Cori said, still caught up on the way Morris grinned when he said it would hurt 'a little'.

"Nonsense." Morris dismissed her with a wave of his hand and opened the jar that contained the shadow of a centipede. It crawled out quickly, and though the Literature Elemental tried to defend itself, the elemental was swiftly overpowered and then devoured by the shadowy arthropod, which now had letters and characters and sentences of its own crawling across its dark length. The Literature Centipede looked over at Morris, and Morris pointed at Cori with an excited and sadistic nod.

Cori backed out of her chair quickly, but the centipede was quicker. It went down the desk and crawled up her leg. Cori was surprised how crisply she could feel its little legs scamper up her body. At her neck, it burrowed into her skin. It was more than a little painful. She could feel it as it dug its way up into her skull where it got stuck for a time. It scraped and dug, then finally nestled into her brain. Here it stayed and formed its nest by crawling and hollowing out circles upon circles.

"You'll thank me when you're older." Morris said as Cori screamed.

Cori became a newly born literary savant. It was miraculous, and worth the excruciating hours she spent coping with the burrowing pains of her augmentation. Time slowed, and each word rang with meaning no matter how quickly she brushed past the words with her eyes. Her memory became digitized with a flawless and picturesque recollection. It was the greatest gift she had ever received. Cori finished a short novel during her morning cappuccino.

'*Etheric Algorithms in Theory and Practice*'s' instructions and tutorials really weren't all that hard to grasp, once you got a handle on them. Nor were the ideas contained in the *Sombranomicon* which Cori found and read in the hour following. She was a little nervous to try the skills she learned for herself, but starting with the enchantment 'bottomless pockets', Cori found she could weave code with the best of them. She read a guide to the Betwixt and an Astral Bestiary before leaving.

Cori entered her closet and gazed at the chalk geometries which she now understood intimately. She could now use this same entrance to the Betwixt to build her pocket universe. Her clothes lay to either side of the walk in closet, and Cori changed into her new outfit. Her Cloak of the Wraith Whisperer. Her Gauntlets of the Black Rose. Her six eyed mask, with which she might ward off evil spirits. Her Timberlands. Then she stepped through, weightlessly, into the shodden Realm of the Betwixt.

Her nerves crackled as she stepped through dimensions. Colors waded through her like fruity liquid. This place which had once been a great mystery now took on a rational tone after Cori had digested the algorithms involved in its creation. The Betwixt was just another scientific anomaly, like gravity and summoning entities. Creating a pocket realm here would be easy. Cori just had to figure out where she'd like to put it. She needed easy access, but she wanted it hidden. So she went to the inversely mirrored gardens of etheric St. Margaret's, out in the backyard. These Ethereal gardens were detached from the rest of the building, and separated by a large chasmatic gulf, a drop into the Abyss. The sky here was full of stars and ringed planets, and the gardens were unlike anything Cori had ever seen. Plants grew midair, without any need for dirt. They were plants as had never been seen in the Mundane, plants that eat only the light of distant stars. Plants that vibrated sensually.

Just through the gardens were the wooded lands beyond St Margaret's. The trees here smiled at Cori languidly. One in particular had a large knot for a mouth. This resembled a door if you squinted your eyes hard enough. Cori decided to use this knot to press a new spatial bubble into existence. Through the tree, she imposed a tunnel. Up, up, up into the high frequencies, unlocking Bardos as she rose, up into Summerland.

It was emptiness, and then there was a hazy light, like the sun trying to come through thick clouds. There was earth, and it was good. Just a patch floating in the dim nothingness. Upon this Cori laid flowers and grasses and bushes and a flowing crook amongst the rocks and reeds. She made a glade and a natural veranda to gaze out upon a cosmic landscape of her own design, with a small cocktail bar besides, and sun chairs.

Cori placed a pool that was made of the same stuff as the ocean, with coral and shells and fish which would never poop. She placed palms and fruit bearing trees; new fruits, fruits like a peach pulp coconut which spilled nectar from its cup-like interior, Golden nectar. She added a bungalow, and then a castle-like cathedral some third mile beyond. Vines grew up the masonry of the castle and the stained glass of the arched windows consisted of vivid moments from Cori's own life. Her water birth, losing her parents in a crowd, kindergarten graduation, meeting her best friend Melanie, learning to drive, Melanie's subsequent betrayal with Aurelius, the death of Aurelius, her interview with Morris, her encounter with Keiran. Cori added an overgrown altar, growing with moon flowers, where she could place her six eyed mask and black rose gloves. The rooftop was open, and gazed out upon a broken planet which

Cori birthed in a moment's inspiration. She added a bedroom on a balcony, a stuffed kitchen, and a plump couch.

Her realm was an otherworldly garden of delight. Cori built a library into her cathedral, and a meditation space in the highest castle tower. Water plummeted from a healing spring on the fifth floor, and fell silently into a flowing crook below. Everything was silent. Not in the way that it didn't make noise. Things still made noise, but they were silent.

Cori allowed crystals to grow into and out of the ground. They felt as though they were already there, and she simply had to give them permission to exist. They grew organically, like plants. Of course, everyone knows that crystals are just the fossils of the beings who live deep in the earth's mantle. But these crystals here felt like the living beings themselves. They Emanated and resonated and sparkled in a thousand hues.

Cori finally allowed herself to settle and refresh now that her work was complete. None of the thoughts which plagued her in the Mundane plagued her here. None of those questions of whether she was worthy of love plagued her here. None of the tormenting thoughts of abandonment, none of the immense weight of empathy. Her cathedral was silent, and so was the large circular bed complete with dozens of floofy pillows. Here, she rested. Blissful repose for 48 days. Each day was just shy of an hour in the Mundane by her exhaustive calculations. All this fell short of the 49 it would take to be unwillingly ushered forth to the Villa of Ormen and into Final Liberation. It was a rest to ease her soul for the days ahead, A blank slate with which to start afresh before her coming exorcism, and all that she feared it might entail.

When she awoke finally and returned once more to her cozy room in the Mundane, she stood taller, and held a keen look in the determined set of her eyes. Her worst thoughts plagued her almost immediately, but she fought them off with a new found vigor, and the sight of hope at the end of a long and very dark tunnel.

Chapter 14

It was evening, just after Burrito Bonanza night, and Cori was lost in a foundry of words and knowledge. Her reading augmentation plowed her through piles of medical scrolls and the dry printed logs of the employees of old. She sat with her pipe filled to the brim with a blue lotus tobacco mixture and read by candlelight. Cori had spent the days of anticipation leading to her exorcism here in the archives and the depths of research. Little was of value, but with her new found sonic reading skills, she was able to crunch numbers till she found little nuggets of wisdom. For example, George's main hobby had been hiking. This stood out to Cori. It was an activity by which means he was able to control his depression in the years logged by the psychiatric institute. She also discovered that Keiran lived in Crescent Vale, the town adjacent to her own hometown of Terry Town. It had been nearly an hour with no more important bits, until Cori stumbled upon a half burned page in Agnus' file.

"This is the log of Doctor Gwynyth, daughter of Doctor Gwyndolyn, and first of the line of Molbog Dondarius, concerning patient 0574188 who has recently been admitted to The Psychiatric Facility at Gil-Galad for witchcraft and heresy. Agnus Tomlin, as she was named by her parents, is a ninety two year old quiescent female who seems resistant to traditional measures of therapy. In accordance with the High Inquisitors DSM-VII, a diagnosis of witchcraft is to be most severely rooted out before such ideas can spread to the other patients. As such, Agnus is in isolation until we can further correct her pertinacious attitude. In my softness of heart, I permitted her a doll to keep her company, though this appears to have been folly, as the doll is a new object of occult fascination for Agnus. She has given it the name Vivian, and often holds lengthy conversation with it, though this has only been observed in isolation. With this in mind, I believe I have no choice but to proceed directly to electroshock therapy, lest the Order of Paladins begin to presume my own mind is besotted with arcane fascination."

Cori puffed at her pipe and grumbled. It was the last page by Doctor Gwynyth. "The Psychiatric Facility at Gil-Galad, hmmmm…"

Cori could have sworn she had seen a stack of papers labeled with the same logo in one of the purge boxes from the years before the fall of the Patriarchy. She sought it out utilizing her now photographic memory, and found more logs concerning Agnus Tomlin otherwise known as patient 0574188. Logs by one Doctor Gwynyth.

"I am at my wits end with patient 4188. Electroshock therapy was at first a success, and all of Agnus' esoteric ramblings ceased. There were several productive months where Agnus spoke only of the most mundane fixtures of daily living, and found solace in her scheduled routines. Tea time, cooking, self care. Inquisitor Jafari was most pleased. But recordings revealed her continued obsession with her doll Vivian. At first, this was assumed to be a harmless byproduct of her electroshock therapy, an infantilization, or regression. But soon it became clear by Agnus' responses to the doll that Vivian was now speaking of all the same witchcraft that Agnus had been admitted for. I have tried to approach this with empathy, to prevent Agnus receiving a frontal lobotomy, or worse. It is my professional opinion that Agnus has experienced a depersonalization effect during her therapy, and imprinted a piece of her mind upon the doll. However, I feel eyes upon me at all times now, and there are whisperings amongst the other psychiatrists that I too am coming under the sway of esoteric compulsion. Still, I cannot quiet my mind's own questions, however I try. It is only for the sake of science that I record that I, myself, have heard the doll whisper now. It is a secret that burdens my soul."

Cori threw several papers aside which contained nothing of interest, medication administration records, and genealogies. She grumbled till she found a new document, a certificate of death, by immolation no less. Or, not just one, but two. Agnus Tomlin, and Doctor Gwynyth Dondarius; both tried for terminal witchcraft.

"By God." Cori exclaimed and slammed her palm down on her desk, then accidentally inhaled too much smoke and set off on a coughing fit.

Next morning, more reading. It had been her sole passtime between shifts as of late. Cori warmed up by reading *A Brief History of Void* in which a mathematical theorem is postulated to explain the inevitable spontaneity of consciousness from infinite nothingness. She eased her way further in by reading *The Transmigration of Species*, where a case is made for guided evolution via reincarnation. Then, Cori read eighteen books about horticulture and martial arts and philosophy and elemental psychology.

"Someone here for you, dear." Luke announced to her just as she was on the last chapter of her last book. "A Paladin, I believe." His automaton sputtered, and spat out oil from behind.

"And her hair, how like the sun.

Much as the solstice gleams in promise,

cast a light upon the dark.

Is she incorruptible? I think not.

Yet, to save mine eyes, she has it done.

Yes, I think I am saved

from the terrors of the bleak.

To gaze at her

Is a final gift

for this elderly fool."

Cori paused a moment at Luke's prose, then came up with a diddy of her own. "Oh, what awaits me, dearest Luke? My rest is at an end. For you may see her beauty, but me, am I condemned? The darkness hangs above me, the rack, the noose, the axe. Is this to be my folly, or will I instead ascend?"

Luke smiled clapped his little gremlin hands, his beady eyes widened with joy. "Splendid."

Cori gave a little bow, and left for her room. As she grew in her magickal abilities with her recent spasmodic fits of reading, she was able to create and send a Servile Construct down to the foyer to inform Aislynn O'Cuillen that she'd be a few minutes. The Construct was a miasmatic logarithm crafted in the likeness of Tom Hiddleston, and Cori kept it around on evenings and weekends for this very reason. It wasn't yet of material stuff, but it was just darling to look at and talk to.

Knowing they would be departing on an adventure, Cori wore her various and most expensive gear. She grabbed chocolate chip pumpkin muffins that she had baked in anticipation. She also grabbed other more nutritious foods because she really wasn't sure how long she would be gone. She grabbed Strawburry Shmucknicks from the cupboard, and a breakfast burrito Maya had made the night before that likely wasn't intended for Cori at all. She grabbed canned peaches and croissants, a couple sausages and spices, sweet and sour chicken and a can of dolphin soup. She really should have been preparing more thoroughly in advance. The minutes were dragging. But then, suddenly, she was ready. And then she wasn't. She had forgotten her toothbrush and deodorant and hair tie, and a book for when she couldn't sleep, her phone charger and also a belt.

Really, she could have done all this the night before, but she had been too busy journaling about Sammiel and why she and he could never be; and how unfathomable and oceanic her emotions were.

"Aislynn, I'm so sorry to keep you waiting." Cori said and dragged her pack of food and necessities behind her. "Oh hey Morris."

"Hey." Morris said coolly from behind his sunglasses. He had been on the porch talking with Aislynn. "Anyway, I'm psyched you can go on this little vacay, but then after that we could plan something together, just for us. You and I. I dunno, maybe the Maldives. You in?"

Cori really wasn't sure what she was seeing, but Aislynn appeared to be smitten with this boggling attempt at flirtation that Morris had put on. Morris wasn't even wearing one of his robes, just yoga pants with no shirt. His chest was gray and hairy but he was otherwise well built in the way that skinny middle aged men can be. "Morris, did you dye your hair?" Cori asked, not intending at all to be a damper on Morris' affair, but legitimately surprised by the unnatural black depth of his otherwise salt and pepper hair. She regretted it as soon as she said it.

Morris turned sullen. He looked between Cori and Aislynn. His sunglasses blocked any view of his eyes, but Cori was sure they were watery. "Cori, I wish you well on your journey--" Morris choked out, then quickly excused himself into the foggy darkness of the house.

"Morris…" Aislynn called after him. Then Aislynn sighed. "You must be Cori. I believe we've met before... He's very sensitive, isn't he?"

"He's something." Cori said. "Nice to see you again, Aislynn. Thank you for doing this for me."

"My pleasure. You're all packed and ready? Nice cloak." Aislynn commented on Cori's flowing wraith garments.

"Thanks, sweet armor." Cori responded.

"Thanks." Aislynn said. She was wearing angelically styled mythril chest plate armor with silver chainmail and lapis trim. Blue and white cloth stretched down her legs above her sharpened mythril greaves. A greatsword encumbered her back that looked stylish, yet with a priority on efficacy rather than show. Between her loadout and the ageless wisdom lined in her face, she made for an imposing figure. Behind Aislynn was a gothic stagecoach manned by a cloaked reaper and pulled by steeds of nightshade. Fog surrounded the vessel. Aislynn saw Cori's surprise.

"Morris summoned it for us." Aislynn said, looking back and rolling her eyes. "It's really not that long of a journey. We're just going up to the Chapel at St. Luc up in the Moldivine Mountains. Would be just a few days' walk."

"And who are we going to see exactly?"

"My old mentor, Ichabod. He is the greatest exorcist since Jean Baptiste. You will be in very good hands." Aislynn said this and looked towards the sky with reverence.

The reaper at the helm of the coach beckoned them to board, wordlessly. Inside was a luxurious matinee of red silk, lit by sconces, and made more enticing by a decanter filled with an effervescent green liquid beside two crystal glasses.

"I hope I'm not being too forward to suggest that Morris might have a bit of a crush on you." Cori said, then bounced a bit on the carriage cushions. "Figure we might as well be open with one another if we're going to be traveling together."

"No, not too forward at all." Aislynn sighed, then, "And yes, I've been picking up on some hints."

"And you?" Cori gave a suggestive wag of her eyebrow.

"Me? I'm in a precarious position, I suppose." Aislynn said, and Cori waited for her to elaborate as the carriage lurched forward, swift as the dead. "He clashes with my career aspirations, somewhat."

"But do you like him?" Cori asked.

"A girl has got to have some secrets." Aislynn said with a wink. "At the moment he's coming on a bit strong."

It was very easy to talk to Aislynn, Cori noticed quickly. They had just spoken a few sentences now in total and Cori was already finding her to be a very grounded and amicable sort. She came off as down to earth, candid in speech, and warm in demeanor. She spoke deliberately, and her words were well enunciated. She was very different from the night creatures Cori had been spending all of her time with these days. "Is it working?"

Aislynn laughed. "Not really. And I've told him that, but he isn't getting the hint. Hah. It's not even a hint, who am I kidding? No, there were a few days before he asked me out where he was acting very naturally. But since I told him I had to think about things he's been putting on some new airs."

It was tempting to poke fun at Morris. All the staff at St. Margaret's did so quite regularly. But for all the jabs, Cori had become somewhat fond of him. "He just gets nervous." Cori said. "He's got a little puppy dog heart, but if he really likes you he probably just wants you to think he's--"

"Big and bold and dangerous." Aislynn chimed in. "And rich and manly."

"It's very hard to imagine Morris acting manly." Cori said.

"It's just as hard to watch it." Aislynn said, then crinkled her nose up. "What do you think this green stuff is?"

"Only one way to find out." Cori said. "We've got a long ride."

"Think it'll be breaking any of my oaths?" Aislynn smirked, took the top off the decanter, and poured two glasses.

"I won't tell if you don't." Cori said, and they locked arms as they took a shot from their crystal glasses in unison. It tasted like electrified cinnamon, if cinnamon were green.

The effect was apparent within a minute. They turned into monsters, both of them. Cori grew antlers out of her head, and a fiery glow now echoed from within her pointed maw. Aislynn became a scarecrow, her limbs extended and multiplied.

"Dude." Cori said.

"I'm not sure I'm fond of this." Aislynn grasped at her seat.

"Are you serious? This is awesome." Cori said. She opened her phone and quickly texted lines to the staff group chat. The land became more autumnal and dark outside their carriage windows. "What is this stuff?"

"How are you so calm?" Aislynn asked, her own voice was calm, but she was marveling and horrified at her own dysmorphic hands, which grew eyes and tentacles in place of fingers.

"Not a whole lot scares me anymore since I started working at St. Margaret's. Now I'm just afraid of things like...infinite void. This is nothing." Cori said. Her phone pinged. She opened her phone "Oh it's *All Hallow's Draught,* Morris says. It turns everything into Halloween."

"Please tell me it doesn't last long." Aislynn asked. One of her eyeballs spilled from her scarecrow head.

Cori texted once again, then turned her attention to the world outside as she waited. Pale Riders cackled as they rode under the orange midday moon. All the trees were dead and adorned with hanging corpses, like little satanic ornaments. Cori's phone pinged again. "Should only be a few hours." Cori told Aislynn, whose face might have been growing pale and sickly if her skin wasn't now made of stained burlap. "I figured as a Paladin you could just get all glowy and remove status effects or something."

Scarecrow Aislynn looked sidelong at Wendigo Cori. "You don't know much about Paladins do you?"

"Actually, I come from a long line of Clerics and Paladins."

"Is that so?" Aislynn asked, taking on an extra tone of cordiality that contrasted her scarecrow features and rising terror. "You did strike me differently than the other Necromancers. Every family has got one, don't they?"

"You're telling me."

"Don't let it get to you. Necromancers and Paladins have more in common than you might think. The man we're going to see, there's a reason he left our Order. He had begun to study Necromancy himself."

"I like him better already."

"All the Saints that your houses are named after, St. Margaret, St. Victus, St. Andrew, those are all people that were beatified by *both* the Council of Necromancers and the Order of Paladins. Did you know that?" Aislynn asked, and Cori shook her head, then Aislynn nodded back at her. "That's why my mentor Ichabod left. He said it is only by studying both that we see the truth. I've been thinking about it ever since."

Cori pondered for a time. "I've never felt quite complete as just a Necromancer. Don't get me wrong, I couldn't stand the precepts my family lived under. But I've never felt complete leaving them either. I love everyone at St. Margaret's, but I do feel like something is missing in myself."

"You are not alone. Ichabod had said much the same thing before he left. Ah, talking does help distract me from all of the--" Aislynn motioned to a pile of snake eggs that hatched while the carriage room slithered with tiny black serpents. Some slithered over Cori's wide wendigo eyes. "That."

"Well, allow me to distract you further." Cori said. "I want to learn."

"Learn what?" Aislynn asked.

"Paladin stuff."

Aislynn frowned. "It's strictly forbidden."

"I'm sure a lot of what we're doing is strictly forbidden, isn't it?"

"You're not wrong… Alright. But only if you teach me some Necromancy. I had refused to follow Ichabod when he left." Aislynn popped her eye back into her burlap face, and pulled apart the stitching that kept her mouth nearly sewn shut. "The way Ichabod had explained it to me is that they are two currents. One brings the light of an individual's soul upwards, towards Liberation. That would be the Necromancers. The other brings the light of the Oversoul downwards to Manifestation. By this light we heal and maintain the world, such as it is. But they do not speak of this. Paladins say Necromancers manipulate souls away from their natural order, and end that which may not yet need to end. They think all life is precious, and should be held onto for as long as possible. Those undead you care for, Paladins consider them unclean spirits who should be left to their own devices, or fought against if they pose a threat. But then, Necromancers say Paladins bind things in place, and keep things stuck which need to be free. Necromancers claim we Paladins are committing sacrilege when we resurrect a soul is ready to die and be free."

"But both are useful…" Cori said.

"That's what Ichabod taught me. He said that even the most fervent Necromancer will Resurrect someone they love. Even the most zealous Paladin will bring their deceased Grandmother to a home like St. Margaret's to be Liberated. The hatred is unfounded."

They spent hours divulging secrets and mysteries most profound. They spoke of the unspoken, ruminated on the transmundane, repudiated ignorance, and held civil discourse on the apparent contradictions between their beliefs. Aislynn taught Cori golden healing spells. Cori taught Aislynn dark illusions. Their carriage rolled silently and swiftly through a ghoulish village where witches were being burned at the stake and men became wolves and ravens plucked at the eyes of sleepy children. But slowly, the effects of the drought became lesser, and the land grew lush and everything took on a very joyful and not-at-all-frightening Christmas effect that Aislynn enjoyed very much. Cori, by contrast, was struck with an almost convulsive uneasiness. Luckily, the crash from the drought wasn't terrible, and soon they were at baseline. They had a very ordinary evening of driving through a mushroom forest at the base of the Moldivine Mountain range, riding in a gothic carriage manned by a grim spectre and pulled by nightmares. The mushroom forest was very pretty, and twinkled with fairies.

They set up camp as it grew dark and settled into the ruins of an old cobblestone farm house which still had a partial roof and a fireplace intact. Cori, brilliant with the recent ingestion of countless books, created a construct to do all the work for both her and Aislynn. It was made of crackling ether and a lode of quickly compiled arcane code. She gave it the body of Tom Hiddleston again, but more physical this time. He gathered their firewood and swept the old floors and neatly arranged their luggage and massaged them both in turn. He even took it upon himself to decorate and make the bleak ruins into a home so that by morning there was a breakfast nook and sunflowers in a vase by the window. Cori's powers were becoming immaculate with all her new knowledge and recent acquisition of Paladin spells. It would have caused her great joy if it weren't for the ever encroaching darkness she felt laying siege to her heart. Arcane Construct Tom Hiddleston could see right through her.

"You seem lost to your thoughts. Is everything alright?" Tom Hiddleston asked her in his luxuriously supple voice.

"It's nothing, Tom." Cori said, then, "A little lower. Yesss, right there. Is that a knot?"

"I don't understand how your feet get so tense." said Arcane Construct Tom Hiddleston. He utilized a massage oil that he had made during the night from locally sourced olives that he had stolen off the trees of the locally sourced co-operative olive farm. It was the only functioning olive farm in a five hundred mile radius. There was a small patch in the mountains where olives grew extraordinarily well, and no one knew why anyone thought to try growing olives so far out of their natural environment in that one particular patch to find out in the first place. It was a source of mystery, and many legends had sprung up around it.

"I need shoes with better padding." Cori said. "Oh, I don't know, Tom Hiddleston. Nothing feels right anymore. I have no right to feel sad, I know. Everything is going so well. I have a lot of friends who care about me, a good job, everything to eat. I remind myself to be grateful so often, but I just feel sad anyway. I've just...I've got no right to be sad."

"You have every right to be sad." Tom Hiddleston explained. "Feelings don't lie. If you're feeling sad, that's because you're meant to feel sad right now. Maybe you don't know why you're feeling sad, but there is something valid about your sadness. You have every right to your sorrow. Feel it. Listen to it."

"I do...or...I don't want to. I'm afraid to. Because there's too much sadness. As much as everything is good, everything is so confusing too. I feel like I'm learning too much, too fast. I'm growing too fast. I'm seeing too much of the world and it's just drowning me in numbness and sorrow. Oh god, right there. That hurts. No, don't stop. It feels good, it just hurts." Cori said, writhing under Tom Hiddleston's foot massage.

"I suggest seeking the advice of an expert. It can be hard to reach out to others, especially strangers, but it's ultimately as important as going to see any other doctor."

"I am, that's where we're off to right now."

"Oh, brilliant. Well you're right on your way then, aren't you?"

"Way ahead of you Tom Hiddleston, but thank you."

They only had to ride in the carriage a few hours that morning to arrive at their destination. They passed a small mountain town, Dwyver's Point, famous for being the home of the Tomorrowers, a cult, or *collective* as they liked to be called, that believed they were cosmic praying mantis' in human skin. Soon, they had said, they would shed that human skin and they'd be able to fly through the cosmos on space bending plasma wings. Then they'd fly into a wormhole that leads to the fifth dimension, bypassing the Betwixt and all the classic rules which invariably applied to everyone else.

The Tomorrowers were famous because of their divine lavender bath bombs, and the fact that their prophecy actually came true. The entire population of Dwyver's Point actually did turn into Space Mantises and they did fly off into a nearby wormhole in the Rembulon system of the Milky Way Galaxy. No one saw that coming.

"Ichabod lives in the Chapel at St. Luc up by Culvar's Pass under Mt. Hammurabi." Aislynn said, then asked. "You alright?" Cori gave a very convincing smile, even as the weight of all the world pulled her heart down to blackness. But Aislynn's eyes were clear from her many profound meditations. "Ichabod is going to help, alright?" Aislynn said, and Cori's smile grew weak. "This isn't just you. Try to detach yourself from it. Recognize that it is not the way the world is, but rather the way a demon is making you see it."

Cori nodded, though her struggle was great.

Culvar's Pass was a gorgeous vista overlooking the sprawling Moldivine Mountain range and lands beyond. One stood above clouds and could spot the town of Remedy and the misty cliffs on Lake Talula and the Talula River and Dwyver's point and towns Cori hadn't even thought to explore, being so ingratiated in her various new cultures as she was. The vista caught her breath, and for a moment Cori forgot her heaviness. The air in the mountains was buoyant and fresh and it smelled of clouds and dewy herbs.
    "C'mon, the Chapel at St. Luc isn't far." Aislynn said and stepped from the carriage and motioned Cori to a mysterious stone stairway hidden in the brush. The carriage, driver, and nightmare steeds disappeared in a flash of fire and brimstone as Cori and Aislynn carried their packs upwards, stair by stair through the brush and stone and ivy and wildflower that formed Mount Hammurabi. The higher they climbed the thinner the mountain fog became and slowly revealed their destination, the Chapel at St. Luc's.
    The Chapel at St. Luc's was a modest structure set upon the only floating island cluster in the Moldivine Mountain Range. Suspended in midair by old and frightening deities for reasons no one remembers, the island complex was reachable only by the enormous ropes which connected it to the top of Mt. Hammurabi, and held the islands tethered to this world like a balloon.
    Climbing the enormous ropes was tricky. The curvature and constant swaying in the wind made it a disarming structure, and the clouds were often so thick as to cut off all visibility. Cori's cloak enchantment made her entirely graceful, but the challenge of climbing the ropes was still great, and Cori really wasn't in shape at all. Thus, her struggle was balanced out to be approximately equal to the struggle Aislynn was encountering, in shape but without enchantments. As the ropes grew steeper and the climb grew higher and the wind grew fiercer and Cori's fingers grew achier, vertigo set in with a dizzying panic in the primal parts of Cori's brain. The Panic was nice. It wasn't heavy like the Sorrow.
    It was misty, this high up. The sun disappeared behind the fog of high altitude clouds. In the distance the Chapel could only be seen by squinting the eyes and gazing through a veil. Pleasant and

gloomy, the colors here popped, unrestrained as they were by the harsh lights of the sun. The grass was greener, the wildflowers sparkled brilliantly, and the air itself had a rainbow in every inch. The air rippled, gaseous. It reminded Cori of the Miasma in St. Margaret's, but sanctified somehow.

Crossing from Island to Island via the ropes, the lands below occasionally came into view from a break in the clouds. Cori hadn't even been aware of how far they had climbed, but looking down below Cori thought she could see the gentle curvature of the Earth. And my, how the air had gotten thin.

The Chapel came into view, simple but luxuriant. It emanated warmth like a cottage. Herbs and barrels of wheat and potatoes gathered next to piles of firewood and a well tended but stubborn English garden. The smoky smell of a spicy stew emanated through the extra terrestrial airs.

"Aislynn." A voice from beyond a cypress grove hummed the name gruffly.

"Ichabod."

Chapter 15

Maya pursed her lips as she set to work and repaired the bindings on Keiran's room. Keiran watched her as she worked, levitated in the middle of his room and panted. It was an unusual behavior for him, but he had been otherwise quiet for some time, so Maya left him to it.

"You're quiet." Keiran said.

"Just focused." Maya replied tersely. She painted the paper of the warding sigils with blessed inks.

"You're lying."

"I've got a lot on my mind."

This response made Keiran sullen, and he drew closer to Maya, who recoiled.

"Don't touch me." She said.

Keiran's eyes flashed with anger, then confusion, then despondence. "Then why not just do away with me? Everyone is so convinced that I'm a monster, bind me up already!"

Maya set down her tools and took a deep breath. "I'm not giving up on you yet."

"Only Margaret could save me now…" Keiran said under his breath.

"Keiran, you're not half as hopeless as you think you are. You are a prisoner only in the prison you yourself have built. Now I'm not in my best way right now, and I'm sorry for that. You hurt my friend, and I don't know if you--"

"I hurt your friend?" Keiran asked, his head twitched. "Who?"

"Cori?" Maya said, then added hesitantly "She's been trying to hurt herself since she came in here."

"No…" Keiran said, his eyes now wide and panicked. "I like Cori. I didn't hurt her."

"Maybe you didn't mean to--"

"I knew it. I'm no good." Keiran said and wisped back and forth across the room and held his head. "I'm no good. I knew it. I don't want to be a demon, Maya."

"Keiran…" Maya said, then stepped back towards the door.

Keiran's eyes turned sad and panicked, then began to drip down his face like oil. "I don't want to be a demon. I don't want to. I'm no good. I'm no good. I'm no good."

"She's alright Keiran, she's getting help."

"It's not alright. It's not okay. I'm no good, I'm no good." Keiran repeated this with increasing panic, then hovered listlessly, staring off into space.

Maya stood watching, vigilant, and prepared her defensive magicks.

Keiran looked up towards the sky. A zealous smile overcame his face. "Yes. How could I have been so ignorant? I've been so selfish." He said. His once ephemeral form was growing far more physical. His eyes churned and he gnashed his teeth. He spoke again. "I've been thinking about me, and only me. How I can be happy? How I can avoid becoming a demon? How I can Liberate?" He said, his ghastly eyes dripped across his jovial cheeks and down the length of his body. "But it's not about me, is it? That's what you've been trying to teach me all along."

"Yeah...Yes." Maya responded, surprised and uncertain. "That's...you do listen, huh?"

"I see it, Maya. That's why Margaret was always so content. She helped others. She knew how to heal, and how to Liberate others." Keiran chuckled. "I know what I must do."

"...Is that so?"

"We're...we're going to Liberate everyone." Keiran sighed, his eyes pious and concerned, his smile serene.

"Liberate everyone…?" Maya took too long to process this, and Keiran had come right to the front of her and smiled down at her while he grabbed her by the throat.

"Thank you for everything you've done for me, Maya." Keiran said and strangled Maya gently. She struggled to fire off magicks, but they skirted off Keiran's new form like oil on water. "It won't be in vain."

Maya, not one to be so easily thwarted, phase shifted and disassembled into elementary particles. It was complex magick, and it was not to be taken lightly. It was used only as a last resort, for reassembly was a messy affair and often resulted in a kidney where a heart ought to be. But Maya reformed as best she could outside of Keiran's room where there was an emergency alarm. Here she saw that her toes had been replaced by fingers. Keiran burst through the door just as Maya sounded the alarm and alerted the house. Maya looked towards him, and he looked back at her with pity. A serrated tentacle lashed out of him, serrated like a bread knife, and sawed Maya from shoulder to hip, too quickly for her to respond or heal.

Ichabod was a nimble man. His beard was grey and he was deft of tongue. His severity was creased in his brow, and his kindness pooled just under his eyes. He carried himself like a man who had been in many battles, physical and otherwise. His hand rested casually upon the sword sheathed at his side.

"I wasn't sure I'd ever see you again." Aislynn said.

"I told you we'd meet again. You never did appreciate my eye for the future." Ichabod said and pointed his eyes, then tightened the ropes around his belt line. He wore a V shaped garment with an origin Cori couldn't place. It was none of the styles of the cultures she had personally been exposed to. Peruvian maybe. It was of white linen and a navy woolen weave. "What brings you here?" Ichabod asked, then turned his weary eyes to Cori. "And I'm sorry, I'm afraid we haven't been introduced."

"This is Cori, and she's why I'm here." Aislynn said before Cori could speak. Her voice was forced, as though giving a military report. "Cori has attracted the attention of a class five spirit, dangerously on the cusp of shifting into the demonic. Her life is forfeit without the assistance of an exorcist."

Ichabod's hand came off of his sword, but didn't quite relax either. "I suppose that would be my fault, never having taught you the ways of the exorcist." He said. "Come inside, have some tea." Ichabod led Cori and Aislynn into the Chapel at St. Luc. It was a structure scarcely the size of a home, but magnificent in other less precarious ways. For as small as it was, one could tell that only the finest ingredients had been used in its construction, built only with the hearts of trees, woven elf-like in flowing geometric patterns that gave only the rough semblance of earthly construction.

It had the usual spired shape of a church, but it sported more colors, all painted tastefully as runes and patterns upon the pivotal lines and corners of the structure. The stained glass windows were delicate and shaded well to produce more realistic yet still artistically divine scenes. They showed stories that Cori knew to be of the Paladin pantheon, and stories that Cori nostalgically recognized.

Ichabod served a floral brew of tea with distant hints of tobacco. Incense burned from a brass burner on a chain hung by the ceiling. The kitchen was housed at the entrance with bags of rice, dried beans, and sacks of potatoes. It was otherwise sparse, but ruled efficiently. A wooden tub of fresh water sat by the window. The chapel itself was one room further. Ichabod opened the door for them. The door moved silently on its hinges, heavy though it looked.

The inner chapel itself looked like the beating heart of a tree. Besides the stained glass, everything was made of polished wood and sculpted as deftly as a marble statue. The altar grew from the earth itself, and behind the altar lay a single glowing crystal held in stasis within a golden monstrance that gleamed like the Sun. Ichabod closed the door quietly.

"Keiran is one of the spirits that lays animate upon this world and you work with him to persuade him to move through to his final end, is this correct?"

"Yes. I did my best to help him. My best wasn't good enough, but I tried."

"It may still be good enough." Ichabod said. "If you're willing to work with me."

"I am." Cori said. The words came only with great effort as her soul continued weighing heavily in her heart.

"This isn't going to be easy." Ichabod said to Cori.

Cori was lost to her own thoughts. *What's the use?* She asked herself. *They just want me to see the world in ignorant bliss as they do. What does this man know about my world? He lives up in the clouds and ignores the pain and the tears of everyone down below. Happiness is ignorance. Misery shows some wisdom, at least.*

"Cori." Ichabod said, coming to grasp her shoulders. "Look at me." She did. He went on. "It isn't real. Those thoughts don't define you."

What does he know of my thoughts? Cori asked herself.

"The words, the feelings in your head. Look at them and see them for what they are."

Cori could hardly even see Ichabod. She was growing dizzy, and terribly sleepy.

"It's coming." Cori heard Ichabod say from a distance. It was the last thing she heard. Her soul burrowed into a dark place at the base of her spine where it could lay in rest and powerlessness.

It was like a spillage. It was oil that one could never quite rub clean. Dirty. Rotting. Something in Keiran had touched Cori, some terrible appendage of his vibration mixed and intermingled with her own, and her will crumbled under the pressure of having to carry the weight of someone else's sins. It wasn't all of Keiran. But their consciousness was intermingled. It was spooky action at a distance. What one thought, the other thought. What one felt, the other felt. When one transformed into a demon, so too did the other.

Cori's eyes felt as though they were made of lava, and she clutched at her belly where a sundering void had ripped open. She yelled, and gnashed her teeth, and bit at her tongue as she thrashed.

"I might as well begin teaching you the ways of the exorcist, Aislynn." Ichabod said, with a voice as cool as morning dew. "Now is as good of a time as any. The first thing we must do is isolate the demon from its host. This is best achieved by causing it discomfort. So much discomfort that it chooses to leave. You must remember that they are not used to earthly pains. Long ago this meant subjecting our patient to torture, but now with modern methods we have abandoned this as a primeval method and found that holy relics suffice just fine in causing great discomfort to the attending entity."

"Do you have a holy relic?" Aislynn asked, maintaining grace with her mentor.

"Of course I have a holy relic." Ichabod said. "Take Cori into the sanctuary, I'll be just a moment."

It was an alarm that could mean any number of things in a home such as this. Morris was always prepared for a fire or a flood, and thought it a statistical anomaly that none had yet occurred, considering the house and all its flaws. But the fire panel showed the alarm was coming from the pull box outside Keiran's room, and that did not bode well.

Morris started off walking from the secret rooms beyond his own sleeping quarters, then pulled into a jog. The sound of a man screaming set him to a run next, then a swift glide. Nothing was fast enough as the sounds of a struggle ensued, the clash of metal one metal, and more closely now the sound of slicing bone and spillage, and a cry of rusted tin. Morris arrived in the hall in front of Keiran's room to see Sammiel lashing with dagger chains while sigils burned and Keiran countered each lash with a serrated tentacle. The dance was beautiful, but too brief. Morris stood frozen as he laid his eyes on Luke and Maya, both slain. And in his hesitation, Sammiel joined them. His chain whip daggers could not match Keiran's speed, especially in such close quarters as the halls provided. Keiran pulled Sammiel apart limb from limb with the serrated tentacles that elongated from his demonic backside.

For all his years, Morris had never seen violence such as this. He was, of course, a Necromancer skilled in the arts of life and death. Taboo though it may be, he knew how to resurrect a human life. But putting them back together would be a delicate operation, and would become more difficult as the bodies decayed and their souls wandered further into the Betwixt.

Keiran's eyes were like a goats and melted into odd forms down his face as he smiled off and looked happier than Morris had ever seen him before. The eyes dripped off into more eyes which slithered down the rest of his corporeal body like disgusting little rain drops. Keiran hovered, suspended in the air and tentacles lashed round his body. "Morris." Keiran said. "You've always cared for me, at least. Would you lend me your ear, in the name of that care?"

Morris replied only with an incantation. His arm outstretched, his fingers flexed, and light erupted as a sphere from his palm. A blast of fission energy speared out towards Keiran. It rocked the walls of St. Margaret's and the ceiling caved in and the wall paper set fire. The energy beam shot a hole straight back through to the outside world and even through the clouds beyond, and Keiran was dispersed. The wounded demonic entity fled backwards through the halls, bleeding ink.

Ichabod laid a light blue shroud upon Cori, which glistened softly in the candlelight of the refectory. "The Shroud of St. Anne." Ichabod said.

Cori thrashed under the delicate shroud, and an alien maw slithered and bit from the inside of her stomach. It lurched out from within her guts, and its jaws tore the bloodied shroud to shreds.

Aislynn held her hand to her mouth, "Sweet mother of--"

"The Beast." said Ichabod.

Cori's joints cracked backwards; and she crawled spiderlike towards then up the ceiling. She spoke a foreign language, unearthly, and not of the Mundane Planes. Each syllable sounded like a harshly whispered curse.

Ichabod and Aislynn placed their hands upon their swords. Ichabod's sword was a slender and simple broadsword sheathed at his side. Aislynn's sword was a heavenly inscribed greatsword she carried at her back.

Cori attacked first, her arms extended inhumanly and cut down by the swift draw of both Paladins. She yowled, but resumed a ravenous attack and bit with elongated teeth. She whipped her lengthy and pointed tongue at the Paladins with deadly precision. The thing inside Cori cackled, then asked a question of the Paladins in its foreign tongue which neither Paladin could understand. It lunged again, its fingernails extended and shredded into bony claws. This time she snared Aislynn and ripped her new angler teeth into Aislynn's shoulder, which now hung by ligament alone, bone exposed, her sword arm ruined. More foreign words.

The thing that was Cori spoke too long. Ichabod's blade cut clean through with a fell downwards swoop from shoulder to buttock, severing the entirety of Cori's Demonic Aspect. The two halves of her body fell to the floor with a wet thud. Ichabod immediately thrust himself into prayer.

"Thou cannot abide by the light, and in the light thou now stands." He said, over and over, a mantra. Aislynn joined in, speaking a harmonic chant in between Ichabod's syllables; a rhythmically designed and synchronized prayer; Ichabod's in English, Aislynn's in Spanish.

They held their hands in triangles, each at their chest, Aislynn's right side up, Ichabod's upside down. Light carried forth, and they surrounded the demon and imbibed it in the holy wine of heavenly light. It screamed and shriveled. It hissed, and it smoked. But never underestimate a demon's desire to stay Earthbound and away from the lower planes. To escape the shackles of hell, and the inevitable jaws of Ammut, most would fight harder than a man fighting to feed his hungry kids.

The thing that was Cori raised up even as it burned and shriveled and stabbed at the heart of Ichabod. She narrowly missed as Ichabod jumped back but broke the holy incantation. The thing that was Cori did not recover from the mutilation set upon her by this prayer. Instead she pulled off her own crisped burning flesh and ate it.

Morris had spent several minutes sorting out which kidney belonged to who. The task before him was nearly impossible. Morris sat in pools of blood, and sorted connective tissue with bloodied hands. He learned his employees' bodies more intimately than he had ever hoped to. "Why the hell does Maya have fingers for toes, and toes for fingers? How have I never noticed this before?" Knowing Keiran could come back at any moment didn't help. There was only one dread option available. Morris had to call his boss.

"Morris, I hope you're calling to let me know you're all set and ready for the Quality Assurance Review Tomorrow." Ruth said from the edges of Morris' iPhone. "The Board will be there in the morning. You remember this, of course."

Shit. "The books are all in order." Even if he could get this sorted out, he would still be up all night downloading and signing the documents he should have had three months prior. "Of course I remember, it's right on my calendar, Morris said, pointing down to an imaginary date on an imaginary calendar. Ruth...you remember the email I sent you about Keiran..."

"Who's Keiran?"

"One of the residents. Near demonic. I had been wondering about the protocol for putting him down in the Basement. Soooo...he shifted..."

"Well, I have the utmost confidence in your abilities."

"Ruth, three of my staff are dead, and one is out getting an exorcism. I need your help." Morris said.

"Morris, I'm up in Nova Scotia right now taking care of the St. Andrews Branch. They've had three demonic shifts this week." Then Ruth did a double take over the phone, however that's done. "*Three of your staff are dead?* What are you teaching these people? They should all be trained in Demonic Interference. Didn't you get the memo? No, I know you did, you signed that memo and sent it back to me."

"Ruth please, I'm in way over my head here."

Ruth huffed. "It'll take me a couple hours through the Betwixt." Then she sighed, and spoke shortly and chuckled a little. "Fine, bye. Bye. Bye."

Cori wasn't quite asleep, just changed. It was the Revelation of Monster, the freedom from morality. Freedom from Humanity. Everything was so certain, so simple. Her goal was singular. In sacrificing her own death, she could bestow death upon others. She was a martyr. She would continue her own suffering for the sake of ending the suffering of others.

And she *loved* the taste of blood.

Drinking Aislynn's blood made Aislynn's life her own. Aislynn filled her every sense, and tickled her nervous system. Her metallic life force now coursed in through Cori's veins, and plasma rolled sweetly round her preternaturally sensitive tongue. It tasted like Aislynn's first kiss, and her vigorous training regimens. The aroma was that of her beach house by the sea, with just a hint of chamomile. It had a voluptuous palette, and exquisite mouthfeel.

It was all that Cori had ever wanted, and she was just so perfectly freed from moral obligation, enough to feast without a hint of guilt. She was doing Aislynn a favor.

...And Aislynn burned her for it. She surrendered to the blasphemous will of this "Ichabod" she was so fond of. And she betrayed Cori.

It was hard to stay compassionate towards someone who betrayed you like that, but Cori maintained her composure and vowed that she would still end the life of the Paladin called Aislynn, and thus end her suffering, just like she would end the suffering of anyone else. *Everyone* else. Cori was transcendent now, and could *see* so clearly. Aislynn was just blind. And hateful. Love had a way of creating hate, that much was now obvious.

Pain was an illusion that Cori could now see through. And, now she knew how to warp her own flesh. How cool is that? So they could cut her in half and burn her all they wanted but she would just meld back together and cover her burn wounds with some extra eyeballs or teeth and call it a day.

Cori was just built for this. It was a natural talent she never knew she had. But overall she wanted to end things quickly. She wanted to consume Aislynn alive. It was a carnal desire, and it produced a pleasurable tingle just to think about it.

Ichabod stood in the way with fierce determination in his eyes. He would not make easy prey. But it didn't matter. Cori craved death. It didn't matter whose death it was. Ichabod would see her wisdom before the end.

The close quarters of the chapel made for difficult fighting. She was out of home territory. She'd have to defile the place. And that's just what she did.

The thing that had been Cori called upon a doorway to the Abyss. It was a door that could be found within oneself, Cori now understood. It unlocked in her very core, and thus in the air surrounding her. The vibration of the floating isles of the Chapel at St. Luc's lowered severely.

"Cori, stop this." Ichabod said, his cool composure finally shaken. "You'll sink the islands."

Cori replied in a language she had just learned, yet she felt that she had been speaking it since time immemorial. She said things to Ichabod, things that have no translation in the language Cori used to know. They were things that shouldn't have a translation. Ichabod understood her words though. His eyes widened, and she could sense his despair. Cori hoped he would start to understand her wisdom. Keiran's wisdom. Then, he could help them do good things. They could all work together for a better future. She would just need to taint his soul like Keiran had tainted hers.

The vibrations in the air of the world around them became disturbed and low. Foreign intelligences spilled through the grains of the wood that had once looked so beautiful, now an abomination. Madness oozed from the walls and pews, but Ichabod held his mind as firm as he could. He gathered determination. Ichabod gleamed bright in his aura and held his sword aloft, steady and balanced.

The earth below their feet dropped. The floating islands sank. High above the mountains, they shuddered and lowered; slowly, dramatically.

Ichabod used the distraction to lunge at Cori with a precise jab of his broadsword. Cori went unphased and allowed the sword into her body with a spurt of blood. She grabbed it by the blade, grabbed Ichabod by the head, and allowed the ghouls that hid in her throat to eat the face of the Paladin called Ichabod. The thing that was Cori feasted and danced and bathed in the blood of the Paladin called Ichabod. Spiritual venom dripped into Ichabod's blood. Keiran needed this one corrupted. It was part of the plan.

Cori lost herself to blood reverie and thus distracted, lost her head to Aislynn's blade. Aislynn, who had been forgotten in the celebrations, delivered a keen slice to the neck of the thing that was Cori. Aislynn then chanted a prayer of immense power. Cori's head thudded on the ground, and her body thudded beside it with a sickening *thwack*.

The Paladin's prayer crackled through the air like a lightning coup de gras, and Aislynn was able to call the demon clinging to Cori's soul forward in judgement. It held the soul of the true Cori hostage. Her small and wispy fractal essence was held tight in the devil's maw.

"She is mine." The demon thing that had pretended to be Cori said like razors, but now in English. Cori's decapitated body lay on the ground, the incorporeal spirit of the Keirinian demon above it. The island once in the sky crashed all around. A jolt of momentum like a megaton bomb quaked as the islands crashed into the side of a mountain, and Aislynn was thrown through the air and knocked unconscious.

The last sight which befell her eyes was an angelic Ichabod doing final battle with the darkness in a plane beyond our own. Cori's fractal spirit lifted up and away to planes farther yet than that.

Chapter 16

Cori had been in the Betwixt before, but it was different being fully dead. It was one thing when her blood was leaving her wrists and Keiran carried her to the Villa of Ormen. It was another thing entirely to have her physical body decimated. She had never met Gustaphniir, the Dread Judge. She had never received the licensure of an unbounded soul. Nor had she been harried up to the Crystallatium by armed humanoid jackals. She had never been given a tour of the resplendent palace at Akasha by the mechanical elves either. She didn't remember much, it all was such a blur, but she had been taken to a garden where the elves announced that her 'friends would soon arrive'. It was a cryptic and ominous statement to be sure.

It was much brighter this time in the Betwixt, or more vivid. The colors popped and the sounds of birds were more musical, as though composed. Cori gained in focus and clarity, and found the Betwixt was becoming less like a dream, and more like physical reality. The air itself hummed a song underneath the birds, and melodically with them.

Vivid though it was, it was twilight here in the garden. Flowers moved into Cori, and through her, and became her. All their aroma and longing filled her, their dew and green leaves. Each felt healing, or delicious, or both. It was a magnificent paradise. More than anything, she was glad to feel like herself again.

She had been thinking so much of death, so much of a final rest. She had been craving it so desperately up until the moment she died. Then, with all the weight of the world off her back, she wanted nothing more than to bear their burden once again. Even this sublime garden of delights left her craving the Mundane. To see the burden lifted showed her only how small the burden was.

Cori found a soft stone bench beside a pool full of stars, and she sat, wondering what had and what would become of her. In the pool she could see the Earth as a little blue speck. Above her and beside her stood a metallic monolith of immense proportion and vibrating.

"Cori?" The voice to her left was of metal, and a cool winter wind. Sammiel stepped through the candied hedges and out in front of the pool. Glistening, he released an inner radiance like youth, but older. His body was carved from marble and his silver hair held all the light of the moon. His tattoos were like soft graffiti.

"You didn't die too…" Sammiel said.

"You didn't--" Cori began. "What happened?"

"Keiran."

"Keiran." Cori repeated. "How?"

Sammiel shook his head. "I heard the alarm go off, and ran with Luke. We found Keiran cutting Maya apart."

Cori was about to exclaim her disbelief until she remembered her own gruesome demise. "He took control of me, and I killed the exorcist who was helping me. I almost killed Aislynn too, but in the end she won. Then, I remember a battle as I rose up through the spheres. But it was all too much. I could hardly tell what was going on."

"Did you get judged by that big purple guy with the eight eyes and the beard?" Sammiel asked. "I hadn't expected that. Apparently he's the one who shackles souls to the lower planes."

"I did not see that coming. Why don't they mention that in any of the textbooks? I wonder if Maya and Luke...do you think they'll be coming here too?"

"We'll run into them at some point. Any relationship you have while alive forms a sort of tether, so we will pull into them soon enough." Sammiel grew silent, then looked at Cori. "Are you--?"

Tragedy washed over Cori, and a life unlived came into focus. "I don't want it to be over. It's not fair...it can't be over yet. That's not right, not when I was just about to...when we...Not when I...I'm falling in love with you."

"Me?"

"You absolutely must have known." Cori said and reflected on her earthly actions which now stood out as more terribly obvious than ever before. "Of course you."

"I had no idea…" Sammiel said earnestly. "I mean I knew we liked each other, and I knew I liked you, and I--"

"You're a fool, but I think that's part of it. It's part of why I've become so--"

"Cori, I--"

"I've been relishing it, if I'm being honest. But I'm also so afraid of it." Cori said, and Sammiel's eyes fell downwards in contemplation. "I know first hand how terribly it can hurt. But you are...genuine, in yourself. A genuine ball of contradictions. Looking at you, you're this stylish Necromancer, but then next thing I know you're showing me the socks you knitted for one of your homunculi. Then, sometimes I think you're kind of dumb. But later I'll see you wearing those little glasses you wear and you're studying up on Planar Dynamics. And its… well it's hot, if I'm being honest. But not the moments you think you're being hot. It's all the other stuff you do. Like when you stumbled over your own cooking on meatball night, and you burned the meatballs and you got so upset about it. And then you got embarrassed because you were upset. And I try to pretend it's just a crush because you're a coworker and I can't get caught up in that mess. But then…" Then Cori stopped and sobbed. "And I had just been looking forward to what...to maybe...to a life together...or something. I didn't even know I had been envisioning it, but I was. I was dreaming of it in some far off place in the back of my mind. And I want the life I was envisioning. I want to be with you. I want to get fat with you. I want to make fun of your wrinkles someday. But I don't even want to do all of that so fast, I want to stop right now and just court you slowly. I want to feel the pulse of my veins when I touch your hand. I want to kiss your tears away when you're sad. I want to be MAD at you. I want to get mad at you for doing something that upset me, because that would mean you were close enough to upset me, and then I could forgive you. And--" Cori broke down.

"Cori no…" Sammiel tucked his hand under her chin and lifted her. "We can still...before the end...here." He said, a tremor in his metallic baritone. "I was going to go straight to the Villa of Ormen, I'll admit. But I--I have trouble saying these sorts of things...I also know how bad this can all hurt...but…all of what you just said...me too. I--I love you too."

"We can stay here?" Cori said.

"For a time." Sammiel said. "Or we can travel…"

"Travel?"

"The Crystallatium. Summerland. Sonorous." Sammiel said. "If the theory of the Bardos is correct, we should have 49 days."

"49 days. Right." Cori said quietly, then whispered, "That's not a lot."

"I know, it's not a lot…but it's what we're given."

"Oh, Sam."

"Cori…"

They found magnificent garments hidden away in ancient and sacred vaults. Sammiel clad himself in a black silken robe round his waist and a many winged crown upon his head and eyes. Cori wreathed herself in the thinnest heavenly silks, flower petals adorned her aura forever more.They found steeds to bond with, Rasputin and Eromir, out upon a grassy plateau covered in stardust. They were glorious steeds whose hooves could tread upon clouds, one with the head of an owl, with antlers upon its cranium. The other was a nightmare horse, all shadows and blood. For dinner they stopped at a phosphorescent astral diner that floated in the forest seas of Ascabab. There's some other syllables behind those ones that you have to pronounce while you say Ascabab. Those syllables are Ra-ma. They must be said at the same time for it to be the right name. I say this in case anyone would like to visit. The proper intonations must be made.

The dinner gazed out onto an eternal sunset over the sea, purple mountains at the edges of the sun. They drank ambrosia and feasted upon the most delectable array of mushrooms. The atmosphere was but a silhouette of the full hospitality and heavenly romance that exuded from the place. Cori and Sammiel were served a delectable *jour de fouie,* courtesy of the house.

Sammiel tried, awkwardly, to grasp Cori's hand on the table. His hands were soft, and she let him have hers. The atmosphere was nearly perfect, but lacked proper music. Cori envisioned the Sigil of Mayhew, the Sonorous Entity. She finally had a proper occasion to summon him. She held his sigil firm in her mind, and let it vibrate. It took on visible reality in front of her, her mind was a projector that burned the sigil into the floor.

From below in the sigil came visions of music. Soundwaves pulsated together to form a being, a vibrating sound being.

"Cori, you called."

"Mayhew!"

Mayhew wasn't as implicit in his being as he had been when Cori had last encountered him, and was more corporeal here in this higher realm for whatever reason. He now looked more like an elf, if an elf was music. A tall handsome elf, also naked.

"Mayhew," Cori said, while Sammiel looked on skeptically. "Could you play us some music? Is that how the summoning thing works?"

"It is indeed." Mayhew said, and pulled a lute from his core. Being a master in his craft, Mayhew wove his own music into the very fabric of reality of this entire higher realm. It harmonized, and his song played the melody of the day as his fingers plucked at the strings of his lute. He turnt the mood to a more energetic sort, and added a fun vibration beyond the intimacy of the astral cafe and all its other onlooking customers who looked on with confusion.

"I figured you all might make it up here." Someone grabbed Sammiel and Cori from behind and wrapped them in a tight hug. Maya pressed their cheeks into hers. "I was just looking for dinner, but instead I found two snacks. Whats up?!"

"Maya!" They both exclaimed.

Maya joined in on their feast. It was a purely sensual affair that needed no end, for their stomachs could never fill. They could have easily, and many dead have, eaten for the entire 49 days they were given. Poke bowls and beef stews, chocolate chip cookies and calzones. Each meal left them feeling lighter and healthier than the one before. They drank wine and nibbled sausages, all set to Mayhew's delightful fiddling.

"The Betwixt sure knows how to treat a girl, huh?" Maya asked. "I wonder when Luke will get here. I don't want to stay too long."

"What do you mean you don't want to stay too long?" Sammiel asked between bites of sweetbread.

"Its not going to be easy getting our bodies back. Especially you, Cori. God knows where yours is. Morris will need all the help he can get."

"Whoa, whoa, whoa…" Sammiel said. "We're not going back."

"We're not?" Cori asked and looked between him and Maya.

"No…I mean, no…I've read about what demons can do. We got off easy. We're lucky to be dead. Cori's lucky her soul got away." Sammiel said, his eyes set and determined.

"Yeah, but we're a team. We can make it through this. Morris will help, he can get Dana and Kitsune and Derrick. And it's not just about us, Sam. Keiran was talking about Liberating *everyone*. I hope he doesn't mean what I think he means, but my gut tells me he does."

"Well that's not really our problem is it?" Sammiel said, his voice raised and his smile turned down. "Everyone Liberates at some point. I don't necessarily think it's worth risking being dragged into the Hells to prevent the natural order of things. Besides, it's forbidden."

"What is the matter with you? Since when did you care about Necromancer Dogma?" Maya asked, then looked over. "Cori?"

"I don't--I don't know--" Cori stammered.

Maya set her palm firmly onto the table. "Alright. Not going to pretend I'm not surprised, but I see you've all made your choice. Happy for you. But I can't just sit around waiting." Maya stood from the table.

"Maya…"

"You two enjoy your dinner."

Chapter 17

"And what's her name again? The one with the bigger gall bladder."

"Maya." Morris repeated, seated on the floor and detangling intestinal tracts.

"You change staff so often here, I don't know how I can keep up." Ruth said, eating skittles as she spoke. She leaned against the wallpaper. Ruth wore a tattered beige cloak atop a skirt that was caked heavily with mud at the bottom. She was adorned in skulls, and vials of soda and satchels of candy that were always on her person. She carried a broom with her, a broom covered about with webbing. Her spectacles she kept at her collar, and wore her white and frizzled hair in a bun.

"Maya has been here for five years now." Morris said, itched his cheek, then realized he just smeared blood all over his face.

"Well, I don't remember her." Ruth said. "So, you want me to reanimate your staff while you banish Brian to the basement?"

"Keiran. Banish *Keiran* to the basement. And not reanimate. I want them brought back to life."

"Morris, you know that's forbidden." Ruth said. "The Council would shit themselves all in unison, torture us, kill us, break their own rules to bring us back to life and torture us again. Then kill us again. And then shit."

"Please, don't act like you've never brought someone back to life on the clock." Morris said.

"That was for me, not for you. We will get you new staff."

"Ruth, you know as well as anyone that we're experiencing a major staffing crisis. St. Margaret's is short staffed by half, and we're one of the lucky ones. Who exactly do you plan on staffing me with?"

Ruth thought for a moment, then said, "Like I said, I can reanimate them. St. Agnello's out in Tacoma is experimenting with an entirely undead staff."

"Aren't we supposed to be helping the undead to move on?" Morris asked. "I don't get it."

Ruth sighed. "Neither do I. It's some Bodhisattva thing passed down from the big wigs, the damned leading the damned. I don't know. Corporate mumbo jumbo."

"So, what? Are they gonna be turning me into a Lich now?"

"God, I hope that's next year's benefit package. Could you imagine?"

"Save a bunch on health insurance." Morris said.

"Fine. Fine. Okay, enough of that, are you gonna let me get in here or what?" Ruth pointed towards the pile of human tissue Morris sat amongst. "Not that I want to. You know what will happen if word of this gets out?"

"Yes, yes. You're the best, Ruth. Oh and uh--let Maya know she's got an ulcer developing. Once she's back. You know. Also, something happened with her fingers and toes, fix that up" Morris said, then massaged his temples with his bloodied hands. "I want a shower. Or something. I really don't want to be doing this right now."

"Oh, please. Enough with the whining." Ruth said and popped more skittles into her mouth before settling in among the piles of skin. "I've heard banshees make less of a ruckus about death than you do."

"When was the last time you dealt with an emergency like this?

"I don't deal with emergencies like this. I make my supervisors deal with emergencies like this." Ruth said, sorting the staff skins.

"This wasn't in my job description."

"Other duties as assigned." Ruth quoted. "Be careful to read the fine print. Did you know corporate can take sole ownership of anything you create whilst living in their facilities? I talked to a lawyer friend of mine and she said that could easily be translated to include any offspring that you have while you're employed here."

"Good to keep in mind." Morris said. "Do I have bags under my eyes?"

"You always have bags under your eyes, Morris. Tell me you have a few vials of tears I can use to resurrect your staff so I don't have to dip into my own stock."

"I just sold my last batch the other day."

"You're an imbecile." Ruth said, and drank a vial of clear liquid that could be presumed to be tears, and wiped her face off with a satisfied grin. "Let me know when you're done banishing Ryan. I'm supposed to be up in Algonquin for a Raid at nine."

"I want to go on a raid."

"Get to work, Morris."

Morris sighed, kicked a loose beam of wood that had fallen from the ceiling, then set off down the hall.

Morris held his hands up like karate chops, moving from door to door, hall to hall, and peeked around the edges like a one man swat team. An errant twitch in the corner of his eye or tap upon the walls meant incineration. There were several hundreds of dollars worth of damages already. *Bfwish*....the sound of his fireball as it ignited the cheap drywall.

Into the stairwell, Morris cast a bright flash of disorienting light, levitated in and shot lasers in all directions. Each left a smoldering dent in the walls, the attack rumbled the entire infrastructure, but there was no Keiran to be seen.

His wizard eyes keen, irises large, Morris sniffed for the whifferings of ectoplasm. The scent absolutely enveloped St. Margarets, subtle though it was. But demonic ectoplasm smelled different. More salty, less musk. Somewhat like pharmaceutical medication. He sniffed it out from amongst the more normal types of ectoplasm, and followed. It went down the stairs, to the right.

The Basement.

Eerie dark veins grew along the walls of the lower stairwell, pumping blood into the framework. It probably would have been obvious without using his sniffer or wizard eyes at all.

"Morris."

Morris shrieked only briefly, then unleashed a volley of lasers behind him, and obliterated much of the West Wing. He recognized the voice shortly afterwards. "Maya?" He said to the empty air. It was like grade school all over again, talking to disembodied voices while his peers laughed and laughed. But the school yard kids weren't here now. Most of them were dead or stuck in dead end jobs. Not that Morris was any better off, but after his twenty year high school reunion, it was nice to know they were fully on his level now. He could talk to disembodied voices all he wanted to in his little castle, St. Margaret's.

"Frickin' Eric." Morris said out loud, thinking of that one kid who always gave him crap.

"Focus." Came the gentle whisper from beyond the breeze.

Morris peeled back the thin veil within his mind and found the chilling apparition of Maya, his once protege. From beyond her translucent face he could see her skull and the very masque of death. He wanted to cry, already missing her so. He wasn't used to speaking with spirits who had ascended higher to the planes. The ghosts of St. Margaret's were so tethered as to be easily accessible from the Ethereal. Maya here, on the other hand, smelled of the Crystallatium; and she looked distant like a star. "Maya. Yes. Speak to me." Morris's eyes glazed over. He held his hands out in front of him and looked up through the ceiling, grasping around as though blind. "Speak to me." He hissed.

"I will help." Maya said, her words required great strength of mana.

Morris' eyes rolled further into his head. "Help. You will...help…" He said, to no one in that could be seen.

"Supervise." Maya whispered from beyond the veil.

"Super...vise…" Morris said. "Supervise?" He asked it, but he already knew what she meant. "yes...yes...Maya. Maya. Listen, I need you... go get Cori and Aislynn." Morris resonated each word he spoke, and spoke them with great concentration. "I need help. Living Help. Get Cori and Aislynn."

And Maya left, quick as a shooting star. And Morris fell to the floor, spent.

He had way over done it with the lasers. He left himself with nothing. He was so terribly out of shape. He didn't do yoga anymore, he barely ever went on raids. He couldn't remember the last time he had taken an adventure beyond the walls of St. Margaret's. He'd been dealing with low level zombies and playing Habbo Hotel on the few days of work that he didn't call in for being too sad.

Morris hadn't expected to be dealing with a demon. Or, he had, but not this soon. Or even maybe this soon, but he was hoping otherwise.

A large part of him wanted to trade tasks with Ruth. He rarely tried to impress her. He could just tell her he wasn't up to the challenge and she'd probably do it for him. She'd only leave with her usual impression of him. He was about to go and hand the task back to Ruth, but then Morris thought, *"Why is Keiran going into the basement anyways? Why not just be free?"*

There were no good answer to these questions. Every possible outcome made the situation unbearably bad, but one of them was apocalyptic. And if Morris knew anything about anything, Keiran's reasoning was likely in the apocalyptic vein.

"He wouldn't." Morris said to himself as he thought of the possibilities. "Why would he...No, no, no, no, no…" Morris said, running down the stairs into the basement, caution thrown to the winds.

The Labyrinth below St. Margaret's was not the sort of place anyone should go, ever...even if you absolutely had to. Any demonic bindings into the labyrinth occurred just outside its massive depth, the demonic spirits were offered like sacrifices outside the doors of the Outer Sanctum. But no one ever went *inside*. There was a secret hidden in the basement. A secret only Morris alive knew, him sworn to secrecy by the Supervisor before him, Louis LaBlanc, who told it to Morris before his passing.

How could Keiran know?

Morris barrelled down into the basement, venous stone walls to his sides and guided by the light of his phone. He came to the Outer Sanctum, a great hall lit by oily flames spilled haphazardly around the ground; and the great stone doors to the Labyrinth which stood carven with many host of the damned, their petrified countenances frozen in horror and forever engraved in these door.

In the center, the exorcism altar was placed beneath the dead and underground Elm of a Thousand Sorrows which grew center the hall; under which beings of profound evil would be exorcised and ushered through the doors, never to be seen again. Morris ran past it and to the doors and tugged at them even as the petrified souls of the damned reached slowly towards him.

Morris had hoped never to use the Labyrinth keys. Each looked like an ordinary house key, but with one different colored eye upon it. Morris always felt bad, and wondered if the eyes felt pain while they jiggled around in his pockets. Morris unlocked all three locks in their correct order, color coded with the eyes. He maintained the weight and gravity of his station while he did so, performing the likely useless ceremonies that had been taught to him by Louis LaBlanc, the old supervisor.

The door opened, and Morris stepped into the darkness beyond. A hall, another door. This unlocked and led into a room like a basement. It was the sort of basement like your old neighborhood buddies' basement. It was quiet, and unassuming. But behind the shelving, Morris could see a secret passage glowing orange by the dimmest of candles. And there, behind the secret passage door was a long downward stair, that dim candle held aloft by a wall sconce. So Morris began his journey down into the Labyrinth.

The Labyrinth was cramped, at the start. But Morris had a map, given to him by the old Supervisor, Louis LaBlanc. There was a place near the center but West. The Maw, it was called; it was where Keiran had gone, Morris knew. It was the only reason Keiran would choose to come down here.

The basement corridors skittered with activity. Something slithered, up ahead, along the musty drywall. And then the sound of muttering, incomprehensible. Morris swore to himself, and turned the other direction. He would just have to take the long way. He felt the first stirrings of madness, the exact type of insanity this Labyrinth brought out in those with even the strongest minds. The exact type of insanity that afflicted the old Supervisor, Louis LaBlanc.

You know, really just sanity is a type of insanity. Morris thought. *My mind is freed.*

Unless I....No, no, no, no, no.

Focus.

Morris had to get to the Maw. It was somewhere around there. The Northwestern. It was...a convergence. But is it? Why aren't my thoughts working?

Morris walked. One foot. In front. Of. The other.

You know, really just sanity is a type of insanity. Morris thought. *My mind is freed.*

Unless I....No, no, no, no, no.

Focus.

Morris had to get to the Maw. It was somewhere around there. The Northwestern. It was...a convergence. But is it? Why aren't my thoughts working?

He stepped. One foot. In front. Of. The other.

An Octopus. On the wall.

Kill it. Morris. Kill it.

"But the Octopus is just a child." Morris said. "So innocent."

Just make it to the Maw, Morris. Kill the Octopus.

Unless I....No, no, no, no, no.

Focus.

Morris had to get to the Maw. It was somewhere around there. The Northwestern. It was...a convergence. But is it? Why aren't my thoughts working?

The Octopus slithered up Morris's arm and onto his neck. It reached its tentacles inside of Morris' ears. Its thoughts reached through some cilia, like electricity, too vast for any ordinary human mind to grasp without losing themselves entirely.

But Morris was clever and not to be so easily outwitted. "I am the Octopus." Morris said.

Wait, what?

It was just a single phrase, but it brought about a cataclysmic shift. Their minds were so vigorously intertwined that it was really impossible to tell the two apart. Morris said it, and there was a great deal of confusion on both parts. The whole illusion was uprooted. Some facts stood firm and chief amongst them was "Kill the

Octopus." Morris didn't need much. Octopi are exceptionally squishy when they're not enslaving your thoughts. Morris didn't even bother with Magick, he just plucked the Octopi off his neck and squished it in his fists; its bulbous eyes popped from its brainishly squishy head.

Every encounter with a mind-flaying demon comes with a deep psychic scar, and Morris would spend the rest of his life wondering if he were really Morris, or if he were the Octopi. But he survived, and recalled the story of the resident ghost Xavier who had been so obsessed with knowledge that he had enslaved himself to the pursuit of its study, and so became demonic in his own arcane learning. He was banished before Morris became supervisor, and was left to rot in the labyrinth beneath St. Margaret's.

The Octopus and ex-resident Xavier wouldn't be dead in the sense that demons can't die, but he would have to lay on the floor of the labyrinth suffering a very slow and painful recovery alone in the dark.

Further on, the walls turned cavernous and dripping, still venous and oozing. Then Morris saw one goat that stood on human legs, though not well at all. Hunched, nearly falling, its ribs poked through its chest cavity, it bleated and chased Morris and Morris ran. He knew the story of this creature all too well, and personally. She was their cursed resident from when he was a novice, cursed to be chained forever to the lower planes by an evil enchantress. The resident hadn't even done anything wrong but to look upon the Witch's azalea garden with unclean eyes. The ironic thing was that her name was also Azalea. She was killed in a hiking accident some years later then sent to St. Margaret's as a terribly contorted sprite. Soon, her consciousness gave in to greater darkness. She lost all sense and took on the guise of this blasphemous man-goat hybrid. Only after managing to terminate all the pregnancies in the town of Remedy, numbering six, was she caught and exorcised to the labyrinth.

She bleated as she chased Morris and begged for love. He couldn't fight her. For as pathetic as she looked in her twisted anthropomorphic state, Morris knew her touch alone was enough to necrotize all the flesh in a body. Her breath, like ammonia, hit

Morris' nostrils and sent a wave of dizziness upon him. Then numbness overcame his extremities as he stumbled into a wall at the end of the hallway. Ammonia filled his nervous system.

The goat lady approached. She bleated angrily.

Numb though he was, Morris could still cast hand signs. His muscle memory superseded his lack of kinesthetic sensation. Morris blinked away, several yards, his teleportation spell flawlessly executed. Then he ran an awkward gait, trying to guess at how his legs were supposed to work in his bodies' numb silence.

The walls closed in around him, and the map was proving wrong over and over again. The Labyrinth became more like a cavernous jungle of mushrooms and sunless vines. His legs had not recovered their strength and his mana had not returned when he came upon the Koanish Sphinx. This fabled creature was one of the few in the Labyrinth who had come with the place and had not been bound here as a demonic force. She had the face of a crone, and the withered flesh of a lion who has gone hungry for far too long. A pointed tongue hung casually from her mouth.

"Halt." She said, her blind eyes covered in galactic cataracts. "You stand before Matilda Kali, Keeper of Mysteries and Slayer of Thought. Who wishes to pass through my domain?"

"I am Morris Llewelyn in Flesh, and Absalon of the Thousand Eyes in Spirit. I'd really like to pass without a riddle. I honestly don't understand the whole riddle thing." He pleaded.

"I stand guard before the Maw, wherein St. Margaret lay sleeping. Only those sufficient of Wisdom may pass, lest I feast upon them, their souls passing by any hope of salvation and falling straight into the jaws of Ammut where they will be shredded into non-being. The Passage is locked, lest in your mind you muster the key."

Morris was already looking up the battle stats of a Koanish Sphinx in his iPhone by the end of her speech and found nothing promising. One on one, she would tear him to shreds. Especially in his weakened state. His sensation was only slowly overcoming numb ammonia.

If Keiran was doing what Morris thought he was doing, millions or even billions of lives could be in jeopardy. Morris reasoned with himself that natural disasters are what they are and sometimes it's better to let the earth work itself out. He should probably just go back to bed. Threats of Eternal Oblivion were threats to take seriously. Morris had a lot of plans for his afterlife, and had been seeking Union with the Godhead since he was in high school. One wrong move with the Spinx…

"Can I back out once I hear the riddle? Can I choose not to answer and still live once I've heard it?"

The Sphinx paused to consider. Its sharp crone teeth bit into its long pointed tongue and drew some blood. "Do as thou wilt, if thou art able."

"Well let's hear it, at least." Morris said and stroked the long gray streak in his beard.

"You're Absalon of the Thousand Eyes, you say?"

Morris almost answered 'yes', but knew he needed to proceed with utmost caution. The koan had begun. Koanish Sphinxes were weird like that.

"Where are we right now?"

Morris still did not answer.

"The Labyrinth?" The Sphinx asked, and lurked over. She pulled her crones face close to Morris's, her soupy breath fell upon his neck. "Come now, give me some back and forth." She hissed and licked him, not unpleasantly. "You will know when I need your final answer. The only one that matters."

Her voice sounded oddly soothing, and Morris knew it was okay to repartee. This riddle was more like a game of chess. "Perhaps the Labyrinth, and perhaps not." Morris rebutted, a carefully calculated but defensive move.

"What is in between Perhaps?" The sphinx asked.

Morris looked through time, as though it were. And he remained silent, and he was correct.

"You still may not pass."

"I've already passed." Morris said.

"Have not." The Sphinx said, and it spoke the truth. Then, she swallowed and smacked her dry lips over her pointed teeth and tongue. "Are we the same?"

"There are no answers to these questions, and you know it."

"Why?"

"Words and thoughts skid over Truth like water on oil."

"Do any of your thousand eyes pierce into the Dimensions of Truth?"

"No."

"Why? Are your eyes inadequate?"

"There is no Dimension of Truth."

"Then, what is there?"

"Lies." Morris said, but spoke too hastily, giving the sphinx an advantage. All was lost.

"Wrong." The Sphinx said, and tore Morris' face apart. Morris was laughing and laughing. "Why are you laughing?" The sphinx asked, his nose skin hanging from her mouth.

"Because…" Morris said, snickering at the unfolding and complex layers of irony which form the foundations of our universe. "There is no Sphinx."

"What do you call is?" The Sphinx asked, but there was no Sphinx.

Morris proceeded to stare into emptiness for as long as encompasses the space between Perhaps. Then, he walked onwards to the Maw. It had been a risky endeavor, but he felt quite lucky his concept of self had already been called into question by the Octopus. "There is no Octopus." Morris tried to tell himself, but that was a statement he knew to be a lie. There would always be an Octopus. There was only the Octopus.

Chapter 18

The Cataclysm at Mount Hammurabi, as it would come to be known, shook loose the first snows of autumn as they built in the dark clouds round the peak, and set loose a mighty quake. Aislynn and the lifeless body of Coriander plummeted through both tree and thicket, while Ichabod fell to a fate as of yet unknown. Through this and her landing in moss and loam, Aislynn was spared the mercy of an instant death. Having fallen on her side, the moss formed a gauze that assuaged some blood loss from her mangled arm while Aislynn's preternatural healing mechanisms cared for the rest.

She gazed, hovering just at the farthest reaches of consciousness, into Coriander's open cranium. Cori's head fell and was cushioned by a boulder. Her body was some feet away in the mud.

While many would slip into darkness and be left to their fates, the nuanced magicks of the Paladin Order allowed Aislynn a measure of control where otherwise there would only be luck. She lay in profound pain and her head rang with its desire to slip away into the abyss.

Aid me Tezriel, Aid me Dosriel, Aid me Gabrion, Aid me Dosrah. Aislynn chanted in thoughts too quiet to adequately record. She called upon those Archangels with whom she had made her most familiar pacts. *I call upon the Cardinal Winds. My Mission is not yet complete, and my Covenant lay at your Mercy.* Then she spoke the sacred names of the Most High, which I shall not utter here.

For all one could observe on the outside, there was but silence in response to silence, uttered by a lifeless body by the pond of a forest glade. But from within, Aislynn's prayers were answered with fire. Her vision was engulfed. Her mind seared. This was an inferno like the sun, which swam in a sphere and set winds that could level mountains.

The passive observer would now see a twitch in Aislynn's finger tips, while Aislynn herself saw through to the end of time. The obliteration of molecular structures. Pain and ecstasy engulfed her, and her eyes opened to the forest glade, and to a far duller light than the one she had been observing with her eyes closed. The dust and clouds parted, and a shaft of light engulfed her glistening body.

Aislynn stood. Her knees quivered with both her own weakness and the nauseating sight of her recent companion, body mangled beyond recognition. But aside from this sight there was a predicament far more ingratiating, that of her own survival. Archangels liked to observe a challenge, and were never keen to give any but minimal assistance. Aislynn was still left with a mangled arm, half severed, and the bitter chill of a mountain in autumn which would approach dusk all too soon.

Her arm dangled by threads. Aislynn wasted not a moment. She managed her breath work to shift her consciousness in such a way that it would accept pain in full and utilize it. Then, stepping upon her hand with one metallic boot, she stood swiftly, and with determination. Her scream was like an aftershock to the quakes of the falling island, and for years those hiking in the foothills claimed they heard her call resonating like a banshee widow on moonless nights.

Aislynn clutched at her shoulder stump and gripped tight for pressure. She looked in Cori's blank eyes. *Necromancers be damned, there's no doubt in my mind it's not her time to go. Too young, too soon. I'm going to need to Resurrect her.*

Resurrection was no simple task. It required a great reserve of strength and life force from the one presiding over it. Aislynn did not have these things in abundance just at that moment. She'd need to strike a balance between her own rest and recovery and minimal decomposition of Cori's body. Tears, a strict prerequisite to all resurrection, she could worry about later.

My Archangels will be no more help here. Aislynn thought. *I'll need a Messenger to hear my prayers.*

Being a woman of action, it felt odd to prostrate herself in prayer and beg for assistance from the unseen, even just after the unseen had brought her back into this fold. But there was no way the both of them would make it off this mountain alive in the current state of things. Aislynn felt in her core that both she and this girl she had so quickly begun to call friend still played some part in things to come.

Calling out into the ether, vibrating her words in her core, Aislynn hailed out to the Messenger Angels, who might take pity on her and hear her plight.

Here's to hoping some came to observe the fall of the Chapel. Aislynn thought, then set back to her focused and rhythmic chanting.

In the Betwixt, properly vibrated prayers can carry for many miles. But Maya was no such distance. Maya was already searching the ruins of the Cataclysm and heard the commanding tones "Heed my call, and bring such assistance as you can, I implore you under the names of the Most High."

Maya pranced buoyantly through the Ethereal, layered just slightly overhead. She recognized the voice of the one called Aislynn, whom she had met only briefly on several occasions. The Ethereal forest was of sculpted ice that floated round the trees in flowing patterns, winter flowers bloomed from vines in the frozen trees. Maya dashed quickly to the source of the commotion and found Aislynn kneeling, praying fervently over a set of beads, rocking back and forth and humming while Cori's corpse and severed head lay to the side.

Aislynn's eyes opened with intensity, focused directly on Maya, whom she sensed as one might sense a stranger spying from the bushes.

"An Angel heard my call." Aislynn said aloud.

"Angel? I don't know about all that." Maya replied, but was not heard, for her voice could not resonate so physically. "Thanks though."

"Please." Aislynn vibrated her words again, her hands outstretched to the shaft of sunlight. "The girl will die if I cannot find rest and repose. Guide me, oh Messenger."

"Cori... Jeez, what a rough way to go." Maya said. She kneeled at the side of the Corpse as it was mirrored in the Betwixt. It was blossomed with plants and water gushed from its mouth in a gentle brook. *Not sure she wants to come back.* Maya thought, but then replied to herself "But that's not really my problem, now is it?

Do what you can, old girl." Then Maya looked off with a sight beyond sight for a solution to their woes. "There must be something nearby."

"Please, you must be swift." Aislynn pleaded.

"I'm swiftin, I'm swiftin." Maya replied, once again unheard. She held her gangly little spirit arm over her eyes as mock protection from the sun. In her realm, the sky was alight only with eyes that gazed down in awe. "There." In the distance she saw a cabin, and one that emanated the warmth of good people, and good stock. "Follow." Maya said in as low a frequency as she could muster in the hopes that Aislynn would hear it beneath the silence.

Aislynn did not, but Maya moved off towards the cabin faster than the wind and turned the very currents of the air themselves to usher Aislynn westward. Sensing the import of this subtle shift, Aislynn dragged Cori's body in the direction that the wind pushed. She kicked Cori's head along like a soccer ball.

It was a long and harrowing mile, far beyond the reach of any ordinary man's accomplishment. But women are gifted with a power of perseverance in the face of exhaustion and pain that would set many men to howling on the couch. Aislynn collapsed several feet from the front door of a poorly tended cabin, set about with sleighs and a smokehouse, dogs and hatchets, tanned hides and a tuber garden.

A hermit named Barnie lay napping within, but it was a silent cabin unaccustomed to visitors, and Aislynn's collapse set his dogs yowling. Snagging his boomstick, the buxom lumberjack kicked the front door out and aimed it at the two bodies that lay prostrate in his yard.

"What in the Nine Hells?" Hermit though he may have been, and Hunter he was by trade, it was in Barnie's nature to care for living things. "This one ain't dead yet." Dead things he was not as fond of. He left Cori's corpse on the frigid mountain but took Aislynn inside and placed her by the fire. Barnie gave her a stew of garlic and herbs and marrow while he marveled at the speed of her recovery, for all Paladin magick's work best when coupled with a dose of compassion.

"The girl, where is she?" Aislynn asked.

"The dead one?" Barnie replied, his voice like delicate wind chimes. "She's outside in the snow. The hell happened to her?"

"Excellent, she should not have decomposed much at all. There is time." Aislynn replied and took her first deep breath since the Cataclysm. Barnie's cabin was sparse and muddy, all one room. Vegetables sat in pickle jars above the bed in which several dogs lay napping. The air smelled of smoke, mesquite, pine needles and coupled with the tang of hounds. "What do they call you, stranger?"

"Those that know me call me Barnie." He said warily. He stirred the stew pot, and sipped from the spoon.

"Barnie… You have done so much. More than you know. But I ask you one more thing. I require a vial of tears, and there is only one person I know who collects them. Please, you must bring me down to St. Margaret's Home for the Nearly Departed. The girl outside may be saved yet."

"St. Margaret's?" Barnie asked, stroking the chin of his Siberian Wolfhound. "I deliver meats down thattaway. But ma'am, might it not be easier to shed a tear or two yourself?"

"I don't cry."

"Fair enough." Barnie stood and clapped his oversized hands. "Come on Jupiter, Julius, Jwango, Jorge, Jasper, Jennifer, and Jimmy-o. Need you all to take Papa for a ride." Barnie said this and one by one the dogs came to lick his beard before running out the front doggy door then hitched themselves up to the sled. "I'll take you to St. Margaret's, but then be on my way. I don't care much for the troubles of the world, and you do seem like an awful bit of trouble."

And off they dashed down the mountains into the darkening yonder.

Sammiel and Cori were far beyond all of that. They had managed to find their way to Cori's pocket realm and settled it as a home. Here they cooked chicken burgers and held sleepovers and shared stories of their past. The ruinous castle cathedral of Cori's pocket realm began to feel like home. There was a roaring hearth and brick oven in which they cooked an array of wood fire pizzas. They cozied under silken fur blankets while mysteriously sweet rain pattered at the rooftop of their cathedral abode. And when it was sunny, they basked on the cosmic beach drinking rum-tinis under marmalade skies.

The kiss was coming. Cori knew it. It was in Sammiel's eyes. They gazed so often and longingly at one another. She couldn't believe it had taken this long. She was all down for courting but at a certain point that boy needed to make a move. It was maddening.

She had learned so much about him that she hadn't expected. This buff necromancer with his deathly white skin and silver hair and ebony armors over esoteric tattoos was unbelievably quaint at heart. For all his old ambitions, the things that gathered his greatest interest were small. He talked often of his homunculi and how he missed them and hoped they'd be taken care of, or better yet that they'd take care of themselves. When they'd plan out their days, Sammiel would present ideas like finding an orchard to stroll through and pick fruit while they watched a dangerously close but chilly star set into its many brilliant hues upon an alien planet. Or sometimes he wanted them to just chat in a cafe. Never mind that the cafe was a shanty set upon a comet made of fungi as it spiraled throughout the galaxy. There was still an exquisite quaintness to all that Sammiel suggested, with only a break for the occasional prank which he delighted in playing on Cori, such as making an elaborate display of choking on a bone, so convincing that Cori forgot that they were already dead.

They could have been partying with the party god, or raging in the sonic pools of Sonorous with the demons of Sector 9. These were the things advertised in their after-life brochure that Cori had been certain Sammiel would want to do. But here he was, sipping the most perfect hybrid of chocolate and coffee in this quaint little fungal comet cafe and talking about how he had had dreams of starting a family whilst he was alive.

This drove Cori to greater upset. She too had dreamt of starting a family. And it was perhaps one of her only regrets.

"Sammiel…" Cori stopped him in the middle of what he thought he might have named his children. "I think we should help Maya."

"Hm?"

"I know we've been doing well. I know we have a lot of time left. But I don't want this to be the end. I'm not afraid of dying. But I want to live. Hell, I want to live just so I can die with you again." Cori looked deep into his eyes and hoped for that kiss which never came.

"I can't pretend I haven't been thinking about it."

"I want a family too, Sam. But we can't have one. As perfect as all this is, as all this has been...That's the one thing we can't have here. And...I keep thinking of my Mom. All she had to do to give me life. I have been so angry at her for so long for leaving my Father and I. But I never understood. She would have wanted nothing more than to be with me and my father. Now I'm thinking about how lonely she would have been, to know she was sick with the Crimson Plague, and dying. She had to leave us when she needed us most...And I've just been taking the life she gave me for granted...after everything. Sam, I just can't."

"Cori, I'm sorry, I had no idea. I knew some, but--" Sammiel said. "I just don't know what we could even do to help."

"It doesn't matter." Cori said, grasping his hands in hers, her eyes wide. "We just have to try. That's all. Just try. That's what she would have wanted..."

"But down there we might only get a few more hours together, if we're even that lucky. And what if--"

"What a surprise seeing you here, Cori," came a voice. Cori and Sammiel were startled and broke from each other's gazes, then looked above their comet cafe table where Ichabod stood, clad in his white linen robes which were now more radiant, in-laid with embroidery of a color as of yet undiscovered that bordered past blue. "I knew the strings of fate that bind us made this meeting inevitable, but I still must admit I'm shocked you've remained."

"Ichabod!" Cori exclaimed. "Oh, thank goodness. Sam, this is Ichabod. I told you about him. He's the one who exorcised Keiran from me." Cori looked up at Ichabod, admiringly. HIs eyes were distant and piercing. "Ichabod...I've wanted so badly to thank you. I don't remember much, but I know you're the reason I got away from Keiran in the end. I know things didn't work out as we planned, but you're the reason I have...well...so much... I'm sorry I can't quite find the words..."

"It's nice to meet you Ichabod." Sammiel said and stood to shake his hand. "Cori has told me so much about you."

Ichabod's eyes remained piercing and saw far past Cori and Sammiel as he looked at each of them in turn. "What are you two still doing here?"

"Oh." Cori said, awkwardly. "We were just discussing that actually. Maybe we've been a little caught up in ourselves. We should have been helping...We're going to go back down and see if we can find a way back to life. Ichabod, is there any way you could help us? We need all the help we can get, I think."

Ichabod's brow creased as he looked through Cori, and he stroked his beard. "I expected more from you Cori."

Cori felt a little hurt, but knew she deserved it. "Ichabod...I'm sorry. You did so much...oh God, you even gave your life to make sure I could appreciate mine again...but here I am... Ichabod, I'm so sorry. I can't even imagine how mad you must be."

"Mad? I am beyond anger. I am beyond this endless cycle of pain." Ichabod said and smiled though his eyes looked sad. "Of attachment. Tethering. I've always admired Necromancers, did Aislynn tell you that?"

Both Cori and Sammiel looked at one another. Cori turned back to Ichabod and nodded slowly.

"Neither side sees the whole picture." Ichabod continued, his eyes glowing with sympathy. "Both sides wish to ease suffering, yet both sides are at odds with one another. Necromancers, darkness and destruction, detached from this world and guiding souls along through life and death and back again, releasing them finally from all their bindings. Paladins, light and creation, nurturing their gardens and healing the ill and attached so wholly to this world, defending it from the encroaching forces of all those preternatural beings from beyond which bring destruction. Yet they are so afraid to die. But they both exist in harmony. You see that, don't you Cori?"

Cori was not sure why she was afraid to nod, but she nodded. She was afraid, too, to step away from Ichabod, though she desired this greatly. "Ichabod...what happened to you?"

"All Paladins train their spirits for one final gasp of battle, should they be slain in the fulfillment of their duties. The demon that had once been named Keiran killed my body, but not my soul. And in doing battle with him, my spirit rose. Angel and demon locked in bondage and conflict. He spoke to me, and I had my final Revelation." Ichabod enunciated slowly now. "That we too, Keiran and I, were One."

Cori was glad that Sammiel stood taller. He had been meek for a moment, but then his eyes grew fierce. They both understood something was wrong. Cori drew strength from him, and he from her, they both sharpened their eyes against Ichabod and called upon what powers they had within themselves. They readied themselves, and made their auras great and immense.

"I think it's time you left." Sammiel said, though it was clear that time had long since passed.

"Or, perhaps you do not understand." Ichabod said. "Perhaps you Necromancers are just as feeble minded as the Order of Paladins. Too caught up in yourselves to see the patterns of Destruction and Creation." Ichabod stretched gray wings out of his back, his eyes glowing, his aura burning orange and hot with fire.

"Ichabod, I don't want to fight you. You gave your life to save me, please don't let that be in vain." Cori pleaded.

The cafe barista, an immense and odious mushroom of a man, begged them for peace in his gibbering speech before cowering away. He sensed a fight threatening his comet home. The patrons all sought shelter and the air grew taut with the coming storm.

"In vain? I am Illuminated. I must thank you, Cori, for it was your coming which heralded my freedom. Now I can bring Rapture to all the world." Ichabod summoned forth a gleaming scythe, bone and ivory with all the radiance of the sun. It had an edge sharper than could be allowed within the confines of spatial reality. This materialized in his outstretched palm with a clap of thunder and a solar flare. "From the depths of the Villa of Ormen itself, a weapon that only one who can resist the Void may wield. So sharp it can cut through all attachment and bondage. Without it, there will be billions of lost souls seeking redemption in the coming Apocalypse, and no

Necromancers who can provide it. They will seek Liberation. And I shall be the Liberator." Before Ichabod finished speaking, and perhaps even before he began to move, he flew over and sliced through the air with his bone white scythe where Cori and Sammiel had been standing. Reality tore, and was stitched quickly by the Stitchers who keep watch over such matters.

Cori and Sam had moved with the perfect spiritual speed to which they had grown accustomed. Battles in the Betwixt are tricky like that. Most battles in the Mundane are based on exploiting imperfections and weakness. Without imperfections and weakness, there's an entirely different set of strategies with which to work from. Cori had once read up on it during a reading jamboree in the book "Schubert's Law: A Study on Astral Equivalency". Even with her reading augmentation, she had had a great deal of trouble understanding it.

"It's a chance to start over. To remake our world. To make it more perfect." Ichabod flew over and slashed again, moving at light speed. "But first, I must send you to the Villa."

Sammiel's Fell Daggers extended from bladed chains embedded in his flesh and bone and slashed round Ichabod's attacks so that no touch of the Sacred Scythe Blade neared them. Coiling as serpents, striking as scorpions, Sammiel led the offensive against Ichabod while Cori pirouetted round and confused his motions, and jabbed unexpectedly with her plasma blade in between Sammiel's slashes.

Still, unwilling to meet their combatant to the mortal end, Cori and Sammiel blasted away together and flew meteorically from the comet and past a moon and through Nebulae, down through Oceania and hopping from planet to planet, world to world, Ichabod in hot pursuit. Through gas giants and onwards through the fractalized Crystallatium. It seemed they would never escape, and indeed their only hope was to wear away at his willpower, for there would be no physical exhaustion in the Betwixt.

Cori, for her part, had never had greater will to live. Keiran possessing her and exploiting her latent suicidal ideations had, in the end, had the reverse effect of expelling those thoughts entirely, and left Cori with the deepest lust for life. Her will persevered beyond that of even the most disciplined Paladin. Sammiel, on the other hand, had latent and unexplored reservations, and his will was no match. It was this which slowed him, just a fraction of a nanobit below light speed, and allowed Ichabod's ivory scythe to pierce his soul. This severed him from the Crystallatium, and sent his soul spasmodically to the Villa beyond where he would confront Liberation itself.

Cori, in disbelief, could barely hear the ringing of the bell which halted Ichabod's onslaught. A portal had opened besides Cori, from which Ruth and Aislynn stepped forth. Like an Owl, Ruth held a bell in her left hand, candies in her right and was clad in the regalia of her tattered robes and skulls and jars. Aislynn, a radiant being, was wreathed in mistletoe and her usual gleaming regalia.

"Ichabod?" Aislynn asked, but Ruth had already grasped Cori from behind, forcefully, and pulled her backwards through the portal. Aislynn cast a wary glance at her old mentor, but sensed something amiss, and followed Ruth besides. All together, they crashed through all the layers and vibrations and Bardos of the Betwixt. Tears streamed from Cori's eyes as they fell through the multi-dimensional portal carried on the sound of Ruth's Bell.

Why am I crying? Cori asked herself, still unable to even comprehend that she had just seen Sammiel slain of his attachments before her very eyes. His eyes, instantly, had gone from concerned and loving wells of light, to the dull and neutral apathy one might see in a mask.

She had craved life so deeply, and no sooner had she vowed to come back and start a family with Sammiel than she was being resurrected without him, while he was reaped of all that made him who he was, and sent straight through to the Villa of Ormen.

Chapter 19

Morris entered the Maw, the deepest chamber within the Labyrinth below St. Margaret's Home for the Nearly Departed.

Keiran stood before the tooth rimmed pit that had given the room its name. The room had a rusted color that glinted through the darkness, and chains reached down into the acre sized hole. Hundreds of chains reached down into the pit that was lined with thick molars, like cow molars. Fat lips rimmed the edges of the opening. Keiran gazed below, looking more human than Morris had expected given his advanced demoniac state. The pit groaned a guttural and urine scented gurgle.

"Keiran…" Morris panted.

"Morris." Keiran said, sadly.

"Please…" Morris continued trying to catch his breath. His lungs were aflame. "Please stop this."

Keiran turned around and looked at Morris with every sympathy. Looking down at Morris. "You've been trying for so long to heal me. I can see the toll it's taken on you. On all of you. I don't want to be a burden."

"Keiran, you're not a burden. We love you."

"Love." Keiran chuckled. "I know you do."

"Keiran, I--"

"What did you always say I needed, Morris?" Keiran asked.

Morris didn't have to think long. "P-purpose."

"Well, it's done then. Mission accomplished." Keiran clapped, then laughed. "You are officially relieved of duties mon Capitaine. Ichabod...the Paladin...do you know him? He helped me to *see*. We fought, he and I. Well, he and the shred of me that was in Cori, that wonderful girl."

Morris couldn't believe what he was seeing. Keiran had shifted entirely. He was not that pool of suicidal angst that Morris had known for so long. This Keiran was filled with that latent personality Morris had only ever seen in glimpses. He had fire, and a glint of humor in his ghostly eyes. To the conscious mind, it all looked exceptionally good. There was only the plucky feeling of intuitive horror that took residence in Morris' gut. It might have had something to do with the manic look that stood alongside Keiran's new found sense of humor. Or maybe the way eyeballs still dripped down his body like rain drops. Or maybe it was the way in which he stood besides the apocalyptic warhead that resided within the Maw.

"Keiran...please...can you come with me? Can you just...we can leave the Labyrinth. You're right...you're doing so much better. You shouldn't be in the Labyrinth. This isn't the place for you."

"Oh, no no no, Morris. This is exactly where I'm supposed to be." Keiran said, fighting back a smile he couldn't control. "Do you know what's in here?"

Morris hesitated for a time. "Do you?"

"It's supposed to be some big old secret, right?"

"I thought I was the only one who knew…"

"Maybe the only one living. She was my friend, did you know that?"

"I had my suspicions…" Morris replied.

"Her final miracle...Margaret sacrificed herself to bind the Crimson Plague. Now *that's* a purpose. I must admit. But I do think I have a better one. It's a little bit deeper, if I do say so myself, at least on a philosophical level."

"Keiran, do you really think she'd have bound that plague within her own body so she could suffer for the rest of eternity as an embodiment of disease stuck in an abysmal pit if there wasn't a *really* good reason?"

"I think people do a lot of dumb things out of ignorance, and even Saints are human. I know what it's like to be trapped and bound by the chain and weight of suffering like she is...and I want to free her, like I am now. She did so much for me while she was alive. She really tried her damnedest to heal me, and when even that wasn't enough, she respected me and my choices till even the bitter end. She was the only one who cared at the end. And she promised she would see me through to Liberation if I ever lost my way. I will free her, then she can free *everyone*. And we can all start again, in a world less evil. A world of less suffering. You should understand, Mr. Necromancer."

The problem for Morris was that he did understand. He knew plenty of the dynamics of destruction and creation. He pondered them often himself. The plan was entirely sensible, but only if you ignored empathy and compassion. But even then, you only had to ignore them for a little bit. Eventually, life would begin again. The world would start again, and it could be remade even better.

"You're beginning to see the wisdom of my plan, aren't you Morris?" Keiran asked with a plucky wag of his eyebrow.

"I'm familiar with the reasoning. There's just one problem. A little fallacy you've overlooked and probably couldn't grasp." Morris said and felt a little smug because he'd read a couple of books on this. "While I do understand that Destruction begets Creation, the precise people who would execute such a plan of destruction are not the sorts of people you would ever want creating anything."

"Oh, you think so little of me, Morris." Keiran replied, grinning. "For that, I have a contingency. See, I will act as the Destroyer. I've appointed Ichabod as Liberator, to ensure the souls are given prompt Rapture at the Villa of Ormen. And to St. Margaret, I will appoint the title of the Creator of our new world."

"Oh, shit." Morris said. St. Margaret was exactly the sort of person you would want to help build a new world.

"I release St. Margaret, and the plague infects all the land. Ichabod then destroys the Plague with Hanuman's Bone Scythe, freeing St. Margaret. Returned to her original form, I appoint St. Margaret Magistrate of the new world order, and hand her a fresh slate to do with as she pleases. I imagine she will be reluctant. All the best rulers are."

Morris was speechless. The last thing he expected was to agree with Keiran's plan.

"Ichabod will end me as soon as my task is done." Keiran added, just as Morris was going to ask about one of his few remaining reservations. "A proper execution for my sins.Justice. And I can finally rest."

"Uhhhh…" Morris guffawed as Keiran stepped backwards over the lips of the pit, then fell like a martyr into the abyssal Maw. Morris reached out half-heartedly towards Keiran, but was lacking in the necessary motivation to actually stop the coming Apocalypse. A world recreated with less suffering…"Well, damn."

Cori was forced into her base meat sack down in the confines of the Mundane walls of St Margaret's. She woke to the taste of skittles in her mouth, which Ruth was applying generously. Cori had never met Ruth before, so this was a very disconcerting sight to wake up to. A strange woman with scrambled hair and a mad look in her eye breathing hot breath onto Cori's face while dumping foreign albeit sweet objects into her mouth. The only consolation was that she saw her friends near her, who stretched their arms and adjusted themselves to their old meat machines as well.

Maya, Dana, Derrick, Kitsune. But there was no Luke. And most distinctly of all, there was no Sam. Cori was crying as soon as she was reborn. Not from the pain in her neck where her head had been severed from her body then roughly reattached. She cried from the pain in her heart where she knew Sammiel had been sent beyond redemption.

Aislynn stood above her, her hands in a diamond where a golden glow showered down upon Cori. The light breathed life and vitality into her very bones. Beside Aislynn was a big bear of a man wearing flannel and carrying a boomstick.

"How--?" Cori began to say, but was interrupted by Ruth.

Ruth was angry, but laughing. It was a disconcerting mix. "I don't even know what to say to all of you. I mean-- You're all trained necromancers and you couldn't even handle a newly born demon. *Three* staff died? I've got people up in Nova Scotia who take on ancient demons one on one, I mean-- What are you being paid for?"

Cori didn't know Ruth, but it looked like Maya and Dana did. They kept their mouths pursed and didn't make eye contact. Cori followed their lead.

Derrick didn't. "Listen lady, I don't know who you are but--"

"Lady?" Ruth laughed. "I am Ruth Stevens, Director of Operations at St. Margaret's. Morris's Boss. And I expect an awful lot more respect than to be called 'lady'." She said this, but her face contorted into a grimace and lasers shot from her eyes. Derrick howled as his flesh turned to stone, and Ruth continued speaking. "Now we're going to whip this place in order and have it done by yesterday. The Council of Necromancers will be arriving tomorrow morning to conduct a Quality Assurance Review, and we're going to have this place running better than they were before all this mess. I don't know how Morris runs things, and frankly, I don't want to know. While I'm around, I'm going to expect you to do perfectly, but you're going to go above and beyond and do better than that. You, Sia." Ruth pointed at Maya, then her face softened a smidge. "Before I forget, you have an ulcer in your stomach, dear. Best to get it checked out. Cut back on acids and fats." Ruth's face hardened again. "Now let's get this straight. No one here died." Ruth said. "Keiran knocked a couple people in the head. Whatever you may remember while you were knocked unconscious amounts to nothing more than fever dreams at best. The only people Keiran killed are these two gentlemen here, Duke and Spam." Ruth's face went soft again. "A terrible shame. I really liked Duke." Ruth bit into a few skittles again, and then shuddered with a spasm of electricity. "Sia."

"It's Maya." Dana said, but Ruth jabbed two long nailed and red painted fingers directly into Dana's eyes, then immediately healed her bleeding eyes.

"*Maya* and Danielle here will begin finding all the residents and bind them in the living room. Once there, keep order and await further instructions." Ruth grabbed Derrick's hand and returned him from stone to flesh. "Could you hear everything I was saying?" Ruth asked Derrick.

Derrick was gasping for breath like a fish out of water, clinging to Kitsune's skirt while she casually cleaned her nails and paid little heed to any of what was going on. "Yes, but I couldn't breathe, what the hell?" Derrick cried.

"Suck it up, buttercup." Ruth said. "What's your name again? You must be newer."

"Derrick." Derrick said, exasperated and wiping pieces of stone off his skin.

"Okay, Dominic, you look like a strapping young man. You're gonna go with Billie here." Ruth said and pointed to Cori. Derrick was happy about this. "You two are going to go find Morris and help him with the demonic binding in case he's just as incompetent as I think he is. Billie. Dominic can be the brawn, you be the brains. Too much testosterone is terrible for the proper execution of any plan."

Ruth said and looked up and to the left as though remembering a very specific instance. "I'm going to stay here and contact Facilities about getting a repair squad, and then run through the books to make sure Morris is ready for the Quality Assurance review. There's really no point in surviving a demon's wrath if you're all just put at the mercy of Corporate the next day." Then Ruth turned her attention to Aislynn and the lumberjack. "You." She said to Aislynn. "You're a Paladin, right?" Aislynn looked as though she was going to salute in proper Paladin fashion, but she was missing the arm for it, having stupidly left her arm back on the mountain. She had had a lot on her mind. Ruth looked Aislynn over for a moment. "Go to hell." Ruth said, but Aislynn looked like she didn't have the strength to be offended. "Oh, you're no fun. What's your name?"

"Aislynn."

"Alright Aspen, now I'd like to stress the absolute reality that no one here has died. However, if for some reason there is an Inquisition and it is determined by the ignorant that a few people did die, I hope you'll admit that it was you who brought everyone back to life. Are we clear on that?"

"I'm really too tired to even--"

"Good." Ruth said, then turned to Barnie the Hermit. "And you, Porky. What the hell are you doing here?"

"I'd really like to get going, if it's all the same."

"Not a chance. Not till all this gets straightened out. No loose ends."

"Yeah, you're not my boss." Barnie murmured. Ruth approached him, a foot shorter, reached up and looked as though she were going to kiss him before she bit deep into his neck. Blood sprayed and Barnie yowled, then Ruth healed him as quickly as she bit him.

"I am *The* Boss. You're sticking with the Paladin till this is all sorted. Now, all of you, things are getting a little messy. I feel it in my bones. I understand why Duke died." She motioned to Luke's lifeless body. "He barely had a year left in him anyway, and poets are always in love with death. We will give him a proper burial when it's time. But this one." She motioned to the body of Sammiel. "I saw a rogue Paladin slice through our own with Hanuman's Bone

Scythe. I have no idea how he got his hands on that artifact. It's supposed to be kept safe within the Villa of Ormen. But I saw it with my own eyes. It's a shame we lost a good man like that."

"Ma'am." Cori stepped forward. "I'm sorry I haven't met you before. I'm Cori."

Ruth's eyes curled as she shook Cori's outstretched hand. "Yes, yes. I'm sorry about your coworker, Billie. You two seemed close."

A knot developed in Cori's throat. *No Coworkers.* "Ma'am...I need to bring him back too. You brought everyone here back. There must be a way to retrieve him from the Villa of Ormen."

"Billie, people die all the time. We will be able to hire new staff."

The knot in Cori's throat grew tighter, but Cori stood taller. "I...can't accept that. I'm in love with him." She said, looked into Ruth's eyes and felt tears fall from her set and determined eyes.

"Oh, dear. There'll be other loves." Ruth said.

"I'm sure there might be. But I don't care. I need to try to bring him back. There must be a way to bring someone back from the Villa of Ormen."

Ruth looked at her, and contemplated. "The Villa of Ormen isn't such a simple place. You haven't learned about it have you? Morris has always been terrible at new staff orientations. It's not like some locked door that no one has figured out how to open. That would be simple enough. It's not that no one *can* get out. It's that no one *wants* to get out."

Cori looked back at Ruth and still felt as though something was being left out of these vague statements. "Can you...just tell me what you mean? Directly?"

"It's...pleasant, child. To be so carefree. One sometimes doesn't notice how heavy the burdens of life fall upon the shoulders till they're removed. Duty is heavier than a mountain, death is lighter than a feather, as they say."

Cori clenched her fists, and stifled a whimper. The thought of Sammiel being beyond her reach was too much to bear, but it was far worse to imagine herself offering him return only to be rejected.

"The powers are beyond you." Ruth said simply, and clasped Cori's shoulders. "Only the most powerful Paladins are able to resurrect a soul from the Villa, and even then it's a toss up."

"What if Sam isn't *in* the Villa?" Cori asked. "Do we know where he went?"

"Hanuman's Bone Scythe would send him riggggghhhhht into the Villa." Ruth said, trying to end the conversation on a note she knew to be futile.

"I need to...sit...and process this." Cori said. As a necromancer with some control over the ebb and flow of life and death, she had reserved hope that Sammiel was not truly gone.

Ruth's expression shifted from soft and caring to a dictatorial intensity. "No, you will go help Morris with his binding. You're still on the clock, unless I'm mistaken. Emotions can be left at the door. Bye. *Bye.* Everyone else, I need all hands on deck, we've got a lot--"

A rumble interrupted Ruth as she delegated, and an architectural howl. A crack grew along the hallway as the wood of St. Margaret's groaned in protest. The split made its way between the feet of the hermit and amongst the coworkers. Ruth held up her hand for everyone to stay still. The groaning gave way to silence. Then a louder groan emitted from the wooden floorboards, the ceiling and all of St. Margaret's split in two. It opened several feet to the autumn wind outside and the gloom of the late evening sky, ghosties and ghoulies wailed as they escaped their confines and floated upwards to bear witness to this new calamity.

From below, the cyclonic emanations of sick vapors twisted upwards to the sky. A full tornado of Miasma began to spin as the air gained ominous weight. Thick, black, nearly dripping in ooze, the tornado raged upwards filled with faces and limbs. Or not black. Just deep and dark with oily blood. In the center of it all, they spotted a figure rising. A very ordinary and somewhat familiar looking figure hanging with broken chains. Her arms reached up to the heavens as she levitated up and up towards the sky.

Below, the employees and others could glimpse the open top of the underground Labyrinth through the torn framework of St Margaret's Home. The toothy maw looked like an open throat from which the black tornado formed its base. And beside the cyclonic maw, Morris shielded his face from the onslaught.

Ruth looked furious. Cori was terribly afraid of the woman. Everyone was. Ruth made a number of hand gestures which looked curiously like martial arts. Cori wasn't quite sure what she was doing until she saw, from down below, Morris was gripping at his neck, force choked, and dragged through the air up several floors to meet them. He was set down in front of Ruth with a final martial arts gesture like the releasing of breath. Then Ruth grabbed him by the scruff of his neck, slapped his mouth open, and plucked all the teeth from his jaws in one rapid motion.

Morris yowled.

Ruth kneed him in the groin several times. "What happened?" Ruth yelled, kneeing him again.

"Thaint Magwet ith akthually the kwimthon pwague." Morris tried to yammer through his gums. Ruth grew his teeth back with a wave of her hand and a purple magick like fire. "St. Margaret was locked in the Labyrinth after binding an Entity of Pestilence using her own body as a host. Keiran went down there and released her, and the Crimson Plague with her."

Ruth grabbed his shoulders and kneed him in the groin even harder. Morris yowled even harder.

"And-why-didn't-you-do-anything-to-stop-him?" Ruth yelled, spittle flying from her mouth.

"It actually kind of made sense when he presented the idea…" Morris tried to say, but Ruth slapped him to the floor, and kicked him into the floor so many times that Cori heard Morris's ribs snap, and eventually his organs squished.

"So, that's St. Margaret up there?" Ruth screamed at Morris' corpse. But Morris was dead. Ruth brought him back to life, but did not restore his bones or organs. "Answer me!"

"Yasss--" Morris wailed, on the cusp of life and death. "Yassss. I'm sorry. I'm sorryyyyyy…"

Then Ruth restored him fully with another wave of purple fiery magicks, and he was able to stand at full strength, if a little shaken.

"That's it everyone, *now* all hands on deck." Ruth said. "Sia and Danielle, go gather the residents and keep them bound in the living room. Billie and Dominic, go with Morris and take care of the demon. Blondie, Fatso, Nosferatu, I need you to do damage control in Remedy. This will be pandemonium, and I need people taking care of the community. As for myself…." Ruth sighed, and looked up as though praying. "I'm going to have to alert the Council of Necromancers of the threat. I don't think this can be contained. Remember, if anyone asks, no one was resurrected. If they decide people were resurrected anyway, blame the Paladin. Okay. Bye. Bye. *Byeeeee*."

Chapter 20

"Well if it isn't Mr. Pumpernickel himself. Haven't seen you for a hot minute." Lucy Draughtsmith put her hands on her hips and gave a familiar smile to her old high school pal, Chris Pumpernickel. "What dragged you into town?"

"I wasn't sure you'd remember me. How's it going Lucy?" Chris Pumpernickel asked, walking into the aromatic two story shop leaning precariously into the corner of Restwood and Pine. Through a distorted glass frame panel came a warm glow and the multicolored frizz of a display of potions to the street side, amidst the odd and sometimes disturbing assortment of smells that accompanied such concoctions.

Lucy ran the most prosperous potion shop in Remedy, Dank Draughts, renowned for her euphoriants and aphrodisiacs. In medicine, compared to Maude Grimm's shop, she couldn't hold a candle. But people cared more about Lucy's potions than Maude's cures for flus and pimples. The people in Remedy had, overall, very nice skin. It was one of those towns where healthy and attractive people gathered, for whatever reason. Both Chris and Lucy were in their mid thirties and enjoying the stability and ease of mind that that age brings. They had both once been in the Varsity Gladiator league in their respective high schools, though Lucy had been a cheerleader back in the days when boys and girls were separated like that. Their school had lost only three students to the Gladiator Arena in the three years that Chris attended.

Mr. Chris Pumpernickel was also scrumptiously handsome, though this was mostly irrelevant to Lucy who was happily married and enjoyed the freedom from sexual longing that marriage can occasionally bring about. He was a traveling salesman. He sold pickles for the Vanderschmidt pickle empire which had invented an entirely new way of pickling vegetables that made all vegetables infinitely more delicious. They were called Schmidt Pickles, which Mr. Pumpernickel thought was a poor choice of name. But they sold like hot cakes, so he wasn't complaining. You could put virtually any vegetable through the Schmidt Pickling Process, and it would come out tasting as savory as a chicken wing. Cucumbers, radishes, broccoli, lettuce. They all retained their overall nutritiousness, but served as a guilty pleasure like a juicy hamburger. Mr. Pumpernickel could visit big clientele or travel door to door, but his result was always the same. No matter how hungover or surly he might have been on any particular day, those pickles would sell, and in large quantities.

"You know my mom's been sick, so I'm back in town for a while to take care of her." Chris Pumpernickel said.

"Oh geez, not Martha…"

"Yeah, she's been bad off for a while now. My brother Morty's been taking care of her, but I think he needs a break. Can be a real strain to take care of someone for a long time. Her mind's been going. It's been rough."

"Oh, I'm so sorry to hear that." Lucy said, mostly earnestly.

"Eh, it is what it is. I just wanted to take a stroll through town to see how the old gang is doing." Chris said, wearily. "I hear things have been going really well for you."

There was a bit of a commotion outside, but neither of them paid attention.

"Well, did you hear Ernie died?" Lucy asked.

"Nooooo."

"Ah, yes. Few years back."

"Gosh, how old are we? He was so strapping. What happened?"

"Ehhh, it looked like a vampire attack." Lucy said.

"A vampire? A vampire couldn't take Ernie down. I saw him go five to one in the Gladiator Arena when he was sixteen." Chris Pumpernickel protested, and frowned. "He was an Admiral for the Paladins wasn't he? Did something take down his whole squad?"

"Couldn't tell you. Classified information. I'm working off rumors here." Lucy shrugged and started to take more notice of the commotion growing outside. She peered over Chris'shoulders.

"Dammit. I had been hoping to visit him next." Chris tried to gather himself. "Well anyway, I was going around hoping to invite a few of the old gang out to Duke's-- Lucy? What are you looking at?"

"Hold up for a second." Lucy said, then walked out from behind the darkwood counter to where people were pointing and gasping and holding their hands to their mouths in shock. Lucy ran out onto the clumsy cobblestone streets to look North, where everyone else was looking, out to the Moldivine Mountain range. There, up above Mt. Hammurabi had been the floating islands which housed the Chapel at St. Luc's, a famous retreat for only the most daring of pilgrims. But those floating islands were much lower than usual, and falling. The enormous ropes which bound them were slacking and loosing. "Mother of---" Lucy said.

Next to Lucy were Mr. and Mrs. Salamander who held each other with a look of restrained panic in their wide eyes. "What does it mean?" Mrs. Salamander asked.

"It doesn't mean anything." The husband replied with his garbling voice, looking stubborn but uncertain. "The islands are just falling. That's all."

Dark birds were flying en masse southwards, darkening the sky, cawing and pooping as they fled.

"This is it." Shouted Skinny John Silver, Remedy's very own crazy homeless man. His wild tousled hair and shaggy beard was strung about with flowers, top to bottom. He was wearing an old and dirty wedding dress, and carrying a sign that said 'Fart'. "I remember this. This is...it." He said, then began to sing, first looking joyful, then pained. "Live...now. Only...love!" He interspersed his words with both shouting and whispering and singing. "Only love...Only love can save us. Inspire!" Then he proceeded to make a farting sound with his mouth and ran through the streets of Remedy and ripped off his dirty wedding dress.

"Oh, Skinny John." Lucy said to herself and shook her head. She had gone to school with him.

"What a fool." Chris said, coming up behind her.

"I love Skinny John." Lucy snapped back. "I've never heard him say one bad thing about another person. He's just unique."

Chris Pumpernickel rolled his eyes. "Wait, is that the Chapel at St. Luc's?" He asked as the distant cluster of floating islands slammed into another mountain in the Moldivine Mountain Range, many miles away. Several dozen seconds later an enormous rumble came with a roar of earth and thunder. "Jeez, those have been floating up there for millennia. Well, goes to show ya, what goes up must come down."

"I don't like this." Lucy said, but tried to put it out of her mind.

Lucy cleaned up after a slow day at the shop, and distracted herself with thoughts of what shenanigans Lance was going to get into in tonight's episode of the hit reality TV show "Pillage me, Softly," where a churlish group of Pirate Raiders has to find love amongst the stricken widows of towns that they had once burned and pillaged. The real kicker of the series was that the widows didn't know that the men they were dating were the pirate raiders who had once burned down their home towns and killed their late husbands. But the series finale was approaching and it really couldn't be much longer before the widows would receive the big reveal. It was the talk of everyone at the Salon, Deus Ex Capilla, where Lucy's friend Carmen worked and where Lucy spent many afternoons once her own shop had closed.

This afternoon, Lucy dyed her hair like an oil slick. She was looking for a change.

She returned home to the astronomy tower at the edge of town where she lived and her husband, Quinn, kept his business. The observatory was set upon a forested plateau about three miles from the town square. Lucy liked to walk home each day to stay in shape, and when she arrived home she'd take care of her chickens and goats and emu and the docile breed of California Hippopotamus her daughter had goaded her into getting. Lucy had a she-shed outside the main abode where she would go to loom and get away from the world, but today she went right in to see Quinn and Harley, their daughter.

The home was painted in a variety of colors, all corresponding appropriately to the cardinal directions in respect to the principles of feng-shui. I don't know the principles of feng-shui, so I can't tell you which walls those colors were on. But they were Pink, Blue, Orange, and Green. The telescope normally pointed upwards, and her husband was usually asleep at this hour, being an astronomer, but he must have heard the collision, as the telescope was pointed low and towards the north where the Chapel at St. Luc's had collapsed. Quinn was nervously sipping coffee.

"So you know..." Lucy said.

"Truly ominous. Truly." Quinn said. He was eighteen years her senior, and wore a monocle on his right eye, his telescope eye, which had taken damage from years of too close observations. He liked to overdress. You'd never see him out of a suit. This worked well with his afro. Especially when he wore a white suit. Light colored suits contrasted his skin, and made him look downright sexy.

"I just think it's sad. I had wanted to visit there when I retired." Lucy said. "I mean-- I'm not sure I ever could make the climb up those ropes, but Sherpa Sheila from next to the grocery store had guaranteed me she'd be able to get me up there..."

"Saturn is in retrograde." Quinn replied, shaking his head slowly. He was an astronomer by trade, but an astrologer by hobby. He also sold stars to wealthy idiots as a side hustle. "It explains *everything*. There will be more to come. I know it." He could be grim at the best of times.

Harley, their daughter, eight years of age, was too busy practicing with her slingshot to notice her parents' concern. She might have broken something, but her parents were minimalists. Or rather, her father was. Lucy wasn't, but that was why she had her cluttered she-shed where she could escape. It was of great benefit to their marriage.

"Mommy, can I shoot the chickens with my sling shot?" Harley asked her mother, tugging on Lucy's leg.

"Honey, no, we've talked about this." Lucy said. They had had this conversation many times. Harley was absolutely dead set on being a mighty gladiator. This had only gotten worse when Quinn gifted her the sling shot and told her stories of David and Goliath. Lucy was all for gender equality now that girls were entering the gladiator arena, but she felt she wouldn't be keen on a son joining the gladiators either.

"But I don't have any targets in here." She said. "I need to practice so I can be a Gladiator."

"Quinn, you got her the slingshot, can we just get her a dang target?" Lucy asked, sighing. She knew the answer already.

"The more we own, the more we are owned." Quinn said, mechanically.

"A toy even?" Lucy asked, then sighed again. She loved Quinn so so much, but sometimes his habits were grating. Sometimes she wanted to own a damn vase, even if it just meant Harley would break it with her slingshot.

Quinn picked up on Lucy's growing annoyance. "Oh jeez, look at me. And here I didn't even notice you got your hair done. You're gorgeous. I'm sorry honey. I've been lost to my own thoughts. It's Saturn Retrograde. I haven't been giving you much attention. Say...I know. Let's go out for dinner tonight. I'll take you to Roma's on Third. Meemaw can come over and watch Harley."

"Awwww, not Meemaw." Harley moaned.

"I'm sorry, honey. Chris Pumpernickel invited us out to Duke's tonight. I almost forgot to tell you." Lucy kissed Quinn on the cheek. "You're very sweet though."

"He invited *us* out? Somehow I don't believe that." Quinn said, giving Lucy a knowing look.

"Well he...I'm sure that's what he meant."

"I doubt that." Quinn said with disapproval. "I really do not care for him. I see how he looks at you."

Lucy gave a playful push to Quinn. She had a love-hate relationship with his jealousy. "Oh please, like it matters. You know I've only got eyes for you. Ehhh... maybe we should just skip out on it. I didn't give him a definite answer. I just feel bad, I haven't seen them all in so long. After Ernie died, I feel like...you know, you never know when it'll be the last time you'll see someone."

"Well then, you don't know when it'll be the last time we can have a date at Roma either. Existential worry applies to everyone, and everything." Quinn said and pushed up his monocle as it glared in the sun setting through the kitchen window. It turned Lucy on whenever he did that. She wasn't sure why. It was just one of those things. Quinn wasn't aware of this, and she didn't want him to be aware of it. But right about now, he could ask her to do anything. Anything.

"Yeah okay, let's go to Roma." She said, stupid with lust for this brilliant oaf she had married.

Lucy called her mother, 'Meemaw', to babysit Harley for the night. Meemaw was always more than glad to watch Harley. And Harley's only complaint with Meemaw was that Meemaw always insisted on dinners of pea soup. Pea soup was something of an obsession for Meemaw.

The Draughtsmith's got ready for their date over the course of a couple hours. For the most part, Quinn was already prepared, as he stayed in formal wear at all times. Still, he redid his hair and freshened his breath and put on cologne and all after he had taken a frigidly shivering cold shower. Lucy put on what few pieces of jewelry she kept in a small box in her she-shed, and applied makeup in the same place after a scalding hot shower and changing into her little black dress that she saved for such occasions.

Quinn ordered a neon rave palanquin via Uber, and made last minute reservations at Roma. This was very lucky, there usually weren't last minute reservations available at Roma.

Roma was the sort of place where the owner was also the chef and was also a gardener. Vegetables were served in season. The owner's name was Nicki Fitz, and he was friends with both the town Butcher, Connie, who gave him the freshest meat; and also

Big Bob Donahue, the best fisherman this side of the Mississippi. The menu was prepared daily based on what was available.

Quinn and Lucy arrived at Roma at 6:07 pm, 8 minutes in advance of their reservation. Timeliness could be one of their few true arguing points, as Quinn was fastidious about being early. Lucy liked to take her time getting ready, but had learned this was one of the few soft points in their marriage, and so she made concessions. Quinn recognized the effort Lucy had put into this concession, and secretly gushed about it in his heart. He hoped she knew how much he loved her.

An Aramaic gentleman greeted them as host, and ushered them to their seats. There were only six tables in Roma, to ensure the quality of the food prepared.

"Oh, Quinn! Eli and Whitney are here!" Lucy said, excitedly. Eli was the Barista at Quintanilla's Produce Cafe, where they served a variety of coffee and espresso based drinks alongside fresh grilled produce. Eli had Down Syndrome, and was proud of it. Everyone in town knew and loved him for his warmth and mischievous personality. His wife, Whitney, also had Down Syndrome. People tended to find her a bit shrill, but she was known as one of the most caring mothers in town and she did excellent work at the DayCare, caring for the babies and toddlers. "Eli, Whitney, Hi!" Lucy said, sounding very suburban.

Some people would be annoyed at being interrupted during a romantic dinner, but not Eli and Whitney. Eli's eyes curled right up and he gave a big smile. He had plump rosy red cheeks. "Oh hi! Lucy! My Friend." Eli said. Whitney giggled. She was shy when she was seen outside of the daycare, and wouldn't speak.

Quinn shook their hands and gave them each a bright smile, but Lucy was the one who kept the conversation moving. "How's things at Quintanilla's?

"I make coffee there." Eli announced with pride.

"No, no, no. You make the *best* coffee there." Lucy said. And she meant it. Eli had been practicing for years, and to top it all off, he poured love into each cup. You could taste it. It tasted pink and cloudy. "I had one the other day. You keep getting better."

"I know. Did you see my friend?" Eli asked. "Carmen? She said hi to me today."

"I saw Carmen today too! Say, we should all go out sometime. Carmen, her husband Dan, Quinn and I, and you and Whitney. It'd be fun. Have you ever gone to Duke's?"

"I love Duke's!" Eli said.

"Great." Lucy said, and looked over at Quinn smiling. "I'll text you. Next weekend. I think we have a long weekend. I'll talk to you later, Eli. Bye Whitney." Whitney batted her eyes.

"Bye, I love you." Eli said.

"Love you too, Eli. Love you, Whitney." Lucy said, and Whitney blushed. Quinn said 'bye' to the both of them quietly and with a nod. Quinn was more of an introvert.

Quinn and Lucy sat down and opened their menu. The menu was sparse, but each and every thing available looked delectable. You couldn't choose wrong.

"They have Manticore?!" Quinn guffawed. "I don't think I've ever seen that on a menu."

"Must have been Barnie, the Hermit. You can only get those by hunting them in the mountains. And he's the only one with a boomstick license." Lucy knew this because she was friends with the town bureaucrat, Asper Cats.

"God, I love coming here." Quinn said. "Thanks for going out with me. I really wanted a night to ourselves. I'd been thinking about it all day."

"You're so sweet. When am I gonna get bored of loving you?" Lucy asked. She had been surprised by how much she still enjoyed Quinn's company, even after all of these years.

The waiter came over and explained the specials of the night. He was outrageously French. "Ze Specials of ze night include ze Manticore." You get the idea. He didn't come off as rude though. His name was Pierre. He liked to skateboard on the weekends, for what it's worth. "Ze Manticore tail will be served with butter sauce in classique fashion. 'Owever, ze loin will be served under toasted olives and garlic with zis year's 'arvest of tomatoes and a special *stinky* cheeseuh zat compliments ze musk of ze meat. Ze cheese has been cured, compliments of our chef Nicki." Pierre said, then went on, "We also have euhhh, le Papillon."

"Excuse me?" Lucy asked.

"Le Papillon. Euhh--woof woof." The waiter said, truly putting effort into properly mimicking a small dog.

"Oh, I don't know how I feel about that." Lucy said, a little dizzied.

"Oh, come on Lucy. Lighten up." Quin said. "Some people think cows are sacred but we still eat them."

"Euhhh if it 'elps, numerous studies 'ave pointed to le Papillon being ze euhhh---most ecologically...sustainable meat."

"So you're telling me it's green to eat Papillon?"

"So far as meat goes, oui." Pierre shrugged.

Lucy also shrugged and frowned, but weighed her morality. She was morbidly curious.

"As I was saying, le Papillon will be braised in a mint tardigrade zauce with locally zourced 'oney. Zis will come with air fried potatoes sprinkled with feta. We can pair it with a Chardonnay which makes an exquisite combo." Pierre concluded, smiled wide and twiddled his thin moustache. "We 'ave ze lasagna, a customer favorite. It is magnifique, as anyone will tell you. We also 'ave ze pho zoup with roasted duck." Pierre looked back and forth at his customers. "You need ze minute to decide? Would you like me to get you started with drinks?"

"Yes, yes, I think we're both having the concord grape wine." Lucy said. "Right, Quinn?"

"Yup." Quinn said. It was both of their favorite.

"And I dunno, I think I'm ready. Are you, Quinn?"

"Yup."

"Okay, ya know, I think I'm going to have the Papillon. You only live once, right? And...I'll also get a chardonnay. I want two wines. Big."

"Excellent Madame. And for you monsieur?"

"I'll have the lasagna, thank you."

"Oh, you always have the lasagna." Lucy protested, but Quinn ignored her.

"Oui, Monsieur." Pierre said, and took their menus.

Their drinks were brought shortly. The red for Quinn, and the red and the white for Lucy. They sipped quickly for a minute, enjoying the silence but looking forward to the glib flow of conversation the wine would soon bring.

Lucy knew she could break the ice talking about astrology. "So, Saturn retrograde. What's going on?"

"Oh, you know Saturn. It's a rough one. Harsh lessons. Very harsh lessons. Retrograde is no good with Saturn. You want to think you'll be better off sometimes, but the things you lose along the way, it's...well it can be closely balanced at the best of times."

"Well, that doesn't sound good. How long does it last?"

"A few months. We're at the tail end though. Honey, I can't believe you ordered the Papillon. You used to be a vegetarian. I was joking when I said to lighten up."

"Those dogs are so cute, they must taste good. Plus, Pierre said it's environmentally sustainable."

Quinn laughed. "You're just full of surprises, aren't you? And speaking of, I hear you're--"

Quinn was interrupted by screaming outside the restaurant. The whole restaurant quieted. The waiter, Pierre, went outside to check, but he did not return. Quinn said "hold on a second, hon, I'm gonna go check what's going on." Quinn and a few others went outside, Eli included. All Lucy could hear was "Oh holy shit," before she just had to run outside to see.

From the North East rose an unholy tornado in the dark evening sky. It was hard to make it out, but flashes of green lightning highlighted it from time to time. The wind had picked up, blowing northwards, and ominous incantations could be heard in the air.

"Oh, Quinn what's happening?" Lucy said, shocked from her normal flow of consciousness. Then, her eyes widened and she dropped the two glasses of wine she had brought with her outside. "Harley!"

Everyone knew that the whirling tornado of dark smoke was coming from St. Margaret's down on River Road. The people of Remedy knew what peculiar things emanated from within that place, and were ever on the alert for the rise of potential disaster. It was a hot topic every November on the political signs adorning most front lawns. Specters were always escaping the place, stealing magazines and spooking the citizenry. People didn't know the depth of what occurred there, but rumor and suspicion had lent credence to many legends, few of which stretched as far as the reality.

The cyclone of oil and shadows over St. Margaret's coalesced into a lanky and lumbering figure, tall as the mountains beyond. A thin and alien humanoid of red oil and rot smoked and stumbled slowly towards the town of Remedy.

By now, chaos was erupting across the town as the populace foresaw the coming disaster. People were yelling and scrambling to find loved ones, and leaving to gather belongings. No one knew for what or whom this ominous bell tolled, no one had yet made the connection, but no one wished to find out first hand.

Lucy and Quinn stole a rickshaw in their panic to find their daughter, knowing Meemaw refused to learn to use an iPhone. Meemaw, one of the oldest citizens in Remedy. Quinn pedaled and made heroic time through the three mile jaunt. By this time, the distant lumbering giant of shadow and smoldering crimson flame was nearly upon the town.

Lucy and Quinn ran inside, yelled for their daughter, and were met by Meemaw, who was pale as a ghost.

"Meemaw, where's Harley? We have to leave now!" Lucy said.

Meemaw was seated at the kitchen table, depleted of strength, her eyes devoid of hope. "I remember this..." She said, her voice quivered in the way old ladies' voices do. "I remember this from the news. Twenty years ago. It's the Plague I tell you. The Crimson Plague."

And of course, both Quinn and Lucy remembered the demonic plague which had once nearly wiped out half the country before it mysteriously disappeared. Everyone knew that it was spread by a giant entity of pestilence and shadow. Most could remember seeing it on the news. Now the connection had been made, and now they saw their doom. It wasn't the sort of thing they could fight. It wasn't the sort of thing they could outrun. It was a terrible and chilling death, if stories told true.

Meemaw trembled with the knowledge. "We can't let our little Harley suffer the fate of the Crimson Plague." She said, glaring ominously at the kitchen knives.

The parents didn't fault Meemaw, morbid though her thoughts may have turned. The Crimson Plague wasn't the gentle sort of Plague you might wish for when you think of plagues. One didn't simply drown in their own blood as it pooled pleasantly in the lungs. The Crimson Plague was a harbinger of the Demon Rastaphan, if Quinn and Harley's high school arcane textbooks were to be believed. Rastaphan, Lord of Monsters.

It was a plague that began first with feverish sneezing. Constant, ruthless sneezing for several days. Then, slowly, as the sneezing drained life and vitality, victims would find their skin was melting away. They would keep sneezing. Then began the wandering, as the flayed victims wandered the streets in search of new skins. A sort of madness would take them, and they'd try to take the skins of the thus far unaffected. They were often successful, and would dance through the streets in the skin of the fallen. But even if they failed, they'd still be sneezing and spreading their disease wherever they wandered. No amount of preparing oneself and saying "I promise I won't wander" would prevent 'the wandering'. It was a psychological effect of the disease.

Then, on the third day of skinlessness, as the victims eyes rolled up into their skull, and death overcame them, they'd be released from their body, and that part was merciful enough for those lucky enough to finally die. The skinless corpse, however, would eventually stand right back up and be reborn as a monster. The shape of the monster varied, but this is why so many monsters could be found in the wilds. Historians speculate monsters older than the Crimson Plague may have been previous iterations of plague borne beast, and that all monsters come initially from plagues, plagues being a tool of the demon Rastaphan.

Considering all this, Meemaw's subtly homicidal suggestion fell on sympathetic ears.

"Okay...okay, let's all just take a step back and calm down a minute." Quinn said and held out his hands cautiously, looking nervously between Meemaw and Lucy. Lucy had the same look she had when choosing whether to order the Papillon. "There's a chance this could all blow over. We don't know what's happening yet. We can consider these more extreme measures later if... well, if any of us starts to sneeze." Quinn said, but even as he said it they all felt a psychosomatic tickling of the nostrils. Trying not to sneeze was the surest way to begin sneezing.

Meemaw lunged for the knife set, and had to be restrained by Quinn. But Quinn had far underestimated the withered reserves of strength she had left in her old bones. She thrashed and bit and clawed in a desperate effort to provide a sympathetic end to her granddaughter Harley. Lucy worked to stop her mother as well, and lucky for the two of them, her strength waned quickly against their combined forces.

"I have to save her. I have to save her." Meemaw screamed, covered in tears, still reaching for the knives.

Quinn sneezed.

A terrible dread came over the four of them. By now the towering alien figure of pestilence would be standing above Remedy, spreading its vile vapors into the lungs of all the people they knew and loved. Everything was given to despair.

Cori, too, was despairing. What was the point in fighting with Sammiel already gone? She followed Morris disconsolately. Morris was not despairing but confused. And Morris was next to Derrick who did not to grasp the enormity of what lay before them.

Cori wept quietly as she walked. Despondent, the universe was handed, suddenly, to evil. Evil and suffering and darkness and pain.

And it was, at least in some part, her fault. She worked with Keiran. He possessed her. He worked through her. She worked at St. Margaret's. And now the people of Remedy were suffering the consequences of her failure.

She had come to St. Margaret's to do good, but she had unwittingly played the part of a pawn in what looked as though it would be the end of all life on Earth.

There was no St. Margaret to bind the pestilence, this time. And so, Cori marched silently behind Morris, uncertain why her feet even carried her forward. The tragedy was made even worse when she realized she had only just started truly appreciating her life to the fullest. But, perhaps that was why her feet were still shuffling along.

Morris stopped.

They were on the road to Remedy, ominous vapors lay stagnant in the autumn air now that the cyclone had dissipated. Ahead stood the mighty plague anomaly, long limbed and towering hundreds of feet above the town of Remedy, it's black arms swaying like smoking tendrils, it's back burning with the flames of pestilence.

Morris looked up at the towering anomaly and looked back at Derrick and Cori.

"You both know there is no point, right?" Morris asked. "There is nothing we can do against this."

"I think I could take it." Derrick said, looking over and Cori and gently flexing his tattooed bicep.

"Even if we could, we shouldn't." Morris said, rolling his eyes.

Cori looked at Morris and her face contorted, flabbergasted. "What do you mean, 'we shouldn't'?"

"Oh, it's complicated, Cori." Morris bemoaned, trying to be dismissive.

"Don't treat me like a child, Morris." Cori snapped, staring him down and seeing him for the first time as small. Not small as in inferior, but small like her. Small as an equal. Cori flared her aura as she had seen Maya do against Morris, and found to her surprise that Morris hardly fought back.

"You're something else, kid." Morris said to Cori. "I like you, I'm not going to lie. But this is bigger than us. There are cosmic forces at work here. You can't fight the embodiment of Destruction. And you shouldn't. There is a balance to be upheld. Destruction begets Creation. And Keiran has a plan to ensure a good recreation."

Cori guffawed, but Morris outlined what Keiran had told him, and to Cori's shock she found it worthy in concept. She had been studying an awful lot of philosophy since she got her reading augmentation; and the argument was sound. "But it's still stupid." Cori surmised.

Morris cackled in spite of himself. It was the first laughter Cori had heard since she came back to life. Genuine mirth. "What do you mean it's still stupid? You little runt." He smirked.

"I'm sorry it's stupid. If balance really wants to be restored, then it'll be restored despite the fight I put up against it. Maybe the world is meant to be destroyed and reborn. But I'm going to fight like hell before I go down if that's the case. Just because someone is trying to destroy it doesn't mean it *should* be destroyed. And just because it should be destroyed doesn't mean I shouldn't do what I can to stop it."

Derrick looked between Morris and Cori. He was not following any of this. But he tried anyway. "I think if Destruction wants to be a force, then I should be a force of destruction against destruction." Derrick said. He looked proud of his point. Cori and Morris ignored him.

"Okay, I'll concede that's reasonable." Morris said to Cori. "But don't you think this world is…. oh, I don't know… a little shitty? Like maybe it's about time someone did something about that."

Cori had known he would try to say that. He hadn't been himself since Aislynn had been keeping him at arm's length. A bruised heart could really darken the humors. "I thought you were just speaking of balance. You were saying St. Margaret would get to remake the world? Do we really want a Saint remaking the world?" Cori asked, and let that sit. Saints know very little about fun and pleasure; and Morris knew it. You don't invite saints to parties. It is known. "There is no one who could remake the world properly." Cori said, then emphasized, "no ONE. The thing that makes this dirty little world great is that it's a whole mixed bag. There's saints and sinners and everything in between. Part of the beauty of the place is the battle and the strife. And sure I could accept a world with a little less strife. I would fall in love with it, I have no doubt. But… ya know what? I'm already in love with this world. This one that we have right now. Warts and all. And I'm going to fight like hell for it."

There was a pause. Then Derrick began a slow clap. It had certainly sounded inspiring enough for him. Morris frowned and his brow furrowed, and then he followed along with the slow clap. Aislynn and Barnie followed suit, or Aislynn tried to, and by her side

Kitsune scowled. They hadn't been with the other three, but had been running to catch up, and they had heard the speech.

"Spoken like a true hero." Aislynn said.

Morris was thunderstruck by the appearance of his love, then shamed that she had heard his callous dismissal of the world, then perplexed by her missing arm. "Aislynn…" he began.

Cori interrupted. "Morris, there must be a way we can fight this. There must be a way to stop the Crimson Plague, and Keiran."

"Keiran is one thing, but the plague is… how do you stop a plague? You can't just… well I'll admit this plague is unusually well formed as a humanoid body, but it's still just a big old cloud of oil and pestilence and smoke."

"But…" Cori thought for a second, something in her recent memory tickling at her mind. "Didn't you say Keiran was going to let St. Margaret remake the world? How could she do that if she's still possessed by the demon of pestilence?"

"Well, yeah, they were going to have Ichabod chop everything up with Hanuman's Bone Scythe, but that's…"

"So, we need to get the Scythe?" Aislynn asked.

"Well yeah, from a deranged Angelic psychopath." Morris snorted as he chuckled. "Good luck with that."

"Aislynn, do you know anything about Ichabod that could help me to fight him in the Betwixt?" Cori asked. "Fighting is different there. It's not about strength and speed. It's about intellect and strategy, willpower and emotional manipulation." She felt as though she was grasping at imaginary straws, but it felt good to take action, even of the futile sort.

"I hate to break it to you, but if that's the case you're up against a hell of an enemy. Ichabod is an exceptionally well disciplined Paladin. He was a strategic commander in numerous battles. At the Battle of Barimand Quay, he outmaneuvered a host of skilled mages protected by a shield wall of constructs. Outnumbered, he took down a hundred with a dozen. He is a brilliant logistician, and was very much prescribed to the old ideals of masculinity in terms of his emotion." Aislynn replied.

"Now wait just one cotton pickin' minute." Morris interjected. "You're not all actually going to do this? I'm still not convinced it's not evil. Cori made a solid rebuttal but there's still a good chance a saint could remake the world with a great deal less suffering than we see today."

"Absolute power corrupts absolutely, Morris." Aislynn said. "Even saints. It doesn't matter how pure her intentions are. And even if she relinquished her power, there's every chance the world could revert to something much worse with her loss."

Morris looked stumped, then defeated.

"We need to fight for what we have, Morris." Aislynn said and touched his face lightly with the caked blood of her one remaining hand while they stood under the leaves of a sycamore. She kissed his cheek gently. Cori wasn't sure if she was being genuine or manipulative, but Morris didn't seem to think it mattered. He lit up like a lamp. Aislynn held her face close. Cori had never seen anyone look so mangled and seductive at the same time.

"I have been looking for a chance to summon Agamemnon." Morris whispered to her, blushing and more alive than Cori had ever seen him.

"I don't know what an Agamemnon is." Aislynn said back to him, her eyes glittering. Then she turned to Cori, fierce as ever. "Cori…I'm not sure if this will be of any use, but I have seen emotion touch at Ichabod before. He'd only listen to music in solitude, but every so often I'd see him shortly after, and his eyes would be red and puffy. It's the only hint of emotion I've seen out of him other than the basic male stoicism and fury. I wish there were more, but do with that as you will."

Cori nodded. "I can use that. Derrick. Honestly, I think you could be a lot of help here. We have to beat someone up. Do you know how to get into the Betwixt?"

"Uhhhhh…." Derrick replied, bewildered.

Morris looked furious and raised a fist of flaming green energies. "I can put him into the Betwixt, just let me—"

"Morris stop, I'm sure we can figure something out." Cori said as Derrick stuck his pierced tongue out at Morris.

"I know how to get into the Betwixt." Derrick affirmed.

Aislynn stepped forward. "It's settled then, I'll stay here to help the townsfolk out. Medicine has come a long way since the last

Crimson Plague. If we can get this isolated, we may be able to cure the townspeople. Paladins will be showing up any minute now, I bet my remaining arm. I can talk with them and direct them. I am still a captain. Morris, you summon… Agamemnon?"

"Agamemnon, yes, the Lord of Locks and Chains and all things Binding." Morris said, proudly.

"You do whatever you gotta do there to fight off that plague giant. Delay it. Kill it. Whatever you can do. Barnie, Kitsune? Can you help me with the townsfolk."

"Glad to be of help." Barnie said in his delicate mezzo-soprano. He was feeling a little lost in the mix, but enjoying the change to his usual daily routine of pancakes, chopping wood, hunting monsters, and snoozing loudly by the fire with his hounds.

"I'm not. I'm not really what you'd call a helper." Kitsune said, then looked around at everyone glaring at her. "What? I'm just being realistic about my weaknesses. Isn't there anything else I can do?"

Morris sighed. "Help me fight off the Plague Abomination?"

"Ew no. That thing is gross." Kitsune mocked gagging. "Whatever, I'll just figure it out."

"Kitsune we need to work as a--" Morris began, but Kitsune flipped him off while transforming into bats, then flew off in the night sky.

"She can really be a bitch." Cori said, tapping her foot. "Derrick and I will get the Scythe from Ichabod, rescue Sam, slay Keiran, and sever the Crimson Plague, and St. Margaret from it."

Morris shot a confused glance at Cori. "What's it matter to you? Rescue Sam? Let Sammiel go. We're necromancers. 'No man left behind' isn't exactly our motto. I'd love to have him back too, but if he craves the infinite void, who are we to stop him?"

Aislynn slapped her forehead and looked down, embarrassed.

Morris looked around at everyone's reddening faces. "What?"

Aislynn pulled close to his ear and whispered something. Then it was Morris' turn to grow flushed around the ears.

"Hubba whuuuu—?! Cori and Sam?"

Cori nodded. "I know it's supposed to be impossible to retrieve someone from the Villa of Ormen but--"

"It...isn't..." Aislynn said. "I wouldn't say anything, but you seem set in your course, and you need to know. It *is* possible. But for even the greatest Paladin it would be a challenge of the greatest measure. This is not Necromancy, Cori. You must use the skills that I taught you in our time together. Skills of light and manifestation. But even then it is literally impossible. There is no comfort I can give you here. It is impossible. However, beyond the precipice of the Villa of Ormen, laws and logic break apart. In that world, the Land of the Truly Departed, the definition of impossible itself is loosened, and dispersed. Root yourself to the Land you love, and do not let go, no matter how insurmountable the pull of ecstasy and relief. It is impossible, but in that world there is no such thing as possible and impossible, because there is no such thing as anything."

Cori frowned, and nodded solemnly, entirely certain that she did not understand.

Chapter 21

"Quinn? Quinn Draughtsmith, open up. It's Aislynn O'Cuillen." A voice came from beyond the chamber door. In retrospect it may not have been the best idea to announce herself in such a way. Aislynn thought it would instill confidence, but instead it had instilled a fierce look from Lucy to Quinn.

Quinn made to move but Lucy said "Don't you dare."

"Babe, it could be our only hope." Quinn pleaded.

"Oh, she's your only hope now?"

Quinn and Aislynn had dated for nearly twelve years. They had broken up just two years before Harley was born. It was not a point of contentment for Lucy, Quinn was aware. But as aware as he was, he was not conscious of the full extent it seethed in her belly. It didn't openly seethe all the time. Just times like this.

"Babe can we… can we deal with that later?… once we're alive. If we're alive."

"Yeah maybe Aislynn can be your only hope then too." Lucy said, thinking about how hard she could pinch him before he bled.

"It's literally a matter of life and a horrific death." Quinn said, trying to reason and finding it futile.

"No, no, it's fine. Really. Lead on." Lucy said, and Quinn felt nauseous.

Despite all, he got up and answered the door. Aislynn had one arm severed to the shoulder, her other arm carried her great sword upon her back. Her usually glistening armor was caked in dirt and dried blood. She looked about as punk rock as anyone has ever looked. This did not help Quinn's current predicament.

"Aislynn, Hi! What a surprise." Lucy said. To Quinn's horror, Lucy sounded absolutely genuine.

"Hi Aislynn." Quinn said. "Hi Barnie, didn't expect to see you around."

"Hey Quinn. Hey Lucy." Said Barnie. "Me neither."

"Harlot." Spat Meemaw to Aislynn.

Aislynn had her focus turned elsewhere, largely toward the pain of her rapidly healing wounds and trying to save the world.

"Townsfolk are to gather at the Armory." She told them stoically. "We can provide armed transport if needed."

"Aislynn, can you tell us what's going on out there?" Quinn asked, trying to match Aislynn's stoicism while maintaining humility beside his wife's wrath.

"I won't mince words with you Quinn. It's pretty bad."

"Meemaw says it's the incarnation of Rastaphan, Lord of Monsters, come back as the Crimson Plague." Quinn said, nodding over to Meemaw. It felt very odd to Quinn to speak of something he had always perceived as a distant and abstract concept in terms of a current and overwhelming reality.

"Yeah… I'm sorry to say that sounds like the most probable explanation for what's occurring… everything we can see points to that."

"Then we shouldn't be breathing out there." Lucy snapped.

"To be honest, the situation is so close to hopeless that we're not terribly worried about contamination. I've put in a call to the Paladin Order to get healers over to the Armory to combat the disease. Barnie and I have set the town moving door to door to gather everyone. Right now the mission is containment. Prevent the spread. Even breathing the vapors without healing, it should take about 12 hours for the initial sneezies to start, assuming the records are accurate. The best hope we have is to stick together as a populace, give care to the infected, and pray. We can provide you armed transport for your peace of mind. Will you come with us?"

Quinn looked over at Lucy, who looked at him with a look that said that it was his decision, but that he would be judged for the decision he made. He weighed the inevitable and horrible death by plague they would suffer at home versus his wife's wrath should they survive. Not easily did he conclude they should gather at the Armory.

Cori strapped into her Cloak of the Wraith Whisperer and her Timberland Boots and her sharply pointed Gloves of the Black Rose. She donned her metallic six eyed mask, the mouth contorted into an overjoyed grimace, and donned her disjointed black witches hat that was left in a package in front of her door. She ordered the witches hat after enjoying several glasses of Cabarnet several weeks prior, and she was glad it came.

Then, Cori stood in front of her closet door. "For Sam." She said, out loud. *Why?* Because of the way he crinkled his nose when he laughed, damnit. And the way the edges of his lips curled when he was holding back a smile. Because Cori couldn't go her whole life without the little tricks he'd play on her to make himself giggle. Because of the sound of that rusty metallic voice of his, and how it shouldn't be snuffed from making a voice in the world. That's why. Cori wanted to make sure she heard that laugh again, which was so much like bells.

"Derrick, get in here." Cori called out her bedroom door. Derrick walked in, and Cori decided she liked giving him commands. He wore centurion armors that fit into his musculature organically. "You sure you wanna do this?"

Derrick looked at Cori and there was something in his eyes that hadn't been there before. Was that a look of righteous determination? "Hell yeah."

"You realize we could actually die right? I'm not at all sure I can beat Ichabod." Cori said.

Derrick did look afraid. Even wearing his fearsome armor, he was sweating, and he was shaking. But still he nodded, and said with uncharacteristic humility. "I'm in. Let's do this."

Cori nodded, led him forth into her closet, up against the abstract geometries drawn in chalk, then slipped through the cracks into the Betwixt. It was all so much more vivid now that she had died before.

"First, we go to Sonorous." Cori said, her body shifting from physical to cognitive in a menagerie of tangible thoughtform. "I need to ask for assistance. Then we have to find Ichabod. I haven't figured that part out yet."

"You haven't?" Derrick asked; his form abstractifying. "We could just see an Oracle."

"Have you been to the Betwixt before?" Cori asked from between the wall cracks, down a psychedelic corridor of neon vertical lines which stretched through into the Betwixt.

"My Dad is a Warlock." Derrick said. "He's taught me all this stuff since I was a kid."

"You have a Dad?" Cori asked with all the spontaneity of communication of the Betwixt, now that they found themselves in a translucent version of St. Margaret's, shattered as it were in reality, but here the shattered fragments and rooms hovered about in the air like asteroids in space. She had put so little thought into Derrick that him having a family seemed somehow implausible. Derrick could approximately see that Cori felt that way, more or less.

"Yeah, Milton. He's cool."

"Well, okay. Milton the Warlock. I'd like to meet Milton the Warlock." Cori said, then became terribly afraid of the implications Derrick might pull from that. Then Derrick saw even that fear. It was awkward being in the Betwixt with new people. Cori could see that Derrick thought she was good looking but wasn't genuinely interested in pursuing a romantic relationship with her. Cori could see a lot of things about Derrick that made her think that, overall, Derrick was pretty alright. Derrick could see Cori thought that, and thought approximately the same as her, and Cori saw that too. Very quickly they felt like good friends. The Betwixt did things like that.

Cori screeched into the air, 'screeeeee', to call Eromir, her mount. Swiftly it came, long sparkling shaggy white feathers and a face like an owls, the body of a deer; and the antlers too. She mounted and padded Eromir's graceful neck. Then Cori reached a hand out to help Derrick on board, and they took off swiftly. They ran through the unfamiliar countryside to the West of Remedy, here in the Ethereal lands of the Betwixt where water flowed upwards and the ground shifted sometimes like floating islands on the Sea. But the Ethereal was feeling the effects of the plague, and the rivers were black and the grass was dying and the air tasted of lead.

Derrick told Cori of a passage to Sonorous that lay in the Singing Pits of the Dry Lands. Away from the plague they moved swiftly. The Dry Lands were a six day journey by ordinary carriage to the North and West of Remedy, but Cori's mount Eromir was able to get there in twenty minutes, for she rode like the wind and could slip between cracks in space which were prevalent in the Ethereal.

They rode through forest and lake and swiftly to the top of a mountain where could be seen all things.

They rode far into the Dry Lands, and saw many strange things, aliens mostly, but made with all haste to pass them by swiftly. Instead, they found the singing pits which in the Mundane howled in the wind, but in the Ethereal quite literally sang. It was a haunting melody, in a key Cori could not place and had never heard before and would never hear again. It was neither minor, nor major, nor eastern. And into these haunted pits of song Eromir lept and carried Derrick and Cori into Sonorous.

Form ceased in Sonorous, and all was given to song and dance. Dance being tricky because there was no form with which to dance; however there was motion, and the motion was the more important part of dance. Much more important than form. To move in Sonorous was to improvisationally dance to a song you were orchestrating as you moved. Songs flowed effortlessly between one and the next, much like The Grateful Dead, no jarring interjections. Perfectly fluid. As such, they couldn't instantaneously move about just any place. There had to be cohesion. That is how one moves through Sonorous.

"Excuse me, sir?" Cori asked one soulful beatnik.

"I am a woman." She replied, with hostility.

"A thousand apologies. We seek the one called Mayhew, belonging to this Sigil." Cori stretched Mayhew's audible sigil to the waveform beatnik.

"It is me who should apologize, I knew not you had business with our Prince." The entity bowed in a decrescendo. "He can be found at 107.7, the Sequoia."

"Prince?" Derrick asked Cori, but Cori only let out a vague tremolo.

They made it to 107.7 by traversing the Clefts of Wubbz and passing through the Bassline on Vibrato. Cori understood why people liked Sonorous so much. She existed like an Itunes visualizer set to the perfect playlist for the moment. True harmony.

Mayhew's Opera was set high upon the Bastion of Funk.

"Mayhew, I love the jam." Cori said, upon her arrival in his palace. Then she decrescendo'd because it felt appropriate given the regal music Mayhew was surrounded in. "This is Derrick. I must say, your palace sounds beautiful."

It was strange to see Mayhew in his element. Cori hadn't realized what a revered being he was. He sat upon a throne of groove and was attended to by many Sopranos. Cori had always thought of him as a smaller entity, but now saw the true weight of his station.

"Cori! I am most pleased to see you here. I had thought you might never come to visit me again, and my heart was heavy with imagined grief." Mayhew trilled, waving his arms improvisationally. "I acknowledge your friend but find myself jealous of you spending time with others, though I have no right to do so."

Cori ignored these blunt pleasantries, obviously. "Mayhew, I'm in need of your assistance once again." Cori sang, and then told her story in song. A ballad. Mayhew and all his court listened, hearing of Cori's deepest sorrows and tribulations. The troubles of the world of the Mundane, and the dangers she faced. "Mayhew; the only known weakness of Ichabod, this Archangel of death, is music. I need you in this coming battle, or if you could spare some elegies..."

Mayhew paused to consider, his song like a royal exuberance. "These troubles are your own, and we are not much greater than acquaintances, for all we may see resonating within the other. Why should I risk myself against this peril when my realm is not threatened?" Mayhew asked, and for all the implicitness of Mayhew's being, Cori has not expected that response at all. She stammered and was taken aback and this caused all sorts of fluctuations in her rhythm and melody. Mayhew saw all of this, of course. "I am sorry, but it is no simple request you ask of me. This is not playing music for a romantic dinner. I have lived for untold ages, but I have done so by reasonably avoiding excessive risk. I know not what sort of entity this 'Ichabod' is or whether he would seek revenge against me, should we fail."

Cori's being stopped fluctuating, and she said simply, "I see."

"I am sorry, Cori Fleshbod." Mayhew quavered. "I do hope this will not negatively affect the ways between us, which I have hitherto perceived as very good and flowing. Though I feel this hope is in err, considering recent revelations, and I cannot guarantee that for my part I won't have qualms for you even presuming to ask."

"I had… just gotten my hopes up." Cori said. "It's not your fault. I had expected far too much from you."

"I cannot risk myself or those of my court." Mayhew held up his right cleft. "That is not to say I cannot help. Allow me to teach you the art of Sonomancy, Cori. It may serve you well."

Cori looked over at Derrick, who was screamo amongst funk opera. It was a little unpleasant to Cori, but she still thought he was alright. Derrick shrugged, if shrugs were screamo music.

"I have no great time to spare, but I am willing to learn." Cori replied.

"Three days is all it will take me, three hours in your Mundane Realm."

"I am ready." Cori riffed.

Those three days training in the Bastion of Funk were a rigorous testament to Cori's growing willpower. While Derrick showed no musical aptitude, Coriander Lou learned solo's and bass drops, unexpected bridges and distorted harmonies. Doing battle first with lesser pop sprites, Cori lost repeatedly. But she lifted herself again, and again, soon defeating those pop sprites and moving on to defeat waltz's, country ballads, and even a full fledged elegiac ballad, though Cori suspected that fight may have been rigged. At the end of three days, Cori had been given the status of Apprentice Sonomancer, and was donned with several major chords in her soul to prove the measure of her worth.

Together, Derrick and Cori left 107.7, encouraged for their glimmer of hope, and success in their journey thus far. They left Sonorous to raise higher into the Crystallatium and seek an Oracle to tell them of Ichabod's whereabouts.

"Oracles are basically a dime a dozen. Anyone can peer through space and time." Derrick told Cori when they stopped Eromir for roadside smoothies on a carved opal super highway between forested moons. "But you have to be careful which one you go to, because it's not just about them telling you what you want to know. Oracles shape the way things turn out. That's what my Dad told me. Usually when people go to Oracles they're on some grand quest of destiny, so Oracles will guide them to certain results. My dad—"

"Milton the Warlock." Cori interrupted Derrick. She just liked saying it.

Derrick sighed. "Yes, my dad, Milton the Warlock. He said that the future is a web of possibility. There's a lot of crappy oracles who don't know this and just tell you the first future they see. But there are also evil oracles and they will tell you futures that make you give up hope, or make you overconfident and turn you to a bad result. And then there's good oracles."

"We're not looking for the future though, we're just looking for Ichabod." Cori said.

"Yeah, but we will find him in the future." Derrick said.

"Whatever." Cori pouted. She didn't like Derrick knowing things she didn't. "So, who is a good Oracle?"

"Well, there's lots of reviews on Yelp, but you have to be careful of those cause there's a lot of fake reviewers." Derrick said. "My Dad gave me this business card back when I moved out."

'Sileen and Ethwith, The Oracle Twins of 2600 Sweet Perihelion View.' Read the Card, which also further described the price points.

"8000 dollars?!" Cori exclaimed.

"Well, no, that's the symbol for Hell Money there." Derrick said. "Don't quote me but conversion rate is like two to one so it's more like 16k American."

"I can't... I don't have that much money."

"God knows I don't. I'm sure there is financing available." Derrick said, helpfully.

"I'm trying to save the world, isn't that enough?"

"One world in a macrocosm." Derrick said. "I doubt they care. There's a chance you could write it off as a business expense."

"You're just full of helpful tips today aren't you?" Cori said, hands on her hips. "Derrick, I can't believe I'm saying this, but I don't know what I'd do without you right now."

"Why can't you believe that?"

"Never mind. How do we get to 2600 Sweet Perihelion View?"

"Gosh, I have no idea…"

"Really? That's where your vast knowledge ceases?"

"Nah. I know the way. I was just messing with you." Derrick said, finishing his strawberry colada, then climbed back aboard Eromir with Cori.

They rode upon Eromir, Cori affront and Derrick in the back, galloping swift as light as they rose further into the Crystallatium. Through the neuron forests of a nebulae and atop frozen chrysanthemums and even down to the technicolored bubble bogs of Sharad-Zur. Their journey was long and at times arduous but along with their smoothies they purchased a roadside snack of Quazium, a fried food made from a non-carbon based entity that exists upon an internally heated rogue planet. This made it all the more bearable when otherwise the conversation lagged from time to time as ultimately Derrick and Cori didn't have a ton in common besides a newfound mutual respect.

They came to Sweet Perihelion View. Greco-Roman pillars of golden circuitry stood watch over an Olympian Haven where water straight from the Sea of Milk sprang forth in a healing font, surrounded by gardens. In the distance, stars collided in a slow but hopeless dance.

It was a town, an island in the oxygenated void of space. A small diamond shaped mountain covered in well tended marble hovels, floating gracefully in the event horizon of what would inevitably be a supernova of bizarre proportions.

The denizens puttered about the town nonsensically, alien hominids, gray with wrinkled cheeks and brows. They worked strange magick with crystals, which grew in abundance about the town; and experimented with the souls of cats in store front windows.

2600 Sweet Perihelion View wasn't hard to find, just a stone's throw away from the Jasper tree in the center of town. The store was of a marble exterior like the rest but there hung a sign which showed an eyeball divided into many geometric diamond structures. The same logo on the business card Derrick had given to Cori.

"Sileen and Ethwith Magorian." Cori read from the etched door. Then she took a deep breath of the fresh and fragrant air of the Crystallatium, and went in. Incense poured forth from the door. It smelled of Sandalwood and pleasantly burned plastic. It made Cori's head feel as though it were swimming with digitized code. It wasn't incense that smelled of burnt plastic, however. The Magorian Sisters were smoking from a hookah that looked to be a thousand years advanced of vaporizers, with strange oceanic wyrms swimming inside the transparent bottom bulb.

The sisters themselves looked to be about mid eighties with dyed black hair cut in thick bangs and deep set cataract eyes, as are befitting of oracles. They were taking puffs and laughing and hardly noticed Cori and Derrick enter. The Necromancers stood watching the Oracles as the hag sister's eyes turned to the walls and they spoke in well organized gibberish.

The room was centered around the table with the hookah, but upon the wall hung complex brass devices that were clicking and whirring and attempting but failing to do anything of noticeable meaning. The table was of brass and the chairs were of brass and the rest was covered in expensive fabrics and carpets. There was a little nightstand on the left with a cup of hot tea.

"Noi'sian elethin la choim." One sister said to the other, and it bore great significance though Cori could not place why that may be.

They continued to speak in gibberish whilst Cori and Derrick looked back and forth at them and one another, waiting for their presence to be acknowledged. And slowly the reverie died down and both sisters appeared to recognize that they had visitors.

"Where once there are visitors, what is now?" Said the sister whose color scheme was more earthen red.

"A wise question, me. But what do we do with it?" Said the sister whose color scheme was more sky blue.

Their words were now English but neither Cori nor Derrick could make out how to respond.

"You'll have to excuse us, Cori." Said the red sister. "Whose name is Ethwith." She added in response to thoughts that arose in the continuum. "We're speaking from a multitudinous place, it's very hard to translate quite what we mean."

Cori was about to ask how Ethwith knew her name but this was obviously going to be one of those conversations where things like that just happened and it was best to just accept it.

"Agreed." Said "Sileen." In response to me. "Pleased to meet you." She said to you.

Cori felt like she wasn't even a part of the conversation.

Do you have anything to ask? Anything to say? Now would be a good time.

Good. They will respond to your statement or question or silence in your dreams tonight.

"Don't speak for us." Ethwith and Sileen yelled, then slapped the air, and by proxy me. "But he's right."

Cori stood, a little dumb founded, and unable to follow the flow of conversation, limited and singular as she was. "I uh— need your services. I need to find the one named Ichabod."

"Do you have any idea how many people there are named Ichabod?" Sileen responded with a bored sigh, looking at Cori through a kaleidoscope of polished wood.

"I hadn't thought of that." Cori said.

"Don't let my sister fool you, Cori. There's only one Ichabod relevant to your timeline. We know exactly who you're talking about." Ethwith said, beginning a knit.

"And yes, we do have financing available." Sileen said, licking her kaleidoscope like a lollipop.

"Oh Sileen, stop that. It's so gauche." Ethwith Said, knitting with frightening rapidity.

"If I'm going to be limited to a text based organism, I'm at least going to be a prosperous text based organism." Sileen responded, now biting and chewing her kaleidoscope.

Cori was becoming filled with dread, though she could not say why. The conversation between the sisters sounded so deeply earnest. She wanted nothing more than to just move on and be done with the whole endeavor. "Please, can we just… can you tell me where I will find Ichabod."

"Page 193." Ethwith said.

"Oh Ethwith, now you're the one being gauche. Pay her no mind, Cori. Pay me in cash, instead."

"Well, I can't, I need financing." Cori said.

"Financing!" Shouted the sisters. They both jumped to their feet and danced. "Financing! Financing! Financing!"

"Shall we check her credit?" Asked Sileen, her eyes growing wide, her toes twinkling.

"I think it's good!" Said Ethwith, her eyes turning to the wall as she looked beyond the beyond.

"Consensus?" They asked in unison. "She winds up paying us in full! Financing accepted. It is due on the day you pay it, which is February twenty third of next year. You are able to secure corporate funding with this as a business expense."

"Oh!... great." Said Cori.

"Derrick, you're feeling irrelevant and forgotten again. Is there anything we can get for you, dear?" Asked Ethwith, her knitting taking shape as what appeared to be a virus.

"Oh? Well yeah, I could use some tea, maybe." He said.

"I set some out for you on the table to your left before you got here." Said Sileen, and so she had.

Derrick sipped. It was his favorite. Monster Green Tea Level Up Boost!

"Sileen, how exactly do we speak Ichabod's location?" Ethwith asked.

Sileen flipped the pages of a book, then pointed. "Well, he's in the Sea of Milk when she finds him."

"That's good, she hadn't explored there much yet, had she?" Ethwith said, gazing proudly at her living knit virus, completed and floating in the air.

"No, it was hitherto left somewhat vague what it could even be." Said Sileen.

"Where in the Sea of Milk?" Cori asked, still wishing this wretched conversation would end.

279

Sileen looked back in the book, pointed, and quoted, "by the Eros Canal."

"I know where that is!" Derrick shouted.

"Of course you do, dear. You needed to make yourself useful somehow." Said Ethwith.

"Oh, Ethwith." Said Sileen.

Derrick looked sad. Cori understood his pain. She couldn't wait to leave.

"Rude." Sileen responded to that sentiment. "It's not like we're keeping you."

"I'm sorry." Cori responded, half heartedly, pushing her way out the door. "It was nice to meet you."

"Bye." Derrick called through the door before it shut.

"Your dreams… tonight." The sisters said in unison after Cori and Derrick left. "Pay attention."

County Remedy suffered visibly, even in so short a time. The foliage that ought to have been red and brown and yellow with autumn was turning black and letting loose the smells of rot, melting under the vapors released by the towering Plague Anomaly which stood hunched over the town, dripping ooze, skeletal and fetid.

Some miles of distance, Morris stood center a field. "Requesting release of power restrictions coupled with necrotic hymnal, five miles in effect at my coordinates." Morris texted furiously. "Request for Level 0 Access to summon the Colossol Beast Agamemnon from Sector 9."

"All Requests granted." Came the response from Ruth. "May God have Mercy on our Souls."

It was wise of Ruth to consider this a somber moment. It was nothing to be taken lightly. But Morris had been looking forward to summoning Agamemnon. He had locked himself up in the Cloisters for weeks during the summer. He was just itching for a reason, though he had a chill in his bones at the thought of actually putting it into practice.

His phone app 'eVoc' would be of no use, it would only work with smaller entities. Instead, Morris made a circle of oil in the fields beyond St. Margaret's Home for the Nearly Departed, carefully spelling out sacred names and symbols in the oil. Then he lit it all on fire as he felt the Necrotic Hymnals arrive from the Council of Necromancers. The air was full of their dark chanting, and thick with miasma. Morris' circle was as wide as a suburban home, covered now in flames as Morris stood just outside, mixing his voice into the hymnals sent by the Council.

"Ohm Roc Sharah! Be with me, and break thine folds, Great Beast who Lords over Sector 9 and the demons therein. Keeper of the Crucible. Unveil thyself and be free to Feast. My enemies lay before me." Morris said, then cut into his hand with a double edged blade of obsidian. "My blood is yours." He said, and the flames licked at his wounds. "Ohm Roc Sharah! I call thee and thou knowest thy name! Agamemnon! Ohm Roc Sharah!"

The ground quaked, and rolled like a wave out from the flaming sigils of Morris' evocation circle. The ground splintered, then cracked "And what is thy name?" Spoke the Earth itself.

"I am Absalon of the Thousand Eyes, and I call upon thee! Come forth Agamemnon, and take your feast. Ohm Roc Sharah!"

The ground chuckled and quaked then grew silent, even as the necrotic hymnals in the air grew silent. Then the ground tore with a ripping sound like a jet engine, as though a great wound had been opened, spilling the blood of the Earth, magma and flaming oil.

"Yes! Hah Hah, yes!" Morris cackled maniacally, his eyes wide and insane. He raised his hands to the sky and screamed rapturously.

Agamemnon, Lord of Locks and Chains and all things binding. He who holds the God Amygdala bound in the Lake of Distal Mists. He who stifles those that cannot be stifled, and tightens his grip over all those who do violence beyond hope of redemption. In form, he comes as a beastly giant of angled musculature and remorseless beauty. Bejeweled, cyclopean, and sad, having long ago resigned to acceptance of his lot as Prison Warden amongst the cosmos, he stood colossal upon the fields outside the town of Remedy, bearing a great golden sword glowing with heat, the size of a small village.

Morris had not chosen this summoning lightly. One doesn't confine oneself to the Cloisters for weeks without reason and wise council, for they are a danger to even the greatest heroes. Agamemnon, as the Lord of Locks and Chains, was the very designer of the Labyrinth beneath St. Margaret's, having carved it long ago in the dawn of ages. Morris knew this when he debated between summons, unable for a time to choose between Agamemnon, and Cecilia the Voracious; the succubus Grand Marquis of cosmic renown. His ultimate decision against Cecilia was a testament to the use and value he saw in being able to call this Colossal beast.

"Agamemnon." Morris said at a whisper, though heard clearly in the silence of this pre-storm calm. "The Plague Anomaly which stands before you... its true name is Margaret, in binding with the plague demon Rastaphan, Lord of Monsters, and thus Margaret Rastaphan. Bring them far from Remedy, then keep them bound in battle, for they cannot be destroyed in their current form."

Agamemnon might have smiled, but it's eyes remained sad. Then it charged several miles to Remedy in the span of seconds, sound barriers ripped in half with a sonic boom. The plague anomaly Margaret Rastaphan was prepared, seeing all that had transpired from afar and preparing herself against the coming threat. Agamemnon sliced with his sword, severing the very air of the world and beating down winds like a hurricane, but Margaret Rastaphan did dodge, slick as the oil she dripped with, formless, then reformed into her humanoid black skeleton of smoldering plague filth.

Her dodge was not complete however, for Agamemnon followed with a mighty kick, which did plunge Margaret Rastaphan through all the airs to the North and into the mountains beyond, landing with a thunderous crash as has never been heard there or elsewhere.

What else is there to do when Colossal Entities do battle? All that one can do is to watch helplessly, and in awe. Morris created a small and simple construct to get him a lawn chair and lemonade. He hadn't had a drink all day, he realized, and the summoning had left him terribly weary. When next he slept, his sleep would be long and profound. Until then, he had done his part for the world, which he now could watch from a safe distance; like eldritch fireworks and a blaze of glory. Bolts of electricity collided with mountains and gravity loosened as the titans did battle and boulders were crushed and hills were felled and fires of every color shot brilliantly through beastly jaws clenched tightly in the terrific strains of battle.

    This should have been enough to keep anyone awake, but all at once Morris felt a great weariness levied against him, and he collapsed to the ground even before his small construct had returned with his chair and lemonade. And there, Morris slipped away from the world.

Chapter 22

The collective undead of St. Margaret's gathered in the briefing room where the staff most usually held their staff meetings ushered by Maya, while Dana did a shamanic dance to ward and protect the room from powers both of this world and beyond. The house, split on its foundations, groaned with each step and held none of its former helter-skelter cackling mischief. There was a quiet anticipation. Many undead had fled in the initial sundering, and even the society of mice and spiders living in the walls had hurriedly sought shelter, lying to their many thousands of children that they were certain everything would turn out fine.

It had taken Maya and Dana several hours to find everyone. Everything was out of sorts, and no one was where they were supposed to be. Agnus had taken Vivian to the Ossuary, Ernie was by the Hermits Nest in the third floor corridors, George took to haunting the bathroom, and Sarah had hidden in the pantry, and many more of those nameless undead besides who so often go unmentioned and unnoticed. But Ruth had insisted upon the most thorough search, for the portents, she said, were grim indeed. Gathered here round the table and under the ancient banners of the Undead in the staff meeting room, seated round the scale model of Remedy, sconces lit by blue flame, the undead all sat with grave attention and unusual focus.

Dana finished her purifying dance while Maya used chalk to form a grand circle around the room with which they might turn their mystic attentions to the meeting of the damned with their bosses, the Council of Necromancers.

Everyone participated. Those who were spectral swirled and formed a necrotic storm at the top of the room, whilst zombies and skeletons danced macabre. Dana and Maya read alternating verses from the Tome of Dorothy Ungal, the Mad Witch who first brought the Council of Necromancers to this dimension. It was a book that never should have been written, written by a writer who never should have been born.

Ruth had instructed the ritual, having decided the paperwork could wait or was at least in some sort of acceptable order. Drums, chanting, ululating, keening. Like a mad funeral, drunk on bloodlust and moonbeams.

The Council heard the Call. Above, through black necrotic clouds, shone an unholy white light. Like a pale sun on a distant moon, sick with ancient intentions. From it descended the hooded and robed wraiths that formed the Council of Necromancers. This chosen physical form of theirs betrayed not the deep and too old knowledge they carried within their consciousness, but their voices carried it well.

"Speak." Said one.

"There is a disturbance that threatens the entirety of the Council's holdings upon this world. Beginning at St. Margaret's Home for the Nearly Departed, the demon Rastaphan, Lord of Plagues and Monsters, was released by proxy of its host, St. Margaret." Ruth said, holding her pride and calm against this fearsome host. It was always best to be obsessively methodical with the Council, and never err from the point for trivialities or pleasantries. "With it, it carries the Crimson Plague, which will wipe all life from this world if proper course is not observed."

The next Council Wraith spoke in a harsh and shrill whisper, "Was not the entity Agamemnon called to handle this matter?"

"It was, and it does battle as we speak, but it will not win against the Plague Aberration named Margaret Rastaphan. It can; at best, hold her bindings for as long as it can maintain form in this world, which is likely to be as the moon rises once again."

"Do you recognize the cost of your failure, Ruth Stevens, Mist Seeker?" Asked a third, its voice like guttural blood loss.

"I do." Ruth Said. "I seek your council and command, knowing my life is forfeit to your mercies."

The black wraiths convened, their speech silent but loud, and indecipherable. Then they spoke once again in a way humans could understand. "There will be repercussions from other organizations, not the least of which shall be the Order of Paladins. They will blame us, and attempt to intercede in our affairs." Said one.

"This threat we must be prepared to fight. The Paladin's grip tightens on multiple worlds." Said the other.

"But how?" Asked the third Council Wraith.

"Bestow the employees with the Dark One's Blessing." Said the first.

"Preposterous. They are not fit to the task. Their failure has marred the organization for years to come."

"Hmmm." The third growled in a guttural and phlegmy utterance. "I can see the wisdom in it. But I am inclined to agree with Thwith'Lthon." He said, motioning to the second. "They are unworthy."

"Oh no, excuse me, this wasn't my problem." Maya stepped forward, forgetting the fear the Council imparted, Ruth abashed by the interruption. "I'll listen all quiet until you say some nonsense like that. I've watched while stupid regulations get passed and implemented to no one's benefit. I do my job and I do it damn well. If I was paid to handle demons, you'd have someone handling demons. So don't you all float there and tell me about my failures when you're the head of this organization and I've never even seen any of you before. I've been here five years without promotion or recognition and I haven't said a damn word, but don't you come in here telling me my failure reflects badly on this company. You don't have to give me any blessings or anything, I'll handle this all on my damn own, but not for some distant shadow council telling me I don't know how to do my job."

The third wraith interjected. "Ruth, who is this insolent—?"

"Don't you talk about me like I'm not here." Maya said.

The second wraith, Thwith'Lthon, floated down towards Maya. "You poor child. You're confused. You know not to whom you speak. Need I remind you?"

Maya pulled her nose right towards the dark hood of the inter dimensional wraith. "Need I remind you that you're in my circle, I called you here, and thus you are under my command until dismissal. Or did you forget the rules of evocation?" Maya asked, and there was a moment of silence. "You can check this circle and all my preparations, but I assure you it's flawless. And don't get your head all in about vengeance and back lash. You're my employers, and you can fire me, but after that you're dealing with a Class 5 Necromancer with a particular affinity for binding non-corporeal entities. So… if you don't mind doing introductions so late, I am Maya. Good to meet you Thwith'Lthon. And you two must be Argexethoth, and Quixixixix." Maya held out her hand for shaking, then thought better of it and bowed. "I read about you all on Wikipedia."

The first Council Wraith, Argexethoth, emitted a growling and deeply disturbing laughter. "Where exactly did you learn to be so bold?"

"Oh, I'm just tired and underpaid." Maya said.

"She must not be allowed to live." Said the third wraith, Quixixixix.

"Hush." Said Thwith'Lthon. "I am in favor of bestowing the Dark One's Blessing. Do you concur Argexethoth?"

"I do."

"It is decided, Quixixixix." Said Thwith.

"I feel as though it is in both poor wisdom and poor taste." Said Quixixixix.

"Then keep your tongue still so that it taste no more." Said Argexethoth. Quixixixix hissed at Argexethoth, but said no more. "Three sisters in union under the Dark One's Blessing, much as the swamp hags of old. I like it. It is befitting to have a coven of three, blessed as you shall be blessed."

The Council Wraiths chanted, an unholy choir of Tuvan throat singing. And Maya saw, and Dana saw, and Ruth saw. Something appeared before their eyes on the horizon in the space between time. Their eyes turned fiery white, hot like embers, glowing in the gloom of the meeting room. Their bodies lifted in ecstatic revelation, levitating and convulsing in pleasurable spasms as they were inundated with all the knowledge and sight as are unbefitting for mortals to have. All the undead released a blue light from their eyes and mouths, breathing voidlight, and despairing. The three hags moaned as they were filled with power immeasurable, and became at last as gods given flesh.

Meemaw followed Lucy. Lucy followed Quinn. Quinn followed Harley. Harley followed Barnie. Barnie followed Aislynn.

The party wound through the forested dirt road, gnarled and mossy trees clung about by the heavy crimson plague fog that still clung from the now distant aberration's presence. Barnie carried his boomstick at the ready and pointed it into the pitch black of the trees beyond. Quinn carried a lantern that barely permeated even the few feet beyond him. Aislynn, at point, held her greatsword as best she could with her one off hand, up and resting on her shoulder.

There were no threats to be presumed in the surrounding woods. On any ordinary night, Quinn and Lucy would let Harley play in these woods alone. Harley had wandered often and deep to where the fairies roam and into the crystal caves, only once needing to fell a boar that had attacked her. There were few places that felt safer to her. But tonight, terror lurked.

In the distance, great and terrible explosions sounded as behemoths Margaret Rastaphan and Agamemnon pounded fists against one another in the mountains. The sound was muffled by the dense forests that lay between Remedy and the observatory home of Lucy and Quinn Draughtsmith.

"You four are the last ones, I believe. We set Mayor Brighton to getting the Havisham sisters out at their farmstead on the lakeside beach. We were able to gather everyone else in town fairly quickly."

"You could have just called or sent a message, you know." Lucy said.

"We tried." Replied Aislynn.

"I'm sorry, I told you I forgot to charge the phone it was at like 5% when we left the restaurant." Quinn said, mediating as best he could.

Even as they spoke of such matters, Aislynn received a ping on her own phone and checked it. "Excellent. A squadron of Paladins are zeroing in on our location. Commander Duncan at the helm. He's a bit zealous, but competent."

"Duncan?" Barnie chimed in, breaking his characteristic silence and stroking his beard. Then he grumbled, offering no more.

They all heard the approach of grinding gears piercing the silence, and the felling of trees. "Is that them?" Lucy asked, holding Harley close. But before anyone could answer, white and gold, heavily and futuristically armored men wearing gas masks marched from the tree line, followed by a tank which crumbled and splintered the trees in its path.

The brass tank was the size of a small house, and covered in guns, walking like an insect across the forest floor. It was a holy tank, presumably. It was covered in symbols and relics and painted white alongside the brass. It could only be run by a team of six from within, and overall it felt more like a small ship than a tank, but for its one large central cannon.

Aislynn alone stood at attention, whilst everyone else watched somewhat meekly as the ranks of uniformed Paladins surrounded the party. The rest of the military procession gathered into formation surrounding the dreadnaught vehicle, then halted. A caped commander with several winged badges jumped off the holy tank.

"Commander Duncan. It is good to see you. Private Ricky." Aislynn nodded with a frown, and let her sword to the ground for a rest.

"First Lieutenant Ricardo." He corrected her.

Aislynn ignored him, and addressed only Duncan. "I had not anticipated such a show of force. The Plague Anomaly is detained for the time being by another entity named Agamemnon. Though I doubt the Plague Anomaly is a force we could defeat, even with the Chalice X90 or any number of soldiers. I had requested healers."

Commander Duncan, a scarred blonde man with a military haircut and short stature stood in front of Aislynn looking grim. "Commander Aislynn O'Cuillen." He said, and looked at her companions, then turned back to her. "Might I have a word?" Aislynn stepped aside to the edge of the forest with Commander Duncan, who spoke with plain authority. "Aislynn, there are new orders. A sensitive matter, and confidential. You are relieved of duties and you are to report back to headquarters immediately."

"Report back to— absolutely not. I will see this through till the end."

"You are wounded, and in need of treatment." Commander Duncan insisted, his lip snarling with disgust as he gazed upon her torn shoulder stump.

"I was waiting for healers, which I do not see amongst your squadron." Aislynn rebutted.

"Aislynn, the nature of our containment mission has changed. It has been deemed that the Crimson Plague is too great a threat to risk the spread. And it has been further decided that Remedy is already a site of contamination. This is no longer a search and rescue."

Aislynn looked mystified, grappling with her own thoughts as much as what was being said. "I'm afraid I'm not following, Commander."

Commander Duncan smacked his lips and shifted his weight in frustration, then ran his hand down his face. "Aislynn, We are given orders to fight two threats. The Plague Abomination, and all those it afflicts. Brigadier General Picard is mobilizing a force against the Anomaly, we're here to neutralize the second threat."

Aislynn continued looking mystified for a long moment. "Duncan… no. No, no, no. The Order wouldn't…" But Duncan looked at Aislynn and Aislynn looked at Duncan and Aislynn knew. "But… you'll all be infected in the process, what's the point?" Aislynn asked before noticing Commander Duncan's new golden wings badge. Aislynn looked around, panicked, seeing the badges on each of the Paladins in the squadron. "You've been given the Martyrs Wings."

"The highest honor." Commander Duncan Said, sadly.

"Duncan, we're supposed to protect life. This isn't…" Aislynn began, but saw the set in Commander Duncan's face. "I'm not meant to return to headquarters at all, am I?"

Duncan held her eyes firmly and shook his head very slowly. "I'd like to ask you to please make this easy for both of us." Duncan said, and Aislynn saw now the Squadron of Paladins surrounding Quinn, Lucy, Meemaw, Harley, and Barnie grip their swords, and draw.

"Commander, please, reconsider." Aislynn pleaded one last time, more as a matter of course than of actual hope.. "This is a stain upon our Order, and your souls."

Duncan's eyes remained hard. "Aislynn, please kneel, and take your leave of this world with honor."

"We're defenders of Life." Aislynn repeated, now quivering.

"Even unto our own dooms, we will make what sacrifices we must for Life. For the continuation of *all* Life." Duncan quoted in reply. "Kneel."

"I will not." Aislynn whispered with more paralyzing force than any command that could be given. Then she turned a gaze of such ferocity upon him that his bladder loosened. "Duncan, tell your men to stand down."

Even as Aislynn spoke, Commander Duncan made a fell slice across the place her neck stood half a moment earlier. For Aislynn, she was entirely uncertain why or how she had moved before Duncan's slice, but move she did, and with grace.

Saved, perhaps, by divine intervention, the members of her party were not so lucky. By the Commander's slash, an order was given, and the heavily and futuristically armored Paladins of the squadron made to kill the party. A melee ensued while Aislynn did battle with Duncan at the line of trees. Both Barnie and Quinn were prepared for confrontation, and several blasts could be heard, but only one could be seen. For Barnie's part, his boomstick was of no ordinary sort, and instead an enchanted sort that tore several Paladin's limb from limb in a butchery buffet of mayhem; whilst Meemaw utilized a kitchen knife she had hidden in her bonnet, and Harley her slingshot which she held with determination and ferocity. Quinn had a gun of his own, and injured one of his holy assailants, but was the first civilian casualty as he fell lifeless, his eyes stricken with disbelief, felled by the blade of First Lieutenant Ricardo.

"Quinn!" Lucy could be heard screaming, followed by a slice and a gurgle as she too was slain. Their love, their story, their lives before and after, all of it far too much to record with written word, put ever so abruptly and unexpectedly to an end.

Aislynn felt as though her heart might crumble for the near forgotten relic of her emotional past, but Duncan was no man to be trifled with, and she parried him with a too heavy greatsword utilized only by her off arm, stifling her heart's woes under the weight of duty. It was hopeless, of course, as they traded blow for blow. Duncan utilizing his gun-blade with his aged but practiced arm. He would normally have been no match for Aislynn, but for all her wounds, Aislynn could only run away. Defeated in spirit but not in flesh, Aislynn called upon Seraphim, Light Wielders, which brought a flash like the sun upon the earth itself, so bright that no sound could be heard. Aislynn ran, grabbed Barnie from the stunned assailants, grabbed Meemaw and Harley. For though they were all three of them terrifyingly fierce fighters, they were outnumbered by an untold many, and the forests were their only hope.

Through bamboo thickets and across bog planks, they ran swift enough for a brief breather and respite with Aislynn panting orders. "We cannot linger. Their armor enhances their speed. We can outmaneuver them if we are lucky, we can hide, but we cannot outrun them. We must go to the Armory to warn the townspeople. The Paladin Order seeks genocide against the people of Remedy."

But for as breathless as Aislynn and Barnie and Harley might have been, Meemaw in her age was approaching death with her exertion. "You need to go on without me." She said as the weighted footfalls of heavy armor could be heard in the distance, metal upon bog planks. "Harley dear… I haven't been a very good Meemaw today. But please try to remember… all I'd do for you. How much I love you."

Meemaw pushed the group away. "Run." She said, wielding her knife towards the coming onslaught. Harley needed to be picked up by Barnie, and even for as large as he was he could hardly hold her. Harley didn't understand why Meemaw had been talking about killing her earlier. Harley didn't particularly like Meemaw's pea soup. But with a rush Harley could only remember Meemaw reading her bedtime stories and teaching her the properties of herbs and how to wear lipstick, and their picnics by Lake Talula. Harley even hated Barnie, somewhat, for picking her up and dragging her away. Even as she knew that Barnie was saving her life, she despised him momentarily.

Meemaw fought valiantly. A deft duck under a sideways slice ended with a stab under the armpit, a weak spot in the Paladin's plate armor, cut into his heart. On the Bog planks, only one could stand abreast at a time. In their overconfidence facing the old woman, as one fell, another took their place, and Meemaw was no less swift with a blade. The next she parried, jabbing the butt of her knife into his nose, blinding him, followed by another stab to the eye, into the brain. The third, however, had had enough, and learned the lessons of her predecessor. Taking no chances, the towering she-knight called upon eight golden glowing blades of heavenly justice which hovered and surrounded her in a circle. Meemaw looked valiantly upon her demise, then was pierced by the eightfold blade, one at a time, each a different direction into her chest. Collapsing, then beheaded by her assailant, Meemaw's spirit flew swiftly to a Warrior's Death at the gates of the Villa of Ormen.

Pursued by nine others, Barnie turned to fire from his enchanted boomstick, blowing three more Paladins(and two trees) to chunky and near liquified bits. The six remaining harrowed on, pursuing now more cautiously as their numbers dwindled. They crossed a stream and pursued the party through a church yard, five strong, then four.

Their dwindling numbers had gone unnoticed till the remaining four stood back to back and scanned around them. Aislynn and her party observed some half a mile beyond in a farmyard grove while one Paladin shot a crossbow bolt at the shadow in the trees, then another threw a trident because they were equipped with all sorts of wacky but still blessed weaponry.

Then there was a pause, then silence, then the screeching of thousands of bats which erupted from the church bell tower, swooped down from the skies above, grabbed one Paladin and sucked dry their life essence with thousands of tiny bat bites, shriveling their flesh and aging them hundreds of years in just seconds before ultimately dropping them with a dry thud through the leaves to the forest floor.

"Seiko, sore wa yoi aji." Came a voice from the coalescence of bats.

Neither Aislynn, nor Barnie, nor Harley knew what to make of that so instead they thanked their stars and ushered forth, unaccosted by the now effectively distracted Paladins. Through the forests and trees which were growing ill with plague, the trio harrowed onwards towards Remedy.

The Sea of Milk both is and is not a misnomer. People expect milk, white and frothy. It is not. It is more like fragrant golden rose water. That said, true to its name, the water was sweet like breast milk and did indeed spring forth from the bosom of a long dead goddess. That's the legend, and the legend is accurately based in reality, unlike many legends.

Eromir was no use here in the Sea of Milk, Cori and Derrick quickly found out. Eromir can fly, and he can gallop, but he cannot float as a ship floats, nor swim as a fish swims. And in the Sea of Milk you need to float as a ship floats, or swim as a fish swims. Interplanar dynamics get complicated, but Cori was well studied in them and knew exactly why Eromir was unable to traverse this realm. Take her word for it.

It was also a little uncertain what was under-water(or under-milk), and upon the Sea itself. It all blended a bit. Some up here, some over there, some both at once, some none of the above.

So, when Cori and Derrick commissioned a pirate vessel to bare them forth to the Eros Canal, they quickly found themselves floating on the water even as fluorescent whales danced above their ship and queer looking corals grew from the Sea floor above their heads. There were other ships, for the Sea of Milk makes a popular honeymoon destination despite the dangers, tourism being where they draw the majority of their economy. The people of the Sea also have other common exports such as a highly popular hearty stew from Whetstone Isle, made by the merfolk who populate the Sea. But that is neither here nor there. The Sea made for dangerous waters, with many rocky outcroppings amongst whirlpools and waterfalls defying gravity. Only the most experienced sailors could navigate it at all, and only the best of those could do so smoothly enough to make a proper honeymoon voyage for the couples daring enough to make the journey.

Cori and Derrick passed by these vast waterfalls, nymphs and sprites tending to the lotus gardens which lay upon the water, rainbow airs shimmering around their heads as they hopped and danced among the sugar plums. They had just left the seaweed forest and jellyfish gardens, and now they looked to the distance where reef castles floated in enormous bubbles.

"Downward, Ho!" Shouted Captain Boscab, the Pirate. And all the pirate crew clamored and bustled as their ship approached a violently swirling whirlpool vortex. Round and round they dodged the jagged rocks in the golden waters, down into a tunnel where they hit cruising altitude and all the crew was finally able to relax after a tumultuous start to their journey. Cori too was able to ease herself into the voyage, and plot the course for her encounter with Ichabod.

The Astral Cruiser they had taken on this voyage was a small galley called Bethany's Shadow. The sails were electrified spider silk and the prow of the ship was manned by a maiden whose look of vague horror was a little too realistic to give the impression of being sculpted, and rather gave the image of one who has been petrified by a Gorgon, or Basilisk.

Below deck, utmost care had been taken towards hospitality. This being an illicit honeymoon cruise run by one of the most prodigious pirate cartels, most rooms were dedicated spa baths and massage parlors. Cori utilized the time leading to her battle wisely, choosing to ease her body and mind with the variety of spa delicacies available onboard. All the while, Derrick used the gym.

Cori plunged her mind into strategy between her squid facial appointment and her posterior scrub and buff. Between her and Derrick, they had all the advantage Cori could surmise. There were no greater preparations that could be taken. She would convene with Derrick and ensure he provided a proper onslaught while she utilized Sonomancy to weaken his resolve from afar. Then she could light him on fire or whatever else felt appropriate in the moment. It wasn't fail safe, but it didn't need to be. It only needed to be all she could give in the moment.

Cori didn't need to wait for Pirate Captain Boscab's announcement that they had entered the Eros canal, as it became immediately apparent.

The Pirate Crew started to glisten, sweating and hoisting sails, stretching taut their musculature. They looked young, they looked vibrant, and they looked voracious. The effect was undeniable. Everyone became beautiful and huggable and sensual and downright irresistible.

The flowing waters around them grew poignant as Greek statues rose gargantuan above the surface depicting lewd scenes and the texture of goosebumps. Everyone here was 'accidentally' bumping into one another while passing by. Compliments were given freely. Hugs were offered openly. The dulcet tones of Marvin Gaye were played over the speakers as they prepared to dock at Port Lingham, a tropical town of rustic shacks and light pink adobo, set about with neon and exotic flowers.

Cori was rarely tempted by anyone, and especially found herself without eyes for anyone but Sammiel since as early as her first shift shadowing him. His danger and her mission ahead kept her eyes ahead and her mind steadied even as a particularly gorgeous gentleman hauled a barrel of wine upon his shoulder and gave her a casual but undeniably seductive wink. Derrick, emerged from the undercarriage of the ship and found himself battling several severe questions of sexuality as he was both surrounded and titillated by the disproportionately male pirate crew.

The ship was led by a small skiff into Port Lingham, and Cori found the nerves of her anticipated battle intermingled with this new sensuality in a strange bloodlust she had never anticipated.

But where was Ichabod? As told by the oracles, she was in the Eros Canal where she was told she would do him battle. Yet here they were and about to pull into Port whilst Ichabod was nowhere to be found.

Disembarking, feet on the smooth wood of the dock, Cori and Derrick found themselves accosted by glow sticks and painted half nude beach bods of an island paradise for singles and honeymooning couples alike. There were roadside stands for mixed drinks and open coed Roman baths and private clubs and open street dance parties with wandering youths exploring their bodies and minds up against the bodies and minds of their peers. This being the Betwixt, of course, it also carried an element of blending abstraction that lent a moldable and mystic air over the place.

"So, I've been to the Sea of Milk before, but I didn't expect anything like this was here." Derrick said as a wide eyed young man grinded hips against his in one of the many street dance parties.

"Yeah this is… definitely an interesting experience." Cori replied, her senses inundated by the alluring cologne of a nearby topless salesperson. "Not sure why Ichabod would be here, of all places." Cori looked around and noticed that despite the glistening beauty of everyone in the Eros Canal, there were definitely older souls aplenty amongst the otherwise errant youth. "Huh…" She said, then kept to herself in quiet contemplation.

They were doing little besides wandering. They were out of leads and direction. Derrick suggested they split up, which Cori was wary of because she felt he might not come back should he leave now. She had seen he had a penchant for eyeing the real estate photos in the windows of offices.

The food here was as delicious as the bodies of all the people eating it. They stopped for a chocolate coated raspberry ice cream that was thick and creamy and served delicately upon the chest of the chef. Cori ultimately decided to decline, wishing Sammiel was here so that perhaps they could enjoy such a delicacy together. Derrick ate Cori's portion.

The day went on and the sunset was squishable as orange juice and by nightfall things got weird, but Cori was left frustrated. The purple ringed planet which dominated the sky among several moons gave rapturous fervor to the crowd. Each corner revealed scenes that left Cori with more questions than answers, and she decided that perhaps it was time to stray from the crowd and out of the bounds of Port Lingham itself into the semi tropical nighttime phosphorescent forest and beaches beyond where glowing blue algae lapped gently upon the sandy waves. Inside the forest it grew quiet, with silver trees dripping glowing moon leaves like the snow of a silent night. Spherical crystals grew in the trees, with roots intertwining like pathways amongst the brush. Cori could still tell she was by the Eros Canal, but there was a quiet and a solitude towards the sensual pleasures the forest offered that Cori found herself preferring.

It was in this deeper solitude of the forest that Cori found Ichabod, standing peacefully on a boulder amongst the fruits of several lunar trees, the fruit juices dripping down his body as he bit them each in turn.

His angelic wings to his side, relaxed; his body rippled with the years of hard discipline and practice his order brought to him. His jawline was severe and his long gray hair fell over his shoulders, reminding Cori of the way Sammiel's silver hair fell over his shoulders in much the same way. He saw Cori and continued eating, though his wings flexed and revealed his white tattered robes.

Cori, at first, was braced for immediate battle. But soon she saw Ichabod had no intention of attacking her, at least for the time being. Hanuman's Bone Scythe, even, lay at his feet. Instead she stood tall, and held her head high, waiting for him.

"It is good to see you again, Coriander." Ichabod said, after finishing the last of his fruit. He stared at Cori and Cori stared at him, her chest heaving in anticipation. She tried to beat back her hatred for him. *Respect thy enemy.* But all Cori could see was this fallen angel's scythe piercing the one she loved.

Cori held out her arms, her face contorted with grief. "I thought you were trying to end all life. You had tried to kill me. Here I am, Ichabod."

"Keiran is trying to end all life. It is my job to sever the attachments of dead souls. You're not dead." He said, simply. "Why are you here, Cori?"

Cori began stoically. "I'm here for Hanuman—"

"No, no. I know you're here for the Scythe. That can be deduced. I mean why are you trying to get the Scythe?" Ichabod asked.

"I'm not going to let the world I love come to an end. The people I love..." Cori said, clenching her fist, trying to beat back the rising wrath as she yelled. "I'm here to avenge Sammiel."

"Isn't it odd. You, a necromancer, are here to fight for life; while I, a Paladin, am here to guide souls towards their final end? Reality can be so strange sometimes."

Cori looked around herself at the moonlight glow of the trees and the purple ringed planets of the night sky beyond and the light blue phosphorescent waves of the ocean through the trees in the distance, listening to the gentle moans of nearby dryads, which brought a measure of calm to the fire in her belly. "Yeah...." She said, and took a long breath.

"Cori, you know all life ends. And life begins again." Ichabod said, his hands outstretched at his waist. "It's an inevitable cycle. As certain as the sun may shine."

"I know that." Cori nodded, somberly.

"We're not trying to end life. Just to begin it again, and better."

"I know that." Cori said, again.

"Then, why?"

Respect thy enemy. "Ichabod...you know how I've struggled. Keiran could only latch on to my own struggles, the ones I held inside myself. He only had so tight of a grip on me because sometimes... sometimes, I didn't want to be alive." Cori said, her wrath now a clean burning fury, measured and contained. "But just as you've made a vow... just as you've become a force, an angel of death to guide souls beyond to their final doom... I have to become a force for life. To fight for life.... I— I know that I'm going to die. In many ways I'm even looking forward to that. But until then... I'm going to fight like hell to squeeze every damn drop out of this life, and the lives of those around me while I have it. Even when it's hard, and even when it's miserable. Because..." Cori motioned around her. "Because reality can be so strange. And because of love. And.... because I just want to feel one more breath."

Ichabod sighed, and his brow tightened. "I didn't expect you of all people to be given over so wholly to selfishness." Ichabod stretched his arm forward while the glittering ivory of Hanuman's Bone Scythe floated into his fist. He looked at Cori with a jarring and genuine empathy. "I understand." He said. "I came here, too, to squeeze out the last vestiges of all I have denied myself since leaving the Order. But those feelings, those are the things that prevent us from having a better world. St. Margaret will remake things so we're not burdened with such self obsession."

Cori looked at Ichabod and saw not a monster, just one whose will clashed infinitely with her own. She tightened her Gauntlets of the Black Rose and donned her metallic six eyed mask and brimmed witches hat. Ichabod gripped his Scythe and spread his stance brow and widened his wings.

The two stood like statues in their fighting stances. Ichabod, hard and disciplined. Cori, passionate and improvisational. The waves of the shoreline halted and pulled back and brought unnatural silence before a single breeze blew between the two combatants, silver leaves rustling.

Cori flew in first, jabbing the sharp nails of her gauntlet at Ichabod, then kicking low, then high, then following up with kicks from behind. Ichabod blocked, and hit Cori with the bone stave, throwing her back into a tree. Extending the scythe like a whip, Ichabod slashed through several trees while Cori ducked, proving his blade could cut through anything like it was little more than air. Cori focused her efforts on faints and unexpected moves, knowing that above all else she must avoid the blade. She ran towards Ichabod once more, feigned left, then completed a flip kick onto his neck. She attempted to utilize this momentum to throw him to the floor, but was instead grabbed and thrown into the sky where Ichabod launched and assailed her.

Cori battled Ichabod through the sky, slipping round his blade and following it with several shallow jabs, but it could not be sustained; for they were flying as a bird flies and not swimming as a fish swims, and such things were unacceptable in the Sea of Milk. And so, they fell into Port Lingham. Ichabod slashing and Cori attempting to dodge whilst in her free fall. But the clash of cosmic beings roused the attention of the populace below and so must have garnered Derricks attention as well, for he joined the fray only seconds later. He launched from the town like a missile to punch Ichabod in the face, the shock of Derrick's entry leaving a wide opening.

Cori began the Sonomancy she had learned from Mayhew. Sine waves undulated from her palms and formed a resonant circle between while Derrick made a fresh assault. Cori poured all her heartache into the song between her fingertips, which vibrated and pulsed against her flesh.

Ichabod, seeing this, slapped Derrick to the side, then rushed to assail Cori, but too late. Her melody completed, waveforms quaked the ground and formed fissures in the rocks and buildings surrounding. With her great need combined with her souls genuine expression, Cori had formed a delicate masterpiece which wrapped around Ichabod and infected his mind from within. Ichabod, for all his ferocity and discipline, fell to his knees weeping.

Derrick stood to Cori's side while Cori approached cautiously. "Finish him, quick." Derrick said.

Cori shook her head, and walked away from her coworker towards the defeated angel. "Ichabod, what is it you dislike so much about the world?" Cori asked. "I don't understand. But I— but I want to."

Ichabod let out several sobs before he was able to speak. "It's not the sickness of the world, Cori. When has the *world* hurt you, truly? It is not the world I hate but the sickness of humanity. Answer me this, Cori. Your hurt, did it come from the world, or humanity?"

Cori looked down. "Humanity."

"What happened to you." Ichabod asked. His hands upon the ground dampened with his tears, and he was unable to gaze in her eye.

"I was betrayed by someone I loved." Cori said quietly. "Two people, actually."

Ichabod gathered himself, clenched the dust under his fingertips and stood. "And they disgust you." He said, and Cori nodded. He met her eye now "And moreover… you disgust yourself."

Cori nodded again.

"My daughter was taken from me… by some… sick… terrible…" Ichabod began, but choked before he could complete his words. Then he walked closer to Cori. "And for as much as I hate the man who did it… I hate myself just as much. Because we are all one and the same. Everything that maed him who he was and what he was, I have running through my veins as well."

Cori was frozen, her eyes now wide with horror. She did not move as Ichabod walked slowly towards her, his scythe now in hand. She did not move while Derrick was yelling for her to run. And she did not move when Ichabod held the blade of the Scythe to her neck and said "You understand."

The cut was painless, and Cori stood suddenly before the Villa of Ormen under an eclipsed and dying star.

Chapter 23

On a hill just outside and above Remedy stood three sisters, bonded not by blood, but by a Dark Blessing. The world could falter or rise at their fingertips, for they were given unwavering control of the power over both life and death. Their hair wavered under grim wind, the smell of harvest apples and blood. They surveyed the fields that stretched before their view.

Their eyes pierced far, through fog and through trees and even through walls and saw all the happenings within Remedy and beyond. They saw into the Betwixt and into men's hearts and through the collective unconscious, they saw all for miles and miles.

"The Council was correct. The Paladins seek to move against us, and so strengthen their hold on this world." The one called Dana said, reveling in each breath of dark and plague ridden air.

"The plague is stronger now than once it was." Said the one called Maya, as she tested the limits of how far 'beyond' she could see. "Soon, there will be monsters."

"I sense the presence of War." The one called Ruth said, and motioned towards the mountains. "And the one called Agamemnon is growing weary, while Maragaret Rastaphan remains strong. The tides will turn soon, and not for the better."

Behind the three sisters, in the mountains, the metallic Colossus Agamemnon was having his face pounded into the side of a cliff by the oily and rotting fists of the skeletal queen; Margaret Rastaphan, Plague Anomaly. Agamemnon struggled and tried to heave her over him, but she bit into his face and tore his metallic and bejeweled flesh so that magma gushed forth down his body and into the mountainside below. The very hill tops were crumbling and craters were forming under their blows whilst trees flew in a cyclone, lifted with the sheer force of wind created in each punch.

"What are we to do, Sisters?" Ruth asked, standing center, looking left then right.

"The Dead of The Home will not be enough." Said Dana. "We require an army."

"Let us give life to all the Dead, then, sisters." Said Maya. "Let us reanimate all the town and lands beyond. The birds and the bees and the old and the young. We will bring life to all bones, young and old, to rise up and do our bidding."

"Yes. Yes. Crows and ants too. They shall all be under our command." Said Dana.

"Bring life to all bones." Said Ruth, and turned to face the others in the form of a triangle and gripped their hands. "Breathe life even unto the trees."

The air became thick with geometries where they stood. Divisive lines and angles shifted in obtuse airs. Each of the sisters keened, and from each of their voices rose magick which became an undulating eldritch green lotus sphere. Thsi then hovered and plunged into the earth and spread its veins down like life blood through roots and soil.

Around the three hags, the Earth seeped forth the old bones and the bodies of squirrels and deer, and soon the bodies of those who once had died on this, the site of the Battle of Morbid Springs and the Eagle Rock Massacre. Here, hundreds had given their lives in defense of their particular brand of freedom, or in offense of a brand of freedom that violated the former brand of freedom.

Anointed by the Dark One's Blessing, the wide spread reanimation construct shivered into the bones and decaying flesh of long dead soldiers. Hands tore through the grass and loamy clay, zombies moaned and skeletons chittered and grasped at long rusted weapons. All the while the three hags petitioned the wights and spectres and wraiths who traversed the land. They sought bindings in bogs and hidden cairn dappled throughout the miles surrounding. Rotten squirrels mounted undead fox battle steeds, and ghosts stood in formation for front line assault. At the helm,

Ernie, Agnus, Sarah, and George acted as Generals and Commanders to the undead host.

"Kill anyone who wears the white and gold of the Paladin brand." Ruth ripped her voice in her fury, and the whole crowd of undead heard her voice as the greatest compulsion. "Sisters, spread your eyesight into our children. See what they see, and command our forces from afar."

The three sisters' eyes went white and bright as their sight spread into the multitudes and they could see and think and feel as their undead host of animals and humans and insects and plants alike. The army marched towards Remedy.

There was such relief leaving the trees and onslaught of Paladins behind and coming to the open fields before the town of Remedy. Harley had insisted on walking once again, even as she staggered with exhaustion. She looked up at Aislynn and did her best imitation of Aislynn's walk and tried to get Aislynn's attention to show her how useful she could be with her slingshot. But Aislynn hardly noticed her, and scanned the horizon for threats. Instead, she spotted a civilian dancing just outside of town.

"Oh Lord," Aislynn said to Barnie, "we have to get them out of here."

"Aislynn, hold up—" Barnie began, but Barnie ultimately lacked confidence and liked to leave things up to other people when he could help it, even if he thought he knew better. So instead he trailed behind Aislynn while she approached the civilian who seemed to be dancing in a rainfall that wasn't there.

"Ma'am, we need to leave here quickly." Aislynn said and knew immediately that something was off about the woman, dancing as she was amongst the plague fogs. The uncomfortable sensation was punctuated by a rustling nearby on the ground, where a man lay writhing in horror.

Skinless, flayed. The man stood on the precipice of physical death. His muscles and fats were as visible as his eyes, his pain so excruciating as to silence him. And the woman, Aislynn now saw, looked odd not only for her misplaced ecstasy, but for the second set of skin she wore over her own.

"Harley, cover your eyes." Aislynn told the child too late, as the girl had in the span of half a second seen far too much of the world.

"I got my skin back. I got my skin back." The woman said to Aislynn, her eyes wide with joy.

Aislynn drew her sword in front of her and tried desperately to hold it steady. But weariness had begun to set in long ago, and the adrenaline rush that had initially countered the weariness was now wearing especially thin. The prayers and holy incantations that would usually counter even this more thorough form of weariness were themselves wearing thin as well. Her greatsword in her off-hand was too heavy at the best of times. Now, she could hardly lift it from the Earth.

"Damnit." Aislynn said and dragged the sword back behind Barnie. "Barnie please, you have to kill her before she transforms."

Barnie was in shock. He had become a hermit for a reason. He sought peace and solitude and most importantly an escape from the odd quarrels and chaos of humanity. Barnie, for his part, couldn't even understand the words Aislynn was saying, and found himself totally and completely stricken dumb.

"Damnit." Aislynn said. She sheathed her greatsword and grabbed Barnie's arm and pulled him and Harley away from the doubly-skinned woman and flayed man. "Damnit, Damnit, Damnit."

Rushing away and into the town of Remedy, the woman did not offer chase, for she had already found a second skin to satisfy her. That could not be said for the other town residents who had taken up 'the wandering'. They peaked out at Aislynn, Barnie, and Harley as shadows from inside windows and in alleyways.

"I don't know how this is happening so quickly. All records show the plague taking several days to set in." Aislynn whispered to Barnie as they tried to avoid notice behind a dumpster in the alleyway between 'The Oubliette' Nightclub, and Mama Raspberries' Charcuterie.

"Yes, but we had that entity standing directly over the town. Didn't anyone think that maybe that could change the timeline a bit?" Barnie asked.

"I couldn't tell you." Aislynn admitted. "I just got a short debriefing from the Paladins by phone, and they were lying about half of what they said anyway."

A street beggar approached whose face was sliding off the bone, "Please, help me, can't you please spare me your flesh." But Aislynn pulled Barnie and Harley and led them on through the streets even as some of the wandering town residents gave chase. Harley fell and Barnie carried her in his arms.

Aislynn wanted desperately to just forget the Armory and leave the town, but there was too high a likelihood that there were healthy people there who were in need of a defender. Weak with exhaustion though she was, she at least had a sword she could lend to the strongest of them, and powerful oaths she had taken worked in her deepest core. But their party was being accosted by 'wandering' and plague ridden town residents, against whom they found themselves defenseless. Several skinless corpses littered the streets.

The breathless party arrived finally at The Charter School Remedia which lay on the Eastern side of South Apple Street, just across from Remedy's very own mysterious Ancient Obelisk whose hieroglyphs sometimes glowed a vibrant orange on the night of the Summer Solstice, which it was not. Next door, the Armory. It was an imposing fortress of obsidian, set with the symbol of a Heptagram over its massive oak doors, as it was used for both cult meetings, and thrash metal concerts.

The Armory doors had several dozen 'wandering' residents clawing at the oak and the chains which barricaded the doors from entry even as their skins slowly fell from their bodies. The barricade was good, but Aislynn felt incapable of fighting even one of them, let alone a host.

It was even with this despair that on the Southern and opposite end of the street, Aislynn saw the emergence of a Paladin host with three six legged Chalice X90 holy tanks.

"Aislynn…" Barnie said quietly, and frightened. He pointed behind himself to the Northern end of the street, where a host of zombies, ghouls, ghosts, and goblins marched below three beautiful hags who sat upon broomsticks.

"Who's that?" Harley asked, pointing up to the mysterious Ancient Obelisk on the Western side of South Apple Street. Upon this, Aislynn saw a young man, red of hair with goat's eyes dripping along his body. The very air around him warped into frightening thoughts and evil symbols and old and sleeping horned gods.

Back, far away in the Northern Mountains of Remedy, Agamemnon and Margaret Rastaphan were staring each other down. There was a great pause in all the world, and all the various opposing forces took a deep and shared breath of fear.

It was Agamemnon who broke the silence, not with sound, but with a light like a supernova which came first to his eyes then as a laser into the black oily skull of Margaret Rastaphan. A shockwave rolled slowly through the mountains, moving the wind and quaking the earth with a mighty eruption. And the moment it passed, Keiran, the Wandering Villagers, the Paladins, and the Necromantic host all gave themselves to War.

The Villa of Ormen stood closer than ever, an empty temple of hieroglyphs made in honor of no god, etched with the stories of the fallen who lay sleeping in its catacomb walls.

Cori had hoped to find Sammiel standing out on the doorstep, refusing to enter. That somehow everything would be alright, and he'd just be waiting here for her, knowing she would come and refusing to enter the place from which he could not return. But he was not standing out on the steps, and all that could be seen was the Villa, empty and forlorn like an abandoned house.

Instead Cori lost herself in the hieroglyphs, images of the final moments of life for far too many souls. It did not provide reassurance, as Cori tried to root and reiterate her tethers to the mundane world she called home. The central hieroglyph, an empty circle above the door leading into darkness, with a single wax candle lit at its precipice, flickering and dim.

"What are you getting yourself into?" Cori asked herself in the silence of the Villa. *This is probably just some sick new way of expressing your suicidal ideation. Don't kill yourself directly, just martyr yourself for a hopeless cause.* Cori thought this, but knew something felt different. The empty depths of the Villa repelled her now, and she was filled with the deepest terror. The thought of dying *now*, after finally seeing the beauty and allure of a bountiful life, was unbearable. She was wasting time, meandering around the doorway, avoiding her cause. She bit her lip. "For Sam..." Cori said, and marched towards the entrance.

Each step up the stairway was a rasping breath, a gutteral tremor of fear. Painful, lonely, devoid. She saw now the duty of a Necromancer. To provide comfort and warmth in a journey that is otherwise so chilling, and she felt glad for just a moment that she had been able to provide even so brief and mild a comfort as she did. Perhaps she had underestimated her own role.

She came to the precipice of darkness, beyond which lay only Void. Above her, the candle, and the empty circle window. Another step into the unknown, this unknown, the greatest unknown. Even the irrational and disjointed Betwixt followed the laws of form and logic. But the Void was a place so empty, even logic would become dispersed. These theories and more, Cori read in her textbook nosedives to which she had become so accustomed. Another step, and she may never read a book again.

"Nothing is going to prepare me for this, so there's no sense in waiting." Cori said out loud, but still she stood on the soupy precipice of the dark light nothing, paralyzed and unwavering. "Just...*GO!*" Cori said, and she stepped out of form and reason.

So this is what the Oracles see... Cori was. The multitudinous place. There's Sammiel, obviously. *But why? He's resting. I could rest too. We're all...resting...together. It's really not so lonely. Just one big silent family in a cold cold bed. Why aren't I resting with them?*

There's Grandma and Pop Pop. Where's mum? Cori spread her thoughts farther and found how easily she could disperse to the point of non-existence. *No, no, not too far. Not yet. What was it Aislynn had said?*

There was a great shushing from everywhere and nowhere. Right behind Cori, and right to her face. It was nobody.

Fear.

Sorry.

Cori felt eons pass between this thought and the next, her sensations stretched and contorted and dispersed. Something was trying to pull her apart. She was trying to let herself pull apart. What was holding her together?

The Land I Love. That's what Aislynn said.

"Shhhh…"

The Man I Love.

There came a cosmic reprimand by way of the threat of the void waking, a prospect too horrible to imagine. An eyelid half opened, if nothingness could be an eye.

Cori coalesced silently in front of Sammiel. She was afraid to think. All she knew was the hunger to sleep beside him, to rest forever cuddled against his cold chest. But even this hunger grew too loud, and the eyeless eye of the void shuddered half open once again.

Sleep.

Cori was in a dark room, an enclosed space, a half forgotten dream. Sammiel rocked in a chair that was not. *"We can speak here."* Sammiel whispered, as though talking in his sleep. His eyes shuddered back and forth rapidly. *"You mustn't wake the Mistress."*

"Where are we, Sam?" Cori asked.

"The Land of the Dead." Sammiel said. "The True Dead."

"It's so quiet."

Cori lost herself again. She stood in the room, her thoughts so blank they could no longer be described as blank, for that description lends too much sensation to that which she was lacking.

"You must come back Sam, I can't hold on much longer." Cori whispered too now, hardly awake, the pull of emptiness was too great.

"No. The Truly Departed do not return." Sammiel whispered apathetically. *"You will stay here with me. You too, are truly departed."*

Cori didn't know how to convince him. She didn't know how to convince herself anymore. Cori didn't know anything. It might have been serene, if serenity were allowed to exist.

Cori was on the other side of the universe. Cori was still with Sam. Things were breaking down. Things were never really there. Time began to loosen.

"I want you home." Cori said. *"I want to be home with you."*

"That's just a dream." Sammiel replied. *"This is real."*

"It's all real Sam, please."

"Shhhh!" Came the hush of the Void.

"*Come home, Sam.*" Cori pleaded now and for a moment she felt more alive. "*Please. I won't leave without you. I can't.*"

There was a rumble that was not, and a non-eye gazing from the deepest places in the machinations behind our clockwork galaxy.

Cori was out of time, something was waking which should not wake. Something that felt wretchedly forbidden. Something that would tuck the tail even of Ammut and his soul-shredding jaws. It was now or never, and Sammiel remained sleeping in the Dusk of Anatman, barely rousing himself for the pretense of a whisper.

In the gaze of this most forbidden wakening, Cori centered herself next to Sammiel's floating corpse-soul. The void itself shuddered into awareness and rage grew as it was roused from a too-deep slumber. All the souls of the Truly Departed roused in witness as Cori pressed a tender but determined kiss to Sammiel's cold lips.

The Kiss.

Taboo, horror, intrigue. The Truly Dead have never been witness to such an event in their own domain. Sammiel woke with the rest of them in both repulsion and delight and pulled Cori's cool lips apart softly. His tongue lapped against hers like the waves of an ocean. Cori felt the Void crumble under the weight of their passion. In all realms and all worlds, all songs and all hearts ceased their rhythm and offered themselves as sacrifice to the Song of Silence.

The kiss was everything Cori had dreamed of since their night in the garden at St. Margaret's. The frustration and anticipation that had been built unequivocally over the months and relieved in a moment of cosmic alignment, in a place beyond cosmic touch. And Cori was undeniably titillated by the fact that they were being watched by those who are forbidden from watching.

Something happened then that could only happen in the non-rationality of the unspace beyond existence. The one and only way in which the Truly Departed can ever return from a place of non-returning is by no longer being one of the Truly Departed.

Sammiel was not Sammiel. Coriander was not Coriander. In truth, they were neither of them nothing at all. And because of this, they could both of them be nothing at all, and thus both of them became something else. With their forbidden embrace, their dead souls collided, merged, and became as one. Coriander was Truly Departed. Sammiel was Truly Departed. But they were Coriander and Sammiel no longer. They were Soriel. And Soriel was not Truly Departed. Soriel had never walked through the precipice of the Villa of Ormen. Soriel was fresh as a babe out the womb.

Silver haired, androgynous, toned; and with new, more delicate tattoo's, Soriel's eyes glittered. One was green like Sammiel's, and one was smoke stone like Cori's. They were well and tautly muscled, and they radiated power and brilliance as they stepped from the crisp blackness of the Void into the stairs of the Villa of Ormen. Soriel spread their four enormous black wings and looked into the eclipsing sun. Together they knew all they had to do and all they could accomplish. As the love child of two differently flawed beings, Soriel encompassed one singular completion. They were one step further towards evolutionary bliss.

They launched and shredded through space and time and down into harsher and deeper frequencies. The Crystallatium, Sonorous, and down into the Sea of Milk where their wings became fins and they were able to swim as a mermaid swims and so traverse the Sea with ease.

The Sea was more fun to swim through than sail upon, as Soriel jettisoned through Atlantian cities and disrupted their day to day thoroughfare as the mermaids and mermen looked to the skies where a black winged angel soared like a comet through their coral streets, boiling the very water of the Sea.

Past the ice volcano of Juniper Monds, and downwards into Funnel Gulch, Soriel flew and remembered riding these same places with a pirate crew back when she was Singular. Then they jettisoned through the steady waters of the Eros Canal, which cut its way under a rock arch and between two mountains.

The tropical town of Port Lingham was in ruins, and flashes of magickal power could be seen coming from the smoking debris. An errant blue fireball shot from within the wreckage and nearly hit Soriel's bottom left wing, instead slapped away casually from a being beyond trivial destruction.

Scanning the town, Soriel saw that there were two men doing battle, and fiercely. With a torn shirt, and bloodstained white wings, Ichabod breathed in heaving sighs. Across from him, Derrick stood with scorched clothes and scorched chest, his fists pulsating.

A distant half memory came to Soriel where Derrick had once announced his plans of becoming a battle mage. Neither aspect of Soriel had expected to see such a well equipped fighter holding his own against Ichabod, agent of death. As they paused a distance away from each other, the dread angel Soriel landed forcefully in the wreckage.

"That is enough." Soriel commanded, their mind innumerable, for it had traversed both being and non-being.

But the mad angel Ichabod dashed forward and slashed his scythe where Soriel stood, who phased away seamlessly, and followed Ichabod with a kick to the back of his neck. Ichabod groaned and flapped his wings to fly into the sky and hover above the field of battle in the smoky light of this world's star.

"I know your face." Ichabod said, wiping spittle from his mouth, and panting. "But I do not know your name. I should know the name of those with whom I do battle, before ending their being. And be swift, there are many souls approaching who seek Liberation."

Soriel, fresh and clean, spoke slowly and without passion. "You speak to one already Liberated, and Manifested again. I am One who may wield Hanuman's Bone Scythe. I am called Soriel, born of both Coriander and Sammiel. I have come to do you justice."

Ichabod scowled, then spit. "The word justice speaks fowl on your tongue. Speak no more, let battle decide whose is the will of God."

Together the two angels collided in attacks of unimaginable speed and force. Aftershocks quaked for miles around, and storms gathered at the site. Soriel retained the Fell Dagger Chains of their father and dodged the Bone Scythe and slashed in long arcs with fury and conviction. But from their mother they retained a rudimentary understanding of Sonomancy. Between long slashes with their dagger chains came bass drops and dynamic interludes from both fist and figure. Synesthetic harmonics assaulted Ichabod's mind and felled his body and allowed for the first bloodying strike.

Enraged, Ichabod followed with slice after slice of his impossibly sharp scythe, but missed one after the other till one cut through Soriel, shoulder to hip. Ichabod smiled. Soriel looked into Ichabod's eyes. Then Soriel grabbed the Bone Scythe calmly from the shocked hands of its former master. "I am already Liberated. There is nothing here to sever." Soriel said simply, and held Hanuman's Bone Scythe aloft, which glittered in the light of whatever star held itself over this world. "It is over, Ichabod."

"You really don't understand the discipline of the Paladin do you?" Ichabod asked. "Once we begin a battle, we do not stop." Ichabod fought now with new ferocity, and assaulted Soriel with both fists and feet. Derrick joined from the side lines and began a dual onslaught with the dread angel Soriel.

For all his discipline and Will, Ichabod's resolve weakened. He faced the collective might of too many foes filled with righteous fury. A punch to the sides followed by an uppercut was then followed by a downward rip from a fell dagger on a left handed chain. Several more punches followed, and a side step for another slice from the fell dagger. More punches. Ichabod, depleted, could not stop the left handed fell chain from wrapping his body after yet another haymaker to the temple. Bound and wrapped, Soriel approached Ichabod with chains in their left hand, Scythe in their right. They made a single passionless cut across his waist, which severed Ichabod from this world in body and in soul, never again to taste of its nectar or roll in the grasses under the sun.

"Might that I see you once again, Serena, to rest forever by your side." Ichabod said faintly, as the ground roiled with the significance of his death in the cosmic order. Then, his body split into many thousands of butterflies, glowing a light teal green as they sailed upwards and away to the Villa of Ormen.

Neither aspect of Soriel had ever ended any other beings life intentionally, and there was a deep seated knowledge that this was exactly what had been done. So came the end of a man who had led a long and complex life, filled with surprises and upsets and love and laughter; who had once known the meaning of what it was to hear the voices of the flowers sing and to dance as the stars dance. A man who had lost it all to a series of unfortunate incidents which set his life spiraling in a way he could not grasp. But his is another story.

Chapter 24

Soriel had to return down to the low frequency of the Mundane, but Derrick chose to remain in Port Lingham and so assist with the reconstruction efforts. He was quite insistent on the matter. But returning for Soriel, was no simple matter. For Cori had elevated through the Betwixt utilizing her human flesh, whilst Sammiel's flesh lay dormant and lifeless down in the Mundane. And for all their desire to remain as one, they knew it could not be a state which was held indefinitely. It was painful, giving themselves once again to their individuality. They craved their union as the greatest comfort they had known since the womb. But it was time to venture forth once again as Sammiel and Coriander.

Splitting and Separating, ripping from embrace, they held hands as they came down to the Ethereal Sphere besides a torn and splintered St. Margaret's, wherein they found Sammiel's reconstructed body laying dormant upon his midnight black comforter on his curtained four poster bed in his room. Here he had been placed amongst roses and decorated and embalmed. And here in his room he kept a gateway to the Ethereal, open and waiting for Cori to step through into the Mundane with ease. Cori alone, for Cori alone had entered the Betwixt with her physical body intact; while Sammiel was left disconnected and with only his Consciousness. He would require Resurrection.

"It's the best door between the Ethereal and the Mundane for a hundred miles. Took me years to put together." He told Cori before she stepped through. "Do what you can for me."

Carrying Hanuman's Bone Scythe, Cori stepped through and saw Sammiel's room and his several homunculi who were being fed and tended to by a construct that looked to be of Dana's particular style and influences of magick. Indigo and pink bubbles floated from Sammiel's beakers, and tubes carried neon liquid round the sci-fi hamster mazes he had built for his homunculi.

Stepping through the gateway, Cori walked up the steps of the Altar that led to his black four poster bed, and stood besides Sammiel's lifeless corpse. He had been kept pleasantly fragrant, his body lightly wrapped with mummification cloths, with protective sigils painted in dark ink upon the cottons.

He looked peaceful, and Cori hated the idea of disturbing him even as she could feel his soul through the veil. She knew she would have to do forbidden magicks to bring Sammiel back to life, but she refused to be afraid of her own power any longer. And so, her veins aglow with all the iridescent greens of pastures and trees as she called upon the secret teachings she had learned from Aislynn as she learned the ways of the Paladin that would reignite Sammiel's neurons and bring his heart to pounding again. Tears would be needed. In her studies, tears were always needed for resurrective magicks. Cori did not much feel like crying, but under Morris' guidance she had a small selection of vials in her satchel which carried the tears of the recent past. Cori dripped tears of happiness onto Sammiel's face, to symbolize how she would feel when he was brought back to life. Cori called upon the four winds of the four cardinal directions and all the angelic host therein. Then, lowering her own face, she brought her lips to Sammiel's while sparks popped in the air and golden sparkles showered down slowly from the ceiling, a side effect of such holy powers. With the final touch of her lips Sammiel took a deep breath of life, his eyes shocking open as his soul slammed down into the central seat in his mind; his driver in his vehicle once more.

It was hard, somehow, coming back to the lower versions of reality. Struck once again by need and longing and the gross mechanical complexifications of otherwise simple actions such lifting an arm which were so simple in the higher planes. But this was home, and this was where they belonged and for all its grounded rules and odd proportions it was a beautiful place in a different but no lesser way than the Crystallatium or the Sea of Milk.

Cori held the tip of the blade of Hanuman's Bone Scythe to Sammiel's neck, digging it in and drawing just a drop of blood. "Look what I got." Cori said, sadistically.

Sammiel was as one born again, and with some horror in his eyes his evolutionary body realized the mortal ordeal he had been through. To have the blade which had struck him dead still against his neck was a little too much for his psyche at just that moment.

But then he looked up at Cori, whose eyes held as much love as eyes have ever held. And he felt then as he looked at her as though he were a child back home on Christmas morning. He looked up at her and saw the warmth of innocence and home, and he knew then that he would be all right.

"We're going to set things right." Cori said, pulling the scythe away. "You ready to do this?"

Sammiel lunged in to kiss Cori, his mummification wrappings as cold as his hands and pressed his lips against hers, "Just one more, in case everything goes to hell." So Cori kissed him back, passionately. Then they left together, arm and arm to cross the chasms of the newly ravaged St. Margaret's, past the crumbling pillars of the Deep Halls of Albahazred, and into the noticeably quiet, empty, and ghostless hallways of the resident's chambers as Cori explained the situation of their ravaged world. Then, leaving the manor through a crack in the East Wing, Sammiel and Cori harried on to the town of Remedy, knowing not what lay in wait for them.

"Wait." said Sammiel, then spoke several fiery and glowing arcane symbols from the forked tongue that people sometimes got when they performed dark arts. These fell to the ground where they scorched the Earth and Sammiel muttered "Rasputin, Nuagn'thiel Asparath, Elohim raga-thuul." Then Sammiel turned to Cori as a bloody nightmare steed crawled through the very dirt of the earth, clawing and sputtering and snorting, then standing stoically and offered itself as a mount. "Remember Rasputin?" Sammiel asked.

"Rasputin," Cori nodded respectfully, for she knew the steed to be kingly. Rasputin nodded back, blood falling as tears from its eyes. Hooves burned the grass surrounding them, it's tail and mane burning hairs like embers.

"Come Rasputin, Ha." Sammiel kicked, Sammiel holding the reins and Cori prepared with her bone scythe, and they rode swiftly onwards towards Remedy.

The Paladins, numbering only in the hundreds, were vastly outnumbered by the host of thousands of undead brought by the witches and then joined by several dozen of the beplagued residents of Remedy. However, each Paladin was thoroughly equipped with armors and blessed weaponry. On top of this, forming a phalanx in front of their Chalice X90 tank, their practiced strategies were greatly superior. Each shot from the tank left a crater in its wake, and bodies were piling even before the undead met the phalanx of soldiers.

Even so, ghouls were a force to be reckoned with. Swift and strong and not willing to be put down by an ordinary cut, they formed an onslaught of gnashing teeth and thrashing bones whilst spirits flew overhead to drive madness into the mind and gray the hairs and weary the resolve of the otherwise determined Paladins.

Maya, Ruth, and Dana, performed terrible hexes and curses. They bolstered their forces and raised those who were already felled. But each shot of spell work from the witches above was met by a holy shield. Five zombies overpowering one Paladin was countered by a fell slash of a mighty sword cutting through all five bodies at once. On all sides, the forces were balanced. Behind it all, in the mountains to the North, Agamemnon was chaining and binding the body and limbs of the Plague Anomaly, Margaret Rastaphan. For each chain that bound her, Margaret Rastaphan would ooze her way out of it. But for each escape, two more chains took their place, and she was becoming overwhelmed.

Aislynn kept her concern away from the clash and towards the wellbeing of the residents trapped in the Armory, keeping Barnie and Harley close behind while she rushed to the oak doors, thoughts of self preservation left too far behind as she saw an incoming Squad of Paladins, intent on their genocide as they rushed the Armory, the beplagued villagers outside, and the host of healthy citizens within.

The Plagued Residents who had once stood clawing at the door for flesh had found more readily available skins from the approaching Paladin force, and met them in battle at the entrance walkway.

Aislynn rushed to meet them in battle, knowing it to be futile but trusting in her cause. The Paladins would overwhelm the Plagued Residents in a matter of minutes, if not seconds, and she was hardly able to lift her sword. This is when she saw Kitsune sway languidly from out behind the Armory's side, her belly large and bloated, her clothes splattered in blood. She held a smile of lavish delight that rested easily on her face. Her eyes rolled back into her head with sated bloodlust.

"I don't know if I could eat another bite." Kitsune said, readjusting and refocusing her eyes and unhinging her jaw. "But mama always told me to clean my plate."

She moved unnaturally, somewhat serpentine while still on her feet, swaying back and forth but at the speed of a jaguar. Her jaws chomped down onto the armor of one Paladin's arm at the side of the battle as he raised his sword against a Plagued Resident. That same arm was pulled separate from his body like cooked ham off the bone.

Reacting quickly, a Paladin stabbed Kitsune with a holy blade which seared her flesh and brought her to a fit of giggling. Her flesh warped and reworked itself away from the wound. This bold Paladin was split upwards with her nails, which brought a shower of blood. Kitsune opened her mouth and drank of the rain. More Paladins moved against her, and Aislynn utilized this opening till a new force stood between her and her mark.

His feet thudded against the ground and kicked dust into the air. "I know you." said Keiran, with a look of delight. Black tendrils lashed round his body, his breath was blue flames, his eyes dripped. "You were pretty tough last time we met. Not gonna lie. But you're tired, aren't ya?"

Aislynn could barely keep her grip round her sword, and she recognized now the same demonic entity which had taken residence in Coriander Lou, the same that had defeated her at full strength with only a fraction of his being. Barnie was quick to react and fired a hearty blast from his Boomstick. Keiran's tendrils slapped all the boomstick bullet beads out of the air, quicker than the eye could grasp.

"I don't believe we've been introduced." Keiran said to Barnie, then looked at Harley. "Oh, she's far too young to be seeing all of this. You didn't even have the good grace to just end her suffering? That's just bad parenting."

"Leave her out of this." Aislynn spat, but her strength finally faltered. Aislynn fell to her knees, and dropped her greatsword.

"Well that's disappointing." Keiran said and looked at Barnie and Harley for some explanation.

Aislynn's body had been pushed beyond its limits. Aislynn's soul had given all it could give. She had already used every holy magick in her repertoire. She had resurrected the dead, she had resurrected herself, she had augmented her own strength and called upon every angel, every sacred name. Every trick in her book she had used to come as far as she had, and there was simply nothing left. Aislynn tried to pray, tried even to invent new prayers, but her mind was given to silence and unable to conjure even the thought necessary to question the silence.

Keiran walked towards her as her breath weakened. Barnie ran in to deliver a sucker punch like a freight train to Keiran's jaw, and was slapped away for the effort. He skidded several times across the ground like a pebble on water before being slammed into the brick wall of an adjacent building and dented the bricks with his weight. Harley rushed over to Barnie, while Aislynn stared at the ground, expressionless.

Keiran turned his attention from the girl and grabbed Aislynn by the chin and lifted her to face him, then grabbed her by the neck and lifted her off the ground.

"You do know why you failed, don't you?" Keiran asked. He frowned and looked at her with pity. "You're supposed to be a defender of what is right. But here you are trying to prolong the suffering of this world. Here you are trying to prevent my Utopia. Here you are, exposing a child to the horrors of the worst abominations of this world. That's why your God has abandoned you."

Thwack.

The force of the rock hitting the side of Keiran's skull wasn't enough to do him harm. But the force was enough to surprise him, and to leave him momentarily stunned. Harley had turned before getting to Barnie, found her courage and found a rock. With her slingshot in hand, she delivered her shot with profound accuracy. Keiran dropped Aislynn, and Aislynn fell to her knees and gripped her sword.

Beyond, Cori and Sammiel approached the Phalanx of Paladins around their tanks as they clashed with the undead host. "You go." Sammiel said to Cori, then he lept off Rasputin into the thick of the Paladin force and unleashed his bladed Fell Dagger Chains and whipped through the center of the host while Cori sped onwards to the Armory. At first, Sammiel sent several Paladins to easy and early graves with a whirlwind of chains and blades. But they quickly formed ranks around him and made things more difficult. Sammiel kept them at bay with a focused onslaught, but they closed closer and closer, shields at the ready. Then, all was given to chaos as the undead horde broke through, and war became all. Sammiel was forced to defend against a confused zombie, and cut down one of his own before a less confused Paladin tackled him to the ground and began beating him with bludgeoning fists. Sammiel cursed but hypnotized the Paladin through his eyes and used the momentary break in concentration to jab his aggressor's jugular with his dagger chain. Blood covered Sammiels face, his pupils dilated, his vision turned red, and ecstasy overcame him. He stood, and slew another Paladin where he stood, then chained another into binding and stabbed him repeatedly with his other hand. Sammiel howled to the crescent moon, and sent all the undead howling with him. Even the hag sisters above joined, and struck fear into the hearts of the Paladins. Then, Sammiel lost himself.

There was no prayer nor effort of will. Aislynn was. And what she was felt light, and loose. She heard the cheer of all the life of the world as all beings, big and small, cried out to their chosen hero. With her own hope silenced in the face of her exhaustion, she felt only the hope of the rest of the universe, punctuated by the single *thwack* of a rock hurled by a young girl. With her own prayer silenced, she heard only the prayers of all the world, punctuated by a howling from the Nearly Departed and those who watch over them. It was with these prayers that she gripped her greatsword and delivered the upward slice that cut Keiran's face in two, then crumbled where she stood, comatose with her exhaustion. Keiran staggered back, and cried out. He gripped at his face and tried to place the two sides back together. He would be able to, of course, but as he centered his thinking on this he missed the distant galloping as it approached and the neighing of a nightmare steed.

The horseman, Coriander, leapt from the steed and slashed with bone white scythe. Cori cut through and, skidding on the dirt with her speed, gathered her balance with her scythe in tow as Keiran slid apart. He was severed at the third vertebral column and released of all his worldly attachments.

"What is it you see in this damned place?" Keiran asked. His upper torso tried to crawl his way to his legs, his face still split in two. His body began to dissolve into ash. "I just wanted to mean something." Cori got down on her knees and gathered Keiran in her arms, and he looked up at her. "I just wanted to do some good with my life." Keiran wept.

"Shhh." Cori responded. "It's okay. It's okay, you can rest now." Kitsune approached to bear witness, her battles won

"I don't want to go." Keiran pleaded. Half his body dissolved and blew with the wind up into a portal above. "I don't understand any of this. I'm so afraid. I'm so alone."

Cori looked up at Kitsune and their eyes locked, and understanding was shared. "I'll go with him." Kitsune offered, just as the rest of Keiran dissolved, pleading and stammering into the warp hole above; and she followed to offer him company on this, his final journey.

Cori stifled the lump in her throat, and her rising bereavement. She had not anticipated the lingering kinship which she felt for Keiran despite his evils. She knew Keiran's suffering intimately, as it was her own, and the two of them had spent much time together locked in the soul binding embrace of possession. As he parted the world, Cori felt his loss cut her more deeply than she could have guessed. She felt all the numb and confused shock that one feels at the passing of a sibling, one who was known beyond the usual bonds, their presence set deep in the blood.

None of them celebrated the end of Keiran. It was loss and loss alone for each of the survivors who staggered amongst the wreckage. Harley, unaware of even her own heroics, pushed her wet face into Barnie and listened against his chest for breathing. There was none. She cried out for him to wake up, please wake up. Cori checked Aislynn, who was alive, and flagged down Maya from her place in the sky to help her.

If Cori had hoped for some human warmth from Maya when she had seen her, she found none. Maya's eyes were glowing like a gods, distant and inconceivable. "Please take care of her." Cori said, and Maya nodded, without real concern. Cori spoke again. "If I stop the plague, can you stop the battle?"

"The battle is all but won." Maya said, and Cori looked over to Sammiel atop a mound of bodies, his fell dagger chains flashing and slashing in the light of the moon, the clash of steel on steel heard over the cries of men as they met with pain. "End this."

Cori climbed atop Rasputin, and held her Bone Scythe in front of her. She pointed out into the mountains where Agamemnon was applying the final chains to a thrashing Margaret Rastaphan. "Time to set things right." Cori said, then kicked the sides of Rasputin, the nightmare steed, and galloped off Northwards to the great clash of the colossi.

Into the hills, Cori rode with her Cloak of the Wraith Whisperer trailing long behind her and Rasputin, her metallic six eyed mask glaring into the horizon, the ivory bone scythe at her side, covered about in blood and viscera. Even as the plants died beneath Rasputin's hooves, and even as autumn blew a dash of frigid air against her on this crisp and frenzied night, Cori felt as though the land was coming alive and waking from a long darkness. Too many lives had been lost to feel joy, but there was a pervading solidarity that breathed over the land as easily as the cold air.

In the northern mountains, through valleys and byways, musky black oils covered newly eroded sediments. Millions of years worth of disruptions had taken place in the intervening hours. Mountains had crumbled and great fissures had formed that would stump geologists who would dismiss the tales and legends of the battle between Agamemnon and Margaret Rastaphan in favor of more worldly explanations, such as an errant and unaccounted for glacier.

The feud raged on, Cori could hear from her nightmare steed. The grunts and wailings of colossal entities continued to give quake to the ground. Last she had seen, Margaret Rastaphan had bitten into the neck of Agamemnon and caused severe magmatic hemorrhaging. From there, Margaret had escaped her bindings, and from there, Cori had seen no more.

It was from the Ken of Dunmare that Cori looked out at the final scenes of battle. The Ken, a wooded cliff under the rising full moon, once a popular photo op and makeout spot for teenagers, overlooked a newly formed crater, Cori gazed from above upon the wrestling and entwined giants. Iridescent scales were ripped from Agamemnon's face as he lay atop Margaret Rastaphan, crushing and crunching her left humerus bone into a pool of his own spilling magma. Cori looked at the plague anomaly with deep set suspicion. There was something too familiar about this raging creature of soot and oil. She had the oddest sensation that she knew the answer to a burning question, but she could not verbalize either the question or the answer. All she knew was that she feared harming the creature, but knew she must do so despite those reservations.

Margaret howled an inhuman howl with the crunching of her arm, and Agamemnon ran for his village sized sword, lodged into the side of the new crater. But too late, for Margaret Rastaphan was upon his back, and digging at his eyes, ferociously feline. Agamemnon allowed himself advantage and fell backwards with his full weight as a pile drive into the earth below. Then, atop her again, one punch then two, he raised several chains from the earth to bind her hands and feet once more as she gnashed her teeth and cursed the gods.

Cori spared no more time on this poetic vista. She rushed down into the crater on foot, leaving Rasputin atop the Ken of Dunmare. She slid down the snowy sides of the crater and her thoughts left her. She had been in several battles now, and was growing used to the rhythms of war and the tides of action. Questions of mortality and morality and logistical concerns were a hindrance to the ritualistic worship that is battle.

She allowed her fear to be a guiding force. Directing it with her will, Cori did not deny her fear but instead told her fear what to

do. "We must sever Margaret Rastaphan." She told herself. She did not tell her fear to go away, but rather greeted her fear as an old friend. "Show me the way." Cori said, then cut her first cut into the immense and oily rib bone of Margaret Rastaphan.
There was more howling from the plague creature who spat and screamed into the air, and her breath was like urine and dirty feet. But even so, Cori's heart broke with the creatures pain.

Another cut to the vertebrae, and another to the shoulder as Cori drifted swiftly and weightlessly around the battlefield like a moonlight wraith on the wind. Her normally gray cloak was a more dazzling white in this light. She pranced to the side of an immense plague ridden fist as it attempted to squash its assailing insect, then cut in reverse and severed the hand.

Cori was dancing as she had learned to dance in Sonorous, and used that dance to do battle. Her dance, she felt, carried more power with it than even the infinitely sharp Bone Scythe as it cut through all things. But that would be a philosophical mystery too great to expound upon.

As Cori severed limbs and bones, the Plague Entity slowed, and halted as she was bound by Agamemnon as surely as she was being severed by Cori. Then, finally, upon limbs and knees, the Plague Anomaly hunched, and a human sized figure descended from its chest. St. Margaret, lowered with reverence by the tendrils of her sickly prison.

Cori ran to the figure and delivered one final cut with Hanuman's Bone Scythe which severed those final tendrils. The enormous and crowned skeleton of oozing illness evaporated into Ash, swiftly and silently, and the body of St. Margaret was dropped. Cori caught her, and gently laid her upon the dirt while Agamemnon kneeled to the side, lowered his head, and paid homage.

St. Margaret's jaw was strong and her hair was unruly. She was middle aged and thick boned and had a wide freckled nose, brown of skin with smoke stone eyes. She had a determined brow, even as she slept. Cori had expected some Halo or holy airs, but there was nothing that marked this woman as a saint. There were no wings nor auras. Cori was not even sure the woman was magickal. She had very nice gray dreadlocks, though, and was wearing well worn jeans.

Cori knew this woman.

Cori pulled away her metallic six eyed mask with the beautiful grimace and showed her own bewildered face to St. Margaret. Speechless, Cori opened her mouth then closed it, uncertain what words could be given. Cori cried as she caressed Margaret's face.

St. Margaret looked back at Cori and recognition dawned in her weak eyes. "Cori?"

"Mom?" Cori blinked and wiped her falling tears away. Cori stammered for several moments, her eyes like faucets. "I don't understand."

"So it worked... you lived." Margaret said between rasping breaths. "Good. That's good." She said, and coughed out a small laugh. "That's good."

"You... you disappeared." Cori stammered. "You just left. Dad said you left to fight the Plague."

Margaret shook her head, and reached up to touch Cori's face. "Oh, my sweet angel...I did leave to fight the plague. My little baby was sick. I wanted to stay more than anything, but I knew what I had to do. Any mother would have done the same."

"How... I don't..." Cori tried to sputter out the torrent of questions that assaulted her mind, but Margaret held a finger to her lips then kissed her softly.

"Please, tell your father I love him." Margaret's labored breath turned into a liquid rasp. "And I understand if he can't forgive me."

Cori nodded but pleaded with her mother not to leave her again. She squeezed Margaret's arms and pressed her cheek against her cheek, and tried to bring any sensation or noise to the silence of her dying mother. Agamemnon's metal turned to rust and dissolved, his earthly duties fulfilled. Margaret looked out on the moonlight. "How strange it all is..." She said and blinked those smoke stone eyes. The hushed whispers of snowflakes fell on her cheek, then melted deliciously. St. Margaret passed away, struck by the wounds the bone scythe had inflicted on the body she had shared with the Plague Anomaly.

St. Margaret passed away, and somewhere a lone wolf howled a keening howl.

Chapter 25

Cori wept for days after the battle. She was in a delirium of grief and confusion. No one was able to console her for a time, not even Sammiel. She withered and writhed with pain and loss. But weeks passed, and then months, and everything returned to a semblance of normalcy.

They still had dinner late in the evening with all the remaining staff and dead in attendance. George continued his suicidal routines and Ernie wandered the hallways in much the same patterns as he had always done. New hirings were prioritized by corporate to replace Luke, and someone had to take Maya's previous position now that she had ascended to the role of Supervisor, and the Dark One's Blessing had left her as the same Maya that everyone knew and loved.

Samuel and Cori's love blossomed during these days. Cori's grief abated during long hours cuddling in the black silk covers in the Southeast Tower. Having shared so much in the Betwixt, they made exceptionally familiar lovers, and their joy grew boundlessly.

Ruth had woken and healed both Aislynn and Morris from their comatose state when the battle ceased. But during the internal audit following the near apocalypse, the representatives from Human Resources somehow managed to discover the forbidden resurrections performed by Morris and Ruth during the performance of their duties, and they were both forced into exile. They left with Aislynn who was also in exile from her faction. They battled with the wraiths from Human Resources, but no one was hurt, and they escaped safely, and their whereabouts were left unknown.

The Council approved immediate structural repairs, and within hours a team of imps from the Facilities department were reconstructing the foundational and structural damages to the manor. These were a pittance compared to the damages done to Remedy and its peoples, but St. Margaret's was run by a massive corporation and so the peoples of the town were relatively helpless against the Council of Necromancer's outright lobbying powers. Settlements were agreed upon, or forced upon the families, valuing each life at an average $132,000.00 to be paid at the convenience of the Council. The staff were given $800.00 bonuses for their efforts. $38,000.00 and $160.00 were taken out in taxes respectively. The Council also donated a large sum to the local university to expand their Arcane Studies department. This money was not taxed, but much of it was fraudulently laundered by the school's corrupt financial coordinator.

Damages to the village were fixed, St. Margaret's was given a renovation on top of its repair, and looked dazzling from top to bottom. New carpets, new wallpaper, new decor, and a spit shine applied to all of the above. Everywhere people continued their day to day lives as they had been. There were just people missing from those routines, and everything was quiet and mournful.

Maya ruled over St. Margaret's with all the vigor of someone new to the job, as Morris had once done. She was enlivened and empowered by memories of the Dark One's Blessing, as Morris had once been. She had been given a newly repaired and renovated St. Margaret's, as Morris had once been given. The Home for the Nearly Departed was born again, and they were taking on new residents from abroad to correct the rampant financial deficits they had been left with.

"You excited for move in day?" Sammiel asked Cori over breakfast, assisting as she cooked breakfast. "I heard they're more confident in our abilities now, so they're giving us an Aswang."

"What is—?"

"A shape shifting vampire type thing. Coming in from the Philippines. Apparently it'll be able to look and act just like any of us, then try to kill you." Sammiel said and looking strangely titillated by the idea.

"Great."

"You alright?" Sammiel asked, flipping and sizzling a long line of bacon in turn.

"I haven't felt right since…. Everything. I have so many questions, my brain feels like a tornado just rolled through." Cori said, adding an aggressive amount of salt to her eggs.

"Yeah I know. Cori I'm so—"

"Don't tell me you're sorry." Cori said hastily, trying not to snap at him. Sammiel had been nothing but supportive, but emotions are emotions.

"Yeah I know. Cori there's nothing I can say or do that will make you feel better, but I'm here for you."

"It would help if you gave me one of your sweet kisses." Cori said, but Sammiel was already halfway to kissing her. He brushed his lips gently against hers, then nuzzled into her neck.

"You know I love y'all but you need to stop." Maya said, sternly.

"Sorry Maya." Sammiel Said.

"We're not clocked in." Cori retorted.

"You got rooms." Maya said absently, looking back to her checklist and walking on.

"Any leads yet?" Cori asked Sammiel when Maya had left. They had both been looking for new positions within reasonable proximity to one another. They didn't mind Maya's heightened professional expectations so much, and they expected things to get better under her rule. But they both still did have their dreams and aspirations. Lives they hoped to live that couldn't be lived here.

"Well there's the Program Director position open in Siberia, but I'm really not sure that's the best option locationally." Sam Said.

"Yeah, ich, no."

"There's also a Professor of Necromancy position open at the University at Miskatonic."

"That's more intriguing." Cori said. "Go on."

"Well I'm not sure either of us would be qualified, but it's in New England and that place is all sorts of spooky, so they're naturally going to need all sorts of spooky people to fill spooky jobs. We could try."

"We could try." Cori repeated, sighing and distant.

"...I know what will cheer you up." Sammiel said with an uncharacteristically large grin.

Cori's interest was piqued. More by Sammiel's grin than by his words.

"I was going to surprise you tomorrow and just... just take you. But sometimes the anticipation is as good or better than the thing itself." Sammiel said, then paused for too long.

"Sam!" Cori said, smirking for the first time in days and pushing him, then tickling him. "Tell me you big dope."

Sammiel was crazy ticklish and took a while to stop laughing. "Okay... okay. Ah stop. Okay. I planned a date! A date night. A real good one."

Cori couldn't help from feeling satisfied. He wasn't kidding, he did know how to cheer her up. She knew they both had the next two days off but she had anticipated they would both just watch movies and cuddle and whatever else have you. This was a very pleasant surprise, indeed. "Not bad, Sam. Not bad."

"Told you. Be ready tomorrow morning."

"So, where are we going?"

"Oh, that part is a secret." Sammiel Said, flinching back even before Cori lunged in to tickle him again. He ran away through the halls giggling. Cori was about to give chase before the doorbell rang.

Cori heard Maya from afar, greeting their guests cordially. Cori couldn't imagine their first impressions of the place. Maya had filled the foyer with jasmine flowers and the whole house had been outfitted with more gentle and therapeutic lighting. The imps from the Facilities department were complicated to summon, but once they came in they really made an impact. Mostly because they were compelled to do so under powerful occult pacts and bindings. They had not been nice creatures, as Cori had attempted to make conversation with them and found them instead saying things that would most wound her and torment her mind. But their leader had deep and even primordial understandings of interior design. They were not yet finished with their work, and Cori was trying to work out the ways she could request they renovate her room from Maya without overstepping her bounds. As of yet, no inspirations came to mind.

Cori went to greet new residents at the front door and was met by the commotion of several mourning families carrying ghostly fetish objects and followed quietly by the spirits of their beloved nearly departed. They came ritualistically, led by priestesses wearing white veils, marching in rhythmic procession, quiet and dream like. Cori stood at attention alongside Dana, Sammiel, and Kitsune. Beside them were the new hires; Poe, a purple haired space case of questionable gender; Corinthia and Lisbeth, the peculiar lace-victorian twins, both with wavy hair, one platinum blonde, one black haired. They were always holding hands and making jokes that very few could understand. And there was Todd, a hunched and bald fashionista with a hooked nose and a taste for the macabre. There were more openings at the house besides, but Maya was booked for interviews and Cori found some special excitement in spying the variety of characters who came to apply.

Cori had never been aware of it, but Move-in Day at St. Margaret's was something of a grand ritual complete with drum circles, embalmings and show casings. This, however, was the biggest move-in day that St. Margaret's had ever seen in its 20 year history. Seventeen new spirits arrived, and Cori was uncertain how they would ever manage. But Maya struck a confident poise and assured everyone that this would be just one of many good things on the way.

Amidst the Cacophony, Cori could hardly meet the new residents, but one struck her eye. A little twig of a girl with wild pig tails and enormous spectacles hid behind her grieving silhouette of a father. Cori could not comprehend what it would take for a father to bring his child here, but then she had been somewhat in awe of parents as of late.

Cori went to her, and knelt down to her height. "What's your name?"

"Willow." The little spirit girl replied meekly, avoiding eye contact.

"Hi Willow. I'm Cori."

"Hi."

"Now Willow, I got a little secret for you." Cori said. "We're gonna be living together in this house here. And I can already tell that I'm going to like you. So you know what that means?"

"What?" Willow asked.

"That means we're gonna be best friends." Cori said, and Willow gave a shy little smile. "You know what else?"

"What?"

"I already have some friends here who are just your age. I can't wait for you to meet them. Penny is a little girl who likes to play in the walls. And Sarah is a little girl who likes to read."

"Other kids live here?" Willow asked, turning her eyes up and wide to Cori from behind her glasses.

"Yup. So what do you like to do Willow?"

"I like bugs." Willow said, with a little crunching of her nose.

"Bugs?" Cori said, not having anticipated such a response. "Oh Willow… well, do I ever have a surprise for you. There's a whole bunch of gardens in the backyard here and I bet they have all sorts of bugs. Will you go looking for some with me some time?"

"Yeah!" Willow said, and her father gave Cori a sad smile.

"Thank you." The father mouthed silently.

The morning came and went in a blur. There had been Churros served and the priestesses wept loudly for and with the grieving. The priestesses had been painted in celtic tribal fashion behind their white veils and sang mournful songs. They held a lunch feast for all the guests set in the now renovated parlor and dining room which together sat everyone comfortably.

It was during this time that Maya approached Cori, each of them with plates full of weenies and sausages and cheeses. Wine was served, and the mournful guests were beginning to liven up.

"Tristan has arrived." Maya whispered casually to Cori's side.

Cori took a long deep breath. Then another, then several more. "Alright. You can do this, Cori." Cori told herself.

"You alright?" Maya asked. "If you need some back up, I got you."

"No, no, I'm fine. It's just Sammiel meeting him and--"

"I hear he's taking you on a special date tomorrow." Maya said and winked at Cori.

Cori immediately deflated. "Ugh, yeah… about that…"

"Whoa. You're not done with him already are you?"

"No no no." Cori flushed. "Maya... oooh I don't even know how to say this... let alone telling the both of them... but I have to tell them."

"Cori, what's up? What happened." Maya asked, her concern growing as she looked around as though searching for potential threats.

It wasn't done as an intentional communication, but Cori's hand rested upon her own belly as she looked about trying to think of how to say what she needed to say.

Maya saw, and gasped. "No." Then she grabbed Cori by the shoulders and brought her swiftly to the bathroom and locked the door. "Are you sure?" Maya asked, and Cori nodded. "Are you absolutely positive?" She asked, and got another nod.

"I mean, as positive as you can be." Cori clarified.

Maya took a moment. Then she took a deep breath. Then she smiled the prettiest smile Cori had ever seen and hugged her and lifted her into the air, and gave a squeal.

Cori struggled to find the breath to speak. "But like... I don't know, what if Sam's not that serious about this? What if he doesn't want to be with me? He said he did, he said he wanted a family, but like... this is different, this is... this is a whole other thing."

"You don't have to worry about nothin', I'll shotgun him up to that altar, you'll see. He steps out of line, I make his eyeballs melt." Maya said, and meant. There was the Dark One's Blessing glittering behind her eyes.

"That's just it. I don't want him forced to be with me. That's what I *don't* want this to be. I'm afraid he will feel like he, like... has to. Like, then, he has to be with me." Cori said.

Maya stepped back and frowned. "Okay, maybe this is a little more complicated than I thought."

"Yeah..." Cori said.

"Okay... new thought." Maya said. "This is gonna take some tight communication. This is gonna take some careful thinking and planning. You want my opinion? He loves you. But you need to go about this carefully so you don't have to doubt that. You don't want him to feel forced. You want to let him choose freely. Give him time to think. Give him time and space and see what he does. You're gonna have to think this through, Cori."

"Yeah…" Cori said. "I feel like I'm gonna throw up."

"Me too, I got all sorts of butterflies." Maya responded.

"No, literally, I'm going to throw up." Cori said, pushing Maya out of the way and heaving the contents of her stomach into the toilet.

Cori texted Sam to meet her in the foyer, then prepared herself with several buff, robust, and otherwise bolstering incantations, and still she was left nervous. Cori wore the new armor she had earned for her service from the Council of Necromancers. She had thought she too was going to be sent into exile for her forbidden resurrections, but somehow along the way they had not discovered hers, and instead gifted her with a sleek skin tight black jumpsuit complete with black metal plate armor boots, chestplate, shoulders, and arm bands, all glowing a gentle ethereal blue. This was joined by a regal cape and hood of cloth, and though Cori kept the hood down, if she put it up, it was enchanted to make her eyes glow blue with the rest of the ensemble.

She walked out to the foyer and stood at the end of the hall, Tristan stood by the front entrance. He was done up like she hadn't seen him in years. He too had chosen to come in full regalia. He sported a heavy bear fur cloak, lined on top with a layer of straw which was growing moss. Several belts and satchels adorned his waistline, his shirt and pants were made of simple hemp weave and adorned with celtic knots. Atop his head, a crown of antlers. It was a bit much for a simple gardener, but he hadn't always been a simple gardener.

He was an immense man, with tree trunk arms, and a fat belly in an otherwise muscular chest. His dark hair and beard had nearly double the gray in it since last she saw him, and his face looked worried and weathered.

They stared at each other for several moments, taking each other in, before Tristan made the first move and nearly ran to embrace Cori with wet eyes, a warm heart, and a kiss to the forehead.

"You were my little girl when you left home." He said, his voice of sand and sequoia. "Now there is a woman before me, but I still see my girl in her eyes."

"I've missed you so much." Cori said, nuzzling into his chest. "I'm so sorry I didn't call, Dad. I've just been...there's been so much. I'm sorry. I should have written to you, I don't know what's wrong with me."

Tristan lifted Cori's chin to meet his eyes with his grizzly hands, and he shook his head slowly. "I was the one in the wrong, not giving you the room to grow. I, of all people, should have known better. We are together now, that is all that matters. Hah, and this must be Sammiel." Her father looked off to the side where Sammiel stood sheepishly, her father's eyes sharp with cunning and intimidation.

He stomped over and gripped Sammiel's hands in a vice like grip, and Sammiel did his best not to wince. Then he slapped Sammiel on the back, causing him to tumble several feet forward. "Good to meet you, lad." Tristan said.

"Nice to finally meet you." Sammiel said.

"You sure you don't want to come along?" Tristan asked, opening the front door to the winter air, a saddled moose standing several feet outside in the snow.

"I know you two have a lot of catching up to do." Sammiel replied, mystified by the saddled moose.

"Next time then." Tristan replied gratefully, and with a wink.

Tristan helped Cori atop his moose, Karlson, and they walked off at a canter towards Remedy. Tristan caught Cori up on all the family gossip, and spoke of recent tales from their home, Terry Town. He asked Cori of her own tales from the past year, but received only short vague sentiments about work and how it was alright. She spoke a bit of her coworkers but remained otherwise silent. He was not even able to get her to speak in too much detail of Sammiel.

Cori showed Tristan around Remedy, their moose mount drawing more attention than even the walking undead.

"A lovely town, but something grim about the place." Tristan said, for the Council of Necromancers had engaged in a great cover up campaign in regards to the Crimson Plague, with non-disclosure agreements accompanying all settlement payouts, and a few mysterious disappearances of those who refused their settlement payouts.

"I suppose there is a lot to catch you up on." Cori said. "Just, over coffee, maybe?"

Tristan nodded and Cori showed him the way to Quintanilla's, which delighted Tristan with its available menu of beet smoothies and fire roasted buttered corn. But neither was hungry and they instead ordered two Cinnamon Toast coffees, which had been enhanced with a unique concoction that made a sparkly red cinnamon mist rise off of it, perfect for a chilly December afternoon.

They found a quiet corner booth, away from prying ears, and sipped until Cori broke the silence. "Quite a lot has happened."

Tristan replied only with a knowing nod.

"Dad...I need to know what really happened to Mom." Cori said, and for all the wisdom in his eyes, this took Tristan by surprise, then his eyes grew harder, and more angry.

"She left--"

"No." Cori said. "I understand you're angry. I know she left. I need to know why she really left."

Tristan continued to look hard and angry at Cori, but then his eyes softened as she held his gaze with equal measure. "I didn't want to tell you, Cori. I needed...I needed to protect you from the truth. Your mother...She had always been a Paladin, as you know. But she had begun to dabble in Necromancy. There was a close friend of hers...Keiran. He had taken his own life and she was just...so insistent that she needed to help him move on." Tristan sighed. "You know I don't care for Necromancy so much...no offense. I'm going to learn, for your sake. But after your mother... I didn't understand all this...and..." Tristan's eyes grew wet against the hard creases of his face. "Then the Crimson Plague came shortly after. You got sick. And she just...she left. She said she was going to fight it but..." Tristan clenched his fist. "I needed her. *We* needed her. Just stole away in the middle of the night, and never returned."

Cori gripped her father's hands from across the table while his face clenched in pain. "Dad...Mom told me to tell you she is so, so sorry." Cori said, and Tristan's eyes grew wide. "That she understands if you never forgive her, but that she loves you."

Tristan looked at Cori, confused. "You've spoken to her spirit?"

Cori shook her head. "Mom was still alive." Cori said, then let Tristan process this with a long range of emotions that played across his face. Seeing that this parade would not end anytime soon, Cori continued, slowly, carefully. "Dad...Mom is the reason the plague ended. She *is* St. Margaret." Cori said, and recognition in her father's eyes. "You knew…"

Tristan shook his head. "I knew they canonized her. I didn't know...she couldn't have ended the plague. No one could."

Now it was Cori's turn for a parade of emotions. "Damnit, Dad. I was going to work at *St. Margaret's*. Why wouldn't you tell me that?"

"I couldn't tell you your mother just went off to die for some hopeless cause while you were sick. They canonized a lot of people in those days. They told me it was because she died fighting the Plague Anomaly while it stomped across the land, that was all. The Necromancers agreed to it, and the Paladins agreed to it. The Necromancers just liked her because she had been speaking out for their causes, and lobbying for them to the Order of Paladins."

Cori stopped him. "No. I don't know who knew. There were at least some Necromancers who knew. I've spoken to a few people and dug into some records, trying to find out what happened and gather up the details. She led a party of both Paladins and Necromancers to the Plague Anomaly, and offered herself as sacrifice. They bound it to her body, and had her locked away. She chose...so I could live."

"No…" Her father said. "It can't be...that's not possible."

Cori squeezed his hands tighter, their coffee untouched. "They made them all Saints, but Mom was the one in the middle. She did it to keep me alive, Dad. She's been stuck in that pit for years just so I could live." Cori was crying now, and her father was

339

losing control. "She knows how angry you were and she's so so sorry. Dad…"

Tristan stood, nearly knocking over the table, spilling their coffees, and ran out into the streets, frantic. He came to an empty alley and threw a dumpster, then punched several dents into the brick walls, crying out "NO, NO, NO!"

Cori ran up to him and grabbed his shoulders and helped guide him down gently while he fell into a corner and wept. "I would have saved her. I would have done something, I would have figured something out. All that anger, for all these years, and she…" He said, and let out another deep wail.

It took a long while for Cori to help her father. When he was ready, she helped him walk away from town with Karlson the moose, out into the woods beyond where she was able to finally tell him of all that had transpired. Her possession, her struggles, her blossoming love, her battles. Tristan listened quietly now, taking everything in with an open ear.

They spoke for hours more on top of this. Tristan lit a fire in the woods to keep the cold at bay, and they spoke until the sun set and they could stand the cold no longer. They spoke of everything. They laughed together, and cried together, and Tristan left with the glittering promise that he was set to be a grandfather. And he left Cori with the oath that he would live nearby, wherever she and Sam may choose, so that he could be the best Papa the little tyke could ever ask for. And when it was time to part ways, they shared promises to write and call, and that no matter what they would be seeing each other soon.

That night, Cori partook in the most peaceful sleep she could remember having had for many years, snuggled up against Sammiel in his grand black canopy bed.

Cori spent the morning of the next day preparing for Sammiel's little mystery date. It was hard to know how to prepare without knowing where they were going, but Cori found she was glowing no matter what she did to herself. She was rosy cheeked and her hair was lush and shiny and her body was full and she wasn't sure she could look bad if she tried to.

"Well that's one benefit of this little mess I'm in, I guess." Cori said to herself in the mirror.

Sammiel had divulged via text message that their date would be 'an adventure', so Cori wore her usual necromancer's gear, her cloak, her witches hat and some extra wintery layers. Meeting at the door, Sammiel wore his usual obsidian armors with a thick black fur cloak to fight the chill in the air.

"Ready?" Sammiel asked.

"How can I be ready? You haven't told me what we will be doing." Cori said with a scowl.

"Nothing crazy or difficult, don't worry. I know we've all had enough of that." Sammiel replied, then he took on a wispy and mysterious tone, grabbing her shoulder and waving his hand across the air. "Has anyone told you of the legends of Lake Talula?"

Cori shrugged, and smirked at Sammiel's theatrics. "Remind me, why don't you."

"The tale has been passed down for many generations, you see. They say that at the bottom of the lake there is a spirit who sings. She sings of her tale of beauty and tragedy and redemption, and some people can hear her and it's why so many famous musicians come from Remedy." Sammiel said.

"Okay, yeah, Maya told me something about that." Cori said, her interest piqued.

"They say she's the one who founded Remedy, Lady Elizabeth Talula. And that she doesn't actually lie at the bottom of the Lake, but in a cave on the opposite shore.

"Okay Sammiel, I'm officially interested. Job well done with the non-traditional date. I applaud thee."

"Ahhh but my lady, there is also a treasure involved. The spirit is said to be bound to a pearl that can be found in a grotto at the bottom of a pool. They say it's guarded by the dead, but I figure if anyone can handle that, it'd be us, right?"

"A quest *with* a treasure. Color me impressed, Mr. Sam." Cori said, and walked out the front door. "You've done well."

They hiked down River Road in a frigid cold, but Sammiel had thought of everything and brought bottled ifrits, fire spirits, to keep them warm. Then, as lunch approached, Sam took out a quart of sweet and sour chicken and a king size of reese's eggs to share between them as they walked, and didn't even get mad when Cori ate all the eggs.

"I'm sorry I just blacked out." Cori said with her head in her chocolate stained hands. "Sam, I'm so sorry, you have no idea how I get with Reese's." Sam just laughed and kissed her cheek and pulled her under his furry cloak. Cori looked up at him and rubbed the white stubble of his chin. "Why are you so nice to me?"

"Cause I love you." Sammiel replied simply, then added, "And cause you're weird and I like it, you little freak. Remember Duke's, when you passed out, and your tongue was like lolling out of your mouth."

"Don't even!" Cori said, pushing him as he chuckled. He pulled out his phone and showed her the picture and laughed and laughed, then smooched her then laughed more with eyes like a maniac.

"And you're calling me weird."

"No, no it's the both of us, I know." Sammiel said, grabbing Cori for a short dance in the middle of the snow covered road.

They avoided Remedy as best they could, the people being highly displeased with Necromancers for the time being, and rightly so. But the cold was such that no one was out upon the roads and the world was silent with ice and snow and the smell of distant wood burning stoves. The water of the swiftly flowing river down the hill to the easy was glacial blue and filled with icebergs, but as they came upon the canyons of Lake Talula, they saw the Lake was completely frozen over, and all the cliffs and canyons were dripping crystalline with ice and icicles and odd spiralations of snow.

It was in this wintery silence that Cori first heard the singing.

It reminded her of her adventures in Sonorous, but more profound in its grounded mystery. It was heard behind the ears. It was as though Cori's heart strings were being played like a lute.

"Do you hear it?" Sammiel asked.

Cori looked up at him, mystified. "Yes." For all the magick she had experienced and for all the wild adventures amongst the many planes of the cosmos, this singing struck her with more awe and mystique than the others had been able to with all their pomp and frill.

"Come on." He said and pulled her to an ancient and icy stair.

"Sam, are you sure about this?" Cori asked. "I'm not really in the mood for either of us to die again."

Sam paused thoughtfully, and nodded. "Well, you're just going to have to trust me to catch you if you fall."

"Yeah, but what if you fall? I don't think I could catch you."

He rolled his eyes. "I know you'd figure something out. Come on."

They walked down the stone stairway, alone. Cori grew more elated by the minute. This happened often when she was with him. No matter what mood she started in, it improved considerably in his presence at a consistent and indefinite rate. She was even beginning to forget her troubles, and had to remind herself several times that she had plenty of things to be morose about. But then Sam would turn her way and smile and then Cori would feel like she was floating and then they would kiss and then she wouldn't be able to think at all.

"I've never been down here before." Sam said.

"Me neither."

"Lived here for years, everyone says to visit Lake Talula, never done it. Weird, right?"

Cori had a terrible lump in her throat and was desperately searching for the words she needed to speak to Sam and with finality, end her torments. Inspired by Maya's own courage the day before, Cori decided on simply blurting it out. "Sammiel, I have something to tell you."

"Breaking up with me?" Sam jested, jumped down a rock wall and offered his hands in assistance to Cori.

"Focus. This is serious." Cori said, then fidgeted. She had jumped into this conversation hoping a plan or at least courage would present itself, but none did. "I--I need to know you want to be with me...for a long time."

Sam held his hand to Cori's mouth. "Cori, hush." He said. "Not--not right now."

Cori's heart sank like it had shoes of cement. "Oh...okay."

"Please just...we can't talk about it right now is what I mean." Sammiel said. "I think you took that the wrong way."

And she had, and she kept taking it that way.

They reached the bottom of the gorge and Sammiel stepped cautiously over the clear ice of the lake. He beckoned Cori to follow behind him. Several feet underneath, primordial fish swam, large as horses. The wind whipped fiercely and pierced their faces and coats as they tiptoed step by step over the frozen lake in the gorge. Cori scanned the opposite end for a grotto, but could see none till Sammiel pointed it out to her.

"See, over there. There is an ancient carving in the rock, a spiral. Behind that is where the cavern is." He said, and the ice groaned under his feet.

They made their way to the rock hewn spiral and left the fierce winds of the ice lake as they passed behind what appeared to be the walls of the canyon and into a small cave, marked by two statues of meditating male saints, their hands in Abhaya mudra. Sam and Cori had both grown quiet by now as they spelunked and squeezed through a long tight passage, where anxieties pressed in on them from all sides.

Within it was much warmer, even summery, a silent grotto like a shrine, the ground a thin coating of water with paper lanterns gracing its surface and swaying gently. The edges were lit by hundreds of candles upon rocks, tended most likely by the local monastery.

"Sam...it's--"

"Beautiful." They said together. The song was loud here, and their hearts were frolicking. At the back was one single pool, lit with a gentle phosphorescent pool. Above this one was a massive two story tall statue of a female saint, her hands in Varada mudra. Plants were growing round its sides. They looked to the bottom of this one, and could see a small glimmer through the blue.

"Who is going in to get it?" Cori asked, and Sammiel gave her a long look. "Oh no, not me."

Sammiel began to take off his gear, his plate armors dropping with heavy thuds in the cave sand. "Us." He said, and revealed that he had quite obviously been working out.

Cori became flushed. She had seen him nude by now, of course, but it still warmed her blood and woke her butterflies to do so, each and every time.

She pulled off her cloak of the wraith whisperer, her timberland boots, her wide brimmed hat, and her gauntlets of the black rose. She removed the tee shirt and pants underneath, but kept her underwear on, to tease him. Sammiel did not.

He stepped into the blue grotto pool and kicked his legs, treading water as he reached up to grab Cori and bring her in. She submerged into the song of the pool, which was fluttering with love and bubbles.

They waded water and hugged, holding each other close, and kissing. Sammiel had a mint in his mouth, not one to miss any details. Cori crossed his velvety tongue to grab it from him and pull it into her own, and bit it between her teeth. Sammiel pulled her hip into his hips.

"I believe I have something to retrieve for you." He said, and did a backflip dive backwards into the water, and down through the pool below. Cori followed, and chased him underwater.

All around was lit by a healthy bacterial phosphorescence, and lined with plants and animals of coral. At the bottom, a clam. Sammiel hovered near the clam and reached in to grab something glittering white. Then he kicked gently to Cori, and grabbed her hand.

Cori looked down as Sammiel placed a ring upon her hand with organic silver, a diamond band, and a single central pearl which gleamed with rainbow opalescence. Cori looked at it confused, and un-thinking, then looked up at Sam confused as well. His eyes curled, then he swam upwards. Cori followed.

Cori surfaced and asked, "What's this? Is this the pearl? I didn't know it would be a ring."

"Coriander Lou Ryel." Sammiel said, enunciating each word slowly, his voice of rusted tin, now an unusual silver.

"Don't you dare use my full name." Cori chided, but was beginning to go wide eyed with comprehension. These things are harder to understand when you're the person they're happening to.

"Cori Lou."

"That's even worse!"

"I have found you to be such a source of mystery and wonder in my life already, in this short time we've known each other. You have kept me consistently happy in your presence since the moment I met you. But since then, we have seen something deeper of one another that goes beyond the ordinary crush and rush of oxytocin and love. I've seen you in strife, only to grow bolder. I've seen you in despair, but holding the fire of hope. I've seen you angry, but still ready to listen. We've accomplished the impossible together. I have...simply become better with you around. I feel smarter and healthier and more alive. You radiate warmth. You're not always certain of yourself and sometimes you're terribly afraid, but you always keep pushing forward. But then, I've seen you want to bite my head off when your metabolism is acting up, and for some reason I think that's cute. I could.... I could go on and on. I'm really... really rambling here." Only then did Cori notice that Sammiel's face was beet red, the first she had ever seen his usually white face turn so. "I want to keep this going. Whatever this is, it works, and I want it to keep working. You are someone I could call family. To start a family. Coriander...Lou... Ryel... will you marry me?"

Cori still stared at the ring on her finger in disbelief. It's not that she hadn't envisioned this before, but somewhere within she never believed it would actually happen.

"Sammiel...Alexander...Prescott." Cori said and looked up at him from the ring, her eyes warm and buttery. She bit her lip painfully. "If you would have me, nothing would please me greater than the honor of spending my life with you, through the difficulties and challenges that life throws at us. To call you family, and create a family. You have treated me with respect and honesty. You have remained unabashedly yourself, even when 'yourself' is kind of a goof. I've seen your lazy days where all you want to do is lie down and eat in-between naps, and I've seen that even when it's one of those days, you're still ready to get up and help me out if I ask. I've seen your productive days when nothing can stop you, but even when you could conquer the world you'll stop and give me a foot massage, just so long as I stop using arcane construct Tom Hiddleston for all my messaging needs. He's disbanded, by the way, like you asked."

"I thank you." Sammiel Said with a nod and puffy red eyes.

"You're just stupid beautiful. You don't even need a great personality, look at you. But you do and you've got such a way about you. I would love to spend my life with you. I want to see what this whole 'getting to know someone forever' thing is all about, and why old married couples seem to like each other so much, even when they badger each other constantly."

Then they kissed. It was fireworks, and the song of a drowned spirit. A meteor shower sprang forth in the sky, visible even in the daylight. The worldwide fertility rates increased. Astronomers marveled at the appearance of several unexpected supernovae, occurring concurrently. Many thousands of Buddha and Angel looked on from their lotus seats and swirly clouds. It was mystic. It was majestic. And that was all before they made love. As for that part, I am forbidden from speaking of it. There are some things which must only be experienced, and never spoken of. Of these, 63% involve the tantric arts. Writhing. Coiled. Tight like a spring, or a python.

It was in the good natured languor, post ecstasy, that Cori sat up from the warm cave waters. Cori rested Sammiel's hand on her lower belly, then looked at him, her eyes half open like the Saint statue above.

It was now Sammiel's turn to miss obvious cues, because something was happening to him that he had envisioned, but never expected to actually occur.

"Sam...Did you really mean it when you said you wanted to start a family?" Cori asked.

"Yeah." Sammiel did, still confused, but then added a more certain "Yes."

"What if one was already on the way?" Cori asked, batting eyelashes at him while he still remained oblivious.

"That'd be great." Sammiel said, looking for the meaning behind Cori's words.

"You're such an oaf, you know that?" Cori said, then pulled Sammiel in for a hug and whispered in his ear. "We're having a baby."

Sammiel said nothing, but gripped Cori tighter, too tightly even, and when she pulled away she saw only the most genuine smile that could have graced his lips, edges curled with delight, reaching to his eyes.

They returned to St. Margaret's with tousled hair and lively spirits, and Cori got to show everyone and anyone who would look her new ring, enchanted so that she might never forget these moments of pure and unadulterated joy which resonate throughout the deep seated knowledge that once one has loved and been loved in return, they shall never truly be alone again.

Made in the USA
Middletown, DE
14 August 2021